Misophonia

Misophonia

A Novel

DANA VOWINCKEL

Translated from the German by Adrian Nathan West

HARPERVIA

An Imprint of HarperCollins*Publishers*

MISOPHONIA. Copyright © 2023 by Dana Vowinckel. English translation copyright © 2025 by Adrian Nathan West. All rights reserved. Printed in the United States of America. No part of this book may be used or reproduced in any manner whatsoever without written permission except in the case of brief quotations embodied in critical articles and reviews. For information, address HarperCollins Publishers, 195 Broadway, New York, NY 10007.

HarperCollins books may be purchased for educational, business, or sales promotional use. For information, please email the Special Markets Department at SPsales@harpercollins.com.

Originally published as *Gewässer im Ziplock* in Germany in 2023 by Suhrkamp Verlag Ag

FIRST HARPERVIA EDITION PUBLISHED IN 2025

Designed by Yvonne Chan

Library of Congress Cataloging-in-Publication Data has been applied for.

ISBN 978-0-06-337455-3

25 26 27 28 29 LBC 5 4 3 2 1

In memory of Norman Golb

Contents

Prologue

He stayed once for kiddush, the big meal after Friday-evening prayers. He sat at the head of the table, the room packed, hardly enough chairs for everyone. It might be better if he left, he said, but no, they wanted him to stay, wanted him to sit at the head of the table, next to the gabbai. They observed as he nodded at the first offer of vodka before gracefully declining, as he carefully cut his food with his plastic knife and fork. He looked a little big for his chair.

There had been three courses: hummus with salad, something with curry, then cake, all from a kosher caterer. He seemed especially to enjoy the vegetables, of which he took a second helping.

He laughed politely if anyone remarked something funny, and when posed a question, he responded neither tersely nor pedantically. They learned that he lived in Prenzlauer Berg, that he'd been in the same apartment a long time; so he liked it, sure, and he'd gotten lucky, the rents in Berlin were a nightmare. They asked him where he'd lived before, and he said Hannover, which surprised them, considering his foreign accent.

They tried to get him to gossip about the Central Council of Jews in Germany, but apparently, he had no bones to pick with the Central Council.

Up close, he looked tired.

He left before Birkat Hamazon, relayed his goodbyes, his thanks, nodded to everyone, wished them all a peaceful Shabbes.

They agreed one and all that he was intriguing, this cantor, friendly, and the one with the best voice.

They wondered if he was lonely where he was returning to. Whether anyone was there waiting for him. He didn't have a ring on, but what did that mean, really, there were fewer people with rings than there were people that were lonely.

Part One

It was always loudest just before the prayers. They commenced at 7:03 p.m. in summer, 6:03 p.m. in winter, or sometimes at 7:07 and 6:07. Exactly five minutes before the hour, he walked through the secured entrance, and the candles had to be lit, that was the job of a woman who had no need of a clock to know when it was time, just seeing him enter sufficed. He would nod politely and climb the bimah, and hear word of children born, partners brought along for the first time, matters major and minor, recipes, the living and the dead. The chitchat would grow louder with every minute past the hour, as if somehow to adjourn the prayers that they had come for. On rare occasions, they had to wait until enough men arrived. Ten men were required for worship. During the pandemic, not so many came, out of fear, from respect, and those who did had to wear masks and sign a list. There were many arguments about whether women ought to count, especially in such times, and even today, there were a few elders who wouldn't budge, old men who wanted things to remain as they always had been, and he went along and tried not to get involved. He was paid for his voice, for cutting through the chatter, not for his opinions about politics with a capital *P*. Or even, perhaps, with a lowercase *p*.

If he took a deep breath for the first time on the Shabbat in question, no one would have heard it, not even he. The first words of his first song would begin to die away, and then, he imagined, a few visitors behind him would breathe more slowly and think: Now we have tranquility, now we have respite. The first verse he sang alone, the second with the diligent sopranos in the women's row. If he turned to his congregation, he might glimpse a timid smile, and someone would decide to try and chant along, because the music was so beautiful. "Yedid nefesh," he sang, "Beloved of my soul, merciful father, bend your servant to your will, may he chase after you like a gazelle, bow to your glory, find your companionship sweeter than honey, sweeter than any delicacy." His relationship with God was never so peaceful as then, when he thought of him as a friend, as vocal accompaniment, gentle and still. As he sang, the faithful kept wandering in, choosing their row, sitting by their friends, their parents and loved ones, nodding and winking, as though to say: Today is Shabbat. He lulled them into a sense of ease. This was his favorite moment, even if the melody wasn't the most beautiful, or the piyyut the most poetic. After a long walk, the shoes came off, and you wrapped your hands around a glass of warm milk with honey. At the end of the song, everything was completely still. The prayers could begin.

* * *

There were little pieces of something, bits of what once had been cherry, maybe, swimming in the yogurt. She hated that. At home, she never had to eat things she didn't like. She liked almost everything, but she hated these bits in her yogurt. Her cheeks grew hot from a longing for home, nostalgia for a place where no one would ever set such a thing before her, where morning meant peppered mackerel, or the best, creamiest feta from the market, or muesli with lots of nuts. Raw onion and lox and cream cheese on the weekend.

Expectant eyes observed her. "Thank you," she heard herself say, "yummy." *Yummy* was a kid's word, but Margarita's grandmother still thought her one. She was already dressed in her uniform: a white starched blouse with pearl buttons and leggings that drooped in the rear—her *house pants*, which she also wore to the butcher's and baker's, but not to the supermarket or restaurants. For these, she had her *outside pants*, black fabric slacks. "Rita," her grandmother said, "why haven't you gotten dressed yet?" The warmth in her head worsened. Her grandparents lived in a house on the South Side of Chicago, near the university, that was three times as big as the apartment in Berlin and at least three times quieter. Each time Grandma brought the yogurt to her lips, she bit down on the spoon. Audible: the whir of the ceiling fan and the click of enamel on silver. A miracle she hadn't chipped a tooth after all these years. Margarita asked herself whether her mother had felt the same disgust, sitting at that same table at fifteen years old and eating with the same silver. Or had she not noticed, or did she bite down on the spoon as well when she ate yogurt. Maybe her mother had also chewed the ice cream that they often had there for dessert instead of licking it. Maybe when she ate a sandwich, you could see inside her mouth. Maybe you could see the way the lettuce, cheese, white bread, and pickles got smashed into a mush.

Margarita spooned it up faster, carefully scraped the sides of the dish, and said, "I need to go to the bathroom." The bathroom was her refuge during those weeks. She liked to shower in the evenings, until the hot water ran out, skipping out on the evening's plans and declaring she was awfully tired and really had to go to bed. She took baths, even when it was nearly a hundred degrees out. She got an inflamed bladder from peeing so often.

Only when her grandparents were asleep, and she could call

Berlin—quietly—did she stop going so frequently to the bathroom. On bad days, she'd beg her father to let her go home, to come get her, and threaten that when she was back in Berlin, she wouldn't speak another word to him, not ever. He said nothing, or sometimes he calmed her down, humming a melody that never varied.

He didn't know where all the pain came from. He knew the circumstances, the longing for home, he knew all that. But he knew nothing about Nico. No one knew about Nico but Anna. Sometimes Margarita questioned if even she still knew about him; in the evenings, when she stared at her phone, when she tried to sleep, she let her hand slide into her underwear and thought about what had happened. Every morning, her heart pounded before she turned on her phone, tapped the green icon, got her new messages, never any from him.

Sometimes, when she really wanted to torture herself, she would imagine Anna kissing him. She knew that would never happen, because Anna had her back. And yet she continued to picture it as she sat on the toilet lid whiling away the time her grandmother needed to finish her yogurt.

She thought of what Nico had said to her the last time they saw each other. Margarita had needed to call her father, because he always worried when she was out. Afterward, Nico had asked her what language she was speaking. "Hebrew," she responded. "Cool," he said. "You're not like a Zionist, though, are you?"

She had never thought about it before. They had talked about it a lot at school, how improbable their continued existence had been, how the country had been founded, why Israel was a safe haven for Jews all over the world, and about the Palestinians, and about terrorism.

"My dad's from there. That's why I speak it. Plus it's cool, it's like a secret language."

"Still you know, colonialism and all that shit, right," Nico had responded, and she'd nodded, not knowing whether her opinion should be different, not having any opinion at all. Then she changed the subject. It felt a little like a betrayal, but against whom, she didn't know. Her father, maybe, but she was already betraying him either way, by meeting with Nico and keeping the whole thing secret from him.

Grandma had finished off her yogurt by the time Margarita sat back down at the table. She smiled at her, and Margarita felt embarrassed that she'd run away. The seething midday heat worked its way slowly into the kitchen. Margarita closed the door to the patio and lowered the blinds so the air conditioner would work better. A week before, she'd screamed herself hoarse at Fridays for Future. Now, even at night, she didn't cut off the AC in her bedroom. Instead, she slept under a thick blanket. Otherwise, she'd freeze.

* * *

Every year, after Margarita's departure, he would cover the mattress on the bunk bed with a covering he'd bought expressly for the purpose of keeping off the dust. Then he'd close the door to her room and would enter only when he called her in the evenings, perched in the chair where he used to read to her for hours on end, and listened to her faraway voice. As he did so, he'd stare at the shelf opposite, lovingly stocked by him and his few friends, who, when Margarita was little, would bring her books whenever they got the chance. They all knew how proud he was that she had begun reading so early. With great earnestness, she would decipher one word at a time. Margarita, the little grown-up, he always called her when she read complete sentences with her stern face, well before the other children around her could even write their names. When he thought about it, he had to laugh. Margarita had scarcely been able to bear the days when he couldn't keep her occupied, when there was nothing interesting going on. Once, he had found her with his key chain and his wallet in her hands, rubber booties already on her feet, in the hallway. She said she wanted to go buy apple juice, they were all out. She would find the supermarket on her own. But it's Shabbat, he responded. She understood.

Sometimes he would take down one of his favorite books to read aloud, the story about Pettson and Findus and the fireworks that she liked so much, or the one about the lonely bear at the playground with its preachy message about never leaving people out. Margarita didn't need to hear that, she had long been the left-out one herself, had borne it soberly and gone on reading until, after a change from the primary school around the corner to the Jewish High School, she'd found a small group of girlfriends. On rare occasions, she had them over. He knew she was at an age when everything was embarrassing, but still, he wished she'd bring them round more often. He could set out a pizza for them, let them sit in front of the TV, listen to them giggle, Margarita would struggle through it, but that was fine, because all things considered, she was happy.

It moved him to know she missed him so bad. He was torn, during her weeks in Chicago, not knowing whether to take her at her word and book her the next ticket home or to tell himself: she doesn't mean it, it'll pass.

Berlin was cold that summer, July full of misty days. On the way to the synagogue, he thought of the heat of Jerusalem, of the many shoes whose soles he'd worn through there. The walk seemed short when he thought of Israel. During those weeks, he was assigned to evening prayers, and on days when he had time, he liked to go on foot. There was a time when he'd used the minutes before his departure to put everything on the hot plate, which was left on the entire Shabbat, turn on the kettle, even bake challah, so it would all be ready when he got home. For a few years now, Margarita had been permitted to stay home when he went to sing. On his return, he would sing again, this time just for the two of them. As quickly as she could, Margarita would light the candles with a match and say the prayers. After dinner, they'd play Monopoly. He lost, because he spent his money too quickly and seized everything he could, while Margarita quietly collected rent from him. Often, she was so tired from the school week that she almost fell asleep over the game board in the evening.

On the long summer days while she was gone, an unfamiliar but pleasant calm settled in. Apart from the holidays, he gave bar mitzvah lessons once a week. They consisted mostly of preparing the young men for their reading of a section of the Torah and the haftarah. The prospective male and female rabbis and cantors he instructed on the side had now all left for yeshivas across Israel to study the Torah. So he could sleep in and do the shopping less often, read the paper in the morning, take long walks through Berlin. At the same time, these days were bitter, a sort of preparation for the fact that in a few years, Margarita wouldn't be there at all, that if things worked out as she wished, she'd be studying medicine somewhere in southern Germany and coming home only on break between semesters. Her friend Anna had taken her to her grandparents' place on Lake Constance, and she seemed to think now that there existed places that weren't sad in winter. The covering would soon be spread over her bed the whole year.

He, too, had spent periods at yeshivas. The last time was two years before Margarita was born. As cantor for Berlin, he also sang at weddings, at funerals, and on days of remembrance; people mostly died in winter, and the days of remembrance were in the dark season as well, which made sense: you had to be able to imagine evil in every street in Berlin. In spring and summer, no one cared to waste the good weather on sorrow. On May 27, people preferred a first swim at the Prinzenbad to polishing Stolpersteine. And that summer, there were no weddings. Just divorces, and no one sang at those.

The security guard hired by the Jewish Community, who stood sentry before the synagogue next to the policemen that people no longer trusted after that Yom Kippur a few years back, nodded to him from afar. He handed over his shoulder bag in the narrow secure entrance. Inside were his organ donor's card, his passport, an emergency credit card, still unused, his phone, and a photo of Margarita.

It began. Lighting of candles, Yedid Nefesh, a few psalms. The conversations persisted as he uttered them softly, almost soundlessly. Sometimes attendance was so sparse that there was little whispering, just listening and prayers in accompaniment. When it got too loud, when the cries of children distracted him, he would raise his arms high in a gesture of appeasement. For some reason, the children tottering through the pews of the synagogue seemed to respect him, too. They couldn't see it when he was standing there with his back to them, but their horseplay made him grin. It distracted him, but it didn't disturb him. He liked children, and he knew there was no such thing as children without noise.

After the psalms came the Lekha Dodi. It must have had as many melodies as it did verses. His, the one he liked most, was brisk and a bit melancholic. It sounded best when a few higher voices sang along in canon, drawing the *lekha* out as long as possible. "Onward, my friend, to meet the bride, onward, onward," they sang. "We will greet the Sabbath's countenance. Onward, my friend, to meet the bride, let us greet the Sabbath's queen. Lekha Dodi, likrat kalah, pnei schabbat, nekabelah."

He liked that Shabbat became a bride, that one fled into her arms, and that the song sounded especially pretty when sung by women's voices.

The synagogue was full for an unremarkable evening in summer. Sunlight fell on the bimah through the stained glass windows, and a few spots of light blue danced on the pages of his open prayer book. It smelled of lacquer and the sticky hands of children.

He recognized the voices of many of those chanting. He sang the last verse especially loud, and they followed along. He wondered whether they were audible from the sidewalk, and what the passersby might be thinking.

* * *

Grandma shoved a meat loaf into the oven. She was getting ugly, Margarita thought, her head was almost hairless, not just wrinkly, but sallow, too. Margarita was certain of it: there was no love there, she didn't love this woman, she didn't like her, she had to be here because she was fifteen and had no say and because it was hoped, as Aba said, she'd one day be grateful "for the time with her grandparents, and for the language." Today she'd be going shopping with Grandma. She used to like going with her. Now she sometimes asked herself whether she was intentionally trying to hate everything; whether she actually enjoyed the drive together to Hyde Park Produce, where the best melons and cherries were, and fresh spinach and green asparagus from California; whether she would miss them, if she were really honest with herself. At that moment, she didn't know what that meant, being honest with yourself. She hoped one day it wouldn't weigh on her so.

To give Margarita something to do, her grandparents paid for a costly summer class at the University of Chicago Laboratory Schools. Last summer, she'd done a three-week cooking class, which had been practical: while there, she'd eaten so much that she was still full at six o'clock dinner. Later, she would often slink into the kitchen for muesli or some toast. Naturally, her grandmother always heard her as soon as she came down the stairs, and ran after her as swiftly as her surgically repaired knee would allow. "Sweetheart, you should have said something! I could have made you something nice! Let me warm you up some chicken, or a bit of the kugel I made for you." Kugel, that was noodles baked in milk in the oven, like a sweet casserole. Authentically Jewish, apparently. What exactly was so Jewish about it, Margarita didn't understand. Nor could her father tell her.

This year, there was another cooking class, but her grandparents had decided one was enough, and so, along with the daughters of rich parents from around the university, Margarita learned to write poems, or at least to try. So far, she'd only managed short stories, inserting line breaks when she finished, making them look like insanely long poems. When she made errors in English, the other girls found it "so interesting."

By foot, it was around ten minutes from her grandparents' front door on Blackstone Avenue to the campus. Detour onto Fifty-Seventh Street, where there was a bakery that offered delicious ice-cold lemonade and chocolate croissants the size of half a loaf of bread. Margarita's father gave her enough money that she could afford a lemonade or a croissant more or less every day. And books. Even lots of them, when she rationed it out well, either at 57th Street Books, where there were new releases—though not cheap—or at Powell's, a used bookstore at the end of the road by the sinister train station that connected Hyde Park with the rest of the city. Inside Powell's, it smelled like a mix of musty cellar, fresh laundry, and old volumes with brittle pages, so brittle you had the feeling they would turn to dust if you rubbed them between your fingers. She had gone there often with her father when she was still too young to fly on her own.

As soon as she turned onto Blackstone Avenue, she slowed her steps. Often she had to grip the railing like her grandmother, pull herself up the small steps in front of the door, stare a minute at the doorbell, before she was ready to endure that *I'm coming, I'm coming*, and seconds later, after the bell was rung, *Just a minute now, I'm coming!*

When the storms came after days of dank heat, she would run out to the yard and let the rain pour over her until her underclothes were soaked, sometimes even until it stopped, amid the unmistakable scent of grass and the big paving stones of the sidewalks: scent of earth, of freshly washed stone, of carefully tended front gardens of aromatic flowers. Her father had once remarked that it was the smell of wealth.

But today was Sunday, Margarita couldn't run around alone as she did after summer school; in the afternoon, her grandmother wanted to go shopping. That was Chicago: shopping on Sundays. On Saturdays her grandparents went to shul, usually, and Margarita had to come along and let her cheeks be pinched. Shopping was on Sundays, and Margarita helped her grandmother carry her bags. This year, she also had to help her out of the car.

Household procedures were strict: breakfast at nine, an hour later than during the week. Then her grandfather spent a few hours reading the paper while her grandmother got a head start on dinner. Margarita, in the meanwhile, would lie belly down on the bed, stare at her phone, read a book, or masturbate, or often all three, one after the other, in thirty-minute intervals. Lunch was at one thirty. After lunch came shopping: first Hyde Park Produce, then Trader Joe's. Everything they bought would be cooked in the coming days: not so much baked, boiled, or sautéed as reduced to mush. Her grandmother managed to burn her pancakes on the outside while leaving their interiors runny. Her lasagna noodles were already falling to pieces before they even went into the oven. Margarita's prose poem about spongy lasagna had made everyone in class laugh. But she had been ashamed of her German accent. And then, on the walk home, she'd been ashamed of her previously shameless meanness.

Now she was lying on the bed and waiting for lunch, for yet another meal to be over, for another day to lurch closer to its end. She stared at an empty page in a notebook, then at the black screen of her phone, then back at the page, a constant back-and-forth. At some point she wrote to ask Anna if she was still awake. Her best friend could party the whole summer away, drinking on the banks of the Landwehrkanal and at the Weinbergspark. Her father had said it was cold in Berlin, but still, Margarita imagined Anna, legs bare in high-waisted Levi's shorts, smoking as she rode her bicycle through the night.

Anna was so pretty that she'd automatically become the most beloved person in their clique. They'd met in the bat mitzvah class, where Anna was the only one no one knew, the only one who didn't attend the Jewish High School. Even at school, Margarita always looked after the newcomers. But Anna needed no looking after. She had learned effortlessly how to interpret the melodies, and had soon become the teacher's pet, because she always did her homework.

Only months later, on one of their long winter walks through Prenzlauer Berg, had Margarita grasped why. Anna spoke, in a soft voice, of her mother, who wasn't Jewish, and of her father, whose grandparents had survived the Holocaust. She said that her mother had needed convincing to let her convert. She was afraid Anna would let herself be victimized. Margarita had to laugh when Anna said that: Anna, who never hesitated to ask a stranger for a light, Anna, so painfully good-looking, with her gigantic blue eyes, full lips, golden-blond hair. No one would ever want to harm someone so beautiful, Margarita thought. Anna could choose whomever she wanted to make out with. At the Jewish High School, everyone had known one another forever, the lines were clear. The parents had set the ground rules. But Anna was allowed to do whatever she wanted, so long as she maintained her grades. At the Saturday prayers they had to attend during preparation for their bat mitzvah, Anna showed up alone, as did Margarita. That brought them together. All the others went with their families, but Margarita's father was off singing, and according to Anna, you couldn't have paid her parents to set foot in the synagogue.

And so Anna started to stop by Margarita's on Saturdays, and together they would walk along Oranienburger Strasse, discussing the events of the two days that had passed since their Wednesday lessons. Anna went out on Friday nights. Margarita had to stay home. In her home, Shabbat was holy, and she accepted this for fear of losing her freedom on Saturday evenings, but also because, somehow, it felt right to her.

After their bat mitzvah celebrations, they stopped going to synagogue on Saturdays, instead lounging on the sofa and gabbing or buying falafel sandwiches and walking through the park. Or they'd help Anna's parents with the cooking. Unlike Margarita's father, they had company all the time, every weekend they went to the chic delicatessen on Rykestrasse and bought good wine, all sorts of cheese, and there was pumpkin soup and salmon in puff pastry in winter, and in summer salad and *Flammkuchen*. All of last year, Margarita had been allowed to sleep over at Anna's after those dinners, where she'd been given a small glass of sparkling wine. In recent months, she'd met Anna's friends afterward, played drinking games in the park, or gone to parties at the homes of strangers' parents. Not long before Margarita had to fly to the US, her friends from the Jewish High School had started coming with them, too. They were shy, and for a while, Margarita found them irritating. She thought herself experienced somehow, since she'd started buying thongs at H&M and taking tequila shots at parties, but she felt she owed it to them to bring them along. A few guys from Margarita's class had heard that she knew people outside their school. She ran into some of them in the park when she was hanging out with Anna and Anna's friends.

Yesterday at summer school, their assignment was to choose a theme that they would write about for the rest of the coming week.

Before then, she hadn't dared write about her life in Berlin, fearing homesickness and being unable to find the right words. Today she wanted to try, but just as she dug out her notebook, her grandmother bellowed, "Rita! Lunch!" Her words echoed through the house. She slowly walked down the stairs. Lunch was eaten at the round kitchen table rather than the long one in the dining room. The dining room table was set only on Friday, Saturday, and Sunday evenings. They sat closer together at the kitchen table. That made the eating sounds even louder.

The meat loaf her grandmother had put in the oven earlier was for dinner. For lunch, there was gazpacho from a jar, because it was so hot out and because her grandmother thought it fancy. Slimy noodles floated in the gazpacho. "We ate this one time in Spain, in that wonderful hotel, remember, darling?" she shouted across the table. Grandpa was hard of hearing. Margarita suspected he turned his hearing aid down on purpose. He nodded amicably and went on slurping his soup. "And I thought it was so tasty," Grandma roared, "it was so tasty, and we were sweating like crazy, the Spaniards, you know, they probably still have no idea air-conditioning exists." At this point, she laughed too loud and too long. Margarita turned in her chair from disgust. "Anyway, sweetheart, I thought I'd buy something special for our Sunday lunch. I always see you making those little sandwiches, and I thought to myself, you'll probably need some carbs, so I added some whole wheat noodles. Is it good, apple of my eye?" Margarita tried to answer, but her grandmother went on talking. "Anyway, hon, we're going shopping once I'm done with my afternoon nap." *Hon* was Grandpa. Margarita was *sweetheart. We* was Grandma and her. Her grandmother smiled to herself. Lipstick and gazpacho clung to her teeth. Margarita felt a bottomless abyss of repulsion and loneliness growing within her.

"Sure," she said, "I'll get ready while you're napping." She stood and went upstairs, without putting her bowl in the dishwasher.

The tears came as soon as she shut her door. She cried until her grandmother called for her. In the staircase on her way back down, she glared at a childhood photo of her mother and thought: You did this to me. You and no one else.

* * *

Lekha Dodi was followed once more by a few psalms he only ever sang the first few words of, to get the congregation started. Afterward, in the synagogue, it was still. "The floods have lifted up, O LORD, the floods have lifted up their voice; The floods lift up their waves. The LORD on high is mightier than the noise of many waters, Yea, than the mighty waves of the sea." He loved his work not only because it allowed him to give guidance, to put the most sacred into words, to share something with each individual, but also because of the literary splendor of the prayers. This the Germans would never understand, no matter how many guided tours they took through the country's remaining synagogues, the ones their grandparents hadn't razed. The significance of reading three times how the rivers roared because they were meant to, because it had been decreed that they should strike and storm and Hashem should overcome them. Hashem, the Most High, incomparably vast, yet smaller than the atoms in the roiling waters, who was all, who abided in all: in him, in the faithful, in the policemen protecting them, in the Landwehrkanal, in green Jordan, in Lake Michigan.

Only in literature did he feel, at times, something approaching those prayers that stole his words away. As though the phrases permeated him, exempting him from this world.

They continued with the Mourner's Kaddish, but he didn't speak along, because he was no longer in mourning. His parents had died ten years before, one not long after the other, he and his sister inherited their apartment on Allenby Street and sold it right away, because the Tel Aviv real estate market was booming. He put aside the money for Margarita's studies. His thoughts drifted back there: to the smell of the apartment when his father became incontinent. An echo of mourning, this disgust at his own parents, which he'd almost forgotten. An echo, too, of Psalm 93: in despair, he had spoken it aloud, over and over, after the two of them died. You were not to utter the kaddish alone, and so he reached for the psalm that was closest to it.

That was the one time in the synagogue he didn't quite have a grip on himself. His voice cracked during the kaddish, and one of the young women who was always there organizing events pulled him aside and asked him whether everything was all right. When he answered that his father had died, she asked if he'd like to take a walk with her. The suggestion pleased him, and for months he was on the verge of taking her up on it. But he resisted, over and over, because he didn't want to bore her or appear unprofessional. Margarita consoled him, as always. When his sister called to tell him their mother had died, heavy tears dripped onto the green telephone. He didn't realize they were his until Margarita crawled into his lap with a roll of toilet paper. Both times, he'd had a babysitter come for the forty-eight hours needed for the burial, he hadn't wanted to bring Margarita along, he felt she was too small for funerals. That gave him time enough to attend the ceremonies, sort through red tape, and buy Margarita books.

He'd had to put on the tefillin in the airplane. He hadn't missed Israel, but on this trip, nostalgia took hold of him, and spun him round in circles until he vomited his heart out that night in the hotel on Rothschild Boulevard. Afterward, cheek on the cool pillow, he whispered Psalm 93 to himself. Repeatedly, he told himself the floods lifted their voice and the Lord on high was mightier, so many sons had lost their mothers, the water's roar resounded, and yet the Most High was louder.

He heard this roar as the mourners uttered the kaddish. Only afterward came the service proper, the evening prayers for Shabbat, everything else was mere preparation.

During the Amidah, he concentrated on staying close to the language, to the language and to the silence of prayer. His relationship to words seemed reversed. Even as he dictated to the congregation its prayers, the words on the paper dictated his own: the strong verbs bent him over their knee, the weak verbs looked on. Everyone wished one another, and him, a peaceful Shabbat. He looked in their faces once or twice and saw a fear he knew from his time in the military, and from the eyes of his parents when the sirens would wail.

* * *

The weekend had passed, despite Margarita's lingering doubts that it ever would. After her midday nap, her grandmother had put on her going-out pants and pressed her bag into Margarita's hand. They walked slowly through the supermarket aisles. She had helped her grandmother bring home the shopping; had helped her put it away, had baked a cake with her, without butter or milk, to be eaten as dessert after the meat loaf; had been allowed to lick out the bowl and had enjoyed it, though she said nothing; had eaten little of the dry meat and the overcooked green beans; had shared the pleasure of the chocolate cake with her grandfather. His eyes sparkled at her across the table as he laid a second slice on the plate, first for her, then for himself.

Margarita well remembered back when she and her grandfather used to count on her fingers, or spent an entire summer drawing Hebrew letters, and he kept guiding her hand across the paper. She had been happy, as a seven-year-old, to sit on his lap and paint in whirls. She still revered her grandmother then, setting off with her to Bloomingdale's to buy expensive clothes and eat grilled cheese sandwiches and mint chocolate chip ice cream. She resisted holding her hand at every stoplight, and it grossed her out, having to kiss her on the mouth to say thanks. But the deep scorn she now felt was something she hadn't known then.

Once, she was there for Pesach, and her grandparents had taken her to their friends' place, and she had fallen asleep at the table, because of her jet lag and because of how ravenous you got listening to the tale of the Exodus. She was allowed to lie down in the guest bed until her grandfather took her out to the car. She let him carry her. Her father was the only other person she'd have allowed to do that. How strange that this was the same man who now nodded off in front of the TV every evening, spittle dripping onto his shirt. Did he already do that back then? Sometimes she tried to regard her grandparents in a gentler light. But she never managed it.

* * *

The way back was faster than the way over. His phone rang: Margarita's mother. He didn't pick up, because it was Shabbat, and on Shabbat he used the phone only for emergencies. Like when his daughter called.

* * *

"Rita, dear, come and sit with me," her grandmother called from her bedroom. Margarita came over and sat on the bench at the end of the bed, which was always perfectly made. Grandma smiled at her. She smiled back. Today it wasn't hard for her, because Anna had told her that morning that Nico had asked about her. But then her grandmother said, "I'm going to arrange for you to see your mother."

Margarita's heart sank in her chest. "I thought she didn't want to see me."

"Well, I want her to see you. We're so proud of the young woman you're growing up to be. We have a right to show you off!" This last sentence she seemed to find incredibly funny, and burst out in that shrill laughter of hers.

Margarita wondered if it was sarcasm, if even her grandmother found the thought of bragging about her preposterous, and she tried to laugh along.

"Anyway, bubbale, since you're just here for two weeks, I thought I'd try to get a hold of her. We saw her just a month ago, she gave a speech at the university, can you believe that?"

"No way," Margarita said, unmoved. She thought she felt diarrhea coming on, her mouth dry the way it always was those nights when she knew Nico would be there and she imagined how she'd lie with him in bed later, his head in her lap. She had to blink several times to bring herself back to her grandparents' bedroom. Sunlight poured through the wooden blinds, dust whirling in its midst.

"Rita?" her grandmother asked. "Did you hear me?"

Margarita stared at her. "Sorry," she said, "I drifted off."

"I said, I'll call your mother up and arrange something. Your grandpa and I are worried this might be your last summer here. You don't really seem to like it." The loud laughter returned.

Margarita's heart sank even deeper. "No, Grandma, I wouldn't— that isn't—that's not true," she said in her faltering English. The dust seemed to whirl more quickly in the light.

Her grandmother stood. "It's fine, Rita," she said. "We're old. We've seen worse things. We raised a daughter, remember?" This time, she didn't laugh. "Now, go to your room and do whatever you do in there. I'll call for you soon."

Back in her room, Margarita heard her grandmother shut the door. Had her mother felt this way, too, when she used to hide in here? Her grandmother's door stayed closed a long time. At some point her heart stopped beating so wildly, and she opened the book she'd been reading.

They fled each other as best they could, her mother and she.

"Rita," her grandmother shouted, "your father wants to speak with you." Her voice sounded happy. That couldn't mean anything good.

"My father?" Margarita echoed, as if she hadn't exactly understood, and sat down next to her again. Her grandmother nodded and smiled.

"Margarita," her father said in Hebrew, "how's it going? Better than yesterday?"

Naturally, she'd cried again last night on the phone. When the sun rose, she strove to forget the nights before. She tried to convince herself this was what growing up entailed: you practiced during the day, then at night you reverted to a child. She still fell asleep on the sofa when she couldn't manage to in bed, with her father there singing to her softly. She still called him on nights when she felt sad. She didn't answer his question.

"Motek," he said, "we have a suggestion for you."

"Who's *we*." She wanted it to sound like an affirmation, not a question: I see that you're working against me.

"Your mother, your grandmother, and I."

So her mother was in on it, too. Her father made long pauses between his sentences. His slowness had always gotten on her nerves. Now it enraged her. Her grandmother sat next to her and looked at her with a mad grin, as if she were about to share with her the best news in her life. She turned away.

Her father started talking again. "Look, Margarita," he said, "you know how rare it is for me to talk to your mother. She called yesterday to ask me a favor. I think it's a good idea. And I think it's important for you to get to know her better. For your relationship with each other."

"This monologue will get you nowhere unless you get to the point."

"I'm getting there, motek. So, your mother called me—"

"If it's about me, she could have called herself."

"Margarita, let me finish."

She was so angry, she hardly knew what to do with herself.

"Your mother asked whether you might like to go see her in Jerusalem."

Before she could even think about whether she might like it, she'd already begun to formulate arguments against it. "I didn't even know she lived there. Why should I all the sudden want to fly to see her when I don't even know where she lives? When I don't even know what continent my mother is not bothering to take care of me from, why should I be the one to fly there? Why?"

Her grandmother placed a hand on her knee, and she batted it away. "Rita," she said, "why don't you at least give him a chance?" On the phone, her father sighed.

"Rita, Rita, Rita," Margarita imitated her. "You don't even understand what I'm saying."

Her grandmother stared back, wounded. It was true she spoke no Hebrew, and yet she must have understood, Margarita thought, grabbing the windowsill to pull herself up and leaving the room. Her father was trying to talk her down, but nothing helped: she refused to leave here, this musty old house that she'd so hated just seconds before. That she could deal with, she'd resigned herself to hating everything, and she didn't want to have to change her summer plans again. Especially not for a woman who had given birth to her only to run away right after.

"How can that even occur to her?" she said. "What am I supposed to do?"

"Do you want an honest answer, or do you want to keep yelling at me?" her father asked calmly.

She fell silent, noticing that her lower lip had curled up over the upper one, as in a shoddy cartoon, and she was angry at herself, at the child she still was. So she listened.

"Right. Your mother's gotten a fellowship at Hebrew University. She thought it would start in October, but they've already let her move into her office. The point is, she has a lot of free time until the fall, and she suggested you come visit. You'd have a room of your own. And you could practice your Hebrew."

"I already speak Hebrew."

"You know what I mean. Please, Margarita, think it over. You've never been there before. I know it's not easy with her, but she says it would make her really happy. She says you could go to the Dead Sea together."

Margarita sniffled. She tried to imagine arriving at the airport and her mother standing there waiting for her and waving. She couldn't even see her face in her head, that was how long it had been since they'd seen each other. Did she have wrinkles? She must have wrinkles. How old was she? "How old is she now?" Margarita asked, because nothing else occurred to her.

"Forty-eight," her father responded.

"A little old to be traipsing all over the world, don't you think?"

That pushed him over the edge. "No, Margarita, no. Your mother has her reasons. I've never talked about her that way, and you shouldn't, either."

"Then she should have taken care of me," Margarita sobbed into the telephone. "Forget it. I'm not going. I'll be back in Berlin in three weeks. You don't have to pick me up from the airport. I'll catch the bus."

"Motek—" her father said, but she hung up.

Her grandmother leaned in the doorway and put her hand over her heart. Margarita stood and walked toward her. She was so much taller than her grandmother that she could peer down at the crown of her head.

"Sweetheart," Grandma said, "it's all right, there's no reason to get so worked up."

"You have no idea," Margarita said, and pushed past her to reach her room. She wanted it to sound dry, hard, and cold, but all she could hear was her German accent. She slammed the door to her room so hard that it flew back open. Nothing was working right.

*   *   *

He tried to pray, but it made him feel foolish. As if you could just pray everything away like an unfeeling donkey. And still, he put on the tefillin and prayed she would calm down, and maybe even agree to the trip. Prayed she wouldn't hold it against him in a few years, whether or not she went. Prayed that she would make the right decision. Even the roar of the ninety-third psalm, which he always repeated, was no match for his daughter's silence. Never before had she gone so long without talking to him. Three days now. Her grandmother called and told him what Margarita was doing, but it sounded as if she were speaking not of his daughter, but of a zoo animal, reachable only by tapping on the glass. His daughter could already be sitting on a flight back to Berlin and her grandmother wouldn't notice. That would be like Margarita, to leave a shell of herself back in America that would flush the toilet every half hour while she had somehow managed to maneuver her way onto a plane.

*   *   *

In the taxi, she asked herself whether it really could have been her last summer with her grandparents. She tried to catch the scent of the brick house, but could no longer recall it. She sniffed her sleeve, which was wet with tears and still smelled of the laundry room, as if that could change anything. Never again, she promised herself, would she wash this sweater that she'd put on because the AC in the car was so cold it made her teeth chatter. Crying didn't ease her chattering. She hadn't known there were any tears left in her, she'd thought she'd let them all out, but no, they kept flowing, and in the meantime, it was harder not to cry than just to keep crying. She wasn't even ashamed of it, though the taxi driver had already asked her if he should turn back. The preparations had all been made in no time. The months of planning her trip to America now seemed laughable. It had taken just three days to ship her off to the other end of the earth. In her suitcase, her dirty laundry was wedged between the books she'd crammed in there, unwilling to leave any of them behind. Margarita wondered what the laundry would smell like in Jerusalem.

At some point, she'd given in, just because she was exhausted and a little curious about what it would be like to wander around there on her own, what the streets would look like, the houses, how people would glance at her, whether it would be obvious she didn't belong, or whether she'd be one of them, a Jewish girl in a Jewish land. She didn't know how she was meant to imagine Jerusalem. She knew the city from stories from her childhood: it sounded menacing, as if sprung from a fairy tale rather than her father's memory. Now she thought she'd rather have swallowed another hundred years of boredom than be sitting in this taxi right now.

And yet, as they arrived at the airport, she sensed something that resembled anticipation. "Flying home?" the man in customs asked as he stamped her passport. "No," she said, and he responded, "Leaving home?" She nodded and didn't know why. She didn't understand the tears that flowed again, that kept flowing as she was picked up by the woman who would accompany her through the terminal and who asked if she'd like something to eat. Margarita showed her the sandwich, the little bag of chips, the big dill pickle in a ziplock bag, the blueberries in another, the piece of kugel in a third. The woman laid a hand gingerly on her shoulder as she sat in a chair at the terminal. She didn't shove the hand away, just leaned a few inches forward, and the woman left it hovering in the air as Margarita ate her blueberries.

* * *

For years, he hadn't needed to set an alarm, his body knew what day of the week it was, what hour of what day; even when it was pitch dark he could tell the time, often within fifteen minutes. But today, he slept in, and there was no time for showering or breakfast. He'd slept a great deal these past few days. He'd been exhausted, the way you were after a long walk in the sun, or after those nights when Margarita had a fever so high he couldn't shut his eyes as he changed out the cold washcloths. It was raining buckets that morning, but it didn't matter, he had to attend a planning meeting at the Community offices. He threw on his raincoat, found a rusty umbrella on the shelf in the hall, and took the tram, just two stations, but still, he was sopping wet when he arrived. It had been a long time since Berlin had seen a storm like this.

Margarita still hadn't said anything, and he realized that what he'd used to regard as loneliness had actually been gratifying solitude. True loneliness, when the silence loomed, threatening to devour him, robbing him of appetite and sapping and depleting him, so that he napped at midday and woke with a warm sensation in his head, spoke his prayers, walked back and forth up the street, and went back to bed—this kind of loneliness he'd only just now come to know. He'd last felt this way during those months in Hannover after Marsha had gone away, before he'd moved with Margarita to Berlin; she'd rather have crisscrossed the city on unsteady legs, he thought, than sit with her depressed father, who still spoke hardly a word of German, in an attic apartment, its only windows in the ceiling, unable ever to see what was happening outside, the garbage trucks and cargo bikes hidden from her little eyes.

He asked himself—occasionally—if he shouldn't find someone

to share his bed, to hold his hand when the thing happened that must absolutely happen sometime: when Margarita went away. When she would close up like one of the seashells she had found on the Baltic Sea and popped in her mouth with a sly smirk before asking whether God would get mad now, because shellfish wasn't kosher, or whether it would be all right as long as she spit it back out.

The meeting dragged on, they discussed trivialities: private matters that didn't interest him, politics, which he'd have preferred to turn a deaf ear to. At the same time, he looked forward to the afternoon with its mandatory rest. And the next morning, he'd have a whole day to kill, no TV, no reading, no writing—just giving in again to the cloying sleep that had relentlessly gripped him over the preceding weeks.

Leaving the Community's offices, as the others all went to the restaurant next door for lunch, he found it was still raining, but didn't care, no one would see him for the rest of the day. He weathered the storm, leaving the umbrella in his pocket, letting his coat flap open, only the thin scarf, which he always wore to protect his vocal cords, remained in place. He supposed the rain was cold, but he himself was unusually warm. Only halfway home did he start to freeze, and he hoped he wouldn't catch cold.

Freeze Margarita wouldn't, wrapped in a blanket on the plane, tomorrow in the heat of Jerusalem, where she would possibly have a freshly squeezed orange juice in a café and read a book with her mother, whom she would hopefully meet shortly. It bothered him that she might treat Marsha differently from him—him, who still sometimes held a finger under her nose as she slept to make sure she was breathing easy. He had transferred more money to her yesterday so she could buy books in Israel at the shop on Emek Refaim, where there were English titles and a few German ones; he'd have preferred to call her right away to tell her where she could find things to read, but it was raining too hard, and he didn't want to ruin his phone, so he trotted onward until even his socks were soaked, probably his underwear, too, the skin under them felt clammy.

At home he took a bath, lay in the tub until hunger got the best of him, drank cold water from the tap like an animal, took a hot shower, and put on his thickest socks. But instead of getting warmer, he only grew wearier. In the courtyard, a woman was shouting at her child. A cold summer, he thought, was worse than the dark winter days when you could tuck yourself away and there were remedies like tea and strudel. There was no remedy for a cold summer day. There was soup on the stove, he ate from it, it burned his throat when he swallowed. Then he prayed and lay down. In his sleep, Margarita spoke with him at the dining table, shouted at him, threw things, for a moment he thought of striking her, took fright, slept longer, did not dream.

* * *

She'd stopped crying by the time boarding started, but now she had a splitting headache. Laurie, the woman who had accompanied her, told her she wasn't allowed to give her medicine, it was against the rules. But she did take her to the airport pharmacy, where Margarita bought a ten-dollar box of tampons and ibuprofen. Laurie waited in front of the pharmacy with her luggage. From a distance, people might have thought they were mother and daughter, but if they came close, they could see Laurie was wearing a uniform with a name tag on the blazer. And then they'd all think: Wasn't Margarita a little old to still need help boarding? Even on the plane, there was a stewardess responsible for her. Laurie took her all the way to her seat before taking her leave.

It was an overnight flight, thirteen hours, direct, with a little screen in the back of the seat in front of her. Her grandparents had booked a seat with extra legroom, which her father would have never been able to afford. Margarita shoved her backpack under the seat and slipped on her headphones. She knew it would be a while before takeoff, so she closed her eyes to keep from crying more and put on some music, first the reggae that Nico had introduced her to, which she soon tired of, then Bach's cello suites, which she loved. It seemed like days ago that she'd been running restlessly from the bed to the bathroom in the redbrick house. She'd gotten diarrhea just before the taxi arrived and had told her grandmother. She'd had to take Imodium, and she was ashamed that these were the last words they'd exchanged before she left. She only knew the Hebrew word for diarrhea, *shilshul*, and that made it all worse. Her grandmother understood right away and rubbed her own belly, as if she'd have happily done the same for Margarita but didn't dare to.

At some point, a stewardess tapped her on the shoulder and introduced herself in English, with an accent Margarita recognized only from her father. They stuck with this language, since Margarita didn't come out and tell her she spoke Hebrew, too. Margarita was sitting by the window, as she always did when she flew, because everyone thought that was what kids were supposed to do. When her father still used to go with her to Chicago, she had laid her short legs on his lap and slept until he woke her to see something pretty: a sunrise or a view of Greenland from above. The stewardess told her their departure had been slightly delayed. Was there a way she could notify her mother? "It's not a problem," she responded. There was nothing the stewardess could do to help her, anyway.

A woman sat next to her with a giant silver Star of David around her neck smelling heavily of perfume. She smiled at Margarita and said, "We're not even in Israel yet, and already, everything's running late."

Margarita didn't know everything always ran late in Israel.

The air in the cabin smelled stale, dull, disinfected. Someone rammed their knees into her back. She didn't want to turn around and get flustered or make it seem like she was picking a fight. So she closed her eyes again until the plane set in motion. It was twilight in Chicago, and from her window, she could see the skyline: the Hancock Center, the Willis Tower. They blinked as if calling out to her, telling her in Morse code: All this and more you're leaving behind. One last time, she sensed the odor of the freshly cleaned downtown streets, expensive shops, and dapper people; one last time, she heard American sirens. Then the plane took off, and the knees in her back were so sharp that she had to glance back, and though she couldn't see the guy's face well, he couldn't have been older than twenty. He had a sleep mask over his eyes and a travel pillow around his neck. On his ears were gigantic headphones. His hair was dark brown, he had thin, crooked lips; judging by his chin, she'd say he couldn't yet grow a beard. He'd balled his hands into fists and was leaning far back. Margarita decided not to bother him, and shoved the blanket that had been lying on her seat behind her back. Beneath them, the grid of streets and the dark blue lake like a sea. She pressed her forehead to the window.

The sun soon set. At some point, the boy's knees grew less sharp. When she turned around again, she saw him looking at his screen. Their eyes met, and she turned away before he could say something to her. Then she fell asleep: a jerky, uncomfortable sleep. She woke to her neighbor poking her. It was dinnertime. She ate nothing, just drank the apple juice on her tray. Then she had to go to the bathroom. While she was there, the plane began to buck, and she fell from side to side. When they announced that passengers must return to their seats, saliva filled her mouth. She had just dropped to her knees when a knock came on the door. She finished, sat on the floor, and breathed deep. Her mouth tasted sour. The knocking grew harder. She unlocked the door. She didn't

know what else to do. A stewardess, an older one, with a moth-
erly smile and a grayish-blond perm, sauntered in and crouched.
"Can I help?" she asked, and Margarita shook her head. "I had to
throw up, because of the—" Her entire body shook. "Oy," the flight
attendant said, "you poor little thing. I'll get you water and mouthwash, will that help?" Margarita nodded. She was too tired to go on
hating everything. She felt teeny-tiny, as though she were about to
turn six, not sixteen. With effort, she pulled herself to the sink and
wiped the tears from her face. The woman brought her mouthwash
and stood in the open doorway as Margarita gargled.

The airplane lurched harder and harder. Again, without warn-
ing, she had to vomit. The stewardess held her hair, which was
already in a ponytail, and rubbed her back. This time, less came
up. The shaking stopped. She rinsed her mouth a second time and
the flight attendant took her to her seat. The woman next to her was
sleeping again. "Maybe you'd like to switch to an aisle seat? Something closer to the bathroom?" the stewardess asked. There was one
free next to the boy who had been kneeing her.

Woozily, she sat down. She must have stunk of vomit.

The stewardess passed her things back to her: the blanket, the
pillow, the book. "If you need to throw up again, just hit the button,"
she said. "I'm Eloise."

Margarita nodded. The guy smiled at her, a smile she thought
might have malicious joy in it. She looked away and closed her
eyes, but she couldn't sleep any longer. At least the Imodium had
worked. Could be worse, her father always said in his odd Israeli
accent, as if he were singing. She longed just then to hear his voice.

There were five hours left in the flight. It was bright again in the
cabin now, and she took out her book. "Ma at korat?" the boy asked
her. *What are you reading?* It sounded less like a question than a
demand. She showed him the cover of *The Sisterhood of the Traveling Pants.* It told the story of four friends who could all fit into

the same jeans even though their bodies were different, because of their spiritual or trouser-based kinship. What was it about? She said she didn't speak Hebrew well and couldn't tell him. He replied that she'd done a perfect job explaining that her Hebrew was bad. So, then.

"It's about a pair of blue pants."

"Jeans," he said.

"Told you."

He stretched his hand out. "My name's Lior."

She said, "Ah."

He asked her what her name was.

"Margarita."

"In Israel that's what we call . . ."

She didn't understand the last word.

"Bitches," he said in English.

She stared into her book, but saw only a row of words, no grammar, no meaning.

"I'm sorry," he said.

"In Germany," she said, "Lior is what they call morons." She knew the word for moron. *Manyak.*

"I doubt there's many Liors in Germany. What do you do in Germany?"

"I am German." *Ani germanit.* He looked at her inquisitively. She didn't understand his expression, or chose not to. "My father's Israeli," she said.

"What about your mother? Is she German?"

"No. We just live there."

"Because it's so nice?"

"Yeah. Have you ever been to Berlin."

"Aaah," he said. "Berlin! Berlin's not Germany, though!"

"Yeah, sure," she said, returned to her book.

He put on his headphones again.

Snacks were passed out. Both tore their packets open at once, spilled all the nuts into their hands, and tossed them into their mouths, in a synchronized movement.

Slowly, Margarita relaxed. Lior stared, was hypnotized by the screen, she flipped the pages and went on reading. The nuts helped with her nausea. Now she really was hungry and she retrieved the bag with the kugel from her purse. It tasted of her grandmother's cooking: sugary, slightly metallic, reminding her of the coppery form it was baked in. Lior laughed. She looked up. It was the movie. "Kugel," he said. "How Ashkenazi." The airplane jolted once more. "Don't throw up again." It had a friendly ring to it.

* * *

The aircraft was now over Sicily. He'd been staring at the website for hours, stepping away only to make tea. His child inside that plane. When she was little, she'd always had to throw up. He reminded her of that before she took off for America. She said it wouldn't happen. He'd bought her an ice cream because they'd gotten to the airport a bit early. She laughed when he said, *If you have to throw up, at least it will be more colorful.*

A child—that was what she was, he thought, a child with big bones and long hair—should be eating ice cream and meeting friends in the park, not sitting alone on an airplane for thirteen hours while he followed a little graphic twitching one millimeter at a time across the screen.

He knew the plane would eventually vanish, but he didn't know why his hands turned clammy and his mouth was dry, he couldn't have smelled very good. He'd have to wait till she arrived—wait till her landing was announced. The rest she would take care of, he knew that.

He prayed the Shema. *Hear, O Israel. The Lord is our God, the Lord is one.* But really, he thought: Hear, O Israel. Hear, O

Israel, there landeth an airplane. Hear, O Israel, there landeth an airplane, and inside is Margarita Rachel Fuchs. Hear, O Israel, protect my daughter, may the Lord protect her. Hear, O Israel, be her baggage not lost, may she meet with no problems at customs. Hear, O Israel, let Margarita Rachel Fuchs be not cheeky in customs, quiet her heart and make her behave, let her say she is come to visit her mother. Marsha Markovitz.

The first three years of her life, they had been Margarita and Marsha Markovitz, then he'd changed Margarita's name to his, because they would be alone from then on, and he didn't want to be taken for a kidnapper every time they traveled together.

Hear, O Israel, may the landing be smooth. Hear, O Israel, the Lord is our God, the Lord is one. The airplane: right above Crete.

* * *

The last page was exciting. Margarita felt the pressure in her ears, but she wanted to know how the book ended before landing.

Lior tapped her on the shoulder. They were careening downward. The machine was plunging toward the earth nose first. All they could see outside was red soil coming closer. No one screamed, but it was like drowning: in the movies, people made noise when they drowned, in real life they did so quietly. Maybe people crashed quietly, too. The plane banked right, and the sun appeared, a red ball over red ground, a little strip of horizon growing bigger and bigger. She slid to the edge of her seat, as she had on the roller coaster she'd taken with Anna at the Hasenheide, the armrests pressed into her sides, she tried to sit upright, but couldn't. Lior chuckled almost manically, oblivious to his surroundings. He seemed to have no problem with it—with dying—as if he were ready for whatever played out. Maybe he was in on it. She thought of the September 11 documents, which she'd peeked at in secret when her father was giving his evening class at the

Volkshochschule. She looked back and forth between Lior's face and the landscape through the windowpane, which looked two-dimensional, like a photograph someone had wrapped around the plane.

Lior lifted his left earphone and said, "Look. There's Israel."

The sea appeared suddenly, dark blue edged in red. "What's happening," Margarita whispered in Hebrew, "what's happening."

Lior laughed and rubbed her upper arm awkwardly. Strange, him touching her like that, Margarita thought, but oh well, we're about to crash, anyway.

"The pilot circled around again," he told her.

Her ears were ringing, the airplane was still tilted.

"Because the country is so beautiful."

She looked out. Saw red, blue, then a city.

"Tel Aviv," he said, and called it something like where he lived, which as she translated it in her head vacillated between two words, *Zuhause* and *Heimat*. "You've never been here? So what were you doing in Chicago?"

She shook her head. She was getting ill again. Not now, she thought, please not now.

Lior told her she was pale. She stared at her feet. Then he said, "Look." The horizon was straight again. Beneath it were streets, high-rises, sea. The approach. She closed the book. The plane hit the ground. Some clapping. Lior included. "I love coming home," he said, this time in English. Home, she thought, that's it, *Zuhause* and *Heimat* both.

"I was visiting my grandparents in Chicago," she murmured.

Lior took out his earplugs. "Come again?"

"I was visiting my grandparents in Chicago," she repeated.

"Ah," he said. "And here?"

"My mother."

"Isn't she in Berlin?"

"No. She's American, but she lives here." She pointed out the window.

"How come you've never been to Israel, then?"

"Because no one ever invited me."

He looked confused by her words, and she didn't feel like explaining. He stared at her a little too long. "But you don't mind being invited," he said after a while. She didn't know how she should respond. "Or being asked a million questions."

"Maybe," she said, and stared at the display, which showed a stewardess waving pleasantly over and over on an endless loop.

"Get up, people are getting their things out of the bins," Lior said.

"I'd rather wait until there are fewer people pushing."

He squeezed past her and lifted his backpack out of the compartment. Then they both stepped into the aisle.

It was hot, even though the sun had just risen. The heat was dry, almost sandy, the sky rusty in a way, despite the deep blue. A bus took her to the terminal. Lior stood across from her. Through his sweatpants, the outline of his penis was clearly visible, as if he didn't have on underwear. But she couldn't imagine that was it. Maybe his underwear was really thin. She hated herself for peeking. Now she could hardly look away. She hoped he hadn't noticed, he seemed busy observing the runway.

"You got your passport?" he asked.

"Yeah, both."

"Both what? Have you got an Israeli one, too? Doesn't that mean you'd have to do military service?"

"No, I mean my American one. Do you have to do military service?"

"Kamuvan," *of course*, he said brusquely and slung his knapsack over his shoulder. The bus doors opened.

In arrivals she saw ads for tourists, posters for beer with people dancing in clubs. A large family hurried past her, the man and the boys with earlocks, the woman with thick beige pantyhose under her long skirt. The advertisement seemed not to disturb them.

The passport line for foreigners was long, the one for Israelis short. Lior waved to her, then jogged off. Halfway, he turned around and said, "Give me your number?"

In her backpack, all she could find to write with was a pencil and her book. She was too shy to ask for his phone and just punch it in, so she scribbled her number on the dedication page, tore it out, and handed it to him. He smiled at her. Then he really did leave.

Margarita stood in line, her American passport in one hand, her German one in the other. When there were just a few people left in front of her, all of them American, she decided to use the American passport and stuck the German one in her backpack. The passport inspector looked at her wordlessly. Then he said, "Hi." He asked how long she planned on staying in Israel, she answered, "Three weeks," because her father had drilled it into her that she should say that, even though she didn't have a return flight.

"What do you plan on doing in those three weeks?"

"Visiting my mother. In Jerusalem. Her name's Marsha Markovitz."

The man looked up. "Ah. Your mother's Israeli."

She shook her head. "No, American, like me," she said, and forced a smile.

"Where are you from, then?" the man asked.

Her heart beat so fast she was scared he could see it through her sweater. "Berlin," she said. Her grandmother had said she should just be honest. Or at any rate avoid lying. Not withhold anything. She was sweating. She thought of Psalm 93, the only one she knew all the way through by heart.

"Miss," he said, "could you answer a couple of questions over there?" He pointed to a door.

She nodded. She remembered suddenly that she spoke Hebrew. "My mother lives here. She's American, that's why I have an American passport. My father's Israeli, but he lives in Berlin. I live with him, and I'm visiting my mother. I was just with my grandparents, my mother's parents, in Chicago."

He laughed. "Your Ivrit's from your father, then?"

"Yeah," she said.

"We've still got to question you."

A woman in uniform approached. She was at most three years older than Margarita. She said, "Come along," and Margarita bent to pick up her bag. As she did so, she noticed a dampness, and imagined gobs of warm blood sloshing out of her, seeping up her buttocks. She got her period irregularly, this time it must have been eight weeks. And when it did come, so much blood poured out of her that the gynecologist Anna had dragged her to had prescribed iron tablets. Naturally, they were in her desk drawer in Berlin. She squeezed her pelvic floor, as if that would help, slung her backpack forward, tore off her sweater mid-stride, and stumbled as she tied it around her waist to conceal the blood spots in her pants. She was dizzy, and bit the inside of her cheek as hard as she could to stop herself from crying from fear.

* * *

It was six in the morning, seven in Israel, and the plane had landed. The exhaustion that had been his companion those past few weeks returned. His hands and his feet were cold. Heavily, he crawled into bed, placing his phone near the pillow, in case something happened.

It vibrated just before dreams overtook him, as his tongue lay heavy in his mouth. He bolted upright. There was nothing on the screen. How many times had he upbraided Margarita for constantly checking her cell phone, where she harbored things that remained a riddle to him. He wrote: *I hope you got in okay, I love you, your Aba.* Then fell asleep. He dreamed his phone vibrated again, and he kept telling himself, You're imagining it, just like before, you can go on sleeping, she's fine.

He dreamed of the synagogue, dreamed that the Torah scrolls had been lost, dreamed of the Weissensee cemetery with its tomb for damaged scrolls, dreamed he was back there, brought again to his knees by this place, the story of which tore at him, more than the memorials, more than Yad Vashem. The words of the Torah spoke to him: there was Moses, daubed with swastikas, there was Sarah, there was the serpent, speaking German. It was bright. Soon he stopped dreaming.

He lay on his back. When he slept this way, he always had the sensation that a chasm was opening in the mattress and he was falling deeper and deeper into it, and the emptiness beneath his back was the deepest black.

* * *

The woman was friendly as she asked Margarita to open her backpack in the windowless room. She repeated the same questions as the man earlier. Margarita hoped she'd answered everything exactly the same, but she wasn't quite sure what she'd said. She tried to discern something, empathy, antipathy in the soldier's face. Nothing.

The woman asked what her father did in Berlin.

"He's a chazzan."

She was surprised, or pretended to be. The light tubes hummed above them. Margarita had been offered a chair, but had declined, she didn't want to bleed on the cushion. The woman asked if she sang. Margarita was stupefied. She said yes, but then she had to ask herself what.

She thought of the Friday-evening prayers at the nearby synagogue with the female rabbi, where she used to go every week while her father was leading his prayers. She thought of the prayer room on Oranienburger Strasse. Of the soprano female cantor. "Lekha dodi likrat kala, p'nei Shabbat n'kab'lah. Lekha dodi likrat kala, p'nei Shabbat nek-a-a-belah." This melody, how she loved it, was sung on Friday evenings when it was just the two of them at home, when her father was off, his voice resonant, familiar.

"Lo, lo, lo tevoshi," she sang, "be not ashamed, Jerusalem, blush not, why do you bow, why do you groan? Within you, all my poor people shall find protection, the city shall be built upon its ruins." Abruptly, she broke off.

"Any weapons?" the woman asked. "In your bag or in your suitcase?"

"No," Margarita said. But still, she had to open her backpack and show what was inside. The woman pulled out the empty bags, asked what had been in them, Margarita told her, she found the tampons, opened the carton, shook the tampons into the backpack, found the guidebook Margarita had bought the day before at Powell's, a guidebook to the Holy Land from 1980, said nothing of it, she found the wallet and the makeup bag.

After a few seconds' unbearable silence, she shoved the plastic box with Margarita's emptied-out possessions and her laptop, which had sat in front of them the whole time, toward her. "Have fun," she said, opened the door for her, and waved at the man in the customs booth. Though she normally had a good sense of time, when she was buckling down at school or taking the subway at night, Margarita had no idea how long she'd been in that room. Only the blood, which had stopped flowing in the meanwhile and was now slowly drying, indicated a long while must have passed. Her vertigo returned as she left passport control behind her.

* * *

He awoke in a half-light, a gray German morning in his imagination, in truth it was the dreary afterglow of a dark blue sky. He

hated these latitudes, where it got dark so painfully early in winter, it used to scare Margarita when she was a little girl walking
home from grammar school; and in summer, the night was over before you'd even managed to sleep soundly. He thought of the night
before. The dreams following close on one another, the constant
vibration of the telephone. He stretched out his hand. It was an
old iPhone, the first he'd let Margarita have, a few years later she'd
wrangled a newer model from her grandparents and given him
back this one. Many, many notifications on the display. *Missed
call from Margarita (15).* Just one message, though: *Do you have
Marsha's number???????* Plus a missed call from the Community
and a message: a congregant had died and they needed him for a
funeral.

* * *

On the baggage carousel, her suitcase spun alone in a circle, almost human, the way it was waiting on her. She pulled it off as
quickly as she could. Hopefully her mother would have something
to eat. They didn't have much in common, but they both liked good
food, she knew that, or at least thought she remembered it. When
they'd last seen each other, they'd gone to a fancy restaurant in a
skyscraper in Chicago. That must have been the summer before
Margarita started secondary school. Her mother jokingly remarked
that she never had money because she always spent it all on expensive meals. Margarita could no longer say what she'd ordered,
but she remembered how her mother had convinced her to get an
appetizer, entrée, and dessert, and how sick she'd felt afterward.

It was strange, how her mother found her own extravagance
amusing, when her father had told her she contributed nothing to
Margarita's upbringing.

She looked for a bathroom, and in a stall slipped on new underwear, though it was obvious she should have showered first. She

washed her hands long and carefully, until there was no blood left under her nails.

In arrivals, her rolling bag sounded like the cars on the street under her window in Prenzlauer Berg. She looked around for her mother, whose face she could hardly remember, whose size and shape she'd forgotten. Only a few of the women standing there in wait were even remote possibilities. And none of them was her mother.

She decided to take a look outside. Grandma had told Marsha clearly when Margarita would arrive. A slight delay, you had to take that into account. She walked out of the airport. The same sticky air she'd felt on the runway engulfed her, the shouts of people jumping into minibuses. A grandpa in a white garment stretching to the ground with a kind of wreath on his head, two men in similarly long garments, black, though, with payot and hats, speaking a language she didn't understand but that sounded faintly familiar. For a moment, she forgot to look for her mother as she tried to catch what they were saying. Probably they were from Holland, she thought, and kept trying to find Marsha.

How could no one have foreseen her mother failing to show up at the airport when it was obvious she would never bother to pick up on time the child she had neglected for so long? *Rabenmutter,* she'd have called her in German, raven mother. Don't say that, she thought, you shouldn't even think it. The word slipped out of her one time when she and her father had discussed Marsha. He flew into a rage, he had intuitively understood it, though she had said it in German. And now she kept thinking it: *Rabenmutter, Rabenmutter, Rabenmutter.*

She pulled out her cell phone, turned off airplane mode. Nothing, just an update from O2: *Welcome to Israel!*

She tried to call her father. She couldn't try to call her mother because none of the adults had thought to give her Marsha's number. That was your job, she thought. Not mine.

The people were still shouting. Be quiet, she thought, I can't think. Her lips tasted salty, she was starving, her stomach an aching pit, she was thirsty, and she was absolutely incensed. This was a new feeling for her, this rage like an empty white wall. The knowledge that she was right.

Her father wouldn't pick up. She would let it ring three times and then call again, three rings, call again, three rings, call again, quick breath, then once more from the top until she'd tried nine times.

She walked back into the airport, put a water and a sesame phyllo pastry filled with cheese on her credit card, wolfed it down in the cool air. She kept dialing her father's number over and over. At some point, he had to pick up, he slept with the phone near his head. She tried her grandparents, but it was nighttime in America. That was why she was so tired, so hungry for sleep, a shower, the silence of an empty room. Someone asked her if she needed help. She didn't look up, she just shook her head. Thirty minutes had passed since she first tried her father. It was six in the morning in Berlin, seven in the morning in Israel, but still, it was packed and bustling. Margarita's head hurt, her legs, her butt, her belly. Everything tensed together, a hot, twinging pain, like a knot in your hair that you can't brush out, except under the scalp. A throb, gathering in the pit of her stomach, like the longing for home she had already felt, three times, five times over. It came in waves, the moments of reprieve between them hardly longer than the blink of an eye.

Again, she tried to reach her father. She had 10 percent battery left, her backpack weighed heavy on her back. She returned to the café where she had just bought the water, Aroma was the brand, she ordered another bottle, sat on a bench beneath which she found an outlet. She turned on data roaming. How stupid that she hadn't thought of it before. Only Anna had written her, *I miss you, bitch*, blurry selfies from a drunken night in Berlin. What she was looking for she couldn't really say. She googled her mother's name. Then *Ben Gurion Airport to Jerusalem*. She found a website informing German tourists of the best way to reach the city via shared taxi.

Again, she tried her grandparents. This time, it worked.

"Rita?" her grandmother shouted shrilly into the receiver.

Margarita began to sob.

"Oh God," her grandmother shouted. "Oh, dear lord. What happened? What happened, Rita?"

She sobbed even harder.

"Rita, you have to talk to me. Are you in Israel? Are you hurt?"

"No," she managed to get out. "I mean, no."

"Rita, it's the middle of the night here, and you're barely whispering. You need to speak up." Margarita heard her grandfather coughing in the background, then he asked something, and her grandmother roared, "No, hon, it's Rita. I don't know if everything's okay, she won't say!" It sounded as if huge exclamation points were shooting through the phone lines with every word her grandmother said.

* * *

When he called back, the line was busy. He kept trying over and over, with no luck. So he texted her Marsha's number along with the question is everything okay, and a little heart, she'd shown him how to find it on the keyboard. Then he called the Community back. A congregant from the synagogue on Pestalozzistrasse had died, one of the older men, and he was supposed to be there for the funeral. Nothing he hadn't done many times before. He buried people and married people, the weddings were nicer, of course, hope, love, and all that, but also, inevitably, the cynical sense that it wouldn't last. He knew the dead man, Harry, from his Hebrew class, full mostly of flirty young women preparing for their voluntary service, where they'd appease their guilt by wiping the asses of old Israeli men. They always did their homework. One of them had asked him for his number after the course was over, he'd given it to her, they'd had coffee together, he hadn't wanted to think about which of them was more pathetic: him, who'd muddled through it because he couldn't say no and then tried the whole time to avoid telling her about what he did in his free time, because he didn't want to mention Margarita, or her, because she wanted to talk with a real Jew so badly.

Harry Meier had been in the same course as her, year after year he stayed in the same level, too old to learn a new language, but motivated, even determined, to read aloud from the Torah by semester's end. He always did his homework, too. It saddened him that Harry's wish would never be fulfilled. He'd been tender, funny, absent-minded like a child at his desk. Often he brought in his wife's homemade cakes, and they'd eat them together after the others had left. He hoped he'd had a dignified death.

The funeral would be the next morning: enough time to come up with a few words to add to the prayers. The woman on the phone told him when and where, then added, "It's supposed to rain, take along an umbrella."

He drew the curtains after hanging up, went to the kitchen and boiled water for black tea, took the milk from the refrigerator, all this with one hand while he held the mute phone in the other.

After pouring the tea—dark as possible, and with lots of milk, turning it a pretty gray color, he'd always loved that in Europe, black tea with milk—he sat in a chair at the kitchen table and tried to reach Margarita again. It wasn't busy this time, but she still didn't answer.

So he sat there in the same T-shirt he'd slept in and his underwear, drank his tea, the door to the balcony cracked, a child yelping in the courtyard. He hadn't realized how quiet it had been before this yelp. Now the silence struck him as deafening, clear as glass.

* * *

At some point, Margarita's grandmother managed to calm her down, just being silent until the sobbing stopped. That had taken five minutes, easily. Margarita told her, eyes pinned to the entrance to the terminal, what had happened, the long line for passports, Marsha not showing. "Damn it," her grandmother cursed, she'd never done this before, cursing was forbidden, only *darn it* was acceptable, or *what the heck* when something was too expensive for her or the restaurant didn't serve brown rice, because she ate no white rice on account of her diabetes. They agreed that her grandmother would try to reach Marsha, and Margarita hoped there would be a big fight and in ten minutes her mother would be there standing ruefully before her and offering a good explanation. Maybe she was waiting in the wrong place, but Margarita couldn't imagine where else you were supposed to wait, there was only one exit. Over and over, she scanned the people arriving, stepping out of taxis and buses. Her phone rang, she shuddered, but it was only her father.

She'd have to tell him it would work out, but something in her resisted letting him off the hook, freeing him of his worry, which was her only hand against him, the penance for shuttling her from door-to-door, because you were supposed to, because a person was supposed to have a family. Because the two of them weren't enough. Maybe he was scared she'd wind up like him, a cantor with just very few friends. Or get pregnant and let her fear of messing things up yoke her to the baby until it grew up and left her all alone forever. So she didn't answer.

She bought another bottle of water and another puff pastry thing, which she learned the name of: boureka. Her grandmother called back.

"Sweetheart," she said, breathless, "I can't reach her. I'm so sorry. How terrible."

"It's okay. Do you have her address?"

"No. I completely forgot to ask her for it. I'm so sorry, dear heart, I'm so, so sorry. I'm an idiot."

"You think something happened?" Margarita whispered.

Grandma was quiet for a long time. "No, dearest," she said. "I thought she'd changed." Her grandmother's voice was unsteady.

Margarita was so tired, so overwhelmed, so sad, that it hurt. Her wrists hurt, her feet hurt, her breasts hurt, her knees.

"Margarita, love, I think you should wait awhile longer at the airport. If you feel like it, you can catch a sherut to Jerusalem, but I don't really know where you'd go. If you like, I can send you some money through Western Union and you can go to a hotel. Grandpa can call the one we always stayed in. I'm not sure how to do it over the internet."

Margarita made a small throaty noise that sounded like *hrm*.

"Oh, Margarita," her grandmother said, "I wish I could just cut you a slice of chocolate cake and tuck you into bed, snug as a bug in a rug. You know that, right? How much I love you?"

Margarita just managed to produce a *yes*. She tried to breathe in and out as deeply as she could. Until her lungs hurt. "It's okay, Grandma. I'll wait. There's stuff to eat here."

Her grandmother pulled herself together. "What is there? I love Israeli breakfast."

Margarita had to laugh. Food, that was always what mattered most.

"I'll look. Grandma?"

"Yes?"

"What if she doesn't come?"

"If she's not there in two hours, we'll have to find a hotel. Have you talked to your father?" She seemed to have fully recovered her bearings.

"No."

"Dear, call him, please, he must be worried sick. Maybe he has some better idea that hasn't occurred to me."

"He'll just tell me to fly home."

"Then we may have to think that over. Tell him our plan of you waiting a little while longer. Maybe she just forgot to set an alarm."

"Okay," Margarita said. She wished she could have forgotten to set her alarm, too. It must be easy to be her mother.

"Please, call Aba. Grandpa and I are going to get some sleep. We love you very much."

Margarita gulped. "Me, too," she said.

"Okay," her grandmother continued, "bye now."

The line beeped. Margarita stared back at the screen. The cord to her cell phone was so short she had to bend over to make a call. She stretched and looked at the plastic menu on the table. There was the *Israeli breakfast* her grandmother had spoken of: challah, salad, tahini, white cheese, olives, and two fried eggs. In her stomach, it was as if the two bourekas had evaporated. How she'd talked up this trip to herself, traveling alone to Israel, Jewish culture on the streets, something totally new for her. She could have tahini for breakfast back in Berlin.

The phone had enough charge that she could disconnect it briefly. Just as she went to hit the call button, a message appeared on the display. Unknown number. *hey what's up? did you arrived good?* The profile pic was the outline of a young man in front of a setting sun. Lior. She responded in Hebrew: *still at the airport. my mother slept in.*

Then she called her father. He picked up before the first ring finished and started talking. "Margarita, I'm so sorry. I talked to Grandma. Are you still at the airport? Please don't be mad at me, I overslept, I didn't mean to, I had the phone on, do you want to come to Berlin? You can just come home, there's a flight in two

hours, I'll pick you up and you'll never have to leave again. Whatever you want. I messed everything up."

"It's okay," Margarita said. "I'm just stuck here. She couldn't get
it together. Grandma's not even surprised." She hated that tone in
her voice. The bitterness, the resignation.

"I can't get hold of your mother," her father said.

"No kidding," she replied dryly.

"I'm sorry, Margarita. How was the flight, though? Are you okay?"

"Yeah, never better."

She heard him sigh. "How was the flight?"

"Fine. I threw up."

"Lo!" he exclaimed. "Thought you didn't do that anymore."

She had to laugh. He made it sound as if her puking were the
reason he regretted convincing her to go to Israel. She'd asked
herself before whether he'd also thought she needed to do it for
reasons of faith, he who kept Shabbes and kosher while she was
so godless.

"So what do we do now?"

"Where are you exactly?"

"At the coffee shop in arrivals. I'm tired, I feel awful, and I don't
have her address, so I can't just go there on my own. And she won't
pick up the phone."

He took a deep breath. "What do you think is best? Do you want
to go to a hotel and get some sleep?"

She swallowed. Normally, she didn't get homesick until a few
days after arriving somewhere. This time, loud and clear, a voice
was already shouting at her: You want to go home, you want to cry
in the bathtub, you want Aba to make you an omelet.

"Eh," she said. "I can wait. I just don't know how long I should
wait before I go somewhere else."

"Oh, motek," he said, "you sound so tired."

That didn't help her homesickness, again her throat closed up.

"Aba, they questioned me for so long, I had to tell them everything. I even had to sing. Because I said you were a chazzan."

"What did you have to sing."

"Lekha Dodi, that was what I still remembered. And they all wanted to know why I was here. It was awful."

"Yeah, that's happened to me before, too, having to recite something," he said.

A strange thought, that he, too, had been here at this airport. And yet she knew he was Israeli, his language reminded her of it constantly. "Don't you have a passport, though?"

"Yeah, but that doesn't protect you if you were just in Jordan."

She heard his chair scraping the wood floor. She'd have liked to ask what he'd done in Jordan, but he was quicker.

"I'm booking you a room in Jerusalem, I'll call you right back. I need to concentrate."

Lior had written her again. She could come to Tel Aviv and drop off her things with him if she wanted. Her father called back quickly, gave her precise directions for what to say to the taxi driver, told her the name of the hotel. He sounded relieved. Problem solved, daughter safe, probably he would pray now in relief rather than fear, that'd be new for him. Something about that infuriated her, him trying to solve the problem from far away instead of standing up to her tyrannical grandmother and her unreliable daughter. She gathered her things and hurried to the taxi stand.

* * *

He had showered, dressed, eaten. Margarita had talked to him again, there was a safe place for her to spend the day, that meant he could prepare calmly for the funeral.

Even today, he was hardly used to the constant reckoning with death. To people dying, sure, but so often . . . And the way you weren't even really sad sometimes, no matter how much you'd liked the person, unless they died far too early or alone. Or worst of all, too early and alone, but that wasn't common.

Though little time could pass between death and the burial, a couple of days, sometimes just hours, usually a few mourners gathered. At least a minyan, but sometimes even twenty or thirty people, depending on how old the deceased was and how many of their friends were still alive, how large the family they left behind was. The Jewish community in Berlin was small and well connected, and word spread quickly about who died. He scribbled a few notes, how he'd met Harry, what he liked about him, then he translated it word for word into German. Margarita usually did that, she liked to do it privately, retreat to her room, lie on her belly, translate his eulogies and letters to the German authorities as though it were the most important thing imaginable.

He hadn't heard from her since he'd booked the hotel room. It had been expensive, he'd had to dip into his savings, her birthday gift at the end of September would be a bit smaller than usual. It wasn't fair, the room wasn't a gift, it was compensation for her unreliable mother, whom she could do nothing about but whose negligence she still had to pay for.

He decided to go to morning prayer at the synagogue around the corner, promised himself a bit of inner peace, a thought for Harry, for those very last survivors who were dying now without Margarita ever having the chance to really talk to them.

Early on, when he couldn't find a babysitter and she was still too small to stay with a friend for an hour or two on Oranienburger Strasse, he would take her with him when he sang, he'd had no choice: the day care closed at seven in the evening.

The old people had watched her, stuffed her with chocolate, one woman even had changed her diapers. While he prayed, they read her stories printed on thick cardboard. He'd set her on these old people's laps, had told himself so long as there were these kind, gentle people who looked on in disbelief as she crawled between the pews, a child needed no real grandparents, no grandparents to celebrate Hanukkah or a birthday with.

Not all of them had survived the camps, of course, some of the exiles had returned, that was a fine line, almost murdered but not quite as much as those who'd been sent to the concentration camps. Survivors still, almost murdered, but different from how his parents had almost been murdered—his mother, born in Palestine, the child of German immigrants, his father, who could barely remember the Turkish city of his birth—no, the ones sitting in these rows were different, German Jews, nearly murdered by the Nazis, so nearly that they could never forget it, a life without the specter of persecution such as his parents had led was impossible to them. Or so he thought, at least.

In the synagogue around the corner, it was always cooler and quieter than the small one where he led prayers. Almost anonymous. Here, he was a regular resident of Prenzlauer Berg, one of many, and afterward, he'd have a coffee among the people walking around, who seemed never to need to go to work, and they'd never suspect a kippa lay beneath his ball cap or that phylacteries were in his pocket. He had his coffee in one of the hipster cafés where everything was vegan. He read a newspaper, almost two hours passed. Relief that the day was ending.

His phone lit up. *Everything okay* he read. Nothing more. He could breathe. She was fine. She was probably settling in at the hotel room, no doubt with a book she'd bought in America. He worried and cooked, read his notes about Harry, tried in between to call Marsha, to be the first one to yell at her. And he would yell at her, he swore to himself, as he last had thirteen years before, in the middle of the night, when he and Margarita had screamed and she'd been quiet. He answered emails from the Community, read the weekly parsha, wondered what it might have to do with

Harry's life. He sucked a lozenge and did the exercises his singing teacher in Jerusalem had prescribed for him. His worries about his voice were always there, though up till now he'd avoided nodules and hoarseness. He always thought to himself, especially before the High Holy Days, that his voice was his life, his income depended on it, and the only thing he knew how to do was sing.

Part Two

It smelled of old fish and sunscreen in Tel Aviv. Of oranges and vinegar. Of flowers and grease.

Lior had opened the door for her, had said to make herself at home, his parents weren't there, though. He didn't say where they were, he just dragged her suitcase into a living room next to an open kitchen with a sofa in the middle and a carpet of coarse fabric. Let her open her suitcase and handed her a towel that she laid on the toilet lid. Under the shower, her shallow breath turned deeper, she closed her eyes until the sirens, the humming, the many tones mingling with the thoughts in her head went dim. The shower gel in its American bottle was the only thing there that reminded her where she'd been. She pulled on the clothes that had lain at the top of her suitcase. Another deep breath, then back to the living room, slowly blinking.

"You want to lie down for a bit," Lior said, and led her to a room. "It's mine. But it's clean." He seemed shier than in the airplane, and she couldn't understand him well.

"Just a little," she said, "is that okay?"

"Yeah," he said. "Afterward, I'll show you the city and the beach."

The bed smelled clean, not like Nico's, which was full of tobacco crumbs, with sheets that always stank, and balled-up crusty Kleenex on the ground next to it that she'd always told herself were for wiping his runny nose.

Before she closed her eyes, she stared at the mezuzah hanging on the doorframe, and thought of the mezuzah on the door of her home in Berlin, and how a few years back, she'd stopped touching it and kissing her fingers because of the virus, and she'd never resumed the practice. It was a ritual that had simply disappeared. She thought of how her father had unscrewed the mezuzah and placed it on the inside of the door, after rockets, attacks, a night full of bad dreams. Walking to the bathroom in the middle of the night, she had found him in the kitchen spooning up plain yogurt, a weary, sad look in his eyes.

She thought of how she had never understood this fear of her father's, how she had mocked it, the same way she did his fear of letting her walk down the street alone in the dark, whether it was six in the evening in winter or three in the morning in summer. She hoped no one would notice she wasn't at the hotel, that no one would uncover her lie. Hoped there was enough trust there that her father's only fear would be that something could happen to her, and not that he couldn't depend on her.

The room was quiet and white. There was a droning inside her, as though her body hadn't yet grasped it was no longer in an airplane. Her sleep was exquisite and black.

* * *

When the time came, he didn't roar into the telephone, that was Marsha's mother's job. Marsha sounded muddled, as though she'd only just woken up. It was a misunderstanding, she'd thought it was tomorrow, because it was an overnight flight, you know, she'd assumed Margarita was still on the plane and she could sleep in, make the beds in the afternoon, ask him what her daughter liked for breakfast, those were her exact words, "I actually wanted to ask you what she eats for breakfast." He said she could find out for herself, he was snippy, or tried to be, and added, "Margarita's safe now."

"I'm sorry, Avi," she managed to say, he just responded, "Yup" and hung up. He spoke with his daughter again, in the afternoon, once she'd awakened, a raw, groggy voice that said, "Everything's fine, I've slept, I think I need to eat something, no, I haven't heard from her, it doesn't matter, Aba, it honestly doesn't matter," *echt egal* in German. "I've got to go." A few hours later a message: *everything okay. i'm spending the night here. got her address, i'll take a taxi there tomorrow.* He replied, *okay,* and that he loved her. Then he lay there awake in the nighttime, thought of Harry and Margarita, at some point turned on the light. This was what happened when you slept for three days straight. Giving up on trying to sleep always had something liberating to it. To distract himself, he grabbed an Israeli novel translated into German about three women who wanted different things out of their lives. It was grim, morbid, full of brutal sex scenes like so many of the books his friend Bettina lent him—a philosemite and an intellectual, she loved him and Margarita, occasionally used to bring them cake on Sundays, but then she got married. Now, every couple of months, he sat at her kitchen table and borrowed her new favorite book about sex in Israel. He took a secret pleasure in these novels, which made no claims on him, they were late-night reading and awoke no memories of his heritage. In his head, he often translated backward, grinning at the jokes only when they disclosed themselves to him in his own language.

Later he slept another two, maybe three hours before walking to the Weissensee cemetery, the folder with notes under his arm. He started sweating, and had to strip off his jacket on the way. It had gotten warmer these past two days, a muggy heat with no sun to be seen. He'd heard nothing more from Margarita, took for granted she was sleeping, she had a knack for it, could stay in bed till one or two in the afternoon. When he arrived, he turned down the volume on his phone.

In front of the building, the memorial plaque. The last time he was here was in winter. A suicide, a young woman, horrible it had been, heartrending; afterward, at the kitchen table, he'd cried into his chicken soup, Margarita had stared at him, grabbed him Kleenex, sat on his lap the way she used to. He would soon pass her grave site, he'd resolved to do that, anyway it was lucky they'd buried her in the cemetery, the beth din had made an exception for her because of her severe depression.

In the chapel were many people, more than he'd expected, among them old people sitting beside their children on their walkers. One woman picked up her father's fallen kippa and set it back on his head.

The rabbi was already there. They shook hands.

People were talking, that was normal, some of them must not have seen one another for years.

He sat in the first row near a pair of elderly women, one of whom was passing out chocolates that crinkled as they were removed from their wrappers. A third woman sat close by, a little younger than he, in her early forties, maybe.

"Who are you?" she asked. "A nephew come from out of the blue? You won't get anything, there's no inheritance." She looked as if she'd been crying.

"The chazzan," he said. "So no worries, the Community pays me."

She smiled at him. "Oh, you are. I'm his daughter."

The rabbi gave a few introductory remarks: "Today, we remember Harald Meier, born in 1936, father of Hannah Meier and widower of Leonore Meier," and said that Harry came to the children's home in Hamburg after surviving the Shoah, caught up on his schooling, and returned to Berlin, where he worked selling watches at a shop he would later take over. The rabbi asked Avi to continue.

He uttered the prayer in a whisper, the one to be spoken when one had not been at the cemetery for more than thirty days. *Blessed are you, Eternal Lord, who revives the dead. We trust in you to revive the dead.* But death was not to be trusted, you knew only that it would come, he thought. Sometimes awful, sometimes less so, but never to be trusted.

It was a Monday, so the Torah was read from in the morning, Tachanun was said, an additional prayer was uttered at funerals, such were the rules.

God was praised for his mercy and righteousness. "The Lord has given, the Lord has taken away, the name of the Lord be praised."

Who all had the Lord taken away? Millions, but not Harry Meier, not until now, was that mercy? Was it possible to believe in mercy? Harry had never told him how he'd escaped the clutches of history.

Then El Malei Rachamim, impenetrable melody, beautiful and eerie as the specters left behind by great, lost loves, a lament, a bitter avowal of death. "Merciful God who reigns above, may we find repose beneath the wings of your divine presence, among the pure and holy who shine in the firmament. El malei rachamim," he sang, "el malei rachamim," Oh, Harry, who wished to read the Torah so, oh Harry, who should now be safe with his father, Josef, whose name the rabbi had whispered to him.

At funerals you weren't allowed to turn away, you had to sing directly to the public and well, that was the hard part, they had told him that in his training: you had to watch people cry while you sang, and keep a steady voice throughout.

But no one was crying at this funeral, that was strange, his daughter just stared blankly at the floor. The faces of the guests were stern, one woman crinkled her chocolate wrapper. No garments were rent, it seemed no one wanted to sacrifice their clothes.

During the kaddish, all the old people stood. It was stirring, to guide them in mourning, when no one was really sad. That was what the kaddish was capable of. It brought order to mourning. Similar to what the German state had tried with its minutes of silence, or the Israelis with the sirens calling people to silence, the kaddish was a call to mourning, one everyone in the room knew by heart, apart, perhaps, from a few people in the last rows who didn't look Jewish, whose kippot were sitting askew and who furrowed their foreheads, understanding nothing.

The procession to the grave site began. It was slow, and he helped one of the women, holding on to her arm while she leaned on her cane with the other, uttering Psalm 91: "For he shall give his angels charge over thee, to keep thee in all thy ways. They shall bear thee up in their hands, lest thou dash thy foot against a stone. Thou shalt tread upon the lion and adder: the young lion and the dragon shalt thou trample under feet."

The old woman clung tight and smiled at him, they were bringing up the rear. That was unusual, really he should have been leading.

At the grave he uttered the kaddish again. The daughter either couldn't or didn't want to. Then they took three steps back, three steps forward. The old people skidded their walkers a little backward, a little forward.

"May God comfort you, among the mourners of Zion and Jerusalem," he said, and tore up a bit of grass, and the others did this, too. "And they of the city shall flourish like grass of the earth. For he knows, we are but dust." They pitched the grass over their shoulders, it was nearly weightless and floated in the air like the words he sang.

The coffin was laid in the earth, the bands cut. Harry lay inside. Avi thought he would still like to ask him something. Then the rabbi spoke all about Harry: his life, his wife, Leonore, whom he met when he was nineteen at a Purim celebration, their happy marriage, their late good fortune in having a child. When Leonore was forty-two, she gave birth to Hannah, an unexpected blessing. A bit inappropriate, telling that here, Avi thought. Hannah bit her lip and smiled circumspectly. Clearly the old people could hear nothing the rabbi was saying, but they remained chipper as they stared into space. The address was far too long, and digressed, but that was what rabbis did. The longer he spoke, the more important he found what it was he had to say.

At some point, he took a deep breath, the torrent of words seemed at an end, but Avi was still worried about interrupting. Only when he was certain that the rabbi hadn't just taken a pause did he step forward. "I'd also like to say a few words about Harry. I knew him from the Hebrew course I taught a few years ago. Harry was already older, but he was an incredibly good student. Sadly, he forgot a great deal over each semester break. But for me, that wasn't a problem. It meant that every year, I was lucky enough to see him again. He told me a thing or two about his life, but not much." He hesitated. "After class, we ate cake together. For a time, Leonore baked it. It was the best cake I ever ate." Harry's daughter snorted softly. He didn't dare look up to see if she was laughing or crying. "This week's parsha, Nitzavim, is about Jewish values. It says, right at the beginning, that the Torah isn't in Heaven, but close to us, in our heart and in our mouth, that we may perform it. Harry kept coming to my class because he wanted to read from the Torah. I always hoped he'd eventually manage it. But now I would say to him: you lived the Torah, and that is far more important. Harry stood for the Torah on scorched earth, so Jewish life could exist in West Berlin. He told me over and over how he and his wife used to have thirty guests for Pesach and how they dressed as Queen Esther every Purim. Both of them! I think this week's Torah reading is a fitting one, because Harry lived the Torah, even without knowing it; it was close to him, not something far away in Heaven. Baruch dayan ha'emet. May his soul find peace."

Only now did he realize how hurriedly he'd spoken. His face must've been glowing red. Quickly he began to intone Psalm 16. Used his voice to distract from his words. He saw himself as an intruder, someone Harry hadn't known at all and who only now presumed to praise him because he was the cantor.

They washed their hands, one after the other. Then they left the cemetery. The mourners would now sit shiva, perhaps, depending on how seriously they took the whole thing. He hadn't been able to do so when his parents died, he'd had to go home to Margarita, a friend had cooked for her, and that was all the shiva there was.

* * *

When she woke, the light in the room had changed, was golden, no longer muted white. Her arm had fallen asleep. She sat up. How long had she slept? Hopefully Lior hadn't gone and left her alone in that strange dwelling. She took her cell phone out of her bag beside the bed. It was five in the afternoon. She called her father. Told him everything was all right. That she'd managed to get some sleep.

She heard a rustling somewhere in the apartment, as if Lior wanted to let her know he was there. Thankfully. She drank the last sip of water from the airport, ran her hands through her hair, took a deep breath, and opened the door. Lior was sitting on the sofa with a book. He looked up at her. "Boker tov," he said.

"Boker tov," she replied. The two of them looked at the ground. "Thanks for the bed."

"You sleep well?"

"Yeah," she said, nothing more, it was too uncomfortable. He smiled. Where were his parents. On vacation in the USA, he came back early. "Okay," she replied.

The strain was back, but not so bad as before, a puzzling, leftover sorrow, in her knuckles, her feet, her wrists, her knees.

He suggested a bite to eat. "First, the sea," she said.

It was sticky as they stepped out onto the street. When they got to the beach, she had the feeling she understood what kind of city she was in. A city like Chicago, with tall buildings by the sand, with a skyline of high-rises and street canyons. Loud shouting, a big group playing a ball game with paddles, the click-clack their soundtrack. Lior had his hands in his pockets and motioned for her to take her shoes off, just as he'd done. They walked to the water, which was surprisingly warm. The sun was high over the sea, but the shadows were already growing longer. She laughed as the waves struck higher on her legs than she'd thought and her clothing got wet.

After he'd gone with her to take out cash, they went to eat. On the way to the restaurant, an uncomfortable silence reigned, but at some point he took out his cigarettes and he saw she knew how to smoke. That was a thing: some people could smoke, some couldn't, she was pretty good at it. So they smoked until the hummus came, and it tasted so good that she wolfed it down and ordered another, with ground beef on top and an egg. He looked at her in disbelief, but she couldn't make herself stop, the hole in her stomach was too deep. She thought of Nico, how she never ate in front of him because she was always too nervous, and she asked herself whether she found Lior attractive. Her pigging out like this in front of him told her no; anyway, there was no hope, he'd already seen her in the airplane with puke clinging to the corner of her mouth.

Lior asked if she wanted to spend the night in Tel Aviv. She pursed her lips and nodded. Whispered *okay*, stared at the hummus smearing her fingers.

"I'll sleep on the couch, then. We could go get a drink with some friends of mine, if you feel like it?"

"Yeah, sure," she said, a hollow feeling in her chest. Friends. Of course he had friends, he wasn't waiting day in, day out for lost children he could take home with him.

When she was done eating, she wrote her mother. *i'll come to your place tomorrow morning (not too early). grandma gave me your adress.* And a second message: **address.*

They decided to meet near the hummus shop, in a neighborhood full of bars. It was hot, more cramped, more crowded than Berlin, no broad streets, no wide paths, the air damp, tons of people lined up in front of an ice cream parlor. Lior gave her a clammy hand, pulling her up to sit on a platform in front of a bar to wait on his friends. So close to him, she noticed he smelled of sweat. Had he really slept, too? Showered? She asked him.

"Yeah, but neither as long as you did," he said, then the others came.

He introduced her as Margarita from Berlin, and all of them greeted her in English till she responded in Hebrew. His friends looked surprised, but didn't inquire further, and as Lior went for beers, they chatted as though she weren't there, a brusque, un-melodious Ivrit that sounded unfamiliar, newer than her father's and peppered with anglicisms. She lit one of Lior's cigarettes and thought of Anna, whom she hadn't written for a long time. Lior came back and brought her into the conversation, someone shouted at him, gave him a punch on the arm, said, "So good to have you back, dumbass." He laughed, looked aside, caught her eye.

She drank her beer quickly, it tasted good, she hadn't drunk for weeks, not since Berlin, the nights with Anna. Someone asked what she was doing there; she said, "Long story." Did she like it. She nodded shyly. Lior told how they'd met, that something had happened with her mother, that was how she ended up at his place.

Someone said something vulgar that she didn't quite understand, Lior rolled his eyes and grinned. They sank deeper into conversation. Margarita listened, there was more beer, Lior sweated, she learned to laugh at the right times.

She had to go to the bathroom, the way there through the thick mass of people like walking through the dark, sleepy, dizzy, feeling your way along the wall until you reached the door.

On the toilet, she thought of Nico. Nico didn't know where she was. But she knew where he was, smoking weed in front of his computer. She saw him before her, raising his arms, reddish-brown armpit hair poking out of the sleeves of his T-shirt.

She thought of the nights with him, of how jittery she'd been when they saw each other, how often she had tried to make him think he didn't matter to her. She'd never fallen asleep next to him, had always been too nervous. Sometimes, in the middle of the night, he'd stuck his fingers into her underwear, until she'd reciprocated, then he'd remove them. She'd rubbed him until it was all sticky, had lain next to him afterward, in his filthy room at his mother's while his mother was asleep, wishing he would touch her again, but he'd already dozed off.

She thought of how he probably wasn't interested at all in what she was doing in that moment, and flushed.

* * *

He was wide awake when he went home and hummed his favorite Adon Olam melody as he unlocked the door. Margarita used to giggle sometimes and tease him for humming after service, before it started embarrassing her. It would be nice if she were here now, doing her homework; he could make dinner and tell her about the funeral.

He'd have liked to chat with her about the parsha she would have read that week on Shabbat, the one he had talked about at the graveside. You had to challenge her to get her to talk, get her heated with some theory so she'd respond and not just shrug and take out whatever book she was reading at the dining table while he spooned up his soup in silence. Sometimes, nose in her book, she'd grumble that he should eat less noisily. It was a lonely picture, seen from without, he knew that, but it didn't bother him. And when you could get her to talk, she said clever things, thoughtful, fascinated him with her perspectives.

He thought back to their first conversation about the 613 mitzvot that framed their daily lives. Thought back to the hours when he'd tried to explain what had happened to her. Thought of her crimped lips, and how he'd hesitated, she was far too small to need to understand such a thing.

Her big questioning eyes. Why had God allowed that, though? What had the Jews done wrong? We Jews, he'd corrected her. Always those crimped lips, when she slept, when she concentrated, they only relaxed when she laughed. What did they do wrong for people to punish them?

We weren't punished, he said, *we didn't do anything wrong*. He often wondered whether all the German goyim asked themselves that, too, the visitors to the ceremonies of commemoration where he sang, on well-manicured lawns or in the castle where the *Bundespräsident* lived, whether they treated the question as unanswerable as they looked at him and thought: He is a bit different, though, isn't he, a bit strange?

Singing there wasn't emotional for him, he knew he'd strike a nerve with the Germans just by trotting out the Ashkenazi melodies, just by sounding like what they imagined a real Jew sounded like. He did what they had laughed at Paul Celan for, but today, no one dared to laugh. People were surprised when they heard him speaking German, surprised he could even pronounce it. Once, a well-known politician had said it aloud: *With that name and lan-*

guage, I'm sorry, but I thought you couldn't speak German. He had laughed. Said jokingly he didn't have a German passport, either. Thought to himself that he wouldn't accept one, even if they threw it at him. A German child was enough.

* * *

They'd gone to another bar, she and Lior had split a beer, he could tell maybe she was tired; either way, he said he was too drunk to have another on his own.

In the bar, loud music in Ivrit was playing, pop beats, in one track the singer said, "Tel Aviv, ya habibi, Tel Aviv," Lior shook his upper body playfully to it like a belly dancer. Something stirred in her, uncomfortable, needy.

At the table, the talk turned to the most recent shelling, a heated discussion about whether and how you could avoid military service, Lior listened with pursed lips. A girl whose name she hadn't caught asked Margarita curtly and defiantly, "What would you do?" Her eyes swept triumphantly over the group. Margarita thought about colonialism and all, about what Nico had said, but in these people, in this place, she saw nothing wicked or power-hungry. She laughed, timid, and said luckily she didn't have to decide.

They went home not long afterward. On the way, she remembered the empty hotel room and how her father thought she'd be sleeping there. Lying to him made her stomach turn. So did her anger.

After he shut the door behind them, Lior shoved her against it, almost aggressively, her heart skipped a beat, she was nearly scared. It didn't feel the way it did when Nico decided to kiss her, when they were out or otherwise. After that first kiss, Lior asked her whether he could keep going, and she nodded. He shoved his tongue deep into her mouth, but when she tried to return the gesture, he closed his damp lips, kissed her on the neck. It lasted long enough for her to start to like it. They kissed a long time; she had to laugh, he asked her why. Because they'd just met, she tried to say, pulled out her tampon quickly in the bathroom, told him she didn't usually—he touched her again, much longer than she was used to Nico doing. She fell to her knees, she was dizzy from the alcohol, from the scent of his sweat, they were now kneeling across from each other as he pushed his fingers inside her, first in her mouth, then—then she grabbed him, too, he made a small throaty sound and asked if he could go for a condom. "Yes, please," she said; after they'd walked hand in hand to the bed, Margarita awkwardly held her hand in front of her crotch, as if he hadn't already seen her naked.

She wanted it, whispered *please* one more time, it sounded good to her, grown-up. He asked if he could turn the lights on and see her. He stood up, his erect penis didn't look like part of his body, extended laterally in the air as he walked from the light switch back to the bed. It was suddenly very bright. He looked down at himself, saw brown slime on him. She wanted to tell him she was on her . . . They tried to get back to it, but the light made it impossible. She was so drunk that none of it felt real to her; the slime, and she couldn't tell him it was blood and not something else, and slowly he got less hard. She could understand. Every few seconds, whenever she blinked, it got dark, the room started shifting, reminded her of the clicking of a camera. He looked at her, saw nothing, her giant dark-brown nipples, weird, she knew.

She stood up, washed off in the bath, got a fresh tampon, put on the nightgown her grandmother had bought for her at Target. When she returned to the room, Lior was dressed, stretched out on the bed, said sorry. It wasn't her fault, was the light's fault, he was drunk.

He slept on the couch. Margarita didn't sleep, she felt sickened by her own body. In the morning, she packed her suitcase, Lior bought chocolate buns and orange juice, they had breakfast without speaking. He turned on some music. Their fingertips touched, inadvertently at first, then long enough to make her heart pound. It was all too bright, dull; as she rinsed out the glasses he gave her a kiss on the neck. She didn't understand that kiss. Her head hurt.

She left without asking whether they'd see each other again. She hadn't dared. The taxi smelled of vomit and fish. She rolled down the window and felt the orange juice rising in her throat. Fortunately, for a pile of cash it would take her back to Jerusalem. Her headache distracted her.

Her mother was waiting in front of the building in big sunglasses and a white dress that looked like a bedsheet with holes for the head and arms. No sooner had she seen her face than Margarita remembered what she looked like, and she wanted to turn around and leave. One brief impression was enough. She wanted to spare herself the awkward greeting, not knowing whether to hug, so she sweatily dragged her suitcase past her, asked which was the door to her apartment, which room was hers, sat on the bed, and drank her water bottle empty as her mother sputtered that there was cold water in the fridge, the apartment was quiet, and it cooled off at night, unlike Tel Aviv, where you could hardly sleep.

Margarita tried to look at her face a bit longer. As Marsha talked, Margarita thought of the night before, which felt torrid and lost, as though she'd heard the ticking of another clock she hadn't known of till now, one that made you want time to pass much slower. Her body felt raw, and still naked, despite her clothes. Her mother explained why she'd thought Margarita wasn't arriving until today. Margarita thought of the hours she'd spent at the airport and glanced at her. Imagine someone as orderly as her grandmother raising such a daughter. Margarita hoped Marsha could see the contempt in her eyes or at least recognize the depths of her indifference.

The apartment was on the second floor of a building overgrown with violet flowers. A guesthouse belonging to the university. Margarita's room opened onto the courtyard, Marsha's looked out on the street. Something was probably not right with the room if Marsha had voluntarily handed it off to her, or maybe Avi had made her do it, knowing Margarita had trouble falling asleep, that she hated losing control, losing consciousness every night, that she needed calm the way she had in Berlin. The room was spare, but nicely furnished, thick mattress, little desk, white dresser with blue knobs. Cold stone tiles. It smelled clean.

She told her mother she wanted to lie down. She felt as though she'd been standing on her head for hours: tired and disoriented from jet lag, from the night, from the alcohol the day before. From a shame that seemed to cut through everything, from her hangover, her anger at her mother.

* * *

Hannah had written him. A brief email, a *thanks*, the question could they maybe have a coffee sometime. She signed off with *cordially*, then her email signature, which included the word *sincerely*. Cordially and sincerely.

He read the message and asked himself what she actually wanted. Now, on the way to prayers, his distrust vexed him, maybe she wanted nothing more than to talk about her deceased father, learn what he'd done in Hebrew class, maybe she had no idea he'd even wanted to read from the Torah.

It wasn't only daughters that kept secrets from their fathers, he knew, it also went the other way around. So he decided to answer Hannah after Shabbat, overcoming his shyness. He hadn't had to do that for a long time, he had gotten comfortable in this life of his, with few friends who no longer went out and also never tried to persuade him to make new acquaintances, never told him he could soon find a wife if he would just bother looking. Friends who loved

Margarita as if she were their own, worried about her and teased
her if she sat at their Hanukkah table in too much makeup, demon-
stratively bored as she played dreidel with the younger kids. She
was always the oldest, he had become a father early, his friends had
mostly done so only once they'd realized that this was as good as it
got and from then on out it would all be camping trips and buying
ugly furniture.

   He had decided he didn't want that kind of commitment, he had
Margarita, he had his friends, he had his God, a consolation, a presence warming in winter and grounding in summer. One that never
wanted to go camping.

   The synagogue was empty that day, they'd have to wait for there
to be a minyan. As the tenth man arrived, a few minutes after seven,
the other worshippers knocked on the bench, there was laughter,
a brief moment of high spirits, since they could now start; a siren
howled rhythmically. Avi couldn't help but smile, his cheer still
audible in the first syllables of Yedid Nefesh, then he became serious, and a feeling of tranquility spread through him.

   It was less than a month to Rosh Hashanah, when the clocks
would be reset; that's why there were so few people: they were
all getting ready for the High Holy Days, tough times for the synagogue, no one wanted to be standing here today, some must still
be on summer vacation, the school holidays had come unusually
late this year, and there was still warm air to fill up on before the
days in Berlin turned shorter. The darkness that settled over the
city with Yom Kippur was still far off. The wet leaves and the rains
of Sukkot were unimaginable on the pebble peaches of Italy and
in the lukewarm sea of Tel Aviv, places the families that sometimes told him of their vacation plans loved the most. They'd
come back red as crabs and not at all relaxed and welcome the
apples with honey that you could eat in the garden in a parka
and long pants, and they'd look forward to fasting on Yom Kippur

with the delusion that they could drop their vacation weight in one day.

He sang to the nearly empty synagogue. It felt like before—him alone singing the Lekha Dodi, the amen in the kaddish a soft buzz from the men's row—when it had been empty here, dead. Today his voice in the room sounded as it had then, he heard it, how it echoed, and he imagined he could hear growling stomachs during Aleinu, the closing prayer, which he began with a shout, as though an exclamation point followed the *Aleinu*. The silent prayers were over, the inward time of Shabbes had been traded for a common one: *Aleinu l'shabeach la'Adon hakol*, it is our duty to praise the master of all. It is our duty to praise him, he thought, all of us here, the few when there are few, the many when we are many, on this strange ball tracing its path through the universe like a swimmer in a pool without walls.

Whenever he sang, he heard the voice of the cantor in the big synagogue in Tel Aviv, whom he had listened to each week as a boy, sensed the way his father had laid his hand on his shoulder, thought of the cholent, the iron pot with eggs and meat, that would be waiting at home later, of the pureed beets with garlic, of the Birkat Hamazon that they had sung as they banged on the tables, sometimes with his parents' friends, sometimes just the four of them: his mother, Stella; his father, Itzik; his sister, Pnina; and him. He sang Adon Olam as though later he would be running home through the streets of Tel Aviv, as if he were seven years old and still had that fine, high voice that had led his parents to put him in the children's choir, a choir full of Israeli boys, later they all did their military service together, all of them were treated nicer at home than their sisters, even him, nicer of course didn't mean nice, Stella was constantly irritated by his and Pnina's mere existence, they were always eating too much or too little, talking too much or too little. Stella always made him ashamed when she came to pick him up from choir, she was so old, so garishly dressed, he'd told the other kids she was his safta, his grandma, and when she found this out, she'd smacked him across the face, and he had heard her crying at night through the apartment's thin walls.

* * *

Margarita couldn't sleep, she was too amped-up, the blood rushed too loudly in her ears when she closed her eyes. She had called her grandmother, her father, eaten in silence, book in hand, the story of the four girls and the jeans that had accompanied her since Chicago. She had the second part still in her backpack, she'd bought it a week before, thinking ahead. When she hadn't known how hot it was in the country where she now found herself, or what the onset of Shabbat would be like. From her window, she watched everyone ready themselves for it, fewer cars zoomed past, soon there was no one in the streets, all those large families had vanished in all directions. Not long afterward came dinner, without the lighting of candles or prayers. Her mother didn't complain about her reading at the table. She wondered how long she'd have to sit there. Then she fell asleep, not long after sunset.

When she walked out of her room, breakfast was on the table, and Marsha in front of it smiling, saying, "Good morning, sleepyhead," as if she'd decided to be one of those mothers who uses pet names like *sleepyhead* but doesn't dare disturb their child, who might bite. "Orange juice?"

"Mm-hm," Margarita said, nodded, tried to smile a little.

Her mother went to the kitchen and came back with a bottle of it. "Do you know what labneh is?"

"Yeah, Aba makes—" Margarita said, then stopped herself. Would they talk about him?

"Yeah, of course," Marsha said, and pointed to the little bowl on the table filled with thick yogurt. "I bought some." Next to it was a

salad of cucumbers and tomatoes, a little tahini, some kind of fish,
bread.

At Marsha's, no brachah was said. That surprised her. She
wondered whether her father had started doing it on her account.
Her mother looked at the newspaper, visibly uncomfortable, and
Margarita picked her book back up and read through breakfast,
thankful, for this flight into others' language, while she herself was
silent.

The one noise was her mother's chewing, with a closed mouth, at
least, no smacking, no grinding her teeth, she could live with that.
At some point, Marsha made a small noise, *um*, Margarita read the
paragraph to its end, then looked up. Her mother was brushing the
bristly rust-brown hair from her forehead: perfectly made up, full
lips like her own, a face that looked so much younger and more
carefree than her father's and at the same time much more foreign,
with an inquisitive gaze, the irises so dark brown you could hardly
tell where the pupils began.

"It's Shabbat, so there's not much you can really do today," she
said, "but if you feel like it, we could take a walk through the neighborhood and maybe go to the Old City. Just if you feel like it, you
know."

Margarita thought it over. She hadn't really asked herself what
would happen once she was here. "Let's do that," she said.

"Cool!" Marsha's answer was too fast, overeager. As though she
was on edge. "I just mean, I'm glad. I wanted to say that again,
Margarita, that I'm glad you're here. And I'm sorry for the misunderstanding."

It hadn't been a misunderstanding, she thought, Marsha'd just
fucked up. Her grandmother hadn't given her bad intel, she'd never
do that, Margarita was certain. She didn't say she still needed an
hour to get ready. She closed the door behind her, sat on the bed,
thought of Lior, of that last moist kiss on her neck, glanced at her

phone. No message. That was a lot to ask, maybe he kept Shabbat, she didn't know what the young Tel Avivis did when their parents were away.

She finished the book, showered, dressed, then they left. Her mother put on sunglasses and smiled at her cheerfully. She told her where exactly they were, the story of the neighborhood, it was strangely normal, listening to her like that, the streets were still, children playing on the balconies, a few men rushing past, appearing to have emerged from another century. An atmosphere that reminded her of the Saturday evenings with her father. The books she read on the living room rug, lying on her stomach, while he just thought or read himself or asked her little questions. Maybe here, too, behind the balcony doors, the parents were asking their children questions to drive away the boredom of a Shabbat afternoon, while the TV remained off and no one ran errands and no one cooked.

They reached a large street with shops; her mother said, "Here's the former German settlement, kind of like the Zehlendorf of Jerusalem." She understood and nodded. And asked herself when had Marsha ever been to Zehlendorf.

"You want to go to the Old City?" she asked. "It's a ways off, it's got to be dead there, but I really don't know what else I can show you." So they walked to the Old City, it smelled of spices, there were sheds everywhere, more men hurrying about. The Wailing Wall teeming for Shabbat, Margarita would have liked to put a note in one of the cracks, but she knew her mother would laugh at her, Marsha said she could come back another time, "I'm sure they'll let us two on the Temple Mount, too, you can't look at the tip of our nose and tell we're Jewish," *us two* sounded like her grandmother's English and yet was no substitute.

It was true, nothing about them looked especially Jewish: Marsha was wearing a black expensive-looking wrap dress and

Birkenstocks, with a handbag where Margarita had stowed her wallet, her mother had said she wouldn't need it, there was nowhere to buy anything, anyway. Weird to have her carrying her stuff around.

Marsha kept laughing at her, and eventually asked, "Can I take a photo, for your dad?"

Margarita said it was best not to, and walked ahead, she knew Marsha was taking a photo of her from behind, you could hear the shutter on her cell phone; okay, boomer, she thought. Her stomach turned as she imagined her father getting the photo on his old cell phone after sundown, holding it away to look. She missed him. Her mother described how the Old City was divided into quarters, Armenian, Muslim, Jewish, Christian, she told the story of the Temple Mount. "You know what happened to the temples?" she asked, and Margarita responded, "Of course, Aba told me all about it."

Under the burning sun, she showed her the gates, the walls, which you could walk on, all those dates bored her, but not too much. They took the bus home. Margarita curled up in bed and dozed, heard nothing from Lior, the ache in her vulva when she went to the bathroom was proof enough that it had happened.

She heard her mother typing on the computer in the next room over, realized she'd never asked her if she was religious; either way, she apparently worked on Shabbat. Was her food kosher? It flustered, exasperated her, that it wasn't her trying to break the rules, that her mother was breaking them for her. She wanted to be the one to decide which rules mattered.

* * *

He had also sung the morning prayers for Shabbat, weary, halting, had needed time to collect himself, his voice sounded different when he hadn't slept well. In the middle of Hashivenu, he changed the melody, but his worshippers didn't let on, sometimes he found them ungrateful, their neediness, their constant requests, their approaches, and their expectations of him, because the rabbi there didn't do such a good job, and only showed up when he had to, to give his deadly dull sermons. Today, though, he was happy that they just took him as he was, they certainly knew he was tired. He had sat down during the Torah reading and closed his eyes a moment, and the gabbai and one of the women there had invoked the Torah, lifted it, borne it through the synagogue; on another occasion, he'd have liked to do it, but this time he had gratefully declined.

A long week, he thought, truly a long week, you should sing for once, I'll listen along, but they sang softly and off-key, his Saturday worshippers. He had to offset them, his voice grew, he held his breath, this way of making himself bigger he'd learned in his training, the Sephardic Nusach and the Ashkenazi, here he generally sang the Ashkenazi; liberal and open as they'd have liked to be, the worshippers here were creatures of habit, they liked things they were familiar with.

He lingered awhile after the service, one of the women had asked him if he'd like to say kiddush, this time he couldn't say no; even if he never used Margarita as an excuse, he almost always declined, knowing she was likely at home waiting on her midday meal. Today he had no reason to leave, he wasn't in a hurry, and he was a bad liar, even if he was good at keeping quiet. And so he took part in the kiddush, there was lox and cream cheese and dry challah. He felt ill at ease, everyone had something to talk about except, somehow, him. A man in his forties took pity on him and asked him questions: whether he'd had musical training, whether he sang elsewhere or only as a chazzan. "What do you mean?" he asked, and the man clarified: "Like in a band or a choir or whatever. Lots of chazzanim were opera singers, too!" He had to laugh, that made his interrogator uncomfortable, he clearly felt he was being made fun of.

Walking home, he regretted it, the man must have thought him arrogant, and Avi realized he'd answered all the questions with a single syllable, hadn't asked any questions of his own, even if he usually liked talking with people about synagogal music, about Louis Lewandowski, who had transformed the entire liturgy right here in Berlin, about Estrongo Nachama, who had carried on the torch for Lewandowski throughout the city.

He had always asked himself whether that was an unconscious argument for his move to Berlin, that Nachama had been the cantor here, he had never forgotten his story since the first time he heard his voice. In his training as chazzan, Nachama's voice was Avi's companion at night, he'd even bought an extra record player to listen to him. As if Nachama's entire story abided within his voice, Avi thought, his entire strength, his childhood in Greece, his days as cantor in Thessaloniki, then deportation, the concentration camps, where he lost his beloved, while his voice kept him alive, the death march, arrival in Berlin, which was supposed to be a stopover; he met his wife there and returned to the profession of cantor, for the American GIs at Hüttenweg and also in the Rykestrasse. Nachama's Greek passport allowed him to travel back and forth through the two halves of Germany. Something Avi, with leaden steps, took for granted now, crossing a border that was no longer there. It surprised him that his feet could still bear him, that they didn't stick in the flagstones of the sidewalk, making him fall over, stiff as a board. He thought of this voice, after which none other sounded full enough, no melody entirely complete, and he had never even heard it in real life. Nachama, who had left for him something he loved, his community here, who mourned and celebrated and fought and endured together, and that represented the soul of the survivors.

On the day before his death, he had tutored children for their bar mitzvah. Whenever Avi had a new class, he told that story and said that hopefully he wouldn't die the next day. But no one ever laughed. He decided, before the High Holy Days, to watch Nachama's Yom Kippur once again on YouTube with his choir, which was on Pestalozzistrasse with the organ, the synagogue where Avi sang had neither, just a loose chorus of the faithful, and him, but that seemed to be enough.

He thought of his calendar for the upcoming two weeks. No appointments for the whole next week, nothing for Shabbat even, a yeshiva acquaintance in Jerusalem was visiting the synagogue and would be standing in for him. A little time off would do him good, he thought, sleep in, no emails to answer, rest the vocal cords, play piano, just for fun; when he played, the hours passed faster. The empty periods, they had always been there, they weren't depression, he was sure of that, he almost relished them, he saw himself as an artist, and didn't art come from sorrow? Or was that nonsense, relics of a tawdry cult of genius?

Really, nothing kept him from spending the empty weeks bearing down on him not at home, but in the algae-scented wind. Placidly readying himself for the new year, which fell in September this year, hopefully amid an Indian summer, he had just learned that word for the last hot days in Berlin, when the light was already autumnal, the leaves slowly yellowing, the city in sepia, making you melancholy like that John Prine song about the end of summer, for days, for weeks, until Yom Kippur ended and the old year was finally past; Sukkot began and the new year properly commenced. Take a break maybe, he thought. Maybe best to have a change of scenery.

*   *   *

The day after, her mother had to *write something*. She made the same breakfast as the morning before. With a firm rap on the door, she woke Margarita at ten on the dot, unconcerned with her jet lag. "Hi, sleepyhead," she said again, forced, Margarita's laughter in response was no less forced. They had no routine with each other. Margarita didn't even know what to call her: *Mom, Mama, Marsha?* She had avoided it so far. When her mother left, she was still calling her father *Ababa*, she was two then, almost three, he was the one who told her that. But he'd never told her what she'd called her mother. So she just omitted it. They had gone too far now, there was no reason to give her a special name.

Marsha hadn't said what she had to work on, she'd just sat down at her desk after breakfast in her robe, tiny feet bare on the smooth tiles. Margarita hadn't inherited those feet, just the chin and the eyes, Margarita wore a women's ten. She read on in her book, the next volume in the series, stared at her phone, thought about writing Anna to tell her what had happened, opted against it, her mother shouted, "You know you can go out alone, right?" It made her mad that Marsha could tell her what to do or what not to do, but still, she put on her shoes and left.

Wandering through side streets, she found her way to the Old City, bought fresh orange juice and pomegranates. Between the stands, the soldiers, who looked like her and Lior, children's faces behind machine guns.

She walked until she lost her sense of direction, had no idea which quarter she was in. Embroidered kippot were on sale there, patterned plates and vases, in one shop she bought herself a dark red shawl.

The next days were the same, she'd walk to the Old City at midday, wander around, buy juice and falafel sandwiches, devour them with pleasure on a cool stone bench. No one seemed to notice her, no one looked at her, there was too much to do. Slowly a map unfurled itself before her inner eye, and she could tell one street from another. East Jerusalem she had to avoid, that was the only place, there was a gate in the Old City that led there. Apart from that,

Marsha let her be free, she seemed clueless about what a fifteen-year-old should be allowed to do.

Every evening they went to eat together in little restaurants in the large street near the building, Emek Refaim, there was a bookstore there full of English books where she ordered the third volume in the series. The menus were always kosher, after two days this stopped calling her attention. The area reminded her of Prenzlauer Berg a bit, all the boutiques and the cute cafés, but the air smelled different, lemony, in the evenings you could hear cicadas and the whir of wind through trees.

A few days after Margarita's arrival, Marsha told her, bent over a big salad with fried sweet potatoes that were thin and long like shoelaces, that they would leave in three days for a trip: to the north, to Jordan, along the Mediterranean coast through Acre and south, swim in the Dead Sea, maybe see the Red Sea, too.

It seemed to Margarita that she didn't have a say, so she simply nodded.

That night, Lior wrote, *what's up*, and her heart froze. It was late, she'd tried to sleep already, but it was still too hot, her tongue was dry and seemed to quiver. She stared a long time at the message, then put her phone under her pillow, where she could feel it burning a hole in the fabric, so she took it back out, read the message again, repeated the whole routine until she actually was kind of tired, but her sleep was troubled, she kept waking up and checking if he really had written her.

* * *

He should have been preparing for the High Holy Days, for the long stretches of singing, for being thirsty and singing on despite it. But no, he just shut the window, stood there in the large eat-in kitchen, a typical Berlin room, cool and dark in summer, warm and bright in winter, laid the machzor on the kitchen counter, in the slanted cookbook holder Margarita had made for him years ago, stared at the first page of Erev Rosh Hashanah, and shut the book again. He didn't know how he would make it this year, two days of Rosh Hashanah, then Yom Kippur, morning, afternoon, and evening for both, Yom Kippur without eating, without drinking, and then Sukkot at the end. Sometimes he sat at the piano, that was better, it felt less like procrastinating than when he just wrote emails, which anyway would get on his students' nerves, none of them would answer, they were all on vacation.

He cleaned, sorted, emptied the cabinets, stuffed Margarita's old clothes into bags to donate, thought, as he did so, of his training in Jerusalem, that faraway life when he'd once believed he would be married with many children who would run through Rehavia with their tzitzit flying through the air. He'd thought that would be enough for him, an occasional excursion south, or north, a vacation in Europe if they could afford it.

He'd been on the right track, done everything right, bent over his books, sweated it out in sports, swimming, running, track and field, he remembered the girls' fingers feeling his abdomen. After his summons at sixteen, he'd gotten a ninety-seven on the test, the highest score in the military. That meant more tests. And after more tests, the offers. Itzik had left the envelope on Avi's desk. You could see he'd opened one flap and then thought better of it. Avi had done so well at everything he'd made it to gibush for the air force, it could hardly get better, Itzik was completely over the moon, he even bought champagne, and Stella put a whole fish in the oven. That was the key, iron discipline. Now they were a proper Israeli family.

Thin, neurotic Itzik: nothing could have made him happier. Avi thought of him, of how he walked with his shopping cart every day through the Shuk HaCarmel and took a bit of baklava *to try* on every visit, but never bought a single piece, because the stall there was overpriced; he, Itzik, said even then no one but Avi took him seriously, Avi had struggled to make him proud, this man whose entire life had been a struggle to rise up in the world. No sooner had he finished his dentistry studies than he was called up from the reserves for the Six-Day War to care for the wounded in a field hospital, and when he returned, in his telling, there was just no more need for dentists, *Believe you me!* he'd shouted. *Six days can change everything!* But Avi doubted there had ever been such a terrible lack of demand for dentists in the early 1960s.

And so Itzik never made the fortune he'd always thought awaited him, and Stella worked as a receptionist at his office, and then she had him and Pnina soon after, and there was only enough money for a little apartment on Allenby Street, no vacation home in the north, for Itzik this was tantamount to starvation.

Avi started reading and playing classical music early, and this hinted he was a prodigy, and absurdly, guardedly, he began to fear he wasn't one, and worked to make himself clever and strong until the air force picked him up, and maybe he, too, was happy about it, being deeply convinced then that the Israeli state was simply defending itself. But what was self-defense, what was the self of the Jewish state?

The training camp was in the desert. He led the prayers there at first, but soon, as a hobby, he became the chazzan, he knew Lewandowski's melodies, and people liked his voice, on the weekends he'd go home, the air in Tel Aviv seemed thicker to him now, his parents older; in his childhood bed he yearned for the stars above the desert, and under the desert stars, he yearned for his flannel sheets at home with the stars on them. His training began in October 1996, a few months after Operation Grapes of Wrath in Lebanon; he was scared to death and had a boyish, absurdly coltish sense of anticipation.

He really did want to be a pilot, pilots were heroes, the good

guys, with the best bodies and minds in all of Israel, the career
was his for the taking, he thought, and it suited him, flying, rigors,
regimented hours, being good, getting better. He could deal with
six hours' sleep, could deal with being woken in the middle of
the night to throw on his uniform and run around the barracks;
even if he was the one who messed up and everyone had to run an
extra lap on his account, they all liked him and would stay mad
at him only through the morning, never for the whole day. Only
a few times were his weekends revoked, for tardiness and once
because of some drunken antics. Generally he got to go home and
was treated better than Pnina, Stella talked down to her, called her
slutty, she struggled to make it through the last year of school.

He was still far from a real assignment, but his commander had
told him, *You're getting there, rookie*, and a few weeks later, laughing, he said something Avi couldn't forget: that the only thing he
felt when he dropped a bomb was a slight jarring of the plane. And
naturally, your superiors noticed when you heard something you
couldn't forget, they noticed everything.

They didn't let him take his final exam. Looking back, he thought
he'd slacked off intentionally his last few weeks, hadn't wanted *all
that*, really, but maybe that was just something you told yourself
not to have to face up to failure. The reason given was that he'd
started to carp at critical moments, that he was too analytic. Not
war-hungry enough for them, he told himself, really that speaks in
my favor. But of course it hurt.

Earn your wings, they said. Wings meant a pilot's license, a
lieutenant's rank, and a bachelor's degree, instead he got the offer
to serve in air defense, which he agreed to, in the end; they sent
him to a control tower in Negev. The work there exhausted him
more than any physical work he'd ever done, it was the opposite of
wings, an aching back and heavy legs, stuck to the ground, but he
did it because he was convinced that they needed him.

Then came the Second Intifada. June 1, 2001. A woman from his graduating class at school was murdered in a club in Tel Aviv along with twenty other people.

Everyone always said it: *Everyone knows someone*, everyone knows someone who's died, soldiers, terror victims, *everyone knows someone*, this time he, too, was *everyone*.

She had slept with Avi's friend Eitan for a few months. Avi had liked her. She was a good reader and the fastest runner in their class.

The call, the pounding heart when again, in Tel Aviv, explosives tore through bodies, the image of Stella's arms torn off and lying on the asphalt, the arms, that was what he always saw.

He had never turned radical, had never been *against*.

Against what, anyway? Against life?

On September 12, 2001, he cursed his botched training, and what his commander had said seemed suddenly not so bad—sympathetic, even. He had thoughts of revenge, and before he went to sleep, he imagined himself in the cockpit, imagined feeling that jarring.

And for the first time, one Shabbes, bent over their cholent, he and Pnina were in agreement. That frightened him. He'd always found her too nationalistic, too racist, too scared.

He stayed in the tower until his service was over, did his job, envied the fly-boys, felt mistreated, but still: he was able to do his schoolwork at the same time, had chosen Jewish Studies, had attended mostly lectures on Jewish music at the university in Beersheba, played piano often on the weekends at Stella and Itzik's.

He moved into his first rented room at twenty-five, a basement room in Mea Shearim, when he was done with the military he started studying in Jerusalem. Mea Shearim was no longer just Haredim, there were students there, too, now, who couldn't find a room elsewhere in overcrowded Jerusalem. He liked the combination, even if he missed all the nice restaurants and cafés in Tel Aviv.

He could no longer say whether he'd been happy then. These were not the right categories to think in when you were suddenly free. Freedom wasn't happiness. Freedom was lax, laconic, lonely, no one watched him when he was free; when he hadn't been free, he'd been constantly under observation, but he'd enjoyed it.

His parents didn't want to pay for his chazzan studies, singing was a hobby to them, not a job, and he didn't sing so well, did he, and he'd been in the air force and should have made something clever of himself. They didn't want him going to yeshiva and dwelling on Rav Huna's interpretations of the Torah and modern conceptions of the niddah, not one bit, they'd have liked him to study medicine or counterterrorism, *wouldn't that be something*, and after so much dithering, he missed the window, hurried through his training, and always sang too fast until he met Marsha.

Then he started taking his time, sucked in breaths till they reached the bottom of his lungs and the words rang out clear and vibrant, opening a small chamber in him that gave birth to a new voice, bolder but at the same time softer. He finished his studies with the highest grades and was soon booked at synagogues all over Jerusalem, and Marsha accompanied him, he'd hold her hand on Friday evenings walking home or at dinners with friends, and the next morning, attending a different synagogue, he'd find himself holding it again, sometimes it was a new one every week, wherever someone was sick, wherever an emergency had come up.

What was left over from his military service: a distrust of the air, a vague fear of flying, a longing for the empty, hollow hangars of the cargo jets that made you feel so small. Two years before, with a knot in his stomach, he had watched scenes of the evacuation of Afghanistan, and was shaken by an urge to do something.

At least the days had been less lonesome since he'd learned

Margarita was doing well. He would ask her school whether she could have an extra two weeks of vacation, hopefully they'd agree, then she'd be back in Berlin a week before Rosh Hashanah. He responded to Hannah's email, as soon as he sent it he realized he'd made a grammatical error, he hated that, but she wrote him back quickly. They could meet for dinner, Hannah proposed a kosher restaurant in Schöneberg that he had last been to with his parents. Snippy, they'd eaten their dry balls of falafel and slurped down a couple of oysters in the KaDeWe afterward while he sat there next to them with empty hands and the feeling that his entire life had been a conservative rebellion against his parents.

When he got there, Hannah was already sitting at a table in front of the restaurant. He hadn't really noticed her face, it was friendly, and younger than he remembered. He was wearing jeans and a white linen shirt. In greeting, she told him she thought cantors always wore a suit, even on their day off, then she kept apologizing for saying that, even though it made him laugh. Not so much as he would have liked, though, because he was nervous and had to speak to her in German.

She talked a long time about Harry, and at times he struggled to keep up, but he tried to tell a few stories of his own, hoping they wouldn't bore her.

The time flew past. She told him Harry had been born in hiding in Berlin, that his parents had dropped him off in a handbag at the door of Catholic acquaintances on the edge of town, his ten-year-old sister had already been sent ahead on a Kindertransport to England, the circumstances were unclear, these acquaintances had protected him, but he had run away and was deported to Theresienstadt, he never found out what happened to the family. His parents? Murdered, they didn't find out till decades later: Treblinka, his father had been in the *Sonderkommando*, he had piled up the dead bodies, his own wife's, maybe, before he himself was gassed. Hannah's fork hovered in the air. Avi had the feeling his eyes were growing bigger as she talked. At fifteen, Harry found out he had an older sister. She never came back to Germany except for weddings and funerals, Hannah nodded quickly, she clearly meant her father's, too. Avi's neck was stiff, his mouth dry, symptoms of inner turmoil. How improbable it was that she was sitting there now.

He couldn't eat as she talked.

"What about you?" she asked.

"I have a daughter," he said.

"I was talking about the Shoah," she said, and he thought. What about him and the Shoah? Did he have anything to do with the Shoah, apart from his parents being lucky that their own crazy Zionist parents had left their home country for Palestine since they didn't have any possessions, his mother's German parents, born in Breslau, his father's Turkish parents, they'd cast their origins to the sea at the harbor in Haifa, even their language, and they'd never left Israel again. His mother's parents—they met a few years after arriving—had made of Stella a true sabra, a real Israeli, except her name, which she never traded for a Hebrew one, his father held his parents' hands on the ferry from Ankara to Haifa, that was 1935, Itzik told the story of how his grandmother gave him an apple and how he'd thrown it into the sea in anger and sadness at having to leave her behind. His grandmother died a year later, thankfully, because that meant no one could murder her, her husband had been gone for years already, and the other grandparents lived in the mountains behind Ankara, no one cared about them, Itzik had said.

It touched all of them in a way, or else it didn't, many of them didn't want to hear about it anymore, the former Hasidim, who hadn't been allowed to talk about anything else, the left, who thought it shouldn't be used as an excuse, the right, who said it was all a long time ago. The conservatives, who instrumentalized it. And him. He thought nothing. He got lost in unuttered, unutterable thoughts, disparate images coming one after the other.

"Isn't that sweet," Hannah said, "how old is she?"

"Fifteen," he said, and worried a moment about Margarita, was almost shocked that he had forgotten his worries during this friendly meal, they hadn't been in touch once that day, not even through text.

They ordered more wine. Hannah said she had a son who was twenty. "I don't know where all the time went." He looked at her astounded. She'd become a mother at eighteen. Harry was the one who'd brought the kid up, mainly. This idea moved him.

She asked him about his childhood. He told her about the air force, the Germans loved that, the German Jews, too, when he talked about the military, his education in Jerusalem, he left Marsha out of it, supposed she would pop up between the lines, and if she didn't, all the better. Then they traded thoughts about the settlements and their fears for Israeli democracy, Hannah said, "The strange way the Germans report on it doesn't help, either the Jews are unimpeachable or everything they do is evil." He laughed again. Then he realized he hadn't even asked what she did for a living, and when he did, it was emphatically, in hard consonants, she worked in a music school, he struggled to follow the details.

He paid for the food, she paid for the drinks. Kissed him on the cheek to say goodbye. She smelled of patchouli, he hated that scent, but what did it matter to him how she smelled.

He told her about his vacation plans as she pushed her bike alongside him, accompanying him to the U-Bahn station. How strange it was, being in Berlin when Margarita was in Jerusalem. He only ever left the city with her. He tried to say how uncomfortable he felt, not being at home in case she decided to call off her trip or something else happened. It was awkward, the way he expressed it, he wasn't used to talking about his feelings like this, let alone in German.

Hannah hummed in agreement and recalled how she'd gone to a sanatorium when her son was little, it was actually called a mother-child sanatorium, but she had just done the mother part and left him out. As the mothers around her alternately hugged and shouted at their children, she had felt guilty, for the first ten days, anyway; for the rest of the month she was able to sit in the sauna and push her guilty conscience aside. Avi found her cheerful, warm, maybe a little attractive.

On the ride home, he thought over and over of Psalm 15, of Harry, who was hopefully dwelling now on the holy mountain, the Har Kadosh. Even if, following the tradition of his faith, he thought rarely of what happened to the dead, he hoped wherever Harry was now, people were bringing him cakes and he spoke fluent Hebrew and he'd be able to see his father. For he had embodied all those things Psalm 15 promised would be rewarded: he had spoken the truth in his heart, had raised a daughter, a grandson, had given the best of himself, and he that doeth these things shall never be shaken, these words had lingered in his mind since Hannah had spoken to him of Harry, he that doeth these things shall never be shaken. Harry must never again be shaken. He hoped.

And Hannah? Was she shaken? Did she feel it, too, that vertigo, with her laughter that sounded so stable? What an orderly life she seemed to have: Sundays with coffee and cake, bicycle trips to the Brandenburg lakes, all that was missing was sauerbraten on Christmas. Unimaginable, how the life that was her grandparents' by right had been ripped away from them. Unimaginable that she, too, was never shaken, even as she seemed to be trying hard to tell the truth.

His truth, which he hardly knew, his life felt like that: being shaken between worlds, between languages, between years; between years, days, minutes.

* * *

The next day, she met Lior at the beach, she found it on her own after Marsha gave her permission to go to Tel Aviv. Her mother had to work, and Margarita got bored, lay around on the bed, stared at her phone. Marsha didn't seem to care much, for her Margarita was far too young to suspect they weren't just two children meeting by the sea. She even seemed happy to be rid of her for a while.

She gave her a banknote for the train tickets, Margarita didn't want it, the money her grandparents had sent her—which she had wanted to turn down at first before reluctantly accepting, to ease things for her father—was enough.

Lior was playing matkot with a friend when she approached, sweating terribly, butterflies in her stomach, he gave her a high five and kept playing, *we're almost done*, she dropped her things in the hot sand and swam, salt burned her eyes, the water barely cooled her.

A whir of voices from the beach, in Ivrit, which had begun to weave its way into her dreams; she dove, a swishing sound rose, voices, up, down, up, down, someone pinched her ribs, up, Lior, laughing. They went to eat hummus again, this time she wasn't hungry. They spoke about her time in Jerusalem, he asked at one point, "When do you have to go back?"

She swallowed. How naive, thinking she didn't have to go back today, that she could sleep here again. The hummus turned mealy in her mouth. "Eh," she said, "it's not hard-and-fast. It doesn't really matter what my mother thinks."

"Then you can come to the demonstration," he said. "I mean, if you want."

She looked at him. Watched him drag the bread through the hummus, put a little egg on top, stuff the whole thing into his mouth. The way he ate had something repulsive to it, so she looked at his fingers, which were running along the edge of the plate, wiping off the last traces of hummus. Those fingers had moved inside her a few days before. There were no words for how powerfully she wanted to feel them. So she asked what the demonstration was about.

"It's against the government."

"Got it," she said, spoke uneasily of the climate protests she'd been to in Berlin, he said, "Yeah, same thing here," then they went to the meeting point.

There were many people demonstrating. Soon she lost Lior in the crowd. Then he grabbed her hand.

Hebrew words were on the posters, many said *Enough*, others said *Love* or *Justice*.

The music got louder, the people chanted, Lior was bellowing along, too. They stood close together, he was up on his tiptoes, trying to see better; they turned inward, smiled at each other, he looked content, even nearly euphoric. "It's so terrible," he told her, "we have fascists in the government who want an identitarian ethno-state, their hope is for an Israel with no Arabs, only Jews, and Israel only, no Palestine. And it's getting worse and worse."

She nodded and tried to share his outrage. Knew that something made him different from Nico, knew not exactly what.

They stood there forever and smoked cigarette after cigarette until their lungs started to burn. A friend of Lior's came over, brought them beers, cursed Bibi, walked away. Later, the crowd dispersed slowly. At a kiosk, Lior bought a bottle of vodka, and they sat on the curb and drank it. She kissed him.

"Not today," he said. "My parents are home."

She kissed him again and whispered, "We could just kiss."

"How boring," he said, and bit her lips. "Let's make it a goodnight kiss, then. I need to go to bed soon."

Fierce disappointment spread through her.

He looked at her. "Do you know how to get home?"

Maybe it was all the people, maybe it was the harshness of the vodka, that smacked of those nights in Berlin when she always knew how to get home, maybe it was that she wished her father would come pick her up. Maybe it was the heat and the feeling, once again, of being unwanted.

She stood, nodded, walked off a few steps to keep from showing her tears. He called to her, but she kept walking like a headless rabbit toward city hall, where she could probably find a bus that would take her to the train station.

Lior caught up with her. "Ma at rotzah," he said, *What do you want?* Maybe the mood at the protest had riled him; anyway, he sounded annoyed. "I don't know," she responded, snot was running from her nose, she wiped it away with an old napkin from her tote bag.

"I don't know. You can leave. I'm going to go home, I just thought it would be like, like last time, you know."

He looked lost, standing there, said, "Sorry, I've just a lot going on right now. And soon you'll be gone again, anyway."

She sniffled. A weak, wan wave, and she turned back around.

"You know how to get home?" he asked again, she shook her head quickly, pursed her lips. He showed her on his phone.

"If you want, you could just come with me," she whispered, almost choking on her own words.

"Okay," he said.

They rode back to Jerusalem, the train glided softly, everything felt easy, because of the alcohol, maybe, quick, mirthful, free; when she tried to open the door, he hugged her, pressed into her, she could tell he was hard. He nibbled her neck and let her open the door, they snuck into her room, it was only when they were actually doing it that it didn't click, that something felt off. He was entering her so hard, she was worried the smacking would wake her mother.

She felt an inner ache when he pulled back. His sweat dripped into her mouth, tasted salty, distracted her from everything. She didn't want it to end.

There was something patronizing in the way he held her after he pulled the condom off and came on her belly. How he pushed her down, told her to hold still, so he could wipe her off and embrace her. His arm around her torso made her heave, because she knew it would be the last time, and even his fleeting attention she'd never be able to beg for again.

She didn't sleep long, sent her mother a text in the gray morning, told her Lior had come over and missed the last train, *don't freak out, he slept in my bed.* When Marsha knocked hard three times on her door, she had fallen asleep again, or so she thought. Her mother shouted the name of the café she wanted to go to, and said, "You two get a move on," as if it were nothing out of the ordinary for her, Marsha liked to say that when something had surprised her.

Lior sat up. They waited until the front door clicked in the lock. Margarita did the same, but tried not to look at him. "I'm going to shower," she said, he followed her without asking. When they were standing together under the water, she felt more naked than she had in all the hours before, she would have liked to hide, and hoped the water would conceal the black hairs on her butt, the stretch marks on her thighs. When he kissed her on the neck again, as he had in his kitchen, she wondered why. It went no further than that kiss. She dried off, realizing how much she wanted him. The shame. Again.

They walked to the café, unnaturally far apart. Tomorrow she would set off with her mother, and when it was over, she'd fly back to her strange, distant Berlin, to her strange, distant father, to Anna, who had come to feel strange and unreal to her since departing. Margarita was surprised that it didn't even hurt her that Lior wanted no one to know what he had just done with her.

* * *

The island smelled as it had in the weeks he'd spent there with Marsha sixteen years before. It smelled of cinnamon and dough and cherries, it smelled of a promise Germany had made to him. As he trod it, he remembered that, and he knew the word for promise now: *Versprechen*. Back then he could think it only in Hebrew, *havtacha*. The island had made him a promise: that there was goodness, beauty, safety on this foreign bit of earth. Breaking promises was in the country's nature, but here the promise was beguiling, collusive.

He thought of how they'd wound up there: she had wanted to see the North Sea before the baby came, and the rabbi had recommended Spiekeroog, and even if in other respects he found the rabbi a useless stick-in-the-mud, they had taken this recommendation and rented a house in September, in the off-season. Marsha was well along in her pregnancy, and three weeks after they returned, Margarita was born. They walked up and down the beach, Marsha kept talking about all the things she still had to buy, he rubbed her belly and spoke to the baby, whose sex they still didn't know, she ran off to the bathroom ten times a night, and he obeyed her wishes and shaved her legs before they—gingerly—slept together. This last time before Margarita's birth smelled, too, of cinnamon and cherries in his memory, they had done it in the middle of the day. He was less strict in matters religious, since arriving in Germany he'd neither worn a kippa nor prayed daily, as he remembered; he had been ambitious, he sang aloud to Marsha and the baby on the beach when he was sure no one else could hear him. He remembered Marsha's laughter, but also her bewilderment as they landed on that island whose name neither of them could pronounce, with rules they didn't grasp, on the patio of the café where you were allowed to order only tea by the pot. And yet it had been nice, they had enjoyed it, the fresh fish, the waffles, the broad beaches, and the warmth of the fireplace in their vacation house, where Avi had massaged Marsha's feet, an American advice book for new parents lying next to them.

This time, too, the place Avi was staying was small, the Community had lent it to him after he'd announced he would like to take a vacation for personal reasons, he had rarely expressed such desires before. He had spent the weekend in Berlin, asked the neighbor lady on Sunday to water the flowers on his balcony, and on Monday he packed, made sandwiches for the long ride, played piano until he was worn out.

It took an eternity to reach Spiekeroog, you caught the regional train, then the ferry, but you were rewarded with quiet white-sand beaches and cold, rough sea air, important for restoring his vocal cords before the holidays, which he felt ill prepared for after the turmoil of the past weeks.

Over the next few days, he read all the novels the woman in the bookshop back home had recommended after he'd told her what kind of thing he liked. Then he had to buy new books on the island. He sent Margarita photos of the beach, the horses, and all the ways the word *crêpes* could be misspelled: *crépès, crepês, crèpés.*

Hannah wrote him long emails that he responded to over his morning muesli, with a grin on his face and an excitement in his throat that spoiled his appetite.

* * *

Marsha was wearing sunglasses and a caftan that reached the ground. She stretched a hand out to Lior. He shook it, said in Hebrew, "Ah, the tardy mother." She didn't understand him, responded in English, he laughed.

So they spoke English. Lior ordered a coffee. Margarita had one, too. Her mother looked surprised, but thankfully said nothing, the situation was uncomfortable enough. Lior talked about the beach, the best hummus in the city, the protest.

Marsha arched her eyebrows, and they peeked out over her sunglasses. "You seriously went and joined a protest."

Margarita could tell from her tone that Marsha didn't approve, probably she thought she was too young for that, it was too dangerous.

"How old are you?" she asked Lior, he told her he was seventeen.

Margarita had never asked him, and he'd never asked her, now she realized she maybe hadn't wanted to know.

"So do you want to go into the military?"

He looked at her with his big black eyes, said dryly: "I wouldn't say I want to, but I will," and Marsha laughed.

Margarita stared at the paving stones of the patio, feet in worn-out sandals. She felt both of them staring at her, but she didn't feel like staring back.

"So, you protest your own government, but then you'll go defend them with a machine gun slung over your shoulders?" Marsha asked.

"That's right," Lior said.

"Do you understand what would happen if the demands you all are screaming about were actually implemented? Do you not think Hamas is murdering people by raising them to be martyrs regardless of what Israel does? Do you honestly think they're in a position to build their own state?"

Margarita knew it had nothing to do with whether she was old enough to go to a protest. It was about her mother's politics. Margarita thought of spending days in the car with this woman, no, never, not with this pathetic catastrophe of a person who loved putting people on the spot. Lior said nothing. Margarita said nothing.

Then Lior replied, "They're people. And you can't even speak

Hebrew. Your daughter understands this place better than you do."
He hopped up, tipped back the last sip of his coffee, turned away,
and hurried down the stairs to the street. Glanced back, waved to
her. She wanted to race after him, but her mother's eyes held her
back. A deep, dizzying unease suffused her. She stood slowly and
went to the bathroom.

* * *

The hotel in Jerusalem had sent him an email with the invoice:
Our no-show policy states that without check-in or cancellation, we
charge your credit card for the full fee. He was confused, slightly
afraid: What had happened? Had Margarita not told them the bill
was on him? He had written to her, but she hadn't responded. So
he strolled around the island, phone in the pocket of his raincoat.
The farther he went, the heavier his legs grew from worry. She had
called him, though. Had she lied. It had to be a misunderstanding.
Hannah called him some time afterward, a fine drizzle struck his
face. She asked if he was in the mood for company. He said yes,
and told her about his confusion, in part to hear himself speak, to
find a plausible explanation that hadn't occurred to him amid the
breaking waves.

She said: "What I meant was, do you want company for real. I
could use a little vacation before the holidays. Anyway, Margarita
must know what she's doing, she's fine, right? Nothing's happened
to her?"

He said he'd call her back. Margarita had naches, he thought.
And she sure didn't get it from him.

* * *

On the table stood the empty coffee cups, and next to them a few
coins. I'll tell Aba about this, Margarita thought, I'll tell him and
he'll be furious. Then she realized she couldn't tell him, because

he didn't know about Lior and didn't know she hadn't gone to the hotel, her mother had done her a favor by not telling, or so she thought, and this meant she couldn't reveal what the raven had done to her, sticking her beak in and picking around in her business. She'd driven off Margarita's one ally in this godforsaken oven of a country, apparently from the pure wish for a fight.

The rage shot into Margarita's legs, and she took off down streets she had never seen before, as fast as she could without running. First on the hunt for Lior, then because she couldn't stop, because she knew if she stopped, that meant she'd lost, would have to go home; as long as she was still moving, she was alone, independent. The pretty streets with their rows of buildings turned gradually ugly. Children were playing in front of the houses, little boys with swinging payot shouting in the language she had already heard at the airport. A mother in a long dress and opaque hose, not much older than Margarita herself, stared at her in her shorts and white David Bowie T-shirt. Margarita stared back. Climbing the streets, Margarita pressed her hands into her flanks and pushed her pelvis forward. Finally, the narrow alleys expelled her onto a broad promenade, and beneath it, a park stretched out. Jerusalem lay before her, a city in beige, the city was beige the same way Berlin was gray.

She thought of all the times she had prayed in the direction of Jerusalem, on her knees on Yom Kippur, her forehead pressed to the synagogue's cool stone floor, on Saturdays in group prayers for Israel; it surprised her how quickly the words returned for her though she'd never learned them through, like the brachot before: *As for our brothers, the whole house of Israel, remember them in all the lands of their dispersion, and swiftly lead them upright to Zion your city.*

Avinu, avinu, shebashamayim, our father in Heaven, he seemed closer here than elsewhere. Maybe that was what made her light-headed, maybe it was a kind of altitude sickness, maybe she, too, needed a head covering to feel there was still something between them, maybe that was the reason everyone wore wigs, kerchiefs, shtreimels, and kippot. Maybe this proximity drove people mad, made them extremists, as her father called them. "That's not us, nudnik," he'd said to her when she asked whether there was anything worth reading in that book a friend had given her about one of the sects.

She was still light-headed, her steps were erratic, and she was thirsty. Her mother sent her a text: *I am leaving now to go get the rental car and will go to university library afterward. There is plenty to eat in fridge and I will make dinner for the two of us. Please be packed by evening so we can leave 1st thing tom.*, clear-cut, *two of us*, and don't dare bring that moron along, she read between the lines, and if she felt like digging deeper, she could imagine she also heard the word *whore* in there somewhere.

Slowly her faintness subsided, a little wind blew, almost affectionately it dried her sweat. She typed *yeast infection Hebrew* into her cell phone along with the route back home. The street she wound up in was called Tayelet Haas. She entered a pharmacy presided over by a woman in a crooked wig who didn't bat an eye as Margarita passed her the phone because she couldn't pronounce the word, the woman sold her a cream for it, she'd seen it before in Berlin. She walked faster than when she'd come, the itching was killing her, she took a few wrong turns, told herself, reassuringly, that her mother wouldn't be home. She was looking forward to a cold shower and watching a series alone in bed, getting her dinner from the refrigerator, salty chicken on bread with ketchup, a hard-boiled egg for after, unseen, unheard, unnoticed.

She applied the cream as soon as she got home, it helped. Margarita was proud that she'd solved this problem on her own, she knew all about the fungus that plagued her every six months and had confidently gone to the doctor about it back in Berlin.

Her bare butt in her nightgown gave her a feeling of safety, of being home, of not having to be elsewhere any longer, for a brief moment. She ignored her father's call, but wrote him that she'd be in touch tomorrow. He answered her briefly: *okay*.

She thought of Lior. Her head was pulsating as she recalled the night before and tried to reconstruct the feeling of his body heavy on top of her. But she couldn't now, she no longer remembered the smell of his neck, all that was left was the sweetish scent of his penis.

When she heard the key in the lock, it was half-past seven, she slammed her computer shut and pretended to sleep, lay still, breathed softly as her mother rummaged around, moved the dishes, called to her. "Fuck," Margarita heard her say, "is she even there?"

Then the door opened. Margarita tried to inhale and exhale rhythmically, not let her eyelids flutter, the corners of her mouth move. "Ugh, good," Marsha whispered. The mattress sank. Margarita felt a cool, clammy hand on her forehead, then on her cheeks. She kept her eyes closed, even if her mother had to know that she was awake. Marsha stood. "No fever," she whispered. It was a long time until Margarita finally fell asleep, over and over she kept jolting awake.

Her mother made a phone call in English, she could understand only bits of it, a door opened, to the kitchen probably, in the hallway she said, "Yes. She had like half a chicken with a truckload of ketchup."

Margarita heard her grandmother's husky laugh through the cell phone speaker. It reminded her of something that felt like another life.

Much later, after she'd slept and woken up from thirst, she heard her mother's voice again. It couldn't be her grandmother this time. Margarita lay still, not wanting to interrupt the conversation, enduring her full bladder and parched throat, listening to her mother's soft laughter, which she'd never heard before.

* * *

The ferry came at 12:50 in the afternoon. He had been standing on the dock since twelve, in front of a parking lot for handcarts, the island was full of them, his left hand was deep in his pocket, he was talking on the phone with an irritable Margarita.

It had been unseasonably warm. In late morning, he'd gone swimming, first a few cautious laps along the coast, then, feeling braver, straight out into the sea, until the spray stopped burning his eyes, and he was no longer freezing, and every time he dunked his head under the greenish-blue nothing of the water, the salt tasted almost sour on his lips, so different from the Mediterranean. This was simple sea salt, measured and sprinkled over the sea by hand, maybe it hovered down in flakes when you looked away.

The beach was so broad it never seemed full, and when you got some distance away, you could hear seal pups waiting patiently for their mothers that were out fishing, and they turned their heads toward you, the tracks of their flippers carved in the sand between the paths left by their bodies as they crawled.

Margarita roared so long into the receiver that he didn't dare ask about the email from the hotel. He didn't dare ask about anything, he let her go, just tried to find out where Marsha was; "How am I supposed to know where she is," Margarita went on, "she keeps going out and never says where."

He was sure she was exaggerating, but she didn't want to say what had happened, she just shouted that she hated him, hated her family, hated the way her family was torn apart, broken, that she wished she had different parents. Her words hurt. The sun was blazing on the baseball cap he wore over his kippa, and he stared at the horizon, nervous that he might make out the boat that would force him to break off the call before he'd calmed her down, unable even to tell her why he had to hang up, he, who always had time for her. He certainly couldn't tell her he was getting a visit from a woman she had never met.

There had been a fight, he'd gotten that much, and she'd woken up and her mother had disappeared with the key, she was locked in the apartment and didn't know what to do, she was seething with rage, Marsha had left her phone in the kitchen on purpose, obviously; Margarita hissed, "She hates me, Aba, she hates me." In the midst of this, she blew her nose noisily.

He wondered what she looked like, if she had changed, whether her thick mascara was running down her cheeks the way it did when they fought because he told her she couldn't stay at Anna's on a Sunday, Monday, or Tuesday night, because of a bad grade, gym was the only class where he'd let that slide.

An older teacher had once recommended a boarding school in England, or if not in Saxony, *But as a Jew, er, Jew, um, Jewish . . .*

He couldn't exactly remember her efforts to force out the word *Jew*, even as a teacher at a Jewish high school, she couldn't bring herself to utter it; after all, it wasn't called the *Jewschool*. Margarita sobbed, and he couldn't remember what train of thought had led him there.

"Are you even listening to me?"

"Of course. Sorry. Do you want to come home?"

"No," Margarita screamed, "I don't want anything, I don't know what I want, I just want to disappear." Then she was silent.

He asked if she was still there.

"She's coming," Margarita whispered.

He heard a door slam closed. A long whistle reached him across the sea, a short one over the line.

He wiped the pearls of sweat from his clean-shaven upper lip, stood up straight, and put on the friendly smile he wanted to greet Hannah with.

* * *

As soon as she heard the key in the lock, Margarita stopped herself. She sat down, blew her nose, took a deep breath, almost gasping; she must have looked pathetic like Anna's cat when it puked and writhed helplessly because that was all its body was capable of, but it worked; when her mother knocked at the door, she was upright in bed staring at the black cell phone screen in her lap. Marsha opened the thin door too forcefully and it struck the wall, then her arm. Margarita gave her a snide grin.

"I got the rental car," her mother said, "they gave us an upgrade. A fancy car, you can even connect your cell phone."

This sounded like a lament. Margarita couldn't bring herself to ask why she'd been locked in. Couldn't bring herself to say, if there'd been a fire, I would have suffocated. Besides, there hadn't been a fire.

She noticed the wrinkles in Marsha's forehead, which looked deeper than yesterday. Her normally perfect lipstick was smeared. It was sad the way she put on this chic researcher act, probably trying to make it seem like she was better than Aba, when really she was just old and used up. Margarita caught herself thinking it had probably been years since she'd gotten laid. The triumphant thought that she'd beat her there, at least, helped with her anger.

"Did you pack your things?" her mother asked.

Margarita stood, opened the suitcase by the bed, pulled out the dresser drawers one by one, and dumped out the contents. She pushed past her mother, grabbed her toiletries bag from the bathroom, and tossed it, half-open, atop the pile. Then she closed the suitcase, sat on top of it, and pulled the zipper shut irately. Marsha shook her head, went to the bathroom, and put Margarita's toothbrush into her handbag. Margarita grabbed her suitcase, slammed her bedroom door behind her, and walked into the cool stairwell, where it always smelled a little bit like piss.

Marsha followed her out, leather weekender in hand. She lifted her sunglasses and looked at Margarita until she looked back. At first, she was too perplexed to understand what she was saying. "Enough," Marsha hissed. "From now on, you are going to behave yourself." Margarita felt her shoulders tighten instinctively, like a cowering animal, whereas Marsha seemed to grow, unfurl, over-shadow her. "I invited you here, and I expect you to behave. Maybe we don't see each other much, but I expect you to respect me."

Margarita nodded slowly. Her face was hot, her stomach upset; all the blood seemed to have flooded to the center of her body. She nodded until Marsha opened the building's front door and pointed which way to go. Together, they loaded the heavy suitcase into the car, and it really was fancy, as Marsha had announced. Margarita didn't spend much time in cars, really just in America or in the musty backseat of Anna's parents' Opel. Or in the taxis her father sent to pick her up from slumber parties, sheepish in her pajamas in the hallway of some apartment in Berlin, in her pajamas in the back of the taxi, in her pajamas back at home in her own bed, which seemed suddenly so luxurious. But it had been a long time since she'd needed to be picked up. As she got into the rental car, she thought of how she'd give anything for the cool, sticky upholstery of a taxi driving her straight to Husemannstrasse.

The traffic was dense and noisy. Marsha mumbled a curse, honked, Margarita had always asked herself who were these peo-ple who honked when everything was at a standstill, and now she knew: those people were her mother. She was ashamed, and at the same time knew she'd have found it funny only days ago, Marsha leaning her entire weight against the steering wheel, hands under her torso, and laying constantly on the horn. On the radio was one of the songs from the bar where she had been with Lior and his friends. So far away already, that evening. Would it continue to recede like that, every memory turning into a film from another life that she could never fully show to anyone?

Marsha laughed in desperation as they continued not to move. Then she started cursing. Not like Margarita's grandmother, but real swear words, *for fuck's sake*, *shit*, words they weren't allowed to say at summer camp. Margarita didn't know why Marsha was in such a hurry, but she also couldn't make herself ask. "Wait," her mother said, and leaned into the backseat, rummaging around in her handbag. "Get us a few bottles of water right quick." She pointed to a kiosk on the side of the road. "We don't have any with us."

Margarita didn't know how to react. Was Marsha planning to abandon her? What if the congestion let up all at once? "Um," she said.

Marsha pressed a banknote into her hand. "Buy yourself a pop if you want to." *Pop*, that sounded just like her grandmother. Margarita opened the door and ran off. The traffic didn't budge, the honking was a noisy concert outside the car with the windows rolled up and the air-conditioning blasting; and Margarita dawdled a few seconds over the cooler with the lemonades, grabbed a Diet Coke, put it back, already tasting the hollow flavor of the sweetener, chose a real Coke instead. With two big bottles under her arm and the Coke in hand, she went to the cash register, where she had to whisper *slicha* several times before she was served. Just as she was paying, the traffic started moving with a metallic jerk.

Of course, Margarita thought, and sprinted back without waiting for her change, the bottles were slippery, the rental car was on its way to the next crossing, the light had turned green, the honking from behind spurred her on. By now she'd switched the can of Coke to her armpit, and the tops of the two bottles were burning in her hands. The car edged away, it was a wide street, four lanes, and Margarita was too scared to walk between the cars. Panic spread through her. Would Marsha really just leave her there? Her cell phone was in the car. Without her cell phone, she was stranded. So she made her way onto the road, kept whispering *slicha*, then *slichslichaslicha*, the honking got worse and worse, someone shouted something, after slicha came *shit*, *shitshitshit*, until she finally reached the passenger door. Marsha winced. "ARE YOU FUCKING CRAZY," she roared as Margarita shut the door. "ARE YOU INSANE YOU COULD HAVE GOTTEN YOURSELF KILLED, RITA." Until now, her mother had avoided calling her by her name, and now she was using not the one she had given her but the one her grandmother had. Margarita snorted. "Your father would kill me," Marsha hissed. It was so ridiculous Margarita burst out laughing. Her mother thinking of her father's reaction when she could almost have been run over by a car.

"I thought you were going to drive off," she laughed, and her mother looked at her with something wounded in her eyes, then the traffic stopped again, the kiosk not yet out of view.

"You're crazy," Marsha said.

The traffic eased again, until they reached a junction. "Fuck, wrong way," she tried to merge again, was now honked and cursed at herself, but she managed it, and now they were on the highway passing under the enormous sign that read *Nazareth* in three languages.

As the car rolled on unobstructed, Margarita opened her Coke. So much pressure had built up in the can that the brown liquid sprayed her neck, ran down her shirt, over both hands, onto the upholstery, it had been sitting in her lap when she opened it. "Fuck," she said, and now it was her mother who laughed, that girlish laugh she'd heard through the door the day before, and soon Margarita joined in as she licked the cola from her wrists. They laughed all the way out of town. And the silence afterward wasn't uncomfortable, it was more a compromise than an emptiness, a silent truce about which there was nothing to say.

* * *

Hannah was wearing a black T-shirt with a thin white crust under her breasts, salt from her sweat, it was hot, especially for Spiekeroog, almost eighty degrees, dried mud clung to her sandals. He wondered where it was from. Had she gone to Brandenburg over the weekend? Did she maybe have a small house there she went to sometimes with her son? Or had she just walked through the mud in the park in Schöneberg after a rainy night?

 They brought their suitcases into the apartment, which was on the first floor of a residential building, then he showed her the village, the beach, ordered iced coffee and almond cherry cake at Backdeck, after that she had to lie down, stretch her sturdy legs, thighs bulging under the fabric of her chinos, while he sat in an armchair and pretended to read. At six in the evening, she woke, she was *ravenous*, she said, and he was too keyed up to cook in peace, so he recommended they go to the best restaurant on the island. The sun was low now, and the light shone through the winding streets of the city center, gold flecks on each corner, happy tourists dragging their children around in handcarts.

 They managed to get the last table on the terrace of the Capitänshaus. The waiter's North German dialect was so strong that Hannah had to translate the day's special for Avi. They ordered wolffish with a sauce of sea buckthorn, which he'd never seen anywhere else but which grew in abundance here. The people of Spiekeroog made sweets from it, teas, jellies and gummy bears, sour juices and sauces. Hannah looked tired and a little disoriented. She laughed at all his comments and looked around frequently, as if she were afraid of seeing someone she knew. Asked if they could still go to the beach.

On the way there, she bought them sea buckthorn ice cream in sticky cones.

The walk past the broad dunes, the last sunlight on the water, where they were just then had to be the most beautiful place in Germany. It was ebb tide, the beach was miles long, no one could be seen far and wide. Hannah took her shoes off, her nails were painted red, her feet sank into the sand with each step, seashells crunched under her soles, they'd been buried there since the water was high. He couldn't help but think again of the invisible hand that had shaped all that, the millennia of rising and falling tides. The bellies of the birds above them glowed white, as on a floating stage. It got cooler, and he pulled on the twenty-year-old sweater that had been tied around his waist. But the wind came through in the places it had been darned, wrapped around his bones, whispered: You're here, you have a life you love, you're here and thinking clearly and being friendly and are excited, because tonight this woman will sleep on the fold-out sofa in the room next to yours. It struck him that it was probably rude to stick her with the sofa, but it was also a bit much to change out all the bedding when she must be tired. He thought of the last time he'd come to the island, one image overlay another, as in a déjà vu, the last time Marsha had slept in bed with him, had walked arm in arm with him down the beach, had held him tight when the wind blew hard, after taking a tumble during her pregnancy, she'd been terrified of falling on her belly. She'd done it in Hannover, at the public pool, the ground was slippery, it had just rained, she was on her way home, she had screamed at him, had screamed at herself, had screamed at the gynecologist in the emergency room later that day, luckily nothing bad had come if it.

"What are you thinking about?" Hannah asked when she caught up with him. "Lovely here, right?" She grinned, revealing incisors framed by full lips under a big, broad button nose. He explained his dilemma. She laughed aloud. "I'll take the couch, obviously," she said, "it's not a problem, you're overthinking it," and she poked him in the side, before they'd gone no further than smiling at each other in greeting. Her dark blond hair, illuminated from behind, looked like a ruffled halo. "Tell me something, though. How am I supposed to believe you're a cantor when you don't even sing? Do you just stop praying when you're traveling on your own?"

He gulped. His legs, from above, looked to him like stilts, too thin in his baggy jeans. He felt abashed, and wished once again to be alone.

"No, I always pray," he said, "I mean, not always, but when I can, in the mornings and evenings, sometimes in the afternoon, as is bidded. Anyway, you know a cantor's not a rabbi, we're singers, we're not priests."

She smiled at him. "Bidded? Bidden, you mean? Like as the scripture commands?"

"Yeah, exactly," he said. The breaking of the waves seemed suddenly very loud to him.

"You're the vain ones, I still remember that," she said, "but you still know your stuff. I can just read the kiddush, the Birkat Hamazon, maybe the Haggadah still."

"That's not bad, though," he responded, "anyway, everyone has to decide for themselves how they want to do things."

She was still smiling. "Is it different to sing, like, to lead a lot of people in prayer?"

He wasn't sure what to say. Felt he was being interrogated, in a way; the tone of the conversation was completely different from the one at dinner or in the emails they'd exchanged. "Eh, yeah. I mean, I don't know. I never really thought about it that way. Thought it through, I mean."

She seemed to notice he was uncomfortable, and bent over to pick up a crushed seashell. "Would you say there's such a thing as bad Jews? Because I'm asking myself at the moment whether my father was a good Jew, or whether it matters or whether it's important that he didn't actually believe in God and couldn't even tell you which animals were treyf. As for me, I barely know the Hebrew alphabet. What you said at the funeral I found so moving, but I also had the feeling, maybe, that you were just saying it because you didn't know he really wasn't a very good Jew."

He had to laugh. So that was what it was about. "No, I don't think there's such a thing as *bad Jews*," he said, making air quotes, "there's just different Jews."

"Do you think you're better?"

He stopped. "No, I don't think I'm better. What I believe is, if I thought I was a better Jew than the others, then I'd be a worse Jew than most."

She nodded. "Thanks," she said. "I'm going to have a crab roll tomorrow, then."

That's not what I meant, he thought, but he laughed.

* * *

They left Jerusalem behind. Marsha told her the north was green, the word she used was *lush*, and all along the Jordan were kibbutzim and farms, vineyards, even. They would spend the night at one of these farms. The next day they'd continue on to Acre and the northern Mediterranean coast. As she deliberated, she softly cursed the GPS app. "How do you say *asshole* in Hebrew?" she asked once, and Margarita said *manyak*, because it was the worst insult she could think of, her father only rarely swore in front of her. Marsha practiced. Every time someone passed her on the right, she said *manyak*, but it sounded strange coming from her, like money-yek. She knows the country, I know the language, Margarita thought, maybe that's enough, but then Marsha shouted, "Oh my God, it's just a loanword, *money-yek*, *maniac*—and I call myself a linguist, for heaven's sake," and Margarita thought, never mind, I don't even know the language, but she hardly cared, the beige on the roadside was so monotonous her eyes started to close. She felt the skin of her thighs go tense as she thought of Lior's body, as she did every time she closed her eyes, if only for a moment; even when she blinked, there he was, the way he thrust inside her, his dirty nails, the thick hair crowning his penis.

She woke when they stopped at a gas station, Marsha had to go to the bathroom. Margarita stayed in the car and observed the family next to them, two kids sleeping in the back, two men up front who kissed before they took off. How happy they must be, Margarita thought, what pleasure, kissing like that. If anyone ever kissed her like that, she'd never complain about anything again.

Soon after they left, she fell asleep again, and was startled awake when Marsha slammed on the brakes. A man in a white garment begged their pardon. He looked like Jesus: long beard, ageless face. Was she dreaming? Had there been an accident? Marsha jerked the hand brake, said, "Out, now," so Margarita got out, the air was dense, muggy, it was loud and smelled like exhaust, people with white garments everywhere. Marsha dug through her bag in the trunk, pulled out a bathing suit and two towels, Margarita pressed her hands into her thighs, it wasn't a dream, they were still sticky from the soda. "Bathing suit," Marsha said, "let's go," and she took her bikini out of the hastily packed suitcase; the robed men around her, tour buses taking off, it felt somehow holy, but the holiness was ruined by the ugly parking lot, the trash on the ground, over the gate it said *Yardenit Baptismal Site*. Marsha smiled. "Don't worry, they won't baptize you by force," she said, Margarita replied, "I didn't know that was an option," and again Marsha laughed, that laugh Margarita had never heard before yesterday.

"Where are we even?" she asked.

"I'll show you," Marsha said, a gleam in her eyes, as if she were sharing a precious secret, here, where nothing was mysterious, romantic, historical, it was more like a ridiculous mishap.

* * *

When they reached the apartment, Hannah said she was in the mood for a shower. She opened her suitcase as he fetched fresh bedclothes from the bedroom closet, a dense silence—was she comfortable or, like him, holding her breath a little? Was this what it was like when two not-exactly-young-anymore people tried to act like what they were doing was normal but their knees were just a bit too stiff to pull it off? How long had it been since he had slept in an apartment with a woman? How long since she had slept in an apartment with a man? Days, hours?

The question made him uneasy, even though he hadn't thought about it once before she'd arrived; he'd just been happy for the company and the chance to talk to someone who seemed to understand him. Now, though, he felt under observation, but also like an observer himself, as though he had to follow her every step to keep from stumbling. As the water in the shower turned on, he made Hannah's bed, then took his siddur and his tefillin from the nightstand, stood at the window, and recited maariv. He didn't usually pray when he had a visitor or something else came up, but today he needed to prove something to himself. Closed his eyes, whispered the Shema as softly as he could, thought of the One, the Eternal, the stars shining over his head, the sea roaring so loud he could hear it through the open window, it could have been the shower, too, though; he wasn't sure just now what was the sound of the sea and what the sound of a shower. He continued with the Amidah, first three steps back, then three forward, tiny, barely audible steps.

He no longer needed the siddur, he hadn't for years, it was just there to have something to hold, the book in the left hand, the bands on the right arm, a symmetry that had been with him his whole life, one he rarely devoted much thought to. He also prayed that Hannah would take a long time in the bath. The movement helped him find the rhythm in his words. The rhythm of the thirteen petitions: for wisdom and knowledge, for understanding and salvation. He struck himself on the chest timidly, he'd done it harder as a young man, the need to feel himself praying was stronger then, now it was prayer that made him feel himself.

His fist was still on his chest as the water stopped flowing. At least I made it this far, he thought, and wanted to go back to the bedroom, but Hannah called to him. She had forgotten to grab a towel. He dug one out quickly. Hannah cracked the door and he shoved his arm wrapped in its ribbon through the gap.

"Oh no," he heard her say as the steam pressed through. "I didn't mean to disturb you."

"No problem," he said. His voice sounded sterner than he'd intended.

"They're so pretty, though," Hannah said, "I always wondered what I'd look like in tefillin."

He didn't know what to say, eventually mumbled, "From what I know, you're not allowed to put them on in the shower."

She laughed and finally took the towel from his outstretched hand. A wet snatch of skin stroked his arm. He closed the door, felt the fine droplets from that contact, wiped them off on his pants, still there was a cool feeling there that distracted him as he retreated to the bedroom and attempted to lose himself in prayer. He hurried through the Modim, nodding rather than bowing twice. His heart pounded as he took off the tefillin and returned to the living room. Hannah was sitting arrow-straight, like an origami boat, in the sofa bed, reading, the edges of the thin mattress curled up under the fitted sheet. He cleared his throat, as though he had something to say, but nothing came out. Hopefully she wouldn't ask whether she could try on his tefillin. It had to be forbidden, he thought, but Hannah was just as Jewish as he; despite their secularism, her parents must have been stricter than his own, to whom religion had mattered no more than their granddaughter in Germany—in other words, not at all—they knew they both existed, gave money, prayed on the big holidays, because that was what you were supposed to do. They had more than enough Judaism in Israel, there were Jews all over the streets; the older they got, the more fanatical they were, and they had other grandkids, his sister's children, who'd lived just a few streets away from them in Tel Aviv, the spoiled brats. Whereas when Harry had wanted to see Jews, he'd had to go to the synagogue, and he'd cried from joy when he found out Hannah was having a child, she had said; it didn't matter that it was out of wedlock, didn't matter that it was a mistake, that she was twenty years old without a penny to her name, Hannah's mother had just said *vos ayn katastrofe.* Hannah didn't explain why her mother had said this in Yiddish.

He smoothed out the bedsheet. The corner of the mattress sprang back up. "Thanks," Hannah said as he stood there, lost, next to the sofa. He felt as if he'd embarked on a journey and didn't know to where. "I think I'll read a little longer. Would you like to call Margarita?"

It surprised him that he didn't feel like it, and he said so: "Surprisingly, I don't feel like it, I'm going to read, too," in his clumsy German, which pained him so; really, speaking German was Margarita's job. When they ate together, she always ordered for him, she didn't like him talking to the servers. She didn't know how humiliating that was, so he just let her do it, and when he ate out alone, he just pointed to the dish on the menu. Hannah didn't seem bothered when he stumbled over his words. Here, he couldn't hide behind his voice, behind his singing, the way he usually did; he had to constantly speak in clear sentences. Just like other people did every day.

He left the door to the bedroom ajar so she wouldn't think he needed her to be quiet. At some point, the light in the living room turned off. He turned his off, too, to keep from bothering her. Just as he was about to take off his pants, he heard her say, "Thanks for letting me come here," her voice young and meek. He didn't know how to answer. Finally, he said, "Sure." Crude. Clumsy. He scolded himself afterward.

The moon shone, a thin sickle, through the skylight over the bed. He thought a long time about that touch on the arm. About how Marsha used to touch him. But now there was not a single cell left in his body that Marsha had ever touched, not a centimeter that Marsha had ever craved the way he had craved her, that greediness, that lust, the memory of sex with Marsha almost painful, the openness with which he had touched her and the greater openness with which he'd let himself be touched. I'm a completely new person, he thought, only my memories are proof that this contact ever took place, and the pain I felt is an echo in the brain cells, you could invoke it, but that didn't mean it was real. It helped him to think that even the skin Hannah had touched would slough off and regrow, nothing left of it but dead cells on a sidewalk or in a drain in the sink.

* * *

The Jordan was milky green, a dense viscousness drifting under a thick canopy of trees. They had changed, Margarita awkwardly, her mother unbothered, Margarita saw Marsha's dark brown nipples and her nappy pubic hair, a body that had harbored and nourished her, and how strange it now was, stranger than her father's, which had never produced mother's milk or grown a placenta. They had put their things aside and clambered over slick branches down to the river, Margarita tense, she'd slipped and fallen into the greenness. Everything was like a dream in the seconds before waking. The water just cool enough to be refreshing, the pull of it so soft that you could easily swim in place; a gentle river, Margarita thought, not like the Chicago River, which was also green, but which you couldn't even dip a toe into. It seemed so far away, in another world, not this one, with the skyscrapers framing it, the Magnificent Mile with its stores with their freezing air-conditioning, the Palmolive Building, its sandstone as beige as Jerusalem, how odd that these places existed on the same earth.

How odd, too, that time had not stood still since she'd gotten there, that her grandmother was still shouting at her grandfather, that she had to heave herself out of the car alone, that right now, she might be eating cherries, chewing with her mouth wide open, gathering the pits in her cheek, and spitting them all at once into the sink, where the garbage disposal would grind them up. That her grandfather was reading the newspaper while Margarita washed off the dust.

Downstream, people were being baptized, their white garments blotted in green, while here all she could hear was rap rattling from the speakers of a couple of young men. As she rowed past them, it smelled of weed. Of Nico. Sounded like him. Her mother, swimming next to her, had wrinkles in her forehead, as if she were concentrated on feeling satisfied, as if happiness were something you had to take seriously.

It was so hot that they hardly had to dry off. They spent the afternoon reading by the river. Once it had cooled off a bit, they drove on to a small farm, two black donkeys in the garden, a pool where Margarita swam a few laps at sundown, deep underwater, to see how big her lungs were, how much of that sticky air she could hold inside them. Under the surface, a quiet blue, quiet in a way nothing had been for weeks.

Margarita's head was heavy at dinner, a long day, she still had to call her father, but when she tried, back in the bedroom, he didn't pick up.

She woke naked, except for her underwear, and bathed in sweat, she had forgotten to turn on the AC. On her phone was a missed message from Anna, a couple of glowing red hearts that made Margarita's eyes burn. She dozed off, the hearts lingering on her retina. Half-asleep, she realized she didn't even know whether the place they were in was dangerous. Maybe a bomb will kill me in my sleep, she thought, and everyone will see my ugly nipples.

* * *

He had dreamed it was Pesach, that the seder had dragged on forever, and he secretly kept eating one hard-boiled egg after another under the table, endless hard-boiled eggs, they disgusted him, upset his stomach, sickened him. At the end of the dream, he threw up in his soup bowl. Countless undigested hard-boiled eggs flowed from his mouth.

When he woke, he felt off, it was early, but not early enough to keep sleeping, so he lay there with closed eyes, fluttering eyelids, and thought about Pesach, which he loved, and what he loved about it, the melodies, the rumbling in his stomach bringing him closer to his ancestors in Egypt, the millennia of hunger for justice, and how creative you had to be, all the things you could bake and claimed you had to bake: chocolate cake without flour, pavlova with the first raspberries if you were lucky, and the holiday fell in late spring. Salads of wild herbs with walnuts and lamb shoulder roasted for hours, caramelized carrots with roast beef, his stomach growled and he thought of the heft of his daughter's body, she always fell asleep during the Birkat Hamazon and he'd carried her home after a long, long seder at Yotam and Ariel's, he saw them both rarely, they had two kids and demanding jobs and still worse lived in Charlottenburg, but they invited them to Pesach every year.

On the second evening, he'd cook, every year for pretty much the same people who came with different company, changing partners and children, or for friends who were there to visit in Berlin. This last seder, Margarita had drunk wine from thimble-size plastic cups that were actually for the vodka after the meal, still, her cheeks had turned rosy. But her face hadn't changed. She clearly had practice drinking. After what had happened at school, he found out why.

His eyelids were now fluttering so much he had to open them. And so he turned to his morning prayers, with the words: *True and certain, settled and enduring, upright and faithful, beloved and cherished, graceful and pleasant, awesome and mighty, right and accepted, good and beautiful is this word to us for all eternity.*

A wonder, he thought, that someone wrote this to tell how beautiful the language God gave us is, and that this person should make language so beautiful in doing so. The Hebrew of the people of Israel, which has never left us. A raincoat made of words, a raincoat of guttural sounds that withstood everything, so that everything had rolled off us. Good and beautiful, this word, forever and ever.

It was just seven when he closed the siddur and removed the tefillin, but next door he heard a rattling from what he thought was the kitchen. Hannah was screwing the moka pot closed. "So you're an early riser, too," she said. "Or did I wake you?" He told her no several times, and asked her to excuse him, he was going to take a shower. After he'd undressed, she shouted through the door that she was going to buy bread. He was nervous, and washed up quickly, so he could set the table before she came back. As he took plates from the cabinet, boiled eggs, stuck a plastic spoon into the marmalade, he imagined doing the same for Hannah in Berlin, her going to the baker while he set the table, Sunday after Sunday, he had to grin, honestly the whole notion was a bit daft. He even lit a small candle, saving the long ones for dinner, it was Friday, he had brought them along with his travel candlesticks, he was excited for

Shabbat, for cooking with Hannah, dishes that would taste good even cold, the next morning they could take their leftovers to the sea for a picnic, maybe even rent beach chairs.

He was looking forward to his first day with her, almost impetuously, he realized, far from the picture of tranquility he always tried to convince himself he was.

* * *

The next morning, they left. Margarita got to jump one more time into the pool, it smelled like chlorine, she pulled her brittle hair into a ponytail.

At breakfast, she asked her mother whether it was dangerous there so close to the West Bank. Marsha didn't answer clearly, instead giving her a long explanation of the *geopolitical situation* as she saw it, described the Iron Dome and the despair of the people who suffered under occupation.

It didn't seem like a bomb would land on them soon, so Margarita dried off in the sun, belly down on the lounger, to hide the love handles she'd put on last winter, which seemed like they'd never go away, even if she tensed her belly every time she sat, following a tip she'd come across on Instagram.

Her hair was still wet when they got back into the car. Marsha told her they'd be driving to Acre, a coastal city with a large Arab population, but not as *segregated* as Jerusalem. Margarita had to ask her what *segregated* meant. It felt hypocritical, her mother talking about racism just now. "You didn't seem to think the situation here was so bad when you were chewing out Lior."

"It's all very complicated," Marsha said, "your father must have told you the same thing. Still, I thought you'd want to see the whole country, not just parts of it."

"What my father told me is there's a dispute about what exactly the entire country is."

"I just thought it would be a good idea for us to travel together, we never see each other, you know?"

Margarita didn't respond.

Acre was small. From a cliff by the restaurant where they ate lunch, boys leaped into the sea and shouted words to each other that Margarita didn't understand. Her mother told her the language was more mixed here than in the Jewish part of Jerusalem or Tel Aviv. Marsha had gotten her university fellowship to study diglossia in Israel, *diglossia*, another new word, she liked it. "For me, as a linguist, it's extremely important not just to talk to people, but to talk about talking, what they feel, what ties them to their language." In this sense, she studied Yiddish and Arabic as *oppressed minority languages.*

Margarita asked how Marsha could research languages she didn't speak.

"It's about the context. When and how people speak languages, if they feel comfortable doing so. What they say isn't so important."

"So if they say, *I'd rather speak Hebrew*, does that matter?"

Marsha laughed. "You're smart," she said. Nothing else.

After the fish cakes, the servers brought them giant sour artichoke hearts oozing with olive oil, so delicious that Margarita and Marsha closed their eyes as they ate them. Marsha left the last one for Margarita. "This is my favorite vegetable," she said, and Margarita replied, "Mine, too." She was happy to find they had something in common, but there was no reason for her mother to know that just then. "Grandma's, too," Marsha said, "it's a Markovitz thing." Margarita smiled, her chest feeling right. She had forgotten that her mother was the daughter of her grandmother. That she, too, was a Markovitz.

The Old City was less bustling than in Jerusalem, easier to get a sense of. Margarita drank an orange juice while her mother tried to haggle over a silk shawl with a hawker in broken Arabic. At least

Margarita couldn't hear her mistakes the way she could in her father's German. Still, Marsha's wrangling embarrassed her. Wasn't it
white supremacy, this very obviously not poor woman putting the
squeeze on an Arab vendor? Or had he set the price so high that it
would have been pathetic not to haggle?

Margarita had hoped she'd learn more about the *conflict* during
her trip, but she only felt more confused. Again, she asked herself
why her mother had gotten into an argument with Lior. Since that
night, the images of him had become less tangible, the longing for
something she had never known had abated, the memories themselves were muffled.

It was so hot that they were soon on their way again, grateful
for the salvation of the car's powerful air-conditioning. Margarita
looked in the little mirror over the passenger seat and arranged her
hair. She stared into a face that had grown darker in just a few days,
the thick brows that she hadn't plucked for weeks and that now
were flourishing, nearly touching her eyelids; into a face that she
hadn't examined carefully for a long time, distracted by so much
else, and that struck her now as unfamiliar, hard-edged, dour.

Marsha pulled into a parking place and took out her phone.
"Your father showed me the beach," she said, "but the kibbutz we
stayed in back then isn't there anymore. I'm looking for somewhere
else to sleep, if worst comes to worst we'll stay in Acre."

"You don't know where we're sleeping tonight?"

"Margarita, as long as we don't run out of money, everything's
fine, it's a small country, we can always go back to my apartment
in Jerusalem."

As long as we don't run out of money—that *we* stuck in Margarita's craw like a hard stone.

"I'm sure you've already realized I couldn't travel like this on
my university stipend. You can write Grandma and Grandpa a nice
postcard."

Margarita tried to swallow the lump in her throat.

They lay in the shadows of a cliff. Marsha read her book, Margarita texted Anna to report on the past few days. *Lol that woman is so weird*, Anna wrote, *miss u!!!* plus a blurry selfie with her mother at the Zionskirchplatz, which Margarita knew so well. How relieving, the certainty of being missed, of missing. *Yeah the old bitch is craaaazy*, she wrote back, an emoji rolling its eyes.

She thought of the nice scent of Anna's apartment. Remembered the hours she had spent there talking in the dark. Anna telling her she'd tried to have sex for the first time, but Anton had been so nervous he couldn't get it up. *A pig in a blanket*, she'd called his member, and Margarita had laughed until she couldn't breathe. A few days later, she was plastered and sobbing into Margarita's winter coat in the Rosenthaler Platz U-Bahn station.

She thought of Anna's father, laughing along with them in the morning at the breakfast table as they recapped, with embellishments, their experiences of the night before, Sigmund, the cat, sitting on his lap.

How long the days were, how long and how full, reminding her of the Berlin winters, those hours of daylight that in their paucity she'd always found so cruel. What she would give now for one of those days, so short that nothing could happen, and dark rather than shrilly bright as it was here. For a day that didn't matter.

More and more people brought out their folding chairs, unpacked food for picnics, and Marsha looked at the time. "Shit, we need to go or we won't be able to check in," she cursed, gathering her things hectically; Margarita jumped up with a start, too, as she did, a black wall appeared before her eyes.

* * *

Cooking together was easier than the day on the beach. Hannah had screamed when she jumped into the water and couldn't even take it for one minute, as for him, he'd have gladly swum far out, to one of the sandbars where, if the seals weren't sunning themselves, you could catch a few strained breaths before swimming back and wrapping up in a towel. But only at high tide, and when Hannah fell asleep in the afternoon sun, the water was already low again.

He passed the time answering a few emails on his phone and texting Margarita. She had apparently forgotten he was away, or at least didn't ask how his vacation was going, anyway she said all was well, טוב, he was surprised she used the Hebrew alphabet instead of Roman letters as usual. He got one last message as he was putting his phone aside, *I miss you*, his daughter wrote. So maybe not all was well.

When Hannah woke, her back was beet red. He offered her the button-down he'd thrown on over his T-shirt. She wore it as they walked to the only supermarket on the island. He saw her sniffing it discreetly. She said they should bake a cake, and assembled the ingredients while he loaded the cart with heartier fare. They walked side by side to the seafood aisle, where fresh fish lay on the counter, and they decided to have whitefish rolls as a starter. As he paid, Anna stood there in his dark green shirt by the door and bit into her roll with closed eyes. He tried to hold on to that moment. Perhaps it would be worth it.

He peeled the potatoes, she pitted the apricots, he made the batter for a quiche, she licked the bowl clean, he washed the lettuce, cut the chives and dill, she beat the eggs until they formed soft peaks, they talked about Margarita throughout. Only when the faucet was running or the hand blender hummed did no one speak.

She asked questions: What was it like, raising his daughter as a single man, did he get help from the government? He said, "Help from Germany, no thank you, just the childcare allowance."

He tried to find out more about her, but she didn't reveal much, that was unusual, him being the one who talked more. She told him that for fourteen years, she hadn't had to do it on her own, she'd met her now ex-partner when she was still pregnant, "Jacob calls him Papa," she said.

There was no way Margarita was still calling Marsha *Mommy*.

He didn't tell Hannah how for years Margarita had screamed *Mommymommymommyaba* after her nightmares; during the first few months, she'd screamed herself hoarse, there were nights when she completely lost her voice, he'd taken the child with her raw throat to day care and gone off to sing, to teach, to sing again, had picked her up, fed her, cradled her, kissed her, asked himself why he'd never gone hoarse himself. At some point she stopped, christened her doll *Mommy* and called herself *Mommymommy*.

It embarrassed him to think of how poor they'd been before his parents died, their greatest luxury had been a year's pass to the Berlin Zoo, which they'd visited every Sunday, and a child's seat for her to ride behind him on his bicycle. After two years, he had renegotiated with the Community, and was able to buy her ice cream at the zoo and meat once a week at the kosher supermarket. She started school, and things got simpler and harder, up early in the mornings, the girls who broke Margarita's new pencils and teased her because of her cute, sharp little ears and, he suspected, because in ethics class she had said she was Jewish; at one of those awful parent nights the teacher had come up to him and asked whether it was true, *I thought she made it up because she wanted to be special.*

He told Hannah this, and she said the right thing, put in words what it felt like when your child was wounded, "You just want to scream at the parents of the little shits until their eardrums burst."

He asked her whether these parents and teachers came all the time to her office at the music school. "Yeah," she said, "they sit there and piss and moan." He liked how vulgar she was, her Berlin way of talking, she must have gotten that from Harry, she cut her vowels short, swallowed her syllables.

They toasted to Harry, a beer before the Shabbat wine she'd

brought along, a handsome Israeli bottle, probably made just a few miles from his daughter's vacation spot; every evening, without comment, Marsha sent him their location on WhatsApp, he had asked her to. He didn't ask her for much, so she stuck to the few rules he did make; a few days ago on the phone, she'd said, "You're not a helicopter father, you're a drone daddy," the conversation had lasted just a few minutes, she hated talking on the phone.

Hannah asked about his parents.

"Dead," he said. "For a while now," he looked around, everything was ready.

"I'm sorry," she said.

"It's fine," he responded, it sounded cold, a son that didn't mourn his parents.

"What kind of people were they?" Hannah asked, "I mean, if you feel like talking about it."

He said: "My mother's name was Stella, us kids both called her that, too, though she wasn't like a star in the least. Still, Itzik, my father, thought she was wonderful. She had a long face, she was always ranting and raving at us, she was, what's the word, eccentric?"

Hannah nodded.

"She was born in Israel, her parents had made Aaliyah in the late twenties, they came from Breslau, they were Zionists. That's why my last name is Fuchs. My father was actually from Turkey, they wanted us to have a yekkish name, even if there was nothing yekkish about us."

Hannah laughed again. For a moment, he didn't know whether she was laughing because he was so un-yekkish with his dark skin and his dreadful accent or whether she was amused at his mother's approximation of feminism.

"It's good they got out in time, right?" she asked.

"Yeah," he said, "my mother wasn't born until 1942, my father was the really lucky one, he was twelve years older, they fled after the Thrace pogroms, they lived in a totally different part of Turkey, but they were scared. He was four when they left, in 1935. My father said he could still remember the crossing, but honestly, I never believed that. The only thing he wanted to do when he came to see me in Berlin was visit the Turkish teahouses. He never could make himself travel back to Turkey, but at the Maybachufer market, he cried. My mother just wanted to go to the KaDeWe, it irked her that he was so sentimental; besides, his family hated her. I can still remember my grandmother Leyla, the way she cooked, the calluses on her fingers were so thick she could reach right into a hot pan. He met my mother because he'd treated her, he was a dentist and he had to pull her molars. She was in her mid-thirties, he was nearly fifty, he thought he'd never marry, and when he died a few years ago, she followed him right after. Heart attack for him, colon cancer for her."

"I'm sorry," Hannah said again in that German voice of hers.

He thought of the joke a rabbi friend had told him, the only rabbi that he really liked. "A German asks you how you're doing, and you tell them *Not so well*. Their response is: *Oh, I'm sorry.*" Then the rabbi paused and added, "*But that's too private.*" He wondered if Hannah was more German than Jewish. Whether it was appropriate for him to wonder that. As if he had the right to interpret such a thing.

"Shall we say kiddush?" he asked.

He took the wine glasses out onto the terrace, then the challah, the plates, a carafe, and finally the candles and matches.

"Outside?" Hannah asked, uncertain. The terrace looked out over the woods, the row house where the apartment was located was at the end of a small path. The chatter from a few balconies farther down was the only sign that people were nearby. What could happen, here on this island, which seemed to be the only place in Germany without *Stolpersteine*? There had probably never been any Jews here, no one knew what Hebrew sounded like, he supposed. "Why not?" he asked, "no one's going to come and kill us, the ferry doesn't leave until tomorrow morning. It wouldn't be worth it."

He couldn't say, naturally, whether the neighbors were Nazis, but he knew he needed a break from everything, he wanted to be rebellious, wanted to say kiddush on a balcony, act as if Halle hadn't happened. As if, after twenty-four hours without eating or drinking, he hadn't run to the Langs' without stopping, from West Berlin to East, to throw up what little was left from the previous afternoon's feast into their nice, clean guest toilet.

Anna's mother had held him tight, "The girls are watching TV, it's still midday break," they were sitting there, their little cheerful almost twelve-year-old bodies on giant cushions, he had kissed Margarita and sat next to her on the couch, forgetting to take off his shoes.

They had turned on the news, two dead, the children froze then, Anna's mother had brought in the sweet honey cake to start with, it was supposed to be a reward, their pale daughters devoured it, not leaving much over for the adults, even though they hadn't fasted; it would be a while yet till their bat mitzvah, so they'd ordered lunch, lots of it, Indian curry and greasy bread.

He had offered to pray for the two dead, whose names they didn't know, and for the survivors, and they were grateful, they muted the TV. He knew how ugly it was to be relieved that nothing had happened to the people in the synagogue, that others had to pay the price and he cared less for them, what did it mean to say they were the others when he was an other himself? And what did it mean, anyway, to say that *nothing had happened*?

In an instant, he saw Margarita differently and had never looked at her the same way since, because she had understood better than him what it was the newscaster was saying. He had grasped something in those shocked seconds: his daughter was German.

She understood the perpetrator's language so much better than he, she even moved comfortably in it. Margarita belonged to the tiny remaining overlap of German Jews after 1945, an overlap he had thought of in relation to his own life, but had never discussed with his Israeli-American daughter.

He said kiddush on the terrace. Hannah said a dry, unmelodic brachah over the candles. He stood behind her, because there wasn't much room, and noticed the fine hairs on the back of her neck. He lost himself briefly in thoughts of stroking that fuzz. She turned around, full wine glass in hand, watching shyly as he sang the kiddush.

When he was finished, Hannah smiled at him. "Thanks," she said, "that was nice." She spoke the brachah over the bread, salted it, and chewed contentedly. Shabbat began, and they set the table and ate. For a moment, he missed Kabbalat Shabbat in the synagogue, missed the simultaneous closing of the books and the nodding at the end. But he knew he needed to enjoy not being there now, in a few weeks he'd be burning the candle at both ends, and then it would be dark again in Germany. He asked himself whether he would sit in the dark at the table with Hannah, whether she would laugh that blithe laughter in his kitchen as well.

* * *

They got there too late, but they were lucky, even though the sun had set, the owner of the dingy hotel had held their reservation and gave them a key. They had to share a room that night. Margarita didn't sleep. Her mother snored, and she stared at the ceiling, stretched her nose in the air to avoid smelling the greasy scent of the pillow. Imagined herself lying in her bed in Berlin.

The longer she lay there, the mustier the room smelled, the louder the snoring was.

How she used to hate her own home, shut up during lockdown,

lessons on a screen, boring conversations with her father, the cold of the classroom. And now, with no preparation whatsoever, she'd been cast into a world she didn't know. She'd imagined Israel as prettier, more exciting. On the screen, the world had been shiny. Here, nothing was shiny.

Exhausted, she stuck in her earbuds. The music distracted her from her thoughts. The first few seconds of sleep—or was it sleep when she knew she was asleep—were interwoven with that song from First Aid Kit, a band Anna had turned her on to: *I'm just like my mother, we both love to run*, the voices, the meaning crystal clear, tangible, and Margarita didn't know whether she was awake or dreaming. In the brief instants of silence before the song started again, she fell asleep.

When she woke, the headphones were lying on the bed.

They would drive on to Tel Aviv, Marsha informed her. She had no problem with driving a car on Shabbat.

"I've already been there," Margarita said, and her mother responded, "Well, I would like to go to Tel Aviv, if I have the permission of the *principessa*."

Margarita sensed that her listlessness annoyed her mother. She knew how pampered, how touchy Marsha found her. She could have raised me differently, Margarita thought spitefully, no one forced her to run away.

After two hours, they reached a small hotel in Jaffa, the reception was open, even though it was Shabbat; Jaffa was the Arab part of Tel Aviv, people there didn't really care about Shabbat, Marsha said. They had separate rooms, with little balconies, even, and a view of the covered market.

Margarita managed to take a nap while her mother was out walking. The empty room was a welcome opportunity to strip off her underwear; two orgasms, another under the shower, all she thought of was Lior, how he was so close to her, she imagined the story had been a different one: that he missed her, and he touched himself when he thought of her the way she did with him.

After the shower, she read the book she'd bought the day before, she'd decided to give a Hebrew one a shot. The silence, the breeze that blew the curtain in from the balcony door—relieving, just as she imagined adulthood.

* * *

It was a windy day, they were wearing jackets and long pants, a foretaste of the German autumn, when the wind tore through the seams of your clothing, not at all like winter in Israel, where it was the damp that crept in through every nook and cranny. His first winter in Hannover had been bitter cold, they'd barely left the house, with the child swaddled in several pullovers and blankets, Margarita and Marsha crying constantly. The synagogue on Haeckelstrasse where he sang was the only place he was ever really warm: the exhilaration of singing made him sweat as if he'd run a marathon.

The Community had put an attic apartment at his disposal. He and Marsha hit their heads on the ceiling constantly. At first they had liked how, in the summer before Margarita was born, they'd been able to lie in bed and see the stars through the skylight, but in late September, with their child there, either it was cloudy or they were too tired to look up. Marsha was lonely, he knew that, but she also hadn't bothered to make an effort, had dropped out of baby swimming, baby yoga, baby coffee meetups, for a long time she said his company and Margarita's were enough, it was just the winter that was getting to her, but then summer came, Margarita no longer had to be rocked all the time, and Marsha applied for jobs and got none of them and started translating instruction manuals from English into German to supplement Avi's meager income. One weekend in Berlin, her mood seemed to lift, and he wrote emails, made phone calls, hit up old contacts from yeshiva, he wanted to surprise her, wanted to do something nice. Not just give up, not run away, where would they go, anyway; they couldn't make it in America, either, and in Israel you could earn money as a chazzan only if you were a famous singer, plus sending Margarita to the military was out of the question for Marsha, so they went on taking their strolls in the park, found a slot in the Jewish day care, Marsha grew angrier and angrier and less and less happy, they started yelling at each other, Margarita started walking. Marsha and he had always been so proud of not needing couples nights out, board games, cards with conversation starters, all those things dumb people relied on because they had nothing to talk about, or because their lives were all about winning and losing, as Marsha used to say, but now he thought they should have given Scrabble a try.

Marsha had left in Elul, it made him shudder to remember that time, she was unloading the dishwasher and she announced to him she wanted to leave Germany, and he could teach piano lessons until he found a job, her parents would lend them money, then she'd cried all day, and her shouting had cut tracks into his heart like the seals in the sand, coarse like the sand that got stuck in his sneakers.

Hannah took her time spreading out a blanket and invited him to sit. He had to strain to listen to her and looked absentmindedly into her face, she was lovely, the pale sand behind her, the gray sea, the hollow between neck and shoulder almost youthful, and he caught himself thinking of nestling his lips in that nook, the thought surprised him so much he tried to pull himself together and follow along.

He had the sense she wasn't so much explaining things to him as justifying them to herself. She hadn't sent her son to the Jewish school in the city so he wouldn't have to learn in a maximum-security environment, she said, then apologized, "for you, it's different."

Right, he thought. He knew what it meant to fear desperately for one's child. His decision to shut his daughter in had come no less from fear than Hannah's decision to shut her son out.

Later, they walked back to the village in silence, sat at the kitchen table, and ate the cold leftovers from the night before, the sun still wouldn't go down for a long time. They washed dishes under the glare of the fluorescent lights. Hannah's movements were fluid. He hadn't noticed that before, the certainty with which she moved. Not graceful, but with something clear, something sure in her gestures. He felt the red wine he had just drunk tickling his stomach, not warm, but cool, as though he'd swallowed ice.

* * *

At dinner, Marsha asked about school: what she liked, what she disliked. Margarita told her what *Leistungskurse* were, like AP or honors courses in the US; she would take biology and English and skip physics and French. Her mother listened attentively. It surprised Margarita how greedily she was gathering information about her life.

She told her about her teachers, Frau Schreiber, who taught bio, she was young, they'd gone for ice cream together before the summer break, Margarita had sat down next to her because it made her sad to see her there all alone while all the other students were standing in groups and chatting. They'd talked about their vacation plans, Frau Schreiber would be spending time in the Black Forest with her husband and two kids. She seemed to have a perfect life. Margarita had felt the stares, even her friends hadn't spared her, kiss ass, they probably thought, but grades had already been turned in days before. She also talked about Frau Liebig with her horrifying breath: how dreadful, growing old and bitter and then smelling bitter, too. Frau Liebig had told Margarita one time that with those short-shorts she could never be a cheerleader, she'd be lucky to make it as a whore.

Marsha almost blew her red wine through her nose and out onto the table.

"You go to a Jewish school, though," she said, "isn't it better?"

"What do you mean, better?" Margarita asked.

"I don't know, like the teachers, aren't they—less German?"

"Just being Jewish doesn't mean they can't also be German. Jews can be burganim, too." She didn't know the English word for *snooty*, just the Hebrew one. Probably from school.

"Haha, your father used to always call me that, a burgania," Marsha said. "But anyway, most of the real German Jews are dead."

"I'm a real German Jew," Margarita said.

"No you're not," Marsha countered.

Margarita looked at her, perturbed. "German's my mother language."

"The idea of the mother language is totally outdated. People can have several first languages. If we're being precise, English is your mother language and Ivrit is your father language. You're not a real German."

"It's not like I want to be German, necessarily," Margarita fired back. "I just am, what am I supposed to do about it?"

Marsha took a long swig of wine. "This is exactly what I was afraid of," she said.

Margarita pursed her lips. It was evident that Marsha wanted her to ask *what*, so she could talk on, but she was furious and felt attacked. On her father's behalf as well. She doesn't understand, Margarita thought, but every signature on every report card, every fucking sandwich packed for lunch, every diced apple, it's all German, and Aba takes care of all of it. When he'd seen blood in her underpants in the dirty laundry, he'd bought her giant incontinence pads at the supermarket, they were still in the drawer in the bathroom, for months already Margarita had been buying her own tampons in secret and hiding them in her backpack. He had tried to take care of her.

Margarita decided not to talk to Marsha anymore about school. She didn't talk with her father about it, either, or hardly. For a long time, it had baffled both of them: you were supposed to get good grades, but effortlessly, without striving; you were supposed to be funny, but not a clown. So what, then? For Margarita, nothing. Either she was sassy or she flunked physics or math or she read over the course of a single afternoon the book assigned in sections over the coming week.

Marsha tried to distract from the silence with stories from her own years at the private school where Margarita went to summer camp every year, tidbits that Margarita would just as soon not have heard, about smoking weed and having sex under the bleachers by the basketball court, stories Marsha would never have told if she'd made her hundreds, thousands of sandwiches in the morning, if she'd sat in the principal's office where her father had promised that his daughter would never again take peppermint liquor shots with a friend who wasn't from that school during the theater play.

Marsha wasn't the one who had yelled at her afterward and asked for days on end: Where did I go wrong? Marsha hadn't gone wrong, she just hadn't been there, and her father had done nothing wrong, either, because he had been there.

That was why Marsha could tell these stories that had nothing to do with Margarita. Because her life had nothing to do with Margarita.

She talked about how Margarita's grandparents had fought until the plates were flying across the room and her grandfather had slept for two weeks in his office at the university. She couldn't remember anymore why.

She talked about Pesach meals in elegant rooms with a paid pianist sitting at a grand piano to provide the evening's accompaniment.

She talked about her parents' friends who had survived the Holocaust and now lived in a building designed by Mies van der

Rohe. She described it the way Americans do, sensationalist, slightly repulsed.

She talked about the Yom Kippur when her best friend—*Linda, you wouldn't know her*—had raided the fridge, polishing off half a roast beef with ketchup while the rest of her family was at the synagogue. "I've never fasted since," Marsha said.

This bit of information surprised Margarita. "And my father didn't mind?"

"It was none of his business," Marsha said. "I'm no less Jewish just because I eat ham on Yom Kippur."

"Uh, right," Margarita said.

"Relax, Rita. It'll do you good. It would do your father good, too. There's no Last Judgment for the Jews, and no confessionals. We're not Christians."

Linda had moved away to the suburbs in the meantime, Marsha said with a theatrical shudder. "Heteronormative utopia. Those people are true burganim."

Margarita wondered if her mother still had any friends.

* * *

The next day, they went walking again, because there was nothing else to do, under racing clouds, as though the Lord could not relax on his one day off, as if having fashioned the Heavens and the Earth and the multitudes upon it, he was now bored and groaning powerfully into the sky. There were just a few people on the beach. Kite surfers bent over their boards in the wind.

Hannah told a funny story about her son, how he had forged her signature on an assignment he'd done well on, thinking that if she knew he was capable of getting good grades, she'd get even angrier about the bad ones. Laughing, he told her that might say more about her than about her son. She took this with humor, said, "I'm only human, I'm probably not any better than that seagull over there."

"I doubt that."

"You think we're better? You think God made us better than the seagulls?"

The word *God*, coming from Hannah's mouth, sounded like a swear word. So *Jew* wasn't only an insult, *God* was, too?

She looked at him, eyes narrowed, as though wanting to see his face better.

He took a breath before answering, but then he understood what he'd been trying to figure out this whole vacation. Hannah appeared to think his faith came first and then his singing, but it was the other way around: his singing compelled him to believe. Because the words he had to sing, those were his job, were words that held for him the meaning of the world, but also its meaninglessness, its happiness, its pain.

It was true that in the beginning was the word, but the word was also the way. It was the word that distinguished them from the seagulls, and it was the word that had no explanation, whose origin one could only conjecture. How many times, how long, had he badgered Marsha as she smoked cigarettes naked in bed, brooding over her dissertation, reading studies, underlining in pencil every concept, every result, every N and P value, diagramming sentences he dictated to her for the Shema Yisrael, because he'd asked her to; she had never been able to answer for him why this first word had existed.

No human being could have performed this miracle unless they were already possessed by language. A miracle he justified with recourse to God, whom he prayed to, while Marsha explained it to herself by working it out in lines and graphs, numbers and statistics.

Marsha had told him that language adapted to the world. The productivity of signs: the capacity to produce endless new words where new ones were necessary, the ability to understand these newly formed words on the basis of that which one already possessed, drawing on their roots, the Hebrew of the Holy Scripture, and even if eight million or so people, market criers and biochemists, bartenders and philosophers, tugged and tore at these roots, still—language stood firm.

He knelt in the damp, cool sand to see if he could do it. Saw Marsha in front of him in her dark red leather coat, so impractical, so chic, a good match for her hair dyed dark and her reddish-brown lipstick. He saw her before him, the way she had done the same thing just a few hundred feet from here, writing in the sand in her spidery hand. And he began to drag his fingers across the ground:

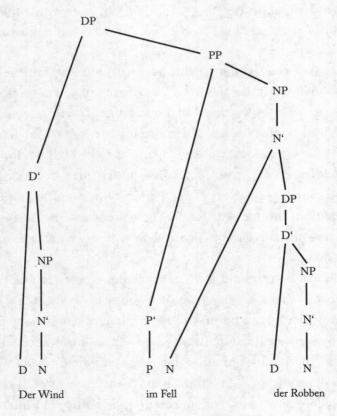

the wind / in the seals' / fur

Hannah looked at him, startled, and asked, "What are you doing?" and he tried to explain what Marsha had taught him years before, when she'd talked for months about nothing but sentence structure: about Chomsky's generative grammar, the X-bar theory, that allowed one to analyze every sentence in every natural language.

This grammar, which had nothing to do with the grammatical rules of individual languages, was called generative because it could produce an endless number of sentences that were *correct* so long as they obeyed the so-called phrase structure rules. And every sentence gave rise to a tree with branches when one depicted its phrase structure. No one could say why this phrase grammar existed in every language that could be spoken, written, or sung, but people knew that it differentiated man from animal, that this syntax was inborn in man and could illuminate human consciousness, because there was a language for human life, life as sign, language as signifier. It seemed to him at the same time the most natural and supernatural thing, bewildering and beautiful that it was thus, that it was this that moved him to prayer. This was, in some sense, evidence that the word had been there at humanity's beginning. That everything depended on it.

He spoke, stumbled, tried too long to elucidate the tree, the nominal phrases, prepositional phrases, in the end he was rasping, his mouth was dry, he said, "Margarita's mother is a linguist."

"Fascinating," Hannah said, "I don't get the tree, though."

* * *

As though their conversation the day before had dislodged something, Marsha could no longer stop herself from telling Margarita about the past. It was almost comically American, and Margarita had the sense that her grandparents had tried to wedge her into a lite version of Marsha's own youth, but the German, the Other, the In-between oozed out of her like cultural foam from all ends.

The jocks and the nerds, the fights with her parents, track and field in summer, ice hockey in winter, Marsha proudly showed her a scar on her shin. She recounted her studies at the University of Chicago, as the daughter of a professor she got discounted tuition, and at twenty-four she'd finished grad school and flown off to Jerusalem to do her doctorate. Margarita's emphatically monosyllabic questions didn't stop Marsha from wanting to tell her more. "It was my first time there all alone, and my first weekend I just wandered the city like you last week, I had no idea what I should do there."

"You were never in Israel before?" Margarita asked, and Marsha answered, "Sure, with your grandparents, but we just went to the hotel, then to Yad Vashem, then back to the hotel."

"Are we going to go to Yad Vashem?" Margarita was supposed to visit the monument two years before as part of the Jewish High School's yearly Israel trip, but the Covid restrictions had made it impossible.

"Maybe for the last part of our trip, I was thinking. I don't know how well you'll cope with it," Marsha said. "As a German and all. Haha." She actually said it like this, *haha*, dryly. "Aaanyway, there I was in Jerusalem, a poor, lonely student, I could barely cook, I still used to have my meals with my parents. And all round there were such amazingly handsome men, but they thought I was weird and stupid, that's how it is, everywhere they think us Americans are stupid, especially when we're cute, which I was, then."

"Haha," Margarita said. And thought of Marsha's rumpled belly, her unruly bush.

"And I had no idea whatsoever what I should do with my life, I mean I don't know if I even do now."

"Yup," Margarita said.

"And then I met Avi, this timid guy who also had no idea what to do with himself, so full of hang-ups, but you know all that, the rest is history."

What is the rest? Margarita thought. Am I history? "How did you actually meet?" she asked. Her father must have told her at some point, but she'd forgotten; in Jerusalem somehow, that was all she knew.

"In a bar. He was there with Yoev, but you don't know Yoev, obviously. He lives in Beersheba with his wife now. It's a shithole."

"So then?"

"I was there alone, they couldn't get a table, so they sat with me. We started talking, and it got late, Yoev left, but your father wanted to stay. He was quite seductive."

Bah.

She imagined her father as a young man in Israel, at home in the language, not an outsider, and she felt ashamed that she'd pestered him, made fun of him so much. It was almost never the other way around, only when he was really at the limit, when she'd been mean and nasty. Realizing who she'd gotten it from, and what her face must look like when she snapped that he always took everything too seriously, knowing that she'd humiliated him over and over, it made her sick. How wretched he was to her, with his accent, his lanky legs in suit pants or jeans that sat too high on his waist, leaving too little to the imagination, though he never noticed; his body long and thin, as if he'd never emerged from puberty, hers on the other hand was too soft, too broad, a reminder that there was no way she'd been formed from his rib alone.

She and Marsha walked side by side through Neve Tzedek, good-looking Tel Avivis were sitting all round drinking lemonade or beer. How gladly she'd have sat with them instead of letting her thin leather sandals grind blisters into her feet. She said nothing, she didn't want once again to confirm her mother's impression that she was spoiled and whiny. When they passed a large fountain on Rothschild Boulevard, Margarita stripped off her sandals and stepped inside, standing in the ankle-high water to relieve herself from the heat.

Then she got out and sat down, to put her sandals back on.

Marsha came close. "Oh no, you poor thing," she said.

Margarita didn't respond.

"You need some blister pads and a new pair of shoes."

Margarita looked around for the nearest pharmacy. Now that Marsha had noticed she was in pain, every step burned. She limped beside her mother, who told her, "Birkenstocks are the only shoes I let touch my feet. That's one good thing about Germany, at least, in case you ever have to leave on foot." She laughed. "Am I allowed to make Holocaust jokes in front of you, or are you too German for that?"

But that wasn't a Holocaust joke. Real Holocaust jokes were different, she knew that, she'd been to parties where people had tried out their quips about crematoria on her.

With her grandparents' money, they bought shoes and sabich, then, belly full and head cool, she let the waves on Trumpeldor Beach tug at her, more timid than those of Lake Michigan, the skyline less monumental, dirtier somehow and less orderly than the one you saw when you went swimming on Fifty-Seventh Street. Margarita couldn't help but think of all the people who had drowned in this sea, it nauseated her, and the water felt warmer then, the salt more caustic.

She lay on her back and dried off and looked into the sky, tried to read, but she kept having to look away, a laugh that could have been Lior's, a shouted phrase.

As the sun fell, they were sitting in one of the restaurants where you could dig your feet into the warm sand, but neither of them was hungry, they just wanted something to drink. Margarita kept looking over Marsha's shoulder to the beach, imagining Lior running past, that she had one more chance to make a last impression, but Marsha tore her abruptly from her fantasies: "Margarita, he's not here. A half-million people live in this city. He's not just going to pop up where you happen to be."

"I don't know what you're talking about," Margarita said, her voice far too loud.

"Lior, obviously; you've been looking for him the whole time. He came across like an asshole, I hope you used birth control."

"No, I'm pregnant now," Margarita snapped, "but it's not your business. I know what a condom is, by the way."

She stared at her mother's wine glass, imagined biting into it, the glass cracking in her mouth, swallowing the shards, being torn apart inside, that would be so much easier than carrying on this conversation.

"Your father didn't warn me you were cheeky," Marsha said, grinning.

"What did he warn you about?"

"If I told you, you'd just do the opposite to spite me," Marsha replied, and snorted, laughing, a quick breath in and out. "He said you were quick to get offended."

Margarita pursed her lips. It was hard not to get offended when someone had just offended you.

"On the phone he said there wasn't much to know, then he gave me a set of instructions longer than you'd need for a nuclear power plant."

"Idiot," Margarita said.

"But he failed to mention you swear too much."

"I don't swear much in front of him."

"Aha!" her mother shouted. "Anyway, he didn't warn me how much you swore, and he also didn't tell me as soon as you got to Israel you'd run off with the first cute seventeen-year-old you came across."

"You forgot me!"

"That was a misunderstanding! I guess your father wasn't kidding when he warned me you got offended easily."

Now Margarita really was offended.

"He also told me you needed nine hours of sleep and regular mealtimes. And that you're shy. And that you get diarrhea a lot."

"I'm not a baby anymore."

"That's clear to me. But not to your father. He's trying to figure out, by the way, how come you never checked into the hotel."

Margarita felt ill. "Oh," she said. She could feel her pulse throbbing again in her tongue. "What did you tell him?"

"First I said he should talk to you, but I don't think he could bring himself to. Then I told him you checked in using my name because you were pissed at me and wanted me to pay for it. And that I did end up paying."

"And he believed you?"

"Naturally," Marsha said, and grinned.

Margarita tried not to smile back. "Did his instructions also say that I was a good liar?"

"Of course not," Marsha said, "if he knew that, you wouldn't be a good liar." She raised her glass as though to toast Margarita and took the last sip.

And there, all at once, between their sweating glasses and the low table, something new arose: common ground. Something forbidden to her father, who didn't want to think Margarita capable of anything bad, who forgot that she'd broken the rules as soon as he was no longer upset, even when she'd sometimes broken them just to upset him. An idea emerged of what life with her mother would be like, a life without constant arguing over how late she could stay out, with no nights where she *stayed at Anna's* and in the morning walked two hours home from Nico's apartment in Charlottenburg because he had told her to go.

Maybe it was a shared stubbornness that she had thought was hers alone, that she hadn't suspected in this woman who had buried her feet in Birkenstocks in the sand just as she herself had.

* * *

After dinner, they moved to the sofa. The corners of Avi's mouth hurt from laughing, and he spoke freely, without chastising himself for his mistakes, he noticed them, but he thought maybe she might even like them, this was the first time he'd ever considered that, that someone might find something appealing about him besides his voice. Hannah's lips were purple from the red wine, her face flushed. She had pulled her knees up to her chest, he had crossed his legs, they fit this way on the small sofa they had folded back together that morning.

"What's your favorite parsha?" she asked, and added, without taking a breath, "Mine's Bereshit, I know, it's mega-boring. But I always thought it was cool how there was chaos on Earth, and then God came and sorted it all out, or maybe not everything, and in the dark, too, and God didn't see anything." She took a sip of wine.

And God called the light Day, and the darkness he called Night. And the evening and the morning were the first day. He nodded. "Maybe."

"Do you believe in evolution?" she asked, her expression dead serious.

He nearly spit his wine back into his glass. "Erm, yeah?" he said. And his mouth was dry like the earth in Bereshit.

"Seriously, though, the Haredim, they're nuts, fundamentalists, just like the Islamists and the Bible-thumpers," Hannah said, again in that excitable German tone.

"For sure," he whispered. She was right, of course, but he didn't know why the conversation had become so suddenly uneasy: Hannah was a Jew herself, she was allowed to judge, even carp. Maybe she wasn't as much a believer as he, but what did that even mean, to believe; after all, it was his job to believe, or so he told himself, so that all those prayers weren't pointless. Scientific knowledge, as he understood it, wasn't a question of belief, those were two different things she was comparing, even if it was true people often confused them. People, but not him. He said nothing, mainly out of fear of explaining to her something she must already know. Margarita already criticized him constantly for mansplaining. He didn't want to give Hannah the impression he thought he was smart for explaining to her the difference between knowledge and belief.

But of the tree of the knowledge of good and evil, thou shalt not eat of it. "My favorite parsha is Noah," he lied, to combat the silence and his raging thoughts, "because he rescued the seals we saw today."

Hannah lifted an eyebrow.

"Cool trick," he said, and she laughed.

As he tried to top her up, he knocked over her glass with the neck of the wine bottle. Pathetic, he thought, now she knows how drunk I am. They both bent over at the same time to grab the falling glass. The sound was jarring. There was red wine all over the tiles, on his white socks, on her naked feet. Classic, he thought, as their heads bumped over the shards. But she didn't pull away, and so he kissed her, it felt utterly different from what he'd imagined, they had to find whose lips went where, he no longer knew how to do it, how to kiss, his tongue struck her teeth; embarrassed, he closed his mouth. Hannah drew her head back.

For in the day that thou eatest thereof thou shalt surely die. Her eyes were closed, her lips pressed together tight, and he began apologizing, I'm sorry, he said over and over, to the shards of glass at his feet, to Hannah.

Eventually she opened her eyes. Lips still pursed, she inflated her cheeks and let the air seep out slowly, with a whistle. Then she stood. He was afraid she'd walk off, but she just got the broom from the hall. The sound of the broom was like someone chewing the shards.

"It's fine," Hannah said, as he excused himself again, "I just didn't see it coming."

He wiped up between her feet with paper towels. Did she mean if she saw it coming now, it would be different? She patted his head as they gathered the last of the shards. As if he were a child. He'd also been afraid of that: a middle-aged woman, moved by pity, patting him on his middle-aged head.

He got a new glass. They toasted clumsily, *last round*, she said, almost stern, he agreed a bit too willingly. She must have noticed he was ashamed.

"So, Noah," she said. "I wouldn't have guessed."

He cleared his throat, bashful, slid as far as he could from her, to the edge of the sofa, though he'd have liked to take her in his arms, try again, more tenderly, more bravely. "It has such a reassuring sound to it," he said, "on the ark, in safety with the animals Noah took with him, floating high over the flood. And how they came out later and God said he would not curse the ground anymore for man's sake, though *the imagination of man's heart is evil from his youth.*"

"But he did," Hannah said. "What was the Shoah if not a curse?"

He said nothing. She gnawed at the corner of her lips, knit her brows.

She did him the favor of not gulping down her glass, and they drank together wordlessly. The wine tasted sour. He kept asking himself what he'd done wrong. Usually he was the one to nip advances in the bud, he'd pretend he hadn't noticed, and when things got serious, he'd use Margarita as an excuse. But with Hannah, it was different. Maybe he only felt attracted to her because he couldn't tease out her motives. Why was she here unless she was interested in him that way, too?

Hannah stood and walked out to the patio. He watched her, lit by the dim glow from the room, the crashing of the North Sea audible,

the sky dark blue. "Oh," Hannah said, "a glowworm," as he followed her outside, and it was true, the tiny insect was there radiant
on her hand. She smiled at him. It had gotten cold.

"I wasn't trying—" Hannah said, and he shook his head, heard
himself say, "Me, neither," but he didn't mean that, what he meant
was: Yeah, but I was.

They looked each other in the eyes, far too long, did that mean
something, or were they just trying to find some kind of common
ground? Why did she have to show him the glowworm? He had the
feeling Hannah was looking through his pupils, which were mere
holes in his eyes, and down into the hollow of his chest to his thun-
dering heart. *Thus did Noah; according to all that God commanded
him, so did he.*

She stepped toward him, not averting her eyes. He was much
taller than her, he had to look down to hold her gaze. He bent over
and kissed her again, a real kiss this time, soft, eternal—kissed her
the way he had kissed Marsha. *And the waters increased, and bare
up the ark, and it was lift up above the earth.*

Sheltering, that kiss. *And Noah only remained alive, and they
that were with him in the ark.*

Hannah pulled away. "Sorry, this isn't working." She turned
around and walked to the bedroom, shaking her head, whispered
shit and went into the bathroom.

He heard the key in the lock, it got stuck, then she managed to
turn it. *And the waters returned from off the earth continually:
and after the end of the hundred and fifty days the waters were
abated.*

* * *

On their second morning in Tel Aviv, Marsha insisted they go
to the market before heading south. It was loud at the Shuk Ha-
Carmel, there was a foul blend of fish and toasted sesame in the

air, Margarita was surprised to find herself far less grumpy now that her feet no longer burned.

Shouting all round. What had been, a week before, a wild bustling in her ears was now crystal clear: dates for ten shekels a kilo. Raspberries. Watermelons, spices. You try, you buy.

They walked down Allenby, because Marsha just had to show Margarita a bookstore there. Margarita asked if they really had time for it.

"I'm spending the rest of my stay in Jerusalem chained to my work," Marsha said. "I want to be able to play tourist with you."

Margarita had briefly forgotten that Marsha would be staying there, that she wouldn't simply vanish into the no-man's-land she'd come from when Margarita returned to her real life.

"This is where your father grew up," Marsha said, and gestured blithely to a building on the other side of the road.

Gray, faded facade, little windows and balconies that looked like you'd do well not to step out on them or sit under them too long. Margarita couldn't believe her father had been a child there, then a young man, that he had stood at that same spot when he was her age.

"It was a creepy apartment," Marsha said, "with stuff piled up everywhere all the way to the ceiling, and it always had a sour smell. His parents hated me. Stella and Pnina were always trying to out-nag each other, Itzik just sat there and asked everybody over and over whether they were flossing."

Margarita took a photo of the building. "I didn't really know them," she said. "Not like Grandma and Grandpa."

"I know. Your father wasn't very close with them. They had such a shitty attitude about their origins and their children's education. And he didn't like how they pretended to be poor. Who would. He was too hard on them, but they didn't make it easy to do otherwise. They were just nasty to him after he ditched the

military, and stingy, especially after he hooked up with me. It
didn't matter that I was Jewish, for them the main thing was to
be Israeli. They could hardly believe he could love someone who
hadn't been in the army and couldn't speak Hebrew. In the end it
turned out they had money, they'd just been hoarding it all."

Margarita looked at Marsha. Had she really criticized Itzik and
Stella for being stingy even though she was a Jew herself? Or had
she just experienced so little antisemitism that she wasn't conscious
of what her words implied?

"It's no wonder he wanted to escape them, first to Jerusalem,
then even farther. They were toxic."

"Why, though?" Margarita asked. She knew almost nothing about
her father's parents, he'd hardly ever spoken about them.

"Eh," Marsha said. "Itzik was from Turkey. He was old as the
hills when I met him, he must have been born before the war, even.
I think Stella's grandmother was from Galicia, but Stella lived with
her parents in Breslau until the end of the twenties, even if none of
them acted it. Their lives had begun in Israel. They were traumatized, of course, like everyone here," she concluded, with a broad
sweep of the hand.

Margarita wondered whether Selma and Dan were traumatized,
too, but she didn't dare ask it aloud. She knew her grandparents
were both children of immigrants from the Russian Empire, last year
she'd learned they were from a place that now lay in today's Ukraine.
They had arrived in America before the world war. Selma had told
her many times about her memories of her parents' Yiddish, their
Russian. The Russian war of aggression dominated world events, and
Margarita had realized since then it was eerily entwined with her
origins. But it remained abstract, more so than the crumbling building she was standing in front of. She imagined traces of the building,
dust, kitchen mildew, splinters, winding through her bloodstream.

Why had her father spoken of his parents only in fragments,

and why had she never tried to find out more, like that child at the seder table who didn't know how to ask a question? Her father had always joked she was like the *simple child* from the Haggadah, because every year, she forgot again why Pesach was the most political of the holidays—because it was about Jewish resistance— and every year she forgot again what the different elements of the Pesach dish stood for, the egg, the parsley, all she could remember was what the salt water meant, the tears of the Israelites in Egypt, tormented by the pharaoh. Or was it maybe their sweat you were supposed to dunk the parsley into?

Margarita jolted. She had missed what Marsha had just said:

". . . and you know how my parents just idolized your father. Right from the beginning. I think for them he's more of a real live Jew than we are, because he's Israeli and because of his job and all. He took them on a tour through Jerusalem back then, and I think my mother would just as soon have married him herself."

"Why didn't you want to, then?" Margarita didn't realize how blunt the question was until she'd asked.

"Your father did," Marsha said, "but I wanted a proper wedding, with a giant party and so on. And we couldn't afford it."

"But that's why you moved to Germany, so you could make more money."

"Is that what he told you?"

"Yeah," Margarita said. "No. I just thought, why else would you . . ." Just then, she could no longer remember why she'd thought her entire life it must have been from financial necessity.

"We moved to Germany so you wouldn't have to do military service," Marsha said.

Margarita held her breath.

"And after that, Stella hated me for good."

Marsha said nothing more, just went on walking, so fast it seemed she was flying over the filthy asphalt of Tel Aviv. Margarita stumbled after her mother to the car, where Marsha cursed, because she'd gotten a ticket.

It took forever for them to make it out of town. After a look at the clock, Marsha struck the steering wheel and announced: "We're driving through the West Bank, otherwise we'll need four hours. This way it'll only take one."

"The car rental people said we weren't allowed to go through the West Bank."

"It's the only way for us to get there."

"I don't want to do anything we're not supposed to."

"Chill, Rita, everyone does it."

"Fifteen years ago, maybe. You have no idea what it's like here now."

"Hey. I'm still the mother here."

Margarita lifted her arms, giving up.

At the checkpoint, her hands were clammy, but the soldiers waved them through. At some point, the Dead Sea appeared, the car followed the serpentine paths through the rubble. On the side of the road were a couple of ibex, and Marsha got excited, telling her they were very rare, Margarita should hurry and snap a photo, but Margarita snapped no photo. So Marsha parked the car and photographed them herself. She motioned for Margarita to get out. Margarita refused, stared at the red mountains through the windshield until her mother was back in the driver's seat.

* * *

The sea glowed a bluish neon green. As if all the visitors to the Full Moon Party on Ko Pha Ngan, where he'd traveled to after his military service, had thrown their glow sticks into the water, as if all the glow-in-the-dark stars over all the children's beds in Germany had been tossed in after them. Avi had walked in the dark at low tide, a half-moon lit the beach sporadically between fast-moving clouds.

You could see the stars. Because there was so little light pollution—
that was a term Hannah had taught him. He walked, as the neon sea
rose over the island and swept back out, to the giant buoy that lay
on the widest part of the beach. Undressed: his sneakers (Margarita:
retiree shoes), his pants, his shirt, his underwear (Margarita: *ugh*).
The water seemed warmer than during the day, a welcome illusion
due to the cooler air. He dived through the glow until his lungs
burned, until he lost his orientation, *never swim drunk*, how many
times had he said that in the military, how many times had others
said it to him, but people also told him the earth of *Germaniya* was
scorched, and here, the sea was glowing.

When he unlocked the door, he was so cold he could hardly
remember coming home, maybe you really shouldn't swim drunk.

"Wow," Hannah said, "you are crazy."

He stripped off his soaked clothes and stepped under the shower,
washed the salt water out of his short hair, stood awhile under the
hot stream, still freezing, felt wonderfully dead and fearfully alive
at the same time, saw his thin, hairy legs beneath him, under his
trunk, which just wouldn't heat up, he was surprised they could
hold him up. Felt as he had before. Hannah knocked and called his
name. "Are you okay?" she asked, and he answered, "Yeah, sorry,"
wrapped his red-blotched arms around his own body, studded with
gooseflesh: thousands of little hard pimples. She asked if she could
come in. The shower walls were of crumbly patterned plastic. The
steam was still thick. He couldn't not say yes, she might be worried.

Hannah sat on the toilet lid. "What did you want from him?" she
asked.

He felt cornered, but he had cornered her that evening, too, so he
didn't complain. "What do you mean?" he asked back.

"Just that, what did you want from him? Why'd you make friends
with him, with my dad. What. Did. You. Want. From. Him." She
said it all slowly, as if she thought he were dumb.

"He was nice," Avi answered, "Harry was just a good guy." He was uncomfortable, looking down at his naked body, observing his penis, which he otherwise never looked at, the naked, red glans, it didn't matter that she couldn't see anything behind the frosted glass. He felt exposed in front of Hannah.

"But what was it about him, why the hell did you have to play missionary with him? That's forbidden, you know that perfectly well." She sounded like a rebellious child.

"I don't understand," he said, "playing missionary? He was already Jewish."

"Look, never in his life would he have come up with the idea of reading from the Torah on his own."

"Eh, he did, though," he said.

"Fine, but why? Someone must have pushed him to it. I never got it, and Mom certainly didn't, either. What did you tell him that made him want to do it? When I was little, we went to synagogue once a year, on Yom Kippur, and the most Jewish thing about us was that we did presents on Hanukkah AND Christmas. He always said it wasn't God that rescued him from Theresienstadt, but a flesh-and-blood man from Switzerland."

"What?"

"Did he tell you it was God? That would take the cake."

"No, he never told me anything."

"Really? Nothing at all? I can't imagine that, with me he never shut up about it, Jacob's third word must have been *concentration camp*, come on."

"I'm sorry."

"You know, I don't need all the religious blah-blah to feel Jewish. My father survived Theresienstadt. I don't understand what he wanted with you."

That stung. "Did you come here to find out?" he whispered.

She snuffled and said, "Sorry, can you speak louder?"

He repeated the question.

"No," she said, "I mean a little, but I also really think you're nice and interesting and all."

"I'm not a zoo animal," he said, audibly this time.

She didn't bite.

"Weird that he never told you, though. A Swiss politician bought his freedom, no idea why, he just paid somehow and got a thousand prisoners out. After that, he stayed in Sankt Gallen. But since the Swiss wanted to deport him to North Africa, he went straight back to Germany after the war, to the orphanage in Hamburg."

"No, he never told me that," he said.

"What was he trying to compensate for? What did you both talk about? Avi, he had no friends, at the funeral, those were all my mother's friends, and his sister, who stayed in England and can hardly speak a word of German. He had no one, he only met the rabbi when Mom got Alzheimer's and went into the Jewish old folks' home, the rebbe looked after her and after him, too, because he could hardly cook, but I always brought him food, and Jacob cooked, too. He was an old Holocaust survivor, and he didn't believe in God, that I can swear to you."

"Maybe he realized I didn't have many friends, either."

"BUT WHY YOU SPECIFICALLY. He could have just gone to play FUCKING bridge with his wife. He didn't need a deathbed missionary."

"Ouch," he said.

She sobbed.

Avi's skin was glowing red. He felt imprisoned in this shower-cage with hardheaded Hannah outside. *Völlig von der Rolle*, he thought in German: completely off the rails.

"That's not how I meant it," she said, "you're so nice, but you're also a true believer, and I think Dad just had different values. After what he'd lived through, there was no more God for him. Maybe you don't understand that. But he just didn't need anybody, he wasn't even lonely, far as I know. He was tough."

He said nothing as Hannah went on sobbing.

He thought. Then he said, "We have the same values. All of us want to live in peace. I'm a singer, I have to pay my rent. I'm not a fundamentalist just because I wear a kippa. And I don't think you have to believe in God. Is it because I'm not German?"

"My God," she said, "no, that isn't what I meant—"

"It's funny, but even you German Jews have something against foreigners. Harry didn't, though. He wanted to read from the Torah, I don't know why, he had this fascination with it. It's really not about why."

"I just don't understand," she sobbed. "We were totally normal Jews. That's all the trauma you need."

Why wouldn't she just leave?

"Then you and I can not understand together," he said.

"You're so, so sweet."

"That wasn't good enough."

"I don't find you unattractive," she said, "I just don't exactly know—I'm going through a phase where—you just have a kind of aura for me, something holy, I can't deal with that. I don't want to do my father the favor, he already idolized you enough. And he wouldn't know the difference anyway, now. And I also don't want to torment you."

"How do you mean?"

"Look, you must want to get married and all that, I don't know, I'm not into that, I just can't see it."

"Hannah, did you just come here to snup around in my life?"

"Snoop," Hannah said, "it's pronounced *snoop*."

"My life's not some Jewish theater you can buy a ticket to," he said. "I'm done showering."

"Okay," she whispered, "I'm sorry."

"Could you please leave?"

"Yeah," she said, and stood up from the toilet seat. "I just miss him so much."

"I know."

"I'm really sorry. I hope I didn't hurt you," she murmured, and opened the door.

"Let it go," he responded.

* * *

The air, like a hot stone pressing down on the people, who shouldn't even be there. No one should be there. This was a foreign planet, not some wellness paradise: hot, stinking water, the salt scratched Margarita's buttocks raw, her hands, too, which she used to hold herself in a sitting position in the Dead Sea, because she kept rising to the surface, the scabs where she'd scratched the mosquito bites on her legs. Bodies, bulging and red, in the slimy broth. Treyf bodies.

Not even the water from the shower was cool. Warm dishwater, then blackness. She saw colors, someone was playing jazz, it was so, so loud. Then no more blackness, she was back, her mother was bending over her, and the bellies of other people. Hotter. Someone brought a Coke. Someone asked if they should call an ambulance, she translated for her mother, her mother laughed, "Lo, lo," she said, she couldn't manage much more than that.

Margarita was terribly weary. She had always thought fainting was stillness, a simple not being there, but it was earsplitting. She needed the lid to come off. Perhaps they were trapped in a vacuum, in the little space between the marmalade and the lid. It was so hot she could explode. Maybe she'd gone to Hell for having sex with Lior. But Jews didn't believe in Hell. A Hell, then, that others had built for them.

The air-conditioning in the youth hostel was way too cold. But still, she was sweating. The sweat burned in her eyes like the sea that wasn't really a sea. Her mother had been so unworried that she came across as harsh, pitiless. "I used to also keel over all the time," she said, got a Coke out of the vending machine, and laid a headache tablet on the nightstand.

A few hours later, she entered, whispered softly, "Rita? Dinner?" seemed secretly to wish Margarita wouldn't hear her. So she pretended not to hear. Stayed still. Felt the corners of her lips tug downward. Outside, past the window, the sun was falling in the sky. When Marsha left, she turned the AC down farther and wallowed in her headache.

The night after she fainted, she couldn't sleep. *Feinted*, she typed into her cell phone, listened to her heart; on the mattress beneath her, a plastic fitted sheet crinkled and crackled. Over it, the thin layer of polyester had covered untold numbers of bodies.

Feinting: all those nights in recent years when so much had changed. Her closeness to Anna, heady with beer and vodka, joints and cigarettes.

Feinting, the last time: a few nights before she flew to Chicago, they'd watched the sun set in Wassertorplatz and had fallen asleep, arms wrapped around each other, on the lawn. All of her tingled from longing.

She wrote her father: *i can't sleep*.

She wrote Lior: *u awake*. Then she erased the message. *Delete for everyone*. Now he'd think she'd written him half a novel, so she retyped: *u awake*.

Both asked: *Ma ze?* What's up? Her eyes hurt. She'd answer tomorrow. As she asked herself what was actually up, she drifted off and woke a few hours later, unable to believe she'd fallen asleep, unable to believe she'd now awakened, how fragile the line was between wakefulness and sleep, no black, no white, no gray, more of an indigo and a royal blue, waking sleep, sleepy wakefulness.

* * *

Avi lay fully dressed in bed. The second morning now with no clanging, no rustling. Hannah was gone, she hadn't even said bye, she'd just slunk off early in the morning the day before. It hadn't disheartened him. Not one bit. He asked himself what he'd been thinking, spending nine whole nights on this sleepy island. The next day, he would finally leave, too.

Hannah was gone, but he didn't care. He lay there and waited, waited for God, who had apparently forgotten him, who would soon punish him for his foolishness, what an idiot he'd been, hoping, real sorrow or real shame was surely in store for those two pathetic kisses, but no, nothing came of them. He didn't care. What remained there was longing, not for Marsha, but for his memories of her, for a long time now there had been so many, he could choose which among them to cling to when he fell asleep, but they always vanished, however much he grasped them tight with arms as strong as Margarita's little baby fingers.

Now they were memories of memories, it all had happened so long ago, he wasn't even sure if they were real.

Memories of memories of a reeling, imponderable life, of a happiness. Memories of memories of his real Shabbes bride, not just one who danced on paper and spoke in his voice.

* * *

There was a knocking at the door, barely audible over her music, as Margarita was packing her things. She pulled off the headphones, and Marsha asked how it was going, one hand behind her back, one hanging clumsily in the air. A ray of sunlight over her face, gleaming in the thin hair over her lip, making her mop of chestnut brown hair look bushier.

"I know it isn't easy, Rita," she said. "You must really like him."

She passed her a book. "I bought it a few days ago for you, but I wasn't sure whether, or how I should—"

"Did you buy that on Amazon?"

Marsha looked at her bemused. "Yeah," she said, and drew her hand back in shame.

"You don't understand anything. You should have just skipped the middleman and transferred your money straight to Jeff Bezos himself," Margarita snapped.

"Breakfast," Marsha said. She sounded hurt. As she walked to the cafeteria in the hotel, she looked stubbornly straight ahead.

The only sound was the kids at the next table over smacking their food. Their eyes met. That loud chewing seemed to torment Marsha, too, mixed with the intermittent sniffling of a snotty nose.

Afterward, they walked in silence through the landscape around Ein Gedi. When you turned around, you saw the salt sea, crusted and blue. Margarita swam in one of the small pools that the waterfalls fed along the paths. She didn't even take off her T-shirt. It was so hot that it would be dry again in minutes. Salty sweat, salty air. A thirst that couldn't be quenched, but at least no more fainting.

There were ibex everywhere. Sometimes they came so close that Margarita could have touched them, and they fought over abandoned bags of chips. Marsha's enthusiasm for the creatures had worn off, and Margarita sensed that she was embarrassed for having been so excited about them the day before.

It was slippery where the creeks flowed over the narrow path. Margarita stuck her hand out when Marsha nearly slipped. Would it go on like this forever, this back-and-forth, insulting and being insulted?

Margarita remembered what her father said when she didn't want to do something: it's a mitzvah. Was squabbling also a mitzvah?

At the end of their wandering, there was water falling several meters over the rocks. Marsha took off her clothes. She had a bathing suit on underneath them. She passed Margarita her big tote bag, climbed under a small barrier, ignored the no-trespassing sign, and stood under the waterfall. Beneath the water, her face looked happy.

Margarita smiled, mortified, as people walked by and stared at her mother. Maybe it was a mitzvah to let Marsha be who she was.

On their way back, Margarita, too, climbed under the barrier, needing to feel the same joy as her mother. The cold water fell over her as though dumped from a bucket, onto her sunburned shoulders and the freckles that sprouted on her nose in summer. The pressure in her head disappeared. She didn't drink the water, and yet it stilled her thirst.

You could buy snacks at the kiosk in the rest area, lemonade, books about the Holocaust. They decided on a sandwich, shared it in the car, with the motor running, so the AC would keep them cool.

When Margarita returned from washing her hands, the book was lying on the passenger seat.

"Today we're going all the way to Eilat, it's the longest stretch so far," Marsha said.

"Why not to Masada?" Margarita asked. They would have gone there, too, on her field trip to Israel, if the entry regulations had allowed it during the pandemic. Eilat was just a place her grandparents and their friends went on all-inclusive vacation packages.

Instead of answering, Marsha asked after a while, as though wishing to figure out or maybe distract from something, "Do you really go to the synagogue with your father every Saturday?"

"With Anna," Margarita said.

"What about Avi?"

"I go to a different synagogue from his."

That was a lie. Since her bat mitzvah she hadn't set foot in a synagogue except, reluctantly, on the holidays, and then she'd usually sat with Anna in the stairwell and whispered. But she wanted it to sound as if she took her Judaism seriously, as if no one could shake that.

In the New Synagogue, she always had the feeling everyone was looking at her askance, because she went there alone, without her parents, and it didn't matter how many times she repeated that her father just happened to work in a different one.

The faithful there were unapproachable. Cold. German. When she thought of the years without Anna, she felt the stagnancy of utter isolation. She dressed wrong, her pants were often too short, her sweaters on backward. She looked wrong. Ugly.

Had she been an ugly child? Was that why Marsha had left? She looked at her mother and thought her capable of anything.

Showily, Margarita opened the book as the car rolled southward, and began to read. She understood almost nothing of the text; even at the bare level of words, much of it escaped her, but she clung to one passage:

> The heart is the organ of desire (the heart swells, weakens, etc., like the sexual organs), as it is held, enchanted, within the domain of the Image-repertoire. What will the world, what will the other do with my desire? That is the anxiety in which are gathered all the heart's movements, all the heart's "problems."

What would the world do with her desire, when it was the world she desired?

She closed the book. Then opened to another section.

* * *

Memories of memories of Marsha's affection, of the angle at which her body bent toward him, of her long fingers on his cheek.

Of her stiff hair, which smelled of Head and Shoulders. How

well they fit together, her arms and legs, her lips, everything else. He got hard when he thought about it.

When he remembered the memories, he was happy.

Dreamer, he heard her saying, *what are you dreaming*, when she used to wake him up, what are you dreaming. About you, he wanted to say now.

Memories of memories, of her prickliness, her restlessness, her boldness, her doggedness.

No hope disappointed was as dreadful as a hope fulfilled then taken away. The only pain the pain of knowing there would never be anyone who could replace Marsha, and that he had waited so long only to learn this in just a few days with Hannah on the island.

Memories of memories of his mulishness. Quickly, he pushed them away.

His dopey proposal at the Cinémathèque in Jerusalem where they had their first date. The ring he hid in the dessert when Marsha went to the bathroom.

She took the ring with her when she left. Took her silk dresses, her wool sweater, three books, her passport.

Were they still engaged?

He remembered the happiness he felt when he'd made her happy, the breathlessness, as though the soles of his shoes were hovering over the ground.

Margarita. She, too, would leave. Would break his wretched heart. If only he could leave himself, he thought, he'd do it.

Really he was just sad because Hannah didn't matter to him, her search for clues in his life didn't matter to him, everything she projected onto him didn't matter. Or his own projections. The Marsha projections.

Between wakefulness and sleep, he heard Marsha's bellowing, he had wished it into existence, that bellowing, into the silence, that wild bellowing as she was giving birth to Margarita, and the deep and desperate one full of the longing for home; at nights, she had begged, begged and threatened, and he hadn't taken it seriously, her raw voice, *I just want to go back, anywhere in the States. Even California. Just not here.* How raw her voice was as she left, as he pleaded.

He had told her they couldn't afford it, private schools, health insurance, he had to find a job first, anyway, and that was impossible, and they'd already promised him a job in Berlin.

The email that reached his inbox weeks later: *I thought you were coming along. Come.*

How furious he'd been, dizzy, bewildered from rage. And how it bewildered him now: he should have gone, he didn't have to give in to it, to that almost hedonistic self-pity, that solitude he used to punish himself. And the worry over Margarita, always, she had picked that name, sung it, whispered it, shouted it. The eternal riddle, why had she left the kid with him. Punishment or acknowledgment.

Often he'd thought of hurting himself, badly, enough that he would stay alive but would no longer be able to care for Margarita, in order to get Marsha back. Let himself be lifted up out of that life he'd fallen into. But he had gone on staggering through that life until it had become a good one, missing just one thing, the love from which it had sprung.

Memories of memories of the scent of her sleeping body.

He spoke no prayers that day. He stared at the ceiling and thought of Marsha's toes, her feet, her heels and her ankles, he explored her body up and down, thought of her voice, her English, the phonetics of it, which she had explained to him herself.

They'd met in a bar. He was twenty-six, she was twenty-eight. She'd fallen so hard in love with him, she followed him around like a puppy, she said that herself, after sex she'd cry from happiness as the light pierced the yellow curtains in his bedroom in

Jerusalem. The bedroom that soon became hers, the bed where she wrote out her dissertation while he drew out syntax trees on her back, *ani ohev otach.*

How she'd put her foot down, she didn't want to learn Hebrew, as a linguist it was the structure of language that interested her, not being able to speak it; she couldn't admit that it was really because of her father, who would always be better at it and wouldn't hesitate to remind her.

How she stretched her nose up in the air when she explained something to him.

How she said: *I'm drinking a glass of stones. Notice how your brain stumbles there.* She showed him that stumbling in a diagram.

How his brain stumbled when it searched for memories. As if there were no mental signifiers left for Marsha.

He called her and asked about their daughter.

"Your daughter's busy feeling offended," she said, amused; her voice had no body, for years now it hadn't, and his brain stumbled, could find no language, simply drank in Marsha's voice, was wordless, senseless, till she hung up.

* * *

Eilat was ugly, in a gaudy way, a pastel-streaked monstrosity. Everything was shrill, garish, excessive, and loud. The people there wore neon clothes on their sunburned skin. The rocks over the Red Sea were like a cheap poster on the wall of a dentist's office. Pixelated, so to speak.

They spent the night at a hotel called Rich Luxury Suites, neither luxurious nor suited to the rich, nor, for that matter, were they suites. There were brown spots on the bedcover, mildew in the shower.

They sat on a little square in front of a shopping center. A guitarist sang "I'm Yours."

All around, people took selfies.

A tacky yellow thong stuck out from the white shorts of a woman at a neighboring table.

A bored child drove a tiny police car in a circle.

The sirens of an ambulance played backup for the guitarist's "Wonderwall." *And after allaiaiaiaiaiai.*

The Red Sea was dark blue. The red mountains were black.

In the half-light, the shop signs glowed ever more eagerly.

"Tomorrow, we'll go snorkeling."

Back at Rich Luxury Suites, Margarita couldn't sleep. When she took off her pajama bottoms, the bed linens skeeved her out, but her pants chafed the sunburn on her thighs.

The next day, they drove to the *coral reef*, a section of coast off-limits to boats, roughly the size of her apartment in Berlin. Margarita had never been snorkeling before. Where would she have—in murky Lake Michigan, in the murkier Baltic Sea? In the Müggelsee in Berlin?

They pulled on their flippers and waddled into the Red Sea. Marsha swam away. When Margarita tried to follow, a big swell hit and she sucked salt water into the snorkel. She stood back up, her feet barely touching the ground, and spit. She tried again, but every time she swam a stretch, water got into the snorkel, and even into the borrowed swimming goggles. She blinked through the tears, took off the snorkel, and waded to a shallow spot. It was hard to go far in the sand with the flippers. Her chest burned as if she'd been drinking Landwirth's Wodka in the U-Bahn station.

Marsha turned around. "What's wrong?" she shouted. Margarita shrugged. Marsha paddled over to her.

Margarita dug her heels into the sand. "I can't do it," she said, "my snorkel's broken or something."

Marsha laughed. "You've just got to lie flat and look down."

There were people in the water all around them. It was hectic

and loud. Just lie down, Margarita thought. "But I can't see anything if I look at the ground." Even she could hear how whiny she
sounded.

"Yeah you can. Fish," Marsha said.

Margarita lay down in the Rich Luxury Sea. Around the lone
bits of coral in the reef swam a few blue fish, which Marsha fawned
over. It was strange, breathing the air above you while your face
was in the water. Margarita didn't like it.

She paddled back to the shore and sat down, the flippers on her
feet in the sand. No more snorkeling, she thought, no more Red Sea,
not ever again. Never again do I want to come somewhere so ugly, I
never want to see such ugliness again.

* * *

There had been a terrible mix-up. A mistake, a wrong turn, and
he had grasped it only when it was too late. Only now, as he took
the glasses from the dishwasher and placed them in the cabinet, the
forks in the drawers, the bowls on the shelf, as he looked around at
everything, back in his clean Berlin kitchen, knowing they would
be filled again, emptied again, would find themselves once more
in the machine that would clean them for him. For fifteen years,
maybe more, he'd believed all he needed was to be full, and then
the life he was leading would be all right. Had looked at the plates,
how they were emptied, his daughter there, growing up in the
world, heard his voice, how it filled up the room. If he was just
full, he thought, nothing could be wrong, nothing hard, nothing
lonely, nothing bleak. He hadn't coveted, hadn't gotten greedy or
stingy, hadn't wanted anything for himself, because the pots and
bowls and years had been full.

And so his thirties had raced past, and then his forties, and
now, all at once, the memories of a hungry life, a hungry time, had
caught up to him. A time after the end of school, in the late nineties

in Israel, military service during a relatively peaceful phase. A time when he'd had an opinion. In Germany it was easier. He didn't have to have an opinion here. In Israel, he had to look. His fear was political. It was political when a bus you just passed exploded in the air, and it was political when someone got on a bus with a machine gun over their shoulder to look around and decide who might blow it up.

And the fear of the others was political, too. Fear in the eyes of people not permitted a state; they, too, placed you in a world, a world you were ashamed of and went along with. Fear made people hungry, it was urgent, it made sure you didn't put things off.

He had moved on hungrily, rooted hungrily around for feelings, even his stomach had always felt empty. In the end, hunger had become his profession, the one thing that could still it was prayer, his voice, it filled his stomach, distracted him until no more distraction was needed, until he was no longer a political being. A fellow citizen, as everyone always said, someone who lived in company with, who didn't play any real role.

And his satiety had chased away the woman who had tried to keep him in the world, to play some role. He'd had too much, demanded too little, so Marsha had gone away, and the hole she'd left behind he stuffed with singing, prayer, ritual. Changing diapers and reading aloud. With banana slices and spelt cookies.

He'd erred. Happiness lay not in satiety. A full life was not the life man needed to live. An apolitical life meant a life without hunger, a life without anger, a deafness. No wonder all his friends were deadly boring, that the only person still hungry was his child while he was constantly trying to shove more and more down her throat until she would finally become numb, like him.

Not even on Yom Kippur was he hungry. Singing distracted him, the knowledge that the honey cake waited for him.

It had been Marsha, with her razor-sharp wit, which she'd bequeathed to Margarita in the crib, with her word-avalanches, her bulldozer arguments. He would never have been full had Marsha stayed, he would have coveted until he had died. He was full only because he was afraid of being hungry.

* * *

The ice cream from the parlor the receptionist had recommended tasted the way Eilat looked: artificial, cheap. Like shampoo. Rich Luxury Ice Cream. It was so revolting Margarita tossed it into the trash. Marsha was furious. She had been since the snorkel outing. Margarita couldn't stop chipping away, to see when her mother would finally explode. To Margarita's satisfaction, Marsha canceled the second night, and they set off on the long trip back to Jerusalem. The mood in the car was miserable, it was already afternoon, they wouldn't arrive until late in the evening.

Margarita fell asleep on the highway. Dreamed of Anna, whom she'd gotten only brief messages from for days, dreamed Anna was sleeping with Nico, his penis in her mouth. Anna told her this like it was good news, it meant Margarita didn't have to worry anymore about having his penis inside her. That was how she put it in the dream. Only when they stopped to fill up did she wake. Marsha got her another ice cream. "I don't deserve that," Margarita whispered.

"Oh, honey," Marsha said. "It's okay. Enjoy it."

Honey. She'd never called her that before.

* * *

It was Thursday, he'd been back since Tuesday, heat wave in Berlin, the neighbors watered the trees in the evening, got their kids to stand under them and threw down buckets of water. Avi sat on the balcony for hours and prepared for the next semester, though he normally planned one week at a time; he had thrown himself into work where there was none.

He went swimming because he was angry, but it was hard, hundreds of people were doggy-paddling around him at the pool in Pankow fighting their own anger.

That night, a young, newly ordained rabbi invited him to dinner, he already had a child, his wife was French, the family elegant in their chaotic apartment cluttered with books. The rabbi's wife asked him if he had a family, too. He talked about Margarita, their reaction was enthusiastic, "Oh, we 'ave to meet her," the man's wife said, and her husband said the same in Hebrew.

Embarrassed, he said that would be nice, but Margarita was very shy. They laughed.

"So are you," the wife said, "no?"

They wanted to know what he was doing in Germany. It had been a long time since anyone had asked him that. He justified it with the political situation, tried to make a joke, finally got around to asking: And what about you?

"Because of school," the rabbi said. And his wife: "I 'ate Israel."

"So does Margarita," he said, and took his leave when the baby began to cry.

He walked past the tourists partying on the Admiralbrücke, the tourists partying on Oranienstrasse, the tourists partying on Rosenthaler Platz. It was good that a new year was starting for him, while they all remained stuck in their stiff old one.

He resolved not to be so harsh with Margarita in the year to come. To let her do more, to enjoy her still being there. To give her the long-yearned-for double bed so Anna could finally spend the night, too.

* * *

Not long after stopping for gas, they came to a standstill. Margarita had slept for an hour, perhaps, and afterward stared out the window at the wasteland, they were driving again through Makhtesh

Ramon, which looked like it belonged on Mars, red, gigantic; they passed a huge prison and villages in the desert, from the road you could see the inhabitants' camels and the date palm farms.

"Must have been an accident," Marsha said, and rested her feet on the steering wheel. Avi would have broken out in a panic about whether they might be forced to sleep in the car, whether they had enough water. Marsha was chilling. Sometime later, she brazenly peed off the side of the road, someone hooted, she made a peace sign. Margarita wanted to puke out the window. Marsha came back and peppered her with questions.

"How did you actually meet Lior? Was it your first time? Was it good?" Margarita answered curtly that sex wasn't just penetration, trying to get her to shut up.

Marsha asked how she was doing. It seemed she had intentionally refrained from asking before because she didn't want to know the answer.

"I don't know," Margarita said, and glared at the black car in front of them.

"Because of that idiot?"

"Can you please not call him that?"

"Sorry," Marsha said, to her surprise. "How was Chicago? I didn't ask yet, did I?"

"Boring. How come?"

"I don't know, we all had the feeling this would be the last time you'd visit for that long, and your relationship with your grandparents wasn't always easy—"

Margarita interrupted her. "Who is *we all*? And what do you mean? How could it be easy? What it is, is weird, you weren't even there, why am I all of a sudden supposed to be best friends with them?"

Marsha looked away. Her eyes gleamed, wet. But Margarita was only getting started.

"You just shoved off. I don't even know what to call you, do you realize that? What should I say? Mommy? And you WON'T EVEN TELL ME WHY YOU LEFT ARE YOU EVER GOING TO TELL ME."

Marsha grimaced and drummed her fingers on her thigh.

"WHY WHY WHY," Margarita roared. "WHY?"

"Can we just drop it, please," this strange mother who wasn't a mother managed to say.

"Why?"

"You are relentless and desperate, Margarita," Marsha said, rested her head on the steering wheel, murmured something. All around, people had gotten out of their cars, were talking, cracking jokes. In the car: another world, claustrophobic, horrible.

"I can't hear you," Margarita said, but she did hear, she had heard her mother ask for forgiveness loud and clear. In her voice was a hatred she reserved for Marsha, one that had lain dormant inside her up until now.

Marsha straightened up. "Margarita," she said, "Margarita, can I hug you?"

She nodded her head as though cast from lead, once up, once down.

Her mother's throat smelled of fresh linens. It was softer than it looked. Her mother pulled her close, weighed heavier and heavier; Margarita's neck got wetter and wetter until loud honking interrupted their embrace. They drove on. Margarita's head was pounding. Twenty minutes later, they were stopped again. Google Maps showed several accidents on Highway 90.

"I hope you know I always loved you," Marsha said.

"Sure."

"It's true."

Margarita decided to change the subject for both their sakes. "It was basically fine with Grandma and Grandpa. They're sometimes strict with mealtimes and all, and it was a little boring. And at night, they keep the TV on so loud I can't sleep. But the house is nice, and they pay for summer school, and they really do love me."

Marsha smiled at her gratefully. "The meal situation is awful, isn't it? You're always being stuffed, and everything is overcooked. And the way they smack their food is just ghastly."

"God, I know," Margarita shouted. "Why didn't you raise them better?"

"I couldn't," Marsha said. "I used to plug my ears at the table. Or take my food up to my room."

Margarita laughed.

"You know what that's called?" Marsha asked.

"What what's called?"

"This sensitivity. To the sound of smacking."

"Someone blowing their nose is just as bad. Or biting their nails, disgusting."

"Yeah," Marsha said. "Or clicking their pen. It's called misophonia. There's nothing you can do about it. It's almost an illness."

"Great. You couldn't pass anything better on to me?"

"I don't have that much to offer."

True, Margarita thought, and her silence showed her mother was right.

"I struggle when I'm there, too," Marsha said. "I'm not so far away, even, but whenever we see each other, it's to eat, and it is an authentic torture."

"So where do you live?" Margarita asked.

"The past few years I've been living in New York."

"Cool. I want to go to New York sometime, too."

"It's gotten crazy expensive."

"I would have liked to visit you," Margarita said, trying to be friendly after she'd bawled her out.

Marsha's face constricted, as if she were about to cry again. Margarita couldn't take that. It drove her crazy that her mother was always so stoic, but now wasn't the time to change. You had to stick to the rules, even the ones you set yourself.

"Margarita, you know things haven't always run smoothly in our family."

Margarita nodded warily.

"So I—I'm back in Chicago. I got a job offer at Northwestern, I didn't want to turn it down. I'm going back in September."

"Whaaaaat?" Margarita shouted, restless. This was getting interesting.

"Grandma and Grandpa don't know yet, I'm not up for the whole rigmarole."

"Does that mean you'll spend the whole summer in Chicago, too?"

"Part of it. I need to take care of some things in New York, too. Don't hold it against me."

Marsha's life sounded independent, undirected, in ways that were forbidden for Margarita. None of it in any way seemed bound up with her being a mother or daughter. It was depressing how Marsha could do everything and she could do nothing. "You're crazy," she said.

"I know. Sorry."

"So when are you planning on telling them?"

"I don't know yet. I don't have a great relationship with them, Margarita. Kind of like you with me."

"Smacking your food is one thing, abandoning your own child is another, don't you think?"

"If only I'd known," Marsha said. Started the car again. "There were other things."

Again they stopped, the congestion had let up only briefly. Traffic jam, Margarita thought, it really was like marmalade, sluggish, the way the cars lurched forward in the heat of the desert afternoon.

"Everything," Marsha said. "My whole childhood. Those were

different times. You know, your grandfather was never home, and he cheated on her, I know that, she doesn't. I found out when I was thirteen, he said he'd beat me if I told her. I thought he was a deviant."

Margarita couldn't imagine her grandfather threatening such a thing. Or even having sex. "Oh, man," she said.

Marsha laughed. "Oh, man, all right." Then she opened the pack of Bamba she had bought at the gas station, and chewed in silence.

They inched forward for a few minutes, then stopped again, and Marsha talked, and it sounded very different from all she had confided to her before: how when she was sixteen, she lived for months with her twenty-year-old boyfriend, who smoked his first joint of the morning in bed in his shared apartment, while Selma was in the psych ward and Dan didn't even know how to make scrambled eggs. She said that afterward, no one ever mentioned the psychiatric hospital again. They told friends Selma had had cancer, that it had been eliminated. She went on to say how her boyfriend had broken up with her, how Margarita's grandfather had thrown an entire casserole dish of gefilte fish against the wall because Marsha refused to eat any of it.

How Grandma had crawled into her room drunk on all fours and threatened to kill herself. How the next day at seder, they acted like nothing had happened. How when Marsha was six, her parents had locked her in the house, and she had smashed the glass door to the backyard, the same one Margarita had opened and closed hundreds of times, to get out and find her parents, and how she'd wandered the streets of Hyde Park until a policeman picked her up.

Margarita said, "You must really be traumatized," because she wanted to sound empathetic.

Marsha made light of it. "In a normal Jewish family, everyone is traumatized, thus no one is traumatized." She told her about lunch at the Quadrangle Club. Margarita, too, was familiar with these lunches at the university club. Marsha talked about life in her Chicago, in Margarita's Chicago, in her house on Blackstone Avenue, in Margarita's house on Blackstone Avenue, in her lab school, in Margarita's lab school. She recounted how Grandma wrote a note every morning and slipped it into her lunch box, always the same message: *I love you.*

That was the one thing that hurt Margarita's feelings.

Boulders and scree around them. No sand in the desert, no coral in the reef. No trauma in anyone.

How hysterical her parents had been, Marsha said, laughing, when she'd told them about her plan to go to Israel: her mother scared, her father elated. That was her biggest fight with her mother. "Your grandfather was proud of me, and she had never been more disappointed. I had everything and more, and I ran away."

"She loves Israel, though," Margarita said.

"Yeah, and as soon as she met your father, it was, eh . . ." Her voice drifted off.

Margarita had the courage to ask, "What did she think when she found out you were pregnant?"

"Oh, Margarita. They were both so happy."

"When did you tell them? After I was already born?"

"A little earlier."

"What does that mean?"

"Margarita."

"When? I'm just asking."

"In the eighth month."

Margarita laughed. "Weak," she said. "Totally low energy."

"It was complicated. We didn't know where we were moving to, we had no money. We wanted you, of course, and we were very much in love, but we were scared."

"You don't have to pretend you wanted to have me."

"Margarita," she said again, and there was pain in her voice, and

Margarita, pugnacious Margarita, enjoyed it. Oh, how she looked forward to her quiet room, to her quiet father, to forgetting this summer. To the first cool days, jacket weather, sleeping in, being alone.

"We wanted you."

"You left."

And again, as if she knew it was the only thing that would quiet Margarita down—like a baby that had to be rocked: her arms the car, the pacifier the packet of Bamba, the lullaby her mother's English—she went on talking.

She spoke of her time in Jerusalem after she'd written her dissertation, and how as a linguist you had to publish one study after another. "The job situation was rough. Plus I was pregnant. And we knew if we stayed, we'd be staying forever. And you'd go into the army, and your father had been in the army, and—

"And—I wanted to go back to America. But not Chicago. I couldn't go back to Chicago.

"Your father could have found a job in New York. But he hates New York. We had been there before. It was too loud for him. Avi wanted to leave Israel. What was I supposed to say: Your kid has to go into the military? I didn't know then that was how it was. Your kid has to serve because I like the weather so much here. Because I like to eat hummus. I liked Jerusalem, but I couldn't even speak Hebrew. And your father was scared. Scared for both of us. Because of all the attacks.

"We wanted you. You were perfect, Margarita, and I thought, I'd go anywhere in the world for you, and then he got the job offer, it was so fast, and there were so many Israelis going to Germany at the time, how bad could it be, we thought, it's just for a while, you were so little, and we were so . . . tired, Margarita, we were tired.

"And Israel was so expensive, and there was mildew spreading on the ceiling over our bed in the apartment, we didn't even notice for weeks because we were so tired . . .

"And your father was so scared. And then, where was I, the job, he got the job in Hannover. They hadn't even heard him singing, they just wanted someone.

"Hannover, Margarita, have you ever been there? The city is so glum. I couldn't stand it. I don't know how else to explain it to you. It was so goddamn gray, and the people at the university were dumb, old, they were gray, too, Margarita. And the Community was awful, there's no way to be plain secular in Germany, either you're a Jew or you're not, our landlord wouldn't let us use a hot plate, the Germans would still love to see the Jews dead, they can't understand how they didn't get them all the first time. Always the same weird questions, and ham everywhere, in the roasted potatoes, in the goddamn lettuce, what the hell is smoked pork doing in a salad. Always that look in your father's eyes, we were constantly leaving our food and walking out until finally we just cooked at home, and you were so helpless, and I was so lonely. And then this tiny thing I had almost forgotten suddenly grew gigantic, a teeny-tiny thing that had never mattered one fucking bit to me, that hadn't even been worth bringing up, all the sudden wouldn't go away.

"We visited Sachsenhausen, Margarita, and people there were taking selfies. They were taking selfies.

"The language, Margarita. How can you stand that language. How can your father stand it.

"And another thing. I don't know how open I can be about this, but there's something you need to know. But your father can't find out. Can you keep something to yourself?"

For a moment, Margarita's brain clicked on. Could she? Could she keep something to herself?

For a moment, she thought: My father isn't my father. That was what would happen in a movie. Marsha had cheated on him.

She'd keep it to herself if Marsha would just spit it out, the curiosity was too much for her, she could keep everything to herself as long as her mother would stop talking, reassembling the building blocks of her origins, moving them around like the entrance to Diagon Alley.

"Margarita, your father doesn't know this. But it isn't why I left, I left because I was deeply unhappy, and Avi didn't understand, and that was my last way out, there was no other way for me to get through to him, I thought you'd both come after me, I waited months for you to come, every afternoon I imagined you running into my arms at the airport. I missed you both, it was the worst heartbreak of my life, and Margarita—you know, men make decisions like this all the time, even if their reasons are different."

Her father was her father. That was a stone that wouldn't budge.

"It's not pretty, but it's the truth. I always regretted how it happened, but it happened."

"Careful," Margarita said. The car swerved, someone honked.

Marsha caught herself: "Anyway, your grandmother is adopted. She would have starved if her biological parents hadn't taken her to the orphanage. Her adoptive mother was Jewish, but her biological mother wasn't. Your biological great-grandparents were Catholic. Not that it matters. It really doesn't."

Margarita didn't know what this was supposed to mean.

"Wait, I don't understand. Did you make that up? When did Grandma tell you? When?"

"When I was a kid. It was never a thing, we're Jews, at least in America, no one there cares about the halakha."

Margarita stared at her, open-mouthed. "And Dad . . ."

"I thought your father would leave if I told him."

"He doesn't know? And then you left him so he wouldn't find out? Seriously?"

"That isn't why I left, Margarita, it played no part whatsoever in my decision. It changes nothing. Not even now."

"Why's it a secret, then?"

"I shouldn't have told you."

Slowly, the significance of the disclosure dawned on Margarita. She knew the rules of the halakha, they'd argued about the law of matrilineality more than a few times in school. The question of whether it was antiquated. It had never really concerned her or at least she thought it hadn't.

"You're an asshole," Margarita said. "You're a giant cowardly asshole and I wish you were dead."

"It has nothing to do with me leaving," Marsha said. "You have to believe me."

"I don't believe a word you say."

"We wanted you to grow up in peace, Margarita. And we didn't know where peace was."

"Peace is wherever you aren't. It's a good thing you left."

It was getting dark, and more and more lights whizzed past them.

"There's no life without pain," Marsha said. "Your father and I, what we wanted was to spare you. And we didn't know how."

Margarita was crying so hard that she gagged. She felt betrayed, she felt her father had been betrayed, and still more, still worse, she was afraid she'd have to betray her father.

"You didn't, though."

Part Three

If he remembered their plans right, Margarita and Marsha would be visiting Yad Vashem today, would experience together the visualization of the horror he'd always wanted to protect her from, without him. Margarita would realize again what had happened. That was the worst. How you had to realize it over and over again.

He looked out the window at the buildings opposite, saw the ground, saw the parquet flooring under him, and thought: everywhere, new carpets overlay corpses underneath, they haven't even been given a proper burial.

He grasped Harry, briefly, grasped his story, too, which seemed to lie fanned out before him. No longer just a sequence of events, but a life.

Grasped the hunger. Grasped the longing for home.

Not me, he thought over and over, that was not me. It could have been me.

Grasped it, so near, and asked himself how he could sit there on an August morning in Berlin on a balcony built on corpses, in a building built on corpses, in a country built on corpses, and how had he dared not grasp that.

Thought of Margarita.

Grasped after the grief in Hannah's eyes, a grief like a mirror, the mirror of a father, became Harry, became Hannah. There was no one who didn't think of someone they'd lost.

Never would he forget, never would he forget, never would he forget how he had first read about the darkest of nights. Had read how the inmates in Auschwitz had said kaddish for themselves, the person who reported this had done the same, and he could report this only because he'd survived his own kaddish.

And Avi, who had just learned to read, bent over the small book on his parents' balcony surrounded by trash, the one place in that apartment you could breathe, had joined in, had said kaddish days later. Had fallen to his knees in prayer, had not bowed before the god who permitted such things, had wondered if he even could bow—no, he had fallen to his knees because his body could take no more.

Not long after, at school, they read about Ka-Tzetnik. Then and there, he had grown a shell, had stopped wanting to understand.

He recoiled now, when he heard a conversation in German in the courtyard. Nazis, he thought. Nazi language. How could he have forgotten?

Would his daughter look into the children's faces? Would she have buried her head in his shoulder if he were there? Would Marsha give her a shoulder to bury her face in?

Had he made a mistake not talking to her about it? Had he really thought he could avoid it?

He thought of the screams. He thought of the pain.

He thought of the monuments at which the shell of his body, borne only by his voice, sang. If his heart had sung, too, his voice would have betrayed it, necessarily, before the chancellor, before the president, when they spoke of the *protection of their Jewish fellow citizens*. If his heart had listened, he'd have broken not into song but into scornful laughter, but his heart didn't hear, nor even could his ears hear their words, the words of the inevitable empty suits, they closed up, went deaf, he needed only to understand what he wanted to hear.

Juden, he heard now and then, but only when they were talking about the dead. The living were *jüdisch*, as he by now understood.

Nothing in Germany had changed, everything in Germany had changed.

It was a gorgeous day in Prenzlauer Berg, and Avi yearned for the racket of Dizengoff Street, the cursing on the bus, the scent of Jerusalem, pinewood and orange blossom, longed for the knowledge that you were among equals when you stepped out onto the street, for a quiet Shabbat with everything closed, for kosher food, everywhere, as a matter of course, for a bookshop full of familiar letters.

* * *

They arrived in Jerusalem after midnight. The silence in the car had grown so oppressive it surprised Margarita that the window hadn't burst.

The anger wouldn't dissipate. When she woke, it was worse than before. It was sticky in her room, disordered, the sun filtered in, caressed her feet. Her mother was gone again, without notice, the apartment still.

So Margarita left, too: packing into her tote bag her cell phone, her bathing suit, a towel, an unread book bought at Powell's, and *A Lover's Discourse: Fragments*, which she had almost finished and would throw into the first trash can she came across. She didn't care for Jerusalem, too beige, sandy, the brittle air full of conflict, what she felt like was going to Tel Aviv and swimming in the sea.

She'd write Marsha later, tell her she'd be back in the afternoon, and in three days her flight would depart. For two days she could shut herself away, coming out only to eat, and the next two years would pass quickly, then she'd be eighteen and wouldn't have to see her mother anymore, no matter what her father said; she could forget she had roots, could set down roots of her own, move to Lake Constance and live her own life without answering to anyone, study medicine and have a sweet Protestant boyfriend and an apartment with roommates and shared meals, work in a café and learn how to sail in the summer.

She got on a bus fully peopled by Haredim, men one and all. They looked aggressively at the floor as she sat down in shorts that dug into her thighs. When a couple of old women got on, each with their respective shopping cart, she called Anna, who picked up, to her surprise, "Yo, what's up," she shouted into the phone, Margarita could have cried from relief, Anna's voice hadn't changed, she was still the same Anna, there was still a world beyond this one.

The men in long coats glanced at her only briefly, but Margarita's language was related to theirs; German, she thought, was like the treacherous brother of Yiddish, which her mother had spoken on so passionately a few nights before. It had driven Yiddish out, or sucked it dry like a vampire, and here she was now, looking like a shiksa and giggling into the phone. Telling what had happened.

"Duuuude," Anna said, then *no way* in English. "You realize this means you might not even be a Jew? So cool, you can finally eat ham, right?"

Margarita didn't respond.

"Sorry, I wasn't trying to hurt your feelings. That was rude. So your father doesn't know?"

"No," Margarita said. "You can't tell anyone, Anna."

"Sure. I wouldn't, you know that. I miss you bad, Margarita, it blows here without you. Just three more days, right? Should I pick you up from the airport? When do you arrive?"

Margarita was so excited she was pushing her toes down into her sandals. As though otherwise, she might fly away. "Totally," she said, "but I'm sure Dad will come, too, is that weird?"

"Nah, of course not, we'll just have to put off your welcome-home cigarette till the weekend."

She had a best friend. She really was still there. "I need to tell you something," she said. Whispered: "I had sex. With a guy I met on the airplane."

"Duuuude," Anna said. "Me, too!"

"Crazy," said Margarita, thinking of Nico. "Who with?"

"Her name's Zoé," Anna said. Softly. Cautiously.

Margarita was overjoyed. "Wow. That's great."

"Really?" Anna sounded timid. She'd never been that way with Margarita before.

"You know you could have told me, right?"

"I was worried you'd think I was into you," Anna said.

Margarita laughed. She didn't even find her own body desirable, and neither did anyone else, so there was no way a stunner like Anna would.

"Dumb, right?"

"And I was worried you were into Nico," Margarita said without really thinking. "Sorry, that sounds super selfish. You're coming out to me and all I can think about is myself. I really just wanted to say how cool I think you are and you can always talk to me and bla-bla-bla."

"Dude, Nico?" Anna snorted with laughter. "Bah. Sorry, girl, but he doesn't do it for me. And this isn't me coming out, that's an obsolete concept." Margarita laughed along with her, but the remark stung.

"Do you ever see him?" she asked; despite everything, she had to know.

"Yeah, of course," Anna said, "but Margarita, he's not worth it. He's been hooking up with a white chick with dreads. You don't wanna go there."

Margarita didn't need to hear more. In the stinking, muggy, rumbling bus, her heart, her kidneys, her pancreas, her clitoris, her fingertips, and her flaking toenail polish said goodbye to Nico. She said as much to Anna. Said, "Okay, gross, donezo, I'm out." Then, interrupting Anna's chuckles, "Who's Zoé, then?"

"You'll meet her," Anna said, "she's super cool, super fun."

Margarita was glad. She said so, because she couldn't think of anything better to say. "I'm glad."

"What are you doing now?"

"I'm going to Tel Aviv."

"All by yourself? You're so wild, can I come along?"

"I wish," Margarita said, shoving past breasts, shtreimels, pantyhose, wigs, mouths stuffed with chewing gum, machine guns at the exit. Saw the bus to Tel Aviv standing at the ready. "Anna, I gotta go. I'll be in touch, okay?"

"Can't wait," Anna said. *Beep, beep, beep.*

When Margarita was sitting in the air-conditioned bus, she logged into her online bank and found with relief that she still had enough money, realized Anna thought Margarita more grown-up than she—what a rush, her going to Tel Aviv on her own—saw that her cell phone battery was at 1 percent, it must not have charged right the night before. And she'd left her cable in the outlet by the bed. "Fuck," she whispered. Used the 1 percent to answer her father, assuming that Marsha would cover for her again, now that she had something on her. Wrote:

I'll be in touch later, my battery's low.
Marsha's making plans for the day.

Anna's picking me up from the airport.

Can you buy peppered mackerel?

He wrote: *Aren't you going to Yad Vashem, motek?*

No tomorrow.

She fired off another message, *love you*, then the phone turned off. She thought of Anna, of Anna's news, thought: Hopefully Zoé won't replace me, realized what she was just thinking, and how she wouldn't think this if Zoé were a guy, it was just bullshit, jealous bullshit.

She didn't think it wise to leave her things unattended on the beach and go swimming, so she lay under one of the many big tents to shield herself from the sun, dug her feet deeper into the sand, and asked herself why she'd even come to Tel Aviv. Was her mother worried about her? Had she even noticed her absence?

She looked for Lior the whole time, of course. In her head raged Marsha, her grandmother, Lior, Nico, her father, as soon as she told him the secret, and she would tell him, if for no other reason than to punish Marsha. Would she tell him? Or was Marsha right, would that mean that for him, she'd become someone else? When she imagined telling him, it stung horribly, it was unimaginable, impossible.

She didn't know what time it was. The sun was still up. Then, eventually, it went down, eventually the sentences in her book made sense.

* * *

It was better once he grasped how little time was left till Margarita's arrival, once he had readied everything for it. She'd wanted peppered mackerel. He would happily fill the whole refrigerator with it.

He knew something had to change in the coming years. That it couldn't go on like this with the worries, the fears. He knew what his yearning meant, his self-pity, Marsha in his daydreams, in his night dreams, his hand around his penis waking him: he needed somebody. He didn't want to be alone. Or should he just buy a dog and wait out the years till death—first the dog's, then his?

Today was Thursday. Margarita would land on Sunday around three. Would she be all grown up?

Should he try online dating? He wasn't so old, younger than most of the other fathers from Margarita's school; he secretly laughed at them with their beer bellies and their bike tours, their scabby-looking hands, their old-man fingernails, smooth and round, rutted.

In March, he'd turned forty-five, had eaten a revolting cake, burnt outside, raw inside; Margarita had given him a potato masher and a book from the secondhand shop, he'd been grateful, but he'd have preferred a drawing.

On the day after, he had given lessons and had imagined the chazzanim-in-the-making were singing for him.

It hadn't been as lonely as he remembered, he was sure of it.

Maybe he needed to make a compromise. Maybe not a Jewish woman. No need to have more kids, that was the good thing; at his age, they wouldn't expect it, maybe, a patchwork they'd be, that word, it had always provoked horror in him, just the sound of it, *patchwork*, like a musty old quilt.

He answered a few emails, someone wanted to record a CD with him, that hadn't happened in a while, he liked the thought of additional income and of being accompanied on the piano, studying new melodies, rediscovering old ones; he sat in the living room in front of his laptop in good humor, it was supposed to be a publicly funded project, he tried to draft a linguistically unobjectionable positive reply, as he did so he sang: "Yismach moshe, yismach moshe."

His cell phone rang while he was cleaning the toilet, he didn't want to handle it with the gloves, he let it ring, there was sweat on his lips, it smelled of sour milk, his knees hurt, he really was forty-five, there was no denying it. He pulled off the gloves and called back. Marsha picked up after the first ring and said his name, then sorry, a white wall before his eyes, he had to sit down on the sofa.

Was this the moment parents always feared? When they were forced to see what their lives would be from here on out, a life with loss?

It couldn't be.

"She's gone," Marsha said.

Rushing sound in his ears. No, not in his ears: his ears heard it, but it was in him and around him, that rushing was everything.

"She ran off, we had a fight, she blew it totally out of proportion, she's gone hysterical," and he stood up, returned to the computer, the email with the good news still open, pulled up the EasyJet website.

Marsha moaned that she didn't know what she'd done to deserve this, why Margarita hated her so much, he asked her what she'd left behind, asked why she hadn't noticed, Marsha said she'd gone to get breakfast, now Margarita was gone, and her phone had been off for hours.

"She's been gone since breakfast and you're only calling me now? Are you fucking serious?"

"I was sure she'd come back!"

"Are you completely out of your mind? You're only calling me now?"

"I'm sorry!" she sobbed.

"If she comes back," he said, "I'm taking her with me, and you'll never see her again."

"Okay," Marsha muttered, "okay, I'm sorry."

In his suitcase he placed four T-shirts, five pairs of underwear, Margarita's birth certificate, his passport in its transparent cover, as if he'd been preparing his whole life to go search for her in Israel. "We'll wait till tonight and see if she shows back up."

"She's tormenting us," Marsha said. "Why the hell would she turn off her phone? Is she *trying* to hurt us?"

"Of course," he said, "of course she is. She's your daughter."

And he added, "Unless she shows up, I'll be there tomorrow morning."

"I'm so ashamed," Marsha said, and he heard her wanting him to say: Don't be, the same could have happened to me, but he hung up, there was a hardness inside him. If she's dead, I'll kill myself, he thought, then he prayed, *Please, please*, he prayed, *please, please, please*.

* * *

The sea was roaring on Frishman Beach. Her stomach let her know it was evening. Margarita thought of evening three days hence, of setting foot in her home, the secret of her shattered origins inside her. The sun was still warm, she had moved a few feet away, tried to ignore the hole in her stomach as she thought of Lior.

Was he mad at her? He had answered her message, though; she was the one who had ghosted.

She imagined walking to his apartment, him being happy to see her, her explaining, imagined him taking her out again to a bar, imagined drunkenness, which was a promise of normalcy, of swaying, stumbling into safety. Dreamed on, dreamed that Anna was actually here. Dreamed Lior took her hand and dragged her to the bathroom in a bar, lifted her up, pushed silently into her, dreamed of his dripping sweat. It was nice, all this imagining, but then she stood up. Wanted to run to the bus station, wanted to go back, then sleep, then sleep again and again, until the homesickness was gone. How had the day passed her by so quickly?

Every time she thought of the dead cell phone in her bag, she winced. Were they looking for her. Did they have faith that she'd come back. Would there be a fight. Maybe she should let Marsha know after all. Maybe it would be better to say it: I'm coming, just chill for once.

She was hungry, she had just enough cash in her pocket for a bus ride back, but when she went to take out cash, she couldn't find the little bag with her credit card and her passport, and she realized it was in the suitcase she had packed in a rush before her trip with Marsha, she realized this the way you realize you forgot your homework, disgusted at herself and her own stupidity. Her hunger was getting worse. Her feet carried her away.

Ma ze, she heard over and over, but when she turned, no one was there, she heard sirens, saw no flashing blue lights, a ringing, a beeping, *ma ze, ma ze*, Margarita, *ma ze*.

His last name was Cohen, she had memorized it, she pressed the doorbell before she could change her mind. A woman's voice crackled through the microphone.

"Is Lior there?" Margarita asked, and there he was standing in the doorway, looking irritated, head peeking out, and Margarita's heart thundered and her feet were so light they almost ran off on their own, as though only her head were subject to gravity. He was wearing short-shorts, his upper thighs bare, Margarita forced herself to look up.

As soon as their eyes met, she started talking fast, got tangled up, all at once, it wasn't her father language, but a foreign tongue, the words guttural as they squeezed past the lump in her throat. She tried to explain, without really saying what had happened, so that he wouldn't think she was lost and out of her mind.

Lior interrupted her. "Just come in."

He hugged her, the hug was stiff, but he stroked her back as they separated.

How weird he must find her.

He guided her to the large living room with the open kitchen, which had been neat and empty when she last saw it. Chaos now reigned. Lior's father was sitting with a girl, maybe eight years old, on the floor and playing Uno Extreme, cards flew out of a machine, the machine made a racket, the two of them glanced over, sized Margarita up, waved as though bringing a girl home with him was just something Lior did, his mother was bent over the dishwasher, wearing jeans and a white T-shirt. A golden retriever greeted Margarita effusively. Lior explained the situation as she stood next to him grinning meekly. She'd have liked to go, but now it was too late.

She asked herself whether Marsha was scared for her. Actually, she hoped Marsha was scared for her.

"Are you hungry?" Lior's mother asked in English.

Margarita told her she spoke Hebrew and nodded guardedly. She sat on a barstool and was served noodles with pesto. Lior sat on the stool next to her and swung his legs. They introduced the girl, Laila, the family gathered around the island, it felt smooth, normal, the dog wandering around, Lior teasing them, they ignored Margarita as she ate, which worked for her. Then they asked her how she knew Lior, Lior calmly told the story of their meeting on the airplane, as if she'd never spent the night with him or he with her, as if their lips had never chewed each other raw, as if he hadn't rubbed his rough nails smooth on her body.

His sister said, "Ima, that girl smells sweaty," Margarita smiled nervously, trying to shrug it off, the father laughed uncomfortably long, that meant it must be true. The mother asked where she lived in America, and she had to admit she came from Germany. Laila said, "I thought the Germans were evil," the father laughed again, and this time Lior and his mother joined in, and Margarita couldn't defend herself, because what was she supposed to say, they were right, eighty years ago the Germans would have gassed her. Unless her adopted grandmother, of all people, had been her salvation.

"It's starting to get late," Lior's mother said. "Where do you need to go, Margarita?"

"Yerushalayim," she responded.

"What? Alone? The whole way? That won't do. Does your mother know where you are?"

"Yeah," Margarita lied.

Lior furrowed his forehead. "And she doesn't have any problem with you wandering around Tel Aviv alone?"

Margarita was ashamed. She had burst in on the life of this family that couldn't imagine people like her, people with nowhere to be.

"I'll take her to the bus station," Lior said. Laila had begun practicing cello. Margarita couldn't make herself say she needed a charging cable to contact her mother, since she didn't have a key, so she remained silent and didn't move.

"Or should she sleep here," Lior's mother said. It sounded like a concession. As if Margarita's silence were so insistent that she had no choice but to offer.

"We've all got to leave early tomorrow," his father said, "and the couch is uncomfortable, she doesn't even have a toothbrush. She could have called at least, you hardly know her, right, Lior?" He seemed to have forgotten that Margarita understood Ivrit.

"I can go to the bus station on my own," she said softly.

"No you can't," Lior said.

Laila shouted, "I don't want a German sleeping here."

No one rebuked her.

Margarita's wrists hurt. "It's no problem, really," she said, she was starting to feel like a beggar.

Lior asked, "Wasn't there some kind of rule about when you had to be home?"

"No," Margarita said, thinking of the dead phone in her tote bag. She remembered she'd said that her mother knew where she was, there was no way she could ask for a charging cable now, especially if she had to go, that would be one more embarrassment in a heap of embarrassments, she'd be giving herself away, they'd all notice she'd lied, that she wasn't supposed to be here, that she'd run away.

"We're not a hotel," Eran said, "we don't even know her."

Margarita had the vague feeling Eran was an asshole. "I don't want to be a bother," she said.

She remembered the girl from elementary school whose parents had said there wasn't enough dinner for Margarita, and she'd had to wait, hungry, for her father, only when she was lying in bed, teeth brushed, did she tell him, and he'd been furious and made her an omelet. What she wouldn't give now to have an omelet in bed.

"It's fine," the mother said. Batya, that's what Lior had called her when he introduced her, Batya and Eran. "What were you doing in America? And what brings you here?"

"Ima, no one cares," Lior said, as though he'd forgotten he was the one who had asked Margarita these same questions on the airplane, that she'd been the one reluctant to answer, and spitefully, Margarita started telling them everything, because it would buy her time. She left out that her mother might be a sociopath or psychopath or someone who didn't love her child; she left out that she might not even be a Jew, she had a gift for invention; finally she asserted she was going to Yad Vashem tomorrow, yes, tomorrow she would go to Yad Vashem and she'd meet her mother there, and this time none of the visitors would be taking selfies.

She went on talking until Lior yawned. Then she said, "All right, I'm going," and decided to sleep on the beach until the first bus left. She would sell it to herself as an adventure, as a story she could tell one day.

She asked to use the bathroom, Batya showed her where it was, she pretended she didn't know, that she hadn't washed vomit from the airplane off herself in the same shower.

When she came back, Eran was laying two sheets on the sofa,

one for over her, one for underneath, he gave her a toothbrush and a set of Lior's old pajamas, Lior rolled his eyes; "What else is she supposed to sleep in?" his father barked, they argued, the dog was dreaming in a basket next to the sofa, whimpering, jerking its paws.

She wanted to ask for a charger now, but they were busy, no one wanted to talk to her anymore, Lior was scribbling out his homework on a piece of paper, Eran took Laila off to bed, Batya made a phone call, something to do with an office lunch from what she could gather. She realized Margarita was staring at her, went to the bedroom, and shut the door loudly behind her. She came out soon afterward to brush her teeth, and Margarita didn't dare ask. She had the feeling any request she made would end with her having to sleep on the beach. She read the last page of Marsha's book in the light of a kitchen lamp no one had turned off. The dishwasher ran, a spray arm struck a plate once every second, a dull clunk, it smelled of food waste.

* * *

For her bat mitzvah, he'd given Margarita a silk prayer shawl with light blue embroidery, beautiful; he had ordered it from Israel months before, and when midnight struck and she still hadn't shown, he laid the tallit with the others in the trunk.

She didn't like to wear it, *It looks like shit*, she'd said last Yom Kippur when he had sent her to Oranienburger Strasse, and he couldn't help but think of her bat mitzvah, how she had read and he was bursting with pride, for months they'd practiced, memorizing the melody points above the letters, when the pitch was high, when low, what to draw out and what to shorten.

Nervously, he paced through the apartment, wrote the Community an email, he had to go to Israel, family emergency, he'd look for a sub, he promised, did not, however, look for a sub, tried to eat something, but in his mouth, the bread felt hard, and he spit it into the trash. Called Marsha every hour. Nothing. It was still dark when he got into the taxi. The plane ticket had cost €458, which he transferred from his savings account. He spoke the Traveler's Prayer while he waited to board, a little for himself, but mainly for Margarita, wherever she might be, sank into the uncomfortable seat, his head nearly grazed his neighbor's shoulder as he drifted off.

When he woke, both his legs had gone to sleep, he couldn't imagine them ever waking up again, wedged between the rows like that; they tingled and ached and he could see himself forced to search for his child on all fours.

* * *

She thought of her cell phone again just before falling asleep, like a forgotten homework assignment, started but then told herself *in the morning*, there was no helping it. Hopefully Marsha was worried. Hopefully she regretted the chaos she had called forth, hopefully she was asking herself when she'd have to tell Avi. Rational as she was, she'd wait twenty-four hours, Margarita was sure of that. So she still had a little time.

Still, though, she lay awake until nothing stirred in the apartment, until nothing was audible but the street sounds; she went on lying there and throbbed, throbbed with want for Lior, only a few feet away. Before she could decide otherwise, her feet took her off on tiptoe, before she could think twice about it and wake everyone with a flush of the toilet. She stood at Lior's door, thought about knocking, it was open a crack, maybe a sign that she should go in, that he was counting on it. She pushed it a little further. "Can I come in?" asked a voice, not hers.

A grunt in reply: "Hrmpf."

She took it to mean *ken* because *lo* would be too much for her,

shut the bedroom door softly, and slid her overheated body between Lior's sheets.

"What the . . . ?" he whispered.

She rested her forehead on his neck, his back was as stiff as a board.

"My parents are here, okay, you're crazy."

"We can do it quietly," she whispered back, edged closer, pressed
her pelvis into him.

"No. Go back to the couch."

Margarita didn't want to listen. Didn't hear him, even. She kissed
his neck, shoved her fingers under the seam of his boxer shorts, ran
them through the coarse hair under the waistband.

Lior closed his eyes, she thought that meant he was letting her,
but then, when she didn't stop, he pulled away.

"Please," she said. Ran her hand through his underwear and
gripped his half-hard penis in her fist. She couldn't believe she
was begging him, but at the same time, what did she have to lose?
Her dignity? The agent at passport control had already stamped
it out.

Lior turned around. He whispered loudly, or screamed softly,
the thick vein in his forehead looked like the one in his dick. "I'd
like to help you," he managed to get out, "but this is starting to
feel psycho, the way you burst in here with no explanation; you
must have noticed how weird my parents thought it was, what am
I supposed to tell them? And now you come barging in, it's just
desperate, I mean we only even did it once."

"Twice," she whispered, he responded, "Whatever, it was a fling,
I thought we'd never see each other again."

Margarita couldn't move, couldn't stand up and go, could only
lie there mute and come up with cheap explanations that felt exor-
bitant to her: "I just wanted to thank you somehow."

"With sex?"

In the yellow light of the streetlamps that seeped into the room, he looked sickly, his facial hair disgusted her, and yet Margarita wanted him to kiss her. "I don't know, I thought you'd be into it."

"That's really sick," Lior said, and now tears streamed over Margarita's face, dripped onto the sheet, no pillow under her head, he wouldn't share his with her, she knew that much, he wanted it for himself, just as he wanted his body for himself, and she understood nothing, nothing at all.

He wiped her cheek, as though it would bother him if she got his mattress wet. "Come on, go now," he said, "we can just forget it, just leave tomorrow before seven, everyone will still be asleep but you won't have to go out in the dark."

"Let me stay here, please," Margarita pleaded, and Lior turned away. She took that as consent. His breathing evened out. When she was certain he was asleep, she snuggled up to him, desperate, threw one leg over his, he shoved it away, now it was there floating in the air and she didn't know what to do with it if it couldn't cling, couldn't encircle, couldn't rest. She tried again. She didn't know what it was that was broken in her, what made her do this, inciting him, provoking him, but it worked, he turned around.

Then he stood, bent over her, picked her up, and she let him, let herself be taken to the couch, laid her head on his chest, let herself be thrown aside like a shoe kicked off when you enter an apartment and left to lie in the hall.

Margarita couldn't sleep. When the sun rose bloodred, scattering bright points of light on the green leather sofa, she walked back to the beach, bag in her fist, which she couldn't unclench, the same as her knotted heart. She was sick with self-hatred. Never would she return to this stretch of earth, which her father had never returned to, either, it wasn't hard to see why, it wasn't even political, but if it were, the settler politics and compulsory military service would be more than enough, the plain fact was the people here were ugly and rude, the country wasn't what you'd call beautiful, everything was grungy, grungy and ideological.

She thought of Lake Constance, its muted constancy, how no one there would have to know who she was, that she wasn't actually Jewish, maybe it was liberating not to be a Jew, but was that even possible.

The amorous subject has no system of sure signs at his disposal, she'd read in one of the last entries of the book Marsha gave her. She didn't know what that was supposed to mean. Stared at the sea, someone swam a trajectory parallel to the beach. She was terribly tired. Ran to a bin to throw the book away, but decided at the last second a book wasn't something you could toss into the trash. Chose instead to make her way to the bus station.

* * *

His cell wouldn't connect to data once they'd landed, he started shaking it, cursing, still shut up in the airplane, turned it on, off, on, and off, had to be patient, his entire life he'd been patient and he didn't want to do it anymore.

It was so hot that not just the light shimmered but the runway with it, the sky, the earth, the entire horizon.

It was eleven. Margarita had been gone twenty-four hours, Marsha said on the phone when he finally reached her, in the airport where the air stood still for a moment as he pulled his suitcase over the smooth marble.

He had thought if he just flew here, she'd be back as soon as he called again.

Marsha stood at the door in her bathrobe, it smelled like coffee, had she really brewed coffee for him. It infuriated him, that she could think of something besides Margarita, that she was making coffee for him, infringing upon him in this way. He hugged her because she left him no choice. And when she freed him, he looked at her.

The first thing he asked her had been burning on his lips for hours. He'd been practicing the words even as he sat in the taxi. "Why did you leave the apartment without talking to Margarita? Maybe she was scared?"

"She was sleeping," Marsha said, the corner of her mouth trembling, she looked at him as if she feared him.

"And now?" he asked.

She shrugged.

It was no time to fight. He called all the big hospitals in Jerusalem, then the ones in Tel Aviv. His Hebrew sounded like a foreign language in his ears, biblical, fusty. The receptionists advised him to call the police in casual, indolent Ivrit. He dialed 100, told them to look for his daughter, the police said forty-eight hours had to pass first.

He rubbed his eyes as he spoke with Marsha, as he tried to blame her and failed. Marsha said she was just a teenager, teenagers ran away all the time, they almost always came back, the police said that, too, and he thought: She could be dead.

Selma called. He heard her voice yelling through the phone, it must have been early in the morning in America, she asked for him and roared louder, "We have to find her, WE HAVE TO FIND HER or I will never forgive myself, oh God, oh dear God."

He laid the telephone on the table, they bent over it and alternated promising that they'd get her back soon.

After they hung up, Marsha went to buy cigarettes.

"To buy cigarettes," he said, and searched for remorse in the look she threw over her shoulder.

When she returned, they decided Marsha would drive to Tel

Aviv and look for her. "Maybe she's just hanging around the beach. Maybe she didn't feel like going to Yad Vashem. Maybe the life-size Yad Vashem she calls home is enough for her."

He scowled.

"Do you have a picture of her? One that you can show people?"

"What, I'm supposed to run all over the city with her photo?" Marsha pulled out her phone. "Here she is in Acre," she said, and showed him an image of Margarita grinning, was she missing her usual half-an-inch layer of makeup there?

"You didn't send me that."

"If I sent you every photo, your phone wouldn't stop dinging." She kept scrolling through her photo album: Margarita walking through the Old City, a video of her buying orange juice in perfect Hebrew, Margarita with a snorkel, an inexpressible love seeming to radiate through the pictures.

"What happened?" he asked. "It doesn't look so bad. I know you had a fight, I know it's hard not to fight with Margarita, but how could it go so wrong?"

Marsha fumbled with her pack of cigarettes, stuck the phone in her purse, snatched a plastic water bottle out of the fridge. "I've got to go," she said, "I don't want to get stuck in traffic." Her shoulders were slumped so far forward it looked like they were about to touch, a little bit farther and the circle would close. He knew she did that when she was ashamed. She left.

Twenty-four times he called Margarita, twenty-four times it went straight to voicemail, sent three texts, *please tell us something, we're not mad at you.*

We.

Margarita forced them to become an entity. Children could do that, he remembered the couple he was friends with who had gone back on their divorce after their son broke his leg in several places, they split up later, though, when he could walk again and moved into his own place and didn't need them.

Now that Margarita needed them, would they have to stay together?

Did she want them to find her?

In his head, alarms were going off so loud he wanted to throw them against the wall, the way he used to in his worst fights with Marsha, when he was trying to blackmail her.

Part Four

Margarita rang the call box. After a few seconds, the buzzer sounded, but just for a second; she almost didn't have time to push the door open. Probably her mother had started to worry and had decided not to go to Yad Vashem without her.

Her bus had been late, she had gotten lost on the way to the apartment, not having a functioning cell phone made it even worse, in the end it had taken three hours, she was tired and thirsty, no hunger, though, not since the disappointment of last night. She was hot, Jerusalem was like a city without wind, without even a breeze, just dry, dusty air. She kept remembering the cold Schlachtensee in Berlin, where she and Anna had jumped all those times from a rented boat, that was how she got through it, thinking over and over of the cool shock of the green water. Finally she'd swallowed her pride and asked the way, it turned out she wasn't far from the apartment at all.

In the stairwell, she briefly rested her cheek on the cool stone, on the landing still out of sight of the apartment; her heart twitched, there'd be a fight; then, though, she could sleep, but around the corner stood her father, eyes gigantic, lips pursed, a furious fish, she hadn't expected that.

She stood on the last step.

They looked at each other a long time.

"Efo Ima?" Margarita asked.

"She's looking for you."

"What are you doing here?" She was scared, she realized, terribly scared of what would happen. She'd so looked forward to seeing him, and now this, now their reunion was utterly fucked.

"Looking for you." He was loud. "Margarita, what is it? Are you out of your mind? Come in right now."

She shook her head.

"If you don't come in here, I will scream until these walls cave in," he said, because he knew her worst fear was him embarrassing her. "I'm so mad, I'm so mad I don't even know where to start. First of all: no going out this fall, no partying with Anna, no new bed, we're flying home and you'll go to school and that's it. How could you scare me so bad?"

"You're the one who up and sent me away!" Margarita shouted, but it wasn't a shout, it came out as a whisper.

"Come in here right now."

"I don't want to."

"What you want doesn't matter to me one bit."

She relented.

As the door closed behind her, he sank dramatically onto the gray floor tiles. "I thought you were dead."

"You said yourself people always know when something bad happens because the police call you."

"That works if I go shopping after lessons and you can't reach me, not when you vanish for twenty-eight hours in a foreign country, motek."

"Don't call me that when we're fighting," Margarita said.

Her father looked up from the floor, where he was sitting with his fists balled on his thighs—looked up, looked at her.

"Go to your room," he said. "Now."

She left.

Through the thin wall, she heard him stand up, heard the chirrup from the speaker of his phone, probably he was trying to reach Marsha. She sat on the unmade bed and bawled in the hope that he'd come console her, her voice rose to siren, to wolf, to Grandma shouting for Grandpa, then lowered again. Her father entered without knocking and said if anyone was going to cry, it should be him. He set down a glass of water. Margarita stared at the wall, her back to him, the door closed again.

She had to go to the bathroom so bad she considered climbing out the window and peeing in the yard out front, but if she did, they'd throw it in her face, say she was trying to run away again.

Naturally, what had to happen happened when she finally dared to leave the room, slipped past her father, who had laid his head on the kitchen table and looked as if he'd folded his long body up and gone to sleep there. No sooner had she pulled down her shorts than the apartment door opened. She heard her father jerk awake, heard that familiar groaning of his that came any time someone disturbed him from the depths of his midday nap, heard him stand up quickly, the toilet seat was cold on the hot skin of her inner thighs.

Three toothbrushes stood in the glass by the sink. She closed her eyes a moment and imagined they were the three toothbrushes of an ordinary family on vacation. She knew something would change as soon as she opened the door, the framework would shift, for the first time in as long as she could remember, her parents would be standing together before her.

She looked in the mirror. Her hair was paler at the tips, her stare insolent, it was hard to look herself in the eyes, she closed them, opened them again, over her broad upper lip were a few fine, dark hairs, probably just one of many features that had repelled Lior. She looked bitter. Could a person at fifteen already be embittered? Yes. She could.

She heard her parents in the hall, her father saying, "She is on the toilet," his English sounded raw, almost German.

Her mother was right outside the bathroom, the handle vibrated, she blathered hectically. Margarita opened the door.

Marsha's mascara was running, gathering in the wrinkles around her eyes. Avi seemed to understand what she was saying, the whole time he kept repeating, "Charah, charah," *shit, shit.*

Marsha said something about a *casserole* that had fallen from a kitchen cabinet onto Grandma's head; "What's a casserole," Margarita asked; "Ofenform," her father said, Marsha covered her mouth with her hand. She pulled Margarita to her and murmured something, Margarita couldn't understand all of it, just "Thank God, thank God" and "I'm so relieved. I'm sorry, darling, I'm sorry." She smelled like cigarette smoke. Margarita was confused. Did Marsha not yet understand she was supposed to be pissed, like her father, and why was her father angry and her mother pleasant, it didn't work, it was supposed to be the other way around.

Marsha told her Grandma was in the hospital, it was probably a concussion, Grandpa was confused, she called them Selma and Dan, she turned to Margarita's father, "He can't even make himself a sandwich." Marsha said, "She was so upset she stopped paying attention," and looked at Margarita, expressionless.

"I'm going to get some food," Avi said. "Whatever happens next, we're not going to talk about it on an empty stomach. You two"—he evidently didn't know what he was supposed to say, swatted the air—"sit tight and hope it's just a bump on the head."

"Thanks," Marsha sighed and took two steps into her bedroom, closing the door behind her.

"Clean your room, motek, and wash up. After dinner, we'll see what happens."

Margarita nodded. "Do you not love me anymore?" she asked as her father opened the apartment door.

He turned around. Something in his face looked broken, dilapidated.

"Oh, Margarita," he said, "of course I still love you. Otherwise I wouldn't have come. Otherwise I wouldn't be in this state."

He took her in his arms, his Aba-arms enclosed her, so tight she could hardly take a breath. She shrank and shrank, and finally he let her go. "Yofi. There are still consequences."

She nodded.

Then he disappeared into the landing.

As she dressed after her cold shower, she heard noises in the kitchen, the crumpling of plastic bags and the chopping of onions, and cucumbers, maybe? She had missed her father, the feeling of safety when he was near, she'd almost forgotten it. The feeling that she could take her pain and anger out on someone who could do nothing but love her in spite of it.

* * *

He convinced her to pray over dinner, catastrophes or no, it was almost Shabbat, Margarita started: "Baruch ata Adonai, Elohenu melech haolam, boreh pri haadamah," she gave thanks for the fruits of the earth, for the baba ghanoush in its plastic container, for the finely minced cucumbers, tomatoes, onions; knowing Marsha, she hadn't once tried to slip the girl a few vitamins. Margarita's Hebrew was sonorous and clear, "Baruch ata Adonai, Elohenu melech haolam, shehakol nihijeh bid'varo," for the labneh, even now he looked forward to it a little, there was nowhere in Berlin where it tasted as it did here, because it was illegal to import dairy from Israel.

In this dingy kitchen, he felt a yearning for home such as he rarely did in Berlin. A yearning for familiar foods, familiar architecture, the language he thought in. The need to walk until he found people, to sit in a bar and talk, and all around him, everyone else spoke Ivrit, too.

He motioned for them to wash their hands, and Marsha, who had just nodded to the *amen* after the prayers, remained seated, "Do you honestly expect me to do that, too?" and Margarita shifted her gaze from him to her before finally doing as he did.

As he began to eat, Marsha and Margarita shot him nasty looks. "Don't smack," Margarita scolded him, there she was again, the German, or else the neurotic daughter of a neurotic American; he closed his mouth as he chewed, could Margarita even imagine how exhausted and hungry he was, or was she lost again in her self-obsession? They chewed, softly, wordlessly, with simple questions: what goes on the bread next, does the salad need salt, am I full yet.

Alas, these questions were eventually answered.

Marsha and he started talking at the same time, gesticulating back and forth, until she stopped long enough for him to take a breath, and then he didn't know what to say. "Where were you?" he finally asked. "And why did you think you could just take off like that?"

Margarita nibbled on a hangnail and shook her head.

"Were you with Lior?" Marsha asked.

Margarita nodded cagily.

Who was Lior?

"Were you mad?" Marsha asked.

"You just left," Margarita said, "so I did the same."

Marsha's eyes said: *You don't have to bullshit us, you know that's nonsense,* but there was something else there, too, that he couldn't read.

He didn't like Marsha being the one wheedling the answers out of their daughter, wasn't this all her fault, anyway. "Who's Lior?" he asked.

"It doesn't concern you," Margarita said.

"It does," he said, surprisingly loud. He looked at Marsha, asked her silently for encouragement, but Marsha was wringing her hands and rubbing her forehead in distress.

Margarita stared into the void, a whitehead in the middle of her cheek, her hair a little greasy. A fifteen-year-old.

"My father's on his way to the hospital," Marsha said. "He thinks Mom might not survive it, they don't know if there's bleeding in the brain. It was that giant ceramic casserole dish, she wanted to make lasagna in the middle of the night, because she couldn't sleep, she was so worried, and she wasn't paying attention. If your grandmother dies because you thought it would be fun to get your revenge by running away, Margarita, I just don't know what I'll do."

There it was, Marsha's hardness, her obduracy, that was the scary side of her. "Marsha," he said, "you can't pin this on her."

"It's fine," Margarita said, looking at the water glass in her hand. "She's right."

He stood up, put the plate in the dishwasher, squeezed Margarita's shoulder, she turned her torso to the side. He felt rejected, as if the two women had united against him. "I was so scared for you, motek," he said in Hebrew, Marsha would understand only snatches of it, all the better, "can I just hold you for a little bit?"

Margarita shook her head.

He felt disoriented, confused, lost, and then there was the new problem, Selma and her injury. "So what now?" he asked.

"I can't just sit around and wait," Marsha said.

"Should we take a walk?" he asked, and they left together, their daughter like a protective barrier between them, he would never have forgiven himself if she'd disappeared. They strolled through his beloved Jerusalem, through Moshava HaGermanit, the German Colony, first through HaMagid Street, where Marsha lived; flowers were blossoming on the walls of buildings, it smelled of sandstone and chicken broth, of roses, on the fences, in the perfume of older ladies, in milk pudding, yes, it smelled of malabi.

They turned onto Emek Refaim. Marsha leaned slightly forward, "Remember?" she asked him, and all he could say was "Of course," and when they reached the corner of Lloyd George Street, Marsha and he stood there, Margarita marched on, between them now was an emptiness and above them their old balcony with a white curtain flapping in the door.

"We lived there," he said, and Margarita paused and looked, responded in English, a sign that she wanted her mother to understand her: "Crazy, I just assumed you were admiring some boring architecture."

If Marsha asked me, he thought, I would climb that wall and throw out the tenants, would bring back the yellow curtain and with it our old lives. But she didn't ask, she'd left him, and he didn't even know if she had a partner, someone she slept with and then cried afterward, who put cold cloths on her forehead when she had a fever. She was wearing a long linen blouse and tight jeans, looked so much younger, so much more worldly than Hannah.

Maybe, he saw, it was a good thing, or almost, that Margarita had vanished, auspicious, maybe, since she'd shown back up and he was here and something was happening, something real.

* * *

Her parents ordered tall glasses of beer, Margarita got a lemonade. They had a half hour until the café closed for Shabbat, they were the only ones on the ample patio.

"We'll talk tomorrow, motek," Avi said, noticing Margarita was waiting to be chewed out again, she was sitting across from the two of them like the accused before a jury. She wanted them to notice she was scared of being punished, so the punishment would be milder.

It was uncomfortably quiet. Margarita tried to think of things she could ask, but the previous night kept replaying in her head, shoving all else aside. She disgusted herself as she replayed that image of her there begging. Her parents exchanged memories and repeated how tasty everything was. I get it, Margarita thought, it's tasty, for her it was really just dreadfully hot.

Marsha's phone rang. She got up and walked a few steps down the street.

When she came back, she was twitching, blood was welling from a scrape on her elbow, a few drops had stained her blouse, red at first, then almost immediately brown; she waved down the server, asked for the check in Hebrew, that much she could manage, and Avi kept asking what is it, all she would do was shake her head. Over and over Margarita imagined the casserole dish striking her grandmother in the head. What kind of noise the blow had made, what her scream had sounded like.

If only she'd charged her phone.

"We need to go to Chicago," Marsha whispered. "We need to leave tomorrow."

The sun was setting as they walked back to the apartment. Margarita lagged behind her parents, whose movements were hectic. It was strange, seeing them together; she noticed that here, Avi didn't hide his kippa under a hat.

She couldn't bring herself to ask what her grandfather had said, her mother was silent and pale, she sat at the kitchen table with her laptop, Margarita's father stood next to her, Margarita remained in the doorway. Marsha cursed, the next day's flights were booked up, there was one in the afternoon that passed through Paris and Atlanta, but it landed only a few hours before the next direct flight on Sunday, the layover in Paris was eight hours. Today was impossible, the best option was Sunday evening. They'd have to spend the fretful hours between in Israel.

"Pray for her, will you?" Marsha asked Avi, and he nodded,

excused himself, Margarita watched him as he donned the tefillin and removed the prayer book from his small, shabby suitcase,
along with her tallit, which you really wore only on the morning of
Shabbat, not Erev Shabbat, she'd never have guessed it was somewhere readily discoverable. She followed him, reached out her
hand, clasped the tallit and stretched it out, prayed the brachah,
kissed the silken corners of the shawl, which she had wrapped
around her fingers, laid it over her head and shoulders.

She stood next to her father, together they both bent forward
in their garments, evening light soaked through the windows and
tinted the pages of the prayer book pink. She noticed that, after
these weeks of translating menus for Marsha, she could weave together the individual letters much faster than before.

When praying, you were supposed to focus on the words in the
book and nothing more, but they said nothing to her, and Margarita
dreamed as she swayed back and forth, dreamed that this was all
just a nightmare.

When they were done, she wanted to say the prayer for the sick,
even if her grandmother wasn't *sick*, sickness made her think of
viruses, infections, not a casserole dish fracturing a skull, but her
father said that prayer was allowed only after the Torah reading,
leaving her disheartened.

Only when she saw his open suitcase in her bedroom was Margarita certain that her father was staying, that he wouldn't be going to
a hotel. He told her he would sleep in her bed and she would sleep
with Marsha in the double bed. As if it were less strange, Margarita thought, for her to sleep with a mother she'd never known than
with her father, the rhythm of whose breaths she knew well, who had
rubbed her head, sung to her, read to her, told her stories, for years
before she drifted off. Because her father was a man and her mother a
woman. If only she could tell Anna all this, but it was dark, and she
was alone, it had always been this way, even when she was a child:

with the darkness came fear, a tugging in the depths of her entrails, she used to call it her *funny feeling*, it overcame her every evening, it was worse when she spent the night with friends, it was homesickness, the moment just before the roller coaster plunged from its highest point, except it lasted for hours. And the same feeling crept into her when her father decided she should sleep with Marsha.

Just before bedtime, Marsha finally told them what Grandpa had said on the phone: Grandma was confused and had been placed under observation. It was probably a bad concussion, there might be internal hemorrhaging, but the doctors hadn't found any so far. She could die, though, and suddenly, it was always possible. Margarita asked to call her, but her mother whispered that it wasn't a good idea.

Her father stroked her head. She shook it, shook all over, from guilt, shrank on the stool in the kitchen, said she was sorry.

"Oh, honey," Marsha said, "imagine all the guilt that *I've* racked up."

Margarita brushed her teeth and lay in bed, so close to the edge that she could feel the corner of the frame under her shoulder. She closed her eyes as Marsha changed clothes, sheet pulled up all the way to her nose.

Marsha lay next to her, on the other edge; Aba could have squeezed in between them, Margarita thought. Her mother turned off the light and began to breathe softly, and Margarita began to cry softly, so her mother wouldn't hear. She thought of Lior, of her grandmother, of how everything had turned into such a mess.

Marsha budged. Margarita bit into her cheek to stop herself.

Her father flushed the toilet, the air-conditioning purred. One more tear fell, the last one, for real this time.

"Rita?" her mother whispered.

She squawked.

Marsha slid closer toward the middle, slowly it became too narrow for her invisible father.

"Rita, what's wrong?"

"Everything," Margarita sobbed.

"You want to tell me where you were?"

Margarita shook her head.

"Let's make a deal," Marsha said.

"Hm?"

"You don't tell my secret and I won't tell yours."

Margarita had to think it over. It felt like a fair offer, especially as she still hadn't fully grasped the secret Marsha had told her or what it meant.

"I went to Tel Aviv," she finally said, "I wanted some peace and quiet, and I wanted to go to the beach."

Marsha propped up on her elbows, resting her face on one hand. Margarita wished Marsha would hug her, but she kept lying there and staring.

"My phone battery was dead. I didn't know how to get back, and I wound up at Lior's." Now she was crying so hard she couldn't breathe. Marsha reached out to her with her free hand, Margarita took it.

"Did he do something to you?" Marsha asked.

Margarita shook her head. "He didn't want me," she sputtered, "I think I'm bad at it."

"At what?"

"It."

"Oh, darling," Marsha said. "Nobody's bad in bed. That's not how it works."

Margarita buried her face in the pillow, as though trying to bore through it.

"Shhh," Marsha said. "It hurts, huh?"

Margarita nodded. "I'm sorry," she wailed, as softly as she could, so her father wouldn't hear her. "I'm so, so sorry." Marsha kept holding her hand. Margarita tried to explain how mean Lior's family had been, too, how she regretted running away, and even more so not charging her phone, and how she'd never, ever have wanted Grandma to worry, or Avi or Marsha, either, but Grandma especially—

Marsha was quiet for a long time. Then she sighed, stroking the back of Margarita's hand steadily, almost mechanically, as if it were a foreign body.

"Rita, you know Lior's not an asshole because he rejected you, right? Men have a right to decide about their own bodies, too."

Margarita pulled her hand away. Her cheeks burned as if she'd been smacked. She turned her back to her mother, and thought about the sofa the night before, which had been just as unwelcoming as the rest of Lior's family. Her exhaustion overcame her disappointment and the knowledge that she couldn't find an argument against what her mother had said, Marsha was right, and the only objection she could come up with was that she *could* be nicer, right, more understanding, wasn't that what a mother's love was all about?

* * *

Margarita slept late, she could do that, in the meanwhile it was twelve, and he was sitting with Marsha on the balcony under a crooked parasol, Marsha had made coffee, a simple breakfast. It was Shabbat, Rosh Hashanah started Friday, but Margarita had asked to come with them to Chicago, what else could he do, risk losing her again, so he called Frau Wagner, who was responsible for sick leave permissions for the Community, they'd find a replacement for him, it was true the guy sang off-key, but he was a safe bet to see them through the High Holy Days.

It started to rain. Margarita woke from her coma as they were cleaning the table.

"Motek, can you smell the rain in the air? Boker tov."

Margarita, still groggy, replied, "It doesn't smell like rain, what the damp does is amplify other scents. It smells like all the things we normally smell, like trash and dog shit."

Marsha arched her eyebrows, looking at her with astonishment. "Who knew!" she said.

"Yofi," he said. "Hungry?"

Margarita shook her head. "Any news from Grandma?"

"No," Marsha said.

"What are we doing today?"

"You and I are going to see your aunt," he said, "you need to meet her."

"It's Shabbes, though."

"For now, I don't mind making an exception, we're taking the rental car. Anyway, we're not flying."

He had called Pnina the evening prior, just before sunset, and told her he'd had to come to Jerusalem out of the blue. She said she didn't live in Tel Aviv anymore, they'd moved to Ra'anana, which didn't surprise him. Pnina had invited him that afternoon. They'd agreed on four, that left them a few hours before the Havdalah, what was there to tell, anyhow; certainly not that Margarita had run off, he would never admit that in front of her.

What would Pnina look like? The last time he'd seen her and her insufferable husband had been at the funeral for his mother, along with two of her four kids; the oldest, Hadassa, must be twelve now, Dvora eleven, Tal, who hadn't even been born then, would be five, maybe, and last came Avishai, whom he knew about only because of a Facebook post. While Margarita was still asleep, he had said to Marsha that the daughters' names all reminded him of the prostitutes in Neve Sha'anan that his Hasidic friends in yeshiva had told him so much about. Marsha had laughed lewdly, with something twisted in her worried face, as if she were defending herself against the laughter that shook her. She was so lovely that something in him went slack when he looked at her too long.

It had been an eternity since he'd driven, he'd gotten a German license, but never used it. It would come back to him, this was

Israel, it was Shabbat and the streets were empty, even Margarita could probably have navigated the arrow-straight roads to the Tel Aviv suburb, in the military he'd had to drive a car half asleep, manage machines that were much more difficult for that matter, the easiest thing about flying was parking after you landed.

Margarita got hungry at some point and pattered into the kitchen.

"We're leaving at two thirty," he said, not sure what else to say.

"Why do we have to go?" Margarita asked. "I thought you didn't even like your sister."

"No back talk." He cut the bread into slices. She ate without thanking him. In Berlin, it got on his nerves when she didn't thank him, but here it made him furious.

* * *

Until it was time, she read in a corner of the filthy balcony, to avoid her hectic mother, her nervous father, the entire oppressive Shabbat mood in the apartment, Avi's never-ending offers of snacks; "Stop working on Shabbat, care work is work, too," she said, and acted as if she didn't notice how deeply that hurt him.

Even in her grandparents' car traveling down Lakeshore Drive, where they took traffic signals as suggestions rather than law, she felt safer, her father drove as if he put too much faith in his dearly beloved God.

Margarita gripped the seat cushions. She let go only when they were finally on the highway, after two wrong turns; he had taken forever to use the GPS, he agreed to it only once Margarita argued that they were already sitting in a car and it was too late to be a stickler about Shabbes. They fought the whole way over, Margarita yowling about how scared she was, her father telling her that her constant complaining wasn't making things any better.

They reached Ra'anana shortly after four. It looked depressing, empty playgrounds and giant supermarkets all round. Big families pushed their offspring through the street in endless strollers, the children had kippot but no sidelocks, the women didn't wear beige hose as in Jerusalem, instead their legs were naked under their skirts and dresses.

They continued to the outskirts, where high fences surrounded single-family homes interspersed with boxy buildings with faded facades. Her aunt greeted them in one of the fenced-in houses. She hugged her brother, shook Margarita's hand, and introduced herself as Pnina. The hallway smelled of Febreze and cumin. She shouted for the children, then spoke to Margarita again in English.

Margarita said she spoke Ivrit. Her aunt arched her brows. She was as tall as Avi, the two of them looked strangely alike, as if they shared all the unfortunate traits and only their individual features rescued their faces from disaster. Unlike Avi, Pnina was round, her body's contours soft in her three-quarter-length trousers and the T-shirt that read *But first, ice cream* next to an ice-cream cone made of sequins.

She invited them into the sunroom. The entire house was tiled, the tiles felt good under Margarita's hot feet. Again, Pnina yelled up to the children on the second floor. Margarita and her father sat at a table full of toys with a bowl of dried yogurt in their midst. A little boy came down the stairs and looked at them.

"Avishai," Pnina said, "this is your uncle."

Avishai shook his head. "Eran uncle," he said.

"No, your other uncle, not Aba's brother," Pnina said.

"Aba," Avishai said.

Margarita's father waved gently and introduced himself. He asked Avishai where his sisters were, and Avishai came back soon after holding the hand of a somewhat larger girl.

Pnina placed a bottle of off-brand cola on the table with a few glasses and a bag of Bamba, then yelled, "I'm counting to three," but didn't count to three. Right away two more girls came down the stairs. Margarita was baffled that they could be related to her.

Avishai's kippa fell to the floor. He kissed it and put it back on his head. One of the girls asked if she could braid Margarita's hair. Margarita sat gratefully on the floor and let the girl do it, even if it pulled. She listened to the two adults trying to converse. Pnina seemed to keep forgetting Margarita could understand, talking about her as if she weren't there.

"She's a cutie," Pnina said, "she's got her mother's face, don't you think?"

She knew Marsha.

"Where's Uri?" Margarita's father asked.

"Shul. Praying Mincha."

"Does he still lead the prayers?"

"Yeah," Pnina said, then whispered, "but not as nice as you."

"Done!" the girl shouted, and showed Margarita's head to the adults. Margarita smiled meekly. Her father praised her hairstyle in exaggerated tones. Then one girl shoved another, shouting broke out, tears flowed, Margarita stood up and went to sit on a stool, the cushion was wet, the damp soaking through her sweatpants; she tried not to let it show, wondering why Pnina's life was so different from Avi's.

"How are you finding Israel?" her aunt asked gruffly, but in Hebrew, apparently she'd finally gotten it.

Margarita vacillated. "Good," she said, "it's different from Berlin."

"I'll take your word for it," Pnina said, "we wanted to visit, but your father said I wouldn't like it."

Margarita leaned her head to one side.

"You can come whenever you like," her father said, "but you'll have to make all your meals in advance, there's maybe three kosher restaurants in the entire city. That's all I meant. And it's really everywhere, the Shoah and all, I mean; it's Germany."

"You think we can't take it or something? Our parents handled it, right?"

"Yeah, but they didn't give a damn about keeping kosher, did they?"

"Me neither, not till I met Uri. You chose this craziness of your own accord."

"If you're just doing it for Uri, you ought to ask yourself if your motivations are the right ones. Besides, I do eat in restaurants where food isn't kosher. I'm free to choose."

"Ah, so you're better than me, then?" Pnina asked.

Margarita saw she was struggling not to cry.

"That's not what I meant," Avi said, "I just wanted to explain why I think you wouldn't be comfortable in Berlin."

"Sure, whatever, I get it. You are better. But at least we can wear a kippa on the street and don't have to cover it with some stupid cap so the Nazis' grandkids won't beat us up, or the Israel haters, or whoever else roams the streets there, don't worry about it, I didn't really want to come anyway, we'll leave you alone in your piece-of-shit country."

Even the siren sounds Avishai made as he pushed a plastic police car through the room went dead.

Margarita's father sucked in a deep breath. He shot Pnina a despairing look, as if remembering that she was his sister, that he might still love her, but then something in his face hardened. "So when are you moving," he asked acidly, "when are you heading off to a settlement to become more and more meshuggene and act baffled when parliament dissolves itself again and cry when someone else gets killed? Germany sucks, fine, but at least I don't have four kids so there are enough to pick up the slack if one of them dies."

Pnina laughed aloud. "You haven't found anyone to have another one with, anyway; your crazy Marsha, who was so much better than your pitiful family, gave you one and hit the road, was she really so great or is it that you just weren't good enough?"

Margarita sat perplexed before her glass of cola.

"And if the Nazis do away with your Margarita, then you'll be all alone. Cool. You can party in Berlin with all the ex-Hasidim and act like you were one of them, but you're not, your childhood wasn't as bad as you think, you're just a snob, that's all, you think you did something brave, you know what's really brave, standing up for your country, doing a real job instead of cashing in blood money, and you know that's what it is," now her tone was triumphant, "they pretend it's a job and shove money up your ass to assuage their guilty conscience, and they don't even know you have fuck all to do with their Shoah, and you think you're better than us? Shame on you, Avi, shame on you," then her father stood, struck the table so hard he knocked the glasses over, and screamed, "Not one shekel, never again, you won't get one shekel from me the next time you come begging and crying about how everything's so expensive, who's the homeowner, you or me?"

Pnina grabbed the edge of the table. Her children stood in the living room next to the sunroom holding hands, the girls stared, the biggest one cried. Cola was running down Margarita's arm.

"We're going," her father said after giving his sister the bird. Observing this, Margarita's mouth opened in an agitated *oah.*

But as soon as they sat in the car, he was asking her forgiveness; his sister was crazy, he said, that sounded like bullshit to Margarita, but she didn't know how she should say that, and besides, she was scared of him just now. From the passenger seat, she could smell his sour breath. After yet another drive through Hell, they arrived in Jerusalem, he dropped her off and said his farewell at the Kotel, alone. Margarita asked if she could go with him, but he said, "No, it's no place for you," that hurt, and she was confused, confused and tired.

After a half hour, which she spent on the floor next to her bed staring at her long fingernails, Marsha asked if she could use a walk, and Margarita said yes, grateful, let her make a sandwich before they left, walked a long ways with her mother until they came to a park.

They sat on a bench, they were the only ones there, everyone else must have been at home or at the synagogue, and Margarita told Marsha what had happened and Marsha cracked up laughing, "Always the same with those two."

Margarita was so relieved to be able to share this with someone who knew that world that she forgot herself and reached out and asked questions and giggled as Marsha trotted out her own stories, and she hardly noticed—only once it had grown quiet—that they were talking bad about her father and that wasn't right at all, but she didn't know what she was supposed to do, she just had to talk about what she'd been through. The sun sank, and the sounds, the peeps and rustles, of Jerusalem emerged.

* * *

He walked with quick steps to the Old City as though into a life he'd forgotten he ever lived, there were more and more people hurrying alongside him, Hasidim, but also people like him, tzitzit flying, kippot on the head, no shtreimels, he walked as fast as possible through Zion Gate into the Armenian Quarter, past the shop where he wanted to buy dishes, a pretty serving dish, maybe a seder plate, he tried not to jostle anyone, hastened farther, nearly fell, the stone had been worn smooth, but he still knew the alleys like the back of his hand, his body was the needle in the compass, the Kotel his north.

He wondered whether Pnina's reproach was true, whether he was—she hadn't used this word, but it was what she'd meant to say—an opportunist. He asked himself whether he had, inadvertently, adopted this Christian notion of good and evil, piety and frumkeit, this absurd idea he and his few close Jewish friends mocked, while the pietistic converts in Berlin really did believe the synagogue was a church, obedience to the halakha was a way of avoiding the wrath of God's hand. He lived as she did, basically, trying to follow the 613 mitzvot, but for him that implied acquiescence, insight, following the rules on account of their beauty and because they were meaningful, at least when you saw the tradition itself as something meaningful. No, unlike them, he didn't follow the rules because he was afraid of punishment. And the Hasidim, why did they follow the rules, was it not out of fear of divine punishment, too, like the former Christians, even if they looked different—fear not of Hell after death, but of chastisement on Earth?

He was almost there, he couldn't believe how crowded the streets were, had it always been this full, was he just old and timid now? He stopped, he was a little dizzy, what if something happened now, the German Ministry of Foreign Affairs had issued warnings to visitors of the Old City, he knew because he'd looked it up for Margarita. He saw himself from above for a moment, as in a cheap series where life swirling around the main character sped up while he stood stock-still.

He pulled himself together. Walked to the Kotel, struggled through the American tourist groups, you could recognize them because they all wore the same T-shirts, branded kippot in some cases, so no one would get lost behind the partition separating the men from women, past the policemen with machine guns pressed to their chests, past Haredim and others who looked like him, Jews reading from the Torah, celebrating and dancing, Jews who here put on their tefillin for the first time, others who were donning it for the thousandth, some who came every week, some who would be here only once in their lives, he made it to the front, gave in, said *slicha* over and over, but why should he beg pardon, this was his home, it was his right to be here. Exhausted, he leaned his head on the sandstone, kissed it, grabbed a tallit and prayer book, they lay there at the ready, so you wouldn't have to take them back home after sundown, he began his prayer, bent left and right and left and right and left in an unsteady wave with all the others, and then the sun went down, Shabbat was over, a real Havdalah, not some sorry theatrics, but people really resting in one another's arms, a Hasidic rebbe sang nigunim, fifty feet away was another one, not Hasidic, everywhere groups had formed, soldiers sang in a big circle, it was a Jewish balagan, something Avi couldn't have performed alone, that he couldn't stage for money, and that he hadn't known he'd missed: it was this that was the object of his nostalgia. He watched the events, the little boys looking rapturously at their fathers, the girls peeking over the fence.

He joined one of the groups, was for once not the head but the body of the prayers, let himself fall and be caught, not by the words this time, not by the meaning or the melody, but by the people around him.

It got dark as they prayed, and the air was cooling. The children even joined in ardently, dragged out the nigunim as long as possible, *lailailailailailailailai*, over and over, *lailailailailailailailai*, their voices like bells fascinated him, when had he last heard such voices? When had Margarita lost this voice? And why had he never managed to interest her in music?

To close, a group of teenagers sang "Am Yisrael Chai," he had to grin at their candor; at the same time, they gave him goose bumps. He asked himself whether he'd been wrong to deprive Margarita of this, whether she wouldn't have been happier here, a normal Israeli teenager, just like all the others, just like him, in the military; he could imagine her chewing gum, joking around with friends on base, not in war, of course, not that. Or as an American teenager, entitled and blissfully unaware of the rest of the world, traveling with a Birthright Israel group, in an American two-parent household, both of them loving each other and her unconditionally, with a bedroom in a Victorian house within walking distance of a synagogue and a university, with summer vacations in Camp Ramah and on the Atlantic coast. Margarita's life, as he prayed, felt suddenly hopeless to him, so he prayed to bring the hope back, for her to one day be able to leave Germany so that he would no longer be fettered to it, either.

* * *

Marsha decided to eat out when Shabbat ended, "Fuck it," she said, "that's what I've got a credit card for." She wanted to go to the Cinémathèque. Margarita would love the restaurant there. Avi sent a text saying he'd come along. Margarita rolled her eyes. They walked across the park, the ground firm, firmer than in Tel Aviv, the footfalls there heavier, the valley starting to glimmer faintly, there it was, Jerusalem in the last light of evening, her father had always talked about it, but till now she hadn't seen it, and it was quite sharp, quite clear, as if the rest of the globe no longer existed. As if there were no Lior, no Nico, as if they didn't matter to her, because Jerusalem existed.

But there was something else: the constant worry over her grandmother, still no news, monitoring in the ICU; that was all Marsha could talk about the whole way there, her fear of losing her mother and how awful the wait was. Margarita felt her shoulders slump farther and farther forward, and between them her heart raced like a hummingbird from guilt and helplessness. She feared another long-haul flight, incommunicado for hours on end, hours during which her grandmother could simply die. Or would everything get better just as soon as she got in the plane, the same way the tram always came right when you lit up a cigarette?

Finally they reached the Cinémathèque. A wave of people pushed through the doors. Apparently a film had just ended. Avi stood by the entrance, looking forlorn.

Silence reigned as they sat down, but Margarita refused to broach any topic. Avi rocked nervously back and forth in his chair. Marsha stared out the window and scratched idly at the sunburn on her arm.

A waitress brought the menus, and Marsha ordered spaghetti Bolognese without looking. Margarita did the same. The thought of eating pasta that hadn't been cooked to mush for the first time in seven weeks made her stomach growl. The school year had started four days ago. She had asked a few friends to take notes for her and emailed her teachers the day before to say that her return would be delayed by a family emergency. She knew the first weeks were always introductory material. She'd been ambivalent about starting that year: she was happy to be done with the core curriculum and get on with her specialized classes, but at the same time, her grades now counted toward her college acceptance.

She already knew most people in her class, they'd been together since seventh year, had gone on the same field trips, to Kabbalat Shabbat at the synagogue next door; had trudged together through Auschwitz not long before the academic year's end, wrapped in Israeli flags the school had passed out, and Jacob from class 10a had thrown up.

Their Bolognese arrived. Marsha sprinkled parmesan over it. Margarita saw her father's sidelong glance. A sudden rage overcame her, maybe because of the emails, maybe because he looked like shit sitting there and sweating into his risotto. She took the little spoon from the dish of parmesan and shook the grated cheese onto her own noodles, but not much of it fell off the spoon, so she kept shoving it back into the dish, finally she had to just tip it, her eyes crossed his, he was staring, she scraped the bottom of the dish, the spoon clinked against the glass, and then she stirred her spaghetti. Marsha hid her smirk behind her hand.

"Bete'avon," Avi forced himself to say. Cautiously, she took a bite. She felt a slight disgust at this mingling of meat and milk, and it irked her that her father wouldn't let himself be provoked. On the contrary, he began to make small talk, mouth full of food. Asked which Margarita liked better, Tel Aviv or Jerusalem. "Eilat," Margarita said, and her parents laughed as though surprised that she sometimes had witty things to say instead of whining.

Afterward, it was quiet again. No one seemed to know what they should talk about. The only things that occurred to Margarita were those they might fight over.

"I signed us up for Yad Vashem. Since we won't be leaving till the evening, we could get an early start on it tomorrow," Marsha said finally.

"Marsha, don't you think that's a bit much?" Avi asked. "We've got to be at the airport at five."

When Avi said *Marsha*, the *r* was so coarse, it sounded like her name was crumbling apart. *Makhsha*, that's how it should really be written, Margarita thought.

"The tickets are for nine. We could go straight from there to the airport, I'll return the car there."

Avi said nothing.

"Any news from Grandma?" Margarita asked.

Her father answered in Hebrew. "She already said she'll tell us if there's anything new."

Margarita looked up from her pasta, seething. "Can't you say that in English?"

Marsha looked back and forth between them.

"He said you'd tell us if there was anything new," Margarita said. "And Yad Vashem works. I'm sure I'd love it there."

"Nobody loves it there," her father said in English, and then, turning to Marsha: "The idea is completely ridiculous, she's totally worn out. She's already been to Auschwitz, isn't that enough?"

"She's lucky to have made it out alive," Marsha said.

Avi rolled his eyes.

"I think a Jewish perspective wouldn't hurt," Marsha said, serious this time. "In Auschwitz, it must be all about the perpetrators."

"Motek, is it just about the perpetrators at Auschwitz?"

She looked up. "Um. I don't know. What do you think?" She didn't understand what he meant. Obviously she didn't have the least desire to drive to Yad Vashem, but she also had not the least desire to prove her father right.

He rubbed his eyes. "I've only gone to Auschwitz for work," he said. He looked sad. Suddenly she felt pity for him.

"You don't have to come, Aba," she said.

"That's not it. I want to protect you," he replied, and he sounded insulted. She had only wanted to make things better, and now they were worse. In silence, she ate every bit off her treyf dish while her parents went on fighting, relieved that they were ignoring her.

* * *

Margarita had bent so far over the plate she looked ashamed, but he knew she bore an expression of rage, defiance, disgust, those downturned corners of the lips, the straight deep lines between the eyebrows were things Avi recognized from himself.

He found himself trapped in an argument he wanted out of, but it was as it always had been, as it was when he and Marsha used to quarrel before; she twisted around every sentence he uttered and saw it as a provocation, or still worse, as idiotic. She got so wrapped up in these political discussions that held little interest for him, he had his own muted opinions, unlike her; everything between them was heated, polemical, impassioned, implacable, whereas on his own, he had a tender attitude toward the world and the daughter he had raised and wanted to protect.

He had said casually, he thought, that Marsha was overloading her, with her grandmother in the hospital, the upcoming flight; what she really needed was to be in her home, in her bed, in her school, and between bites Marsha said, "I think she's tougher than you believe, and this might be the last time she sees her grandmother alive."

"I think she's not as tough as *you* believe," he replied. Margarita had gone to the bathroom, she must have had the smallest bladder in the world, she had already stood up and almost run off fifteen minutes earlier, or was she having a bad period, maybe he should ask? Or was that Marsha's task now that she was having her fifteen minutes of fame, should she be the one to talk to Margarita about her menstrual flow and condoms and dental dams, all open-minded and cool?

"I'm being serious, Marsha," he said, "she's got her entire life ahead of her to go to Yad Vashem. Why right now?"

"For a Jewish perspective, obviously, do you not get it anymore? You're the Israeli here, my goodness; she only knows the German perspective, the eternal defensiveness!"

"We live a Jewish life! She goes to a Jewish school!"

"Being frum is the opposite of education, Avi, you know that yourself. And how many people at this school are actually converts full of guilt because their grandparents were in the SS, hm?"

"What you're saying is unfair. You know perfectly well that music matters to me more than the halakha. I didn't bat an eye when she sprinkled parmesan on her spaghetti, that's her choice. And at the school they have a strong focus on Jewish philosophy, Jewish history, liturgy . . ."

"Yeah, but they're still German, right? My goodness, there's a lot I haven't held on to, but I'll never forget that *Jude* is a curse word in Germany, they won't even allow themselves to utter it aloud, you yourself used to always say that."

"Germany, Germany, Germany," Avi mimicked her. "It's an obsession with you."

By now, Margarita had returned.

"With me? Who's the one who insisted on going to live there? You just had to take the job in Hannover, you swore we'd be back after two years, but no, you had to send applications to Berlin, if anyone has an obsession, it's you!"

"It's terrible what happened," he said, "and I won't try to make light of it, all I wanted to say was that with Yad Vashem tomorrow, we're asking too much of her."

"Oh, but the Israeli teenagers have to deal with it, because they're supposed to be the victims?"

"That's completely irrational. It was a tragedy, we agree about that, but it remains the case that it will still be there next year, we could come back . . ."

Now Margarita laughed aloud. "I hope we never have to come

back," she said. The hatred in her voice frightened him. For a moment, he and Marsha looked at their daughter, who was now once more busy with her phone.

"A tragedy," Marsha said. "It wasn't a tragedy, it was a genocide. Germany wasn't struck by lightning, there was an entire society backing the Nazis, and everything is still there, nothing's been worked through, for crying out loud; why do I have to be the one to explain this to you?"

"You don't have to be," he said, wanting to go on, but she interrupted him: "Avi, it wasn't your beloved God that punished the Jews, it was the Germans, and they murdered them! Your obsession with the Germans makes me sick, with their efficiency and cleanliness and rigor. No god made them evil, no god wanted to kill us, they were the ones who wanted to kill us."

"Why are you so emotional?" he asked, since nothing better occurred to him.

"I'm emotional? You're the one who's acting like we're going to traumatize Margarita just because I want to take her to Yad Vashem."

"I simply don't understand why it's so important to you."

"Because it's our responsibility, Avi. It was a part of my plans for our trip."

"It was also your responsibility to make sure she didn't run away."

"Not that again," Marsha said. "I just have the feeling she barely understands the significance of the ground she's standing on here."

"Marsha, you romanticize everything, you know perfectly well this isn't the Israel of fifty years ago, and what are we supposed to tell her, yeah, the Germans are evil, evil, evil, even though she's one of them? We can't confuse her like that. I feel a strong Jewish identity is resistance enough!"

"You talk like you're reading off a teleprompter. A strong Jewish identity, what does that mean for a person who can't even deal with the Holocaust?"

"Please stop," Margarita said.

"Sweetie," Marsha said, "you have to deal with this. Jews get into fights all the time."

"Sorry, motek," Avi said. "You want dessert?"

Margarita ordered a tiramisu, clutching her phone, typing hectically.

"Where were we?" Avi asked. "Were you wanting to talk down to me more?"

"Yeah, of course, once again I'm the overemotional one and you're the poor single father who just happened to end up in Germany because it was the only place he could fulfill his dream of living off his crooning and putting aside a little pocket change for his housewife."

That had struck home. "You left, Marsha, you shoved off right before the move!"

"You could simply have come along."

"You were trying to extort me."

"You were, too, with your Germany, in America at least we could have had a family, and I could have earned money, but no, you wanted *me* to live *your* dream and be a housewife and go on birthing children like the queen of the Hasids!"

Margarita cupped her hands over her ears.

"Marsha," he said reproachfully, but Marsha had started to cry, and again he felt she was extorting him, constantly extorting him, the stubborn Markovitz women, grandmother, mother, and daughter, with their sobbing and their tears.

She hissed, "My mother's life is in the balance, what's the point of this goddamn argument," and he went pale; it was true, there were more important things.

"I'm sorry," he said, "I'm sorry," and sat there, resourceless, as though his outer shell had slipped away, as though everything had just spilled out onto the table, "I'm sorry," but Marsha kept crying harder and harder. The waitress brought over napkins.

"All this guilt," she burbled, "all this fucking guilt, and the pain,

and the missing, and it was just to prove our points," what a de-
bacle, someone laughed in the restaurant, Schumann's *Träumerei*
played over the speakers, maybe it was a sign that this was a nightmare, not real, but it was real. Shit.

* * *

Her parents obviously didn't know what sound her cell phone made
for voice messages, or else their fight had distracted them; either way,
Margarita kept pressing record and sending them to Anna, and Anna
responded with laugh-crying emojis, and the entire situation eased,
by now Margarita couldn't care less whether they did or didn't go to
Yad Vashem, Anna had said it was terrible but also something you
could scratch off your bucket list afterward, the main things on their
bucket list, though, were going to a Harry Styles concert, bungee
jumping, and bungee jumping at a Harry Styles concert.

While her mother sniveled to her father, she ate her tiramisu.
Everything that had happened this summer had its roots in her
parents' sensitivities and their notions regarding the child they had
in common. As for the child's own sensitivities, her own notions,
nobody cared.

She would never have children of her own. She would study
medicine, help people, open an office somewhere far from Berlin,
she'd never tell anyone she was a Jew, nothing good could come of
it. If she was even a Jew.

* * *

Margarita and Marsha had dawdled so long, Margarita absorbed in
her book, Marsha frozen at her computer, googling for hours on end
all the things that could happen when something heavy fell on a person's head, that it wasn't until late at night that she and Avi packed
their suitcases and Margarita's, gathering things, washing clothes,
drying them with the hair dryer while Margarita slept, they had

tucked her in a little too eagerly, then cursed the clothing thrown sloppily into the dresser, unfolded, dirty mixed with clean, Avi said softly he sometimes put on an FFP2 mask before entering her room.

The next day, they'd fly to Chicago, it felt surreal, as if the stage they were walking on could collapse at any time, or Margarita's grandmother might instantaneously recover and send them all back to their day-to-day lives, and there was no plan for going back, there was only sleepy Berlin, where no one was waiting for them, well, for Margarita, maybe, but even she seemed disconnected from her universe, like a Lena distraught, looking for her Leonce. His daughter reminded him in those days of that fraught figure of Büchner's in one of the few plays he had seen in Germany, at the Berliner Ensemble, ten years ago, easily; the audience was full of philistines, not just the kind with chunky watches on their wrists, but the ones in Che Guevara shirts and harem pants, Jack Wolfskin fleece pullovers, people who used natural deodorants that didn't work. Or was he being unfair, maybe even nasty to the Germans, the way Marsha wanted, like they could never do anything right again?

He slept just a few hours, lay in bed in just his underpants so he could keep an extra T-shirt clean for Chicago. He assumed they'd all stay with Marsha's parents, he was well acquainted with the uncomfortable guest sofa in Dan's library. Where, though, would Marsha sleep, with Margarita in her old bedroom?

Marsha served him a coffee when he entered the kitchen, even before she always got up earlier than him, not because she was an early riser, no, not in the least, but she knew how grateful he was for a cup of coffee in the morning, he guessed she had remembered.

Marsha parked deftly in the underground garage at Yad Vashem, the car full of suitcases and all the trash mother and daughter had accumulated on their trip together. Margarita hadn't let him drive, hadn't even let him ride in the passenger seat, she'd pointed to the back theatrically, Marsha had simply laughed.

He craved once again to finally show what he could do—sing, and well, in contrast to all the other things he was apparently so much worse at than he had told himself. He even went so far as to imagine, with his beautiful voice, he might have survived. No, that was appalling, just the thought of it was an insult to all those who, despite their voices, despite their gifts, despite their infinite love for their children, despite their basic humanity, had been murdered, or not despite, *because*, because they were Jews, and Marsha had been right, it wasn't lightning that struck them down, a machine had been behind it, a German machine, and he had not impeded what Marsha had seen coming clearly fifteen years before: that the aftershocks would also make Margarita reel. A German, one of those who cried not from sorrow, but from shame.

But Marsha didn't look at it that way, Marsha was proud of Margarita, how she walked stiffly through the museum, at just a few places did her tears flow, but silently; when he wanted to hug her, she pushed away. He knew what Marsha thought: Yeah, that's how it is when you think about the Holocaust every day without taking refuge in the naive belief in God. Their daughter had, like her, abandoned the idea that the Almighty had played some role in it, their daughter had grasped what he didn't wish to accept: it had been people. Just people. Efficient, German people. Not machines. And he himself stopped believing, he didn't have to, he was a musician, not a man of the cloth; his piano had once been dearer to him than his siddur, his voice dearer than his kippur.

The exhibition opened with antisemitic signs that had hung on every corner in Germany at the beginning of the thirties, one of them read *Norderney ist judenfrei*, Norderney is free of Jews, it rhymed in German, though. Norderney was on the North Sea, near Langeoog, next to Spiekeroog, but Spiekeroog didn't rhyme with anything, *Spiekeroog ist judenlos*, Spiekeroog is Jewless, it didn't have the same ring.

He wondered if Jews had been forbidden to travel to Spiekeroog, asked himself whether that should matter to him, but when he thought of Spiekeroog, he thought of Hannah, and that made him want to stop thinking of Spiekeroog, but then he wondered how many Jews had even set foot in Spiekeroog since the Holocaust.

He had worried it would be too much for Margarita, but no one listened to him, so he'd gone along, even though no one wanted him there. He lingered on the details that he normally had no time for at the memorial affairs where he sang and was thus a part of the exhibition. Here he wasn't part of the exhibition. He was a visitor, a learner. Here there were moments of surprise that made the blood drain from his head: the meticulous model of Birkenau, the rent faces in miniature. The comic drawn by Horst Rosenthal, a prisoner in the camp in Gurs, Mickey Mouse as a concentration camp prisoner, Mickey Mouse forced to slave away; not Mickey Mouse released, no; not Mickey Mouse deported to Auschwitz-Birkenau, not Mickey Mouse murdered in Auschwitz-Birkenau, no; the comic didn't make it that far, those details were recounted in the attached biography of Horst Rosenthal himself.

How faint he felt as information about Gershon Sirota flickered on the screen, it was almost unbearable to hold the cold receiver to his ear and hear his voice, him singing B'Rosh Hashanah, it crackled, he could whisper along with each word, he knew the prayer, even the recording, Sirota was one of the greatest cantors of the twentieth century, he had died in the Warsaw Ghetto, and as Avi thought of his post, of the synagogue in Berlin, of the function he fulfilled there, he fell to his knees.

Before entering each room, you thought: Here comes the worst part, and the room afterward was always worse. Right away, he grasped what Marsha had said. The Polish and German memorials always expressed their outrage that even the assimilated Jews had been killed, but here, in Yad Vashem, all that mattered was that they had been people. There was no appraisal, it didn't matter whether they'd been Hasidim or put up a Christmas tree in their living room—what mattered was that they were dead. The Germans used to think the Jews who had eaten *Leberkäse* with cream sauce on Yom Kippur deserved less to die than the pious ones, probably they still thought so. The Germans thought the truly awful thing was that *some of them* had been murdered, just totally normal Germans who happened to have had a Jewish grandmother, when these not-so-Jewish Jews were already well on their way to not being Jews at all.

Here it wasn't about the arbitrariness of the racial laws, it was about genocide.

The exhibition had been conceived not for sensitive Germans, for morally superior atheists; how repugnant this smugness of theirs, enervation overtook him as the interviews with witnesses reeled before his eyes, by now they were probably all dead, maybe they'd died in the last war in Europe, even; he was livid at those Germans who said they believed in nothing at all, as though that somehow made them better, anyway they probably did believe in astrology and definitely went to Christmas at their parents' house. What united them all was their refusal to recognize they were Jewish; whether or not they believed in God, whether or not they ate buttered bread with ham, no one could kick them out of this club.

A further surprise: the truly unjust, the irreducibly elusive thing was that you could pose questions only to those left behind, when the ones you needed to ask things of were the dead, the ones who had actually seen what it was like, death in the gas chambers, those who spoke had been spared that, and so even when they recounted the worst of all possible horrors, still, it remained a fragment. Because death was absent.

He thought of his childhood, his Israel: an Israel in spite of the Germans. When had he ceased to see it that way?

In the museum shop, there was a 20 percent discount on Dead

Sea hand lotion. Was there hand lotion in Auschwitz, made with the ashes of Jews?

He sensed something that might have been patriotism. They—the Jews—could buy this hand lotion in the gift shop of Yad Vashem, because it was their narrative. Their decision.

In his head: *Yad Vacream.*

In his head: *Norderney ist judenfrei.*

In his head: a German children's rhyme, stern and pedagogical, of course; the last words something like *Grow up rich and you'll eat ham, as for the poor, who gives a damn.*

In his head: *Shema yisrael Adonai Eloheinu Adonai echad.*

Was he going crazy?

He didn't buy the hand lotion, instead he bought Margarita a copy of the Hebrew translation of *Maus.* At the cash register were German prayer books, he threw in one of those, he didn't know why; just yesterday he'd seen how godless his daughter was and how easily she moved through the world nonetheless. The man in the little booth next to the barrier was in a terrifyingly good mood; as they were driving out of the garage, he'd wished them a spirited good morning, Avi wondered whether he was a psychopath or a normal Israeli.

* * *

Margarita couldn't say whether this pertained to her, whether this was her grief. Now that she knew the secret, she couldn't let it go, she didn't know what it meant to her, and she couldn't ask her mother, because her father was always there; she had tried in Yad Vashem, and her mother had snapped at her, *Not here, are you crazy*, and then she'd had to hold it together, she couldn't lose it, where in the world if not in Yad Vashem were you obliged not to lose it because of your own personal drama?

She was almost relieved to find the racial laws would have

applied to her, too. The Nazis would have declared her a Jew. Whether the halakha would have as well, she couldn't say, and her attempts to find out with the help of the internet had produced an even greater feeling of emptiness, it said there that she must convert as quickly as possible. Convert to a religion that already belonged to her, that she had allowed herself a certain freedom toward, an insolence, mocking and doubt, one because of which she'd already been the target of discrimination. Conversion was a profession of faith, an attempt to belong, but she didn't want to belong anywhere, she thought, not to the perpetrators, not to the victims, the best thing would be to be nothing at all. She watched her parents, how they strode through the exhibition, Marsha almost too stiff, self-satisfied, observing the displays with scholarly regard, reading the plaques at light speed or maybe just skimming them, her father lagging behind, rubbing his lips, sitting down to watch the interviews. Margarita in between.

And everywhere, Jews, the life stories of Jews, their death stories, in the Warsaw Ghetto the daily rations were 184 calories per Jew.

She wondered whether her American grandparents had ever been here. She wanted suddenly to talk to her grandmother about it. Normally, she never wanted to talk to her grandmother about anything, and now she was more interested in her than ever. Only because she might be taken from her. There was no news, Marsha was phoning Grandpa constantly, even from the museum, but it was always the same: concussion, she was disoriented. Wait.

A blond woman on a screen spoke of the Jewish houses in a German her father struggled to understand, he turned on Hebrew subtitles, and it was unsettling to Margarita to read along in a language not made for these words, one unaware of how cruel they were, an impartial language, perhaps; *Beit haYehudim*, sounds normal, a house with Jews, a metaphor for Israel, maybe—Israel, *Beit haYehudim*—another woman told how she was cursed at, *Go back to Palestine*, and Margarita wondered why they all hadn't just gone to Palestine, knew immediately this was a question you didn't ask yourself when you were at home somewhere, the way she was with her father on Husemannstrasse. The woman spoke of herself as a Ka-Tzetnik, a camp dweller, it sounded like a nickname, but it was just the word for what she'd been, sounded almost like *nudnik*, which her father called her sometimes, meaning something like *birdbrain*.

By then they had reached the concentration camps themselves, past the indignities, the antisemitism, the gradual eclipsing of everyday joy; now the subject was music in Auschwitz, the gassed Hasidim, but that didn't reach her, she could think then of nothing but what it would have been like not to be gassed, to survive, to outlive your loved ones, and when she imagined her father out-living her, she felt sick, because there was no world in which he could outlive her, his life was hers, and she constantly forgot how loved she was and how precious it was to be loved. Dying, maybe that was easier? And now everything was harder, because of death, because of all the deaths, because her grandmother might die, be-cause she might have killed her grandmother, and she wished she'd been nicer, not always running off, wished she'd said nice things about her cooking and sat on the swing her grandparents had set up in the garden just for her.

Family names all over. So many names. Names she'd never heard before, names that probably no longer existed. Names that sounded like her own name.

Day-to-day life in the KZ, rusty spoons, shoes, they'd left the hair and teeth in Auschwitz, though; it seemed the Israelis wanted nothing to do with them. The next room: day-to-day life in the KZ part two, Mengele, murdered babies, the selections, people digging trenches where they would then be shot to death, and what, what, what was its meaning for her, and why did she feel guilty because she dreamed in the language of the perpetrators? Even the German

Jews back then had dreamed in the language of the perpetrators. She kept tracing out on her thigh with her finger a word: *corpse, corpse, corpse*, on her sunburned skin some letters vanished quicker than the others, at one point it seemed to read *close*.

At the end, there were two sentences that restored the meaning of it all, with the name Abel Herzberg under them: *There were not six million Jews murdered. There was one murder, six million times.*

She walked out of the museum, onto the terrace overlooking Jerusalem, her parents still behind her; only now did she realize how cold she was, she swallowed deeply, perhaps a tear fell, perhaps two, but no more, and she looked embarrassed at her telephone as a group of Germans around her age walked close to her on the terrace, the guide spoke English, but no one was really listening, someone asked where they could smoke, someone was chewing their gum loudly, Margarita felt wounded, for the Germans she didn't look like a German, and she felt a stranger to the language these idiots were gabbing away in, as if she understood the odd word only by chance. Was this a sign that she was a Jew, a real, proper Jew, the way the Germans made her angry, how personally she felt affronted?

Her parents joined her, and the rage abated, luckily, and she was now a German no more, now, as she saw the two of them, she was only their flesh and blood, she was their Jewish child, sullen and strange they stood before her, Marsha and Avi, and Margarita was taken aback by her own gratitude at being a Jew, chosen, above all: alive.

Part Five

It was a gigantic machine they entered after two hours' delay, there had already been mix-ups when they were asked about the purpose of their trip, Margarita had gone deathly pale and hadn't uttered a word until she fell asleep on one of the uncomfortable airport benches, her exhaustion was surely rooted in worry over her grandmother, her guilty feelings, too much for a child to bear. Marsha, at a loss, kept going to get more food, first sandwiches, then fruit, then water, and eventually beer, which he was grateful for and which made him feel younger than he was.

Once Margarita woke, he took a walk through the terminal. There were cheap electronics in duty-free, he almost bought himself a shaver, there was a KitchenAid mixer on sale for $200, but he could hardly drag it all the way to Chicago and back to Berlin. Enthusiastically, he told Marsha and Margarita about it, and they laughed in his face, called him a Yiddish mamme, at least he could make them laugh, he even laughed along himself a little bit. He went for more snacks. When they could finally enter, they were so stuffed he couldn't even get down the tiny chocolate that came in his seat pocket. They were

separated, him next to Margarita, Marsha a few rows behind, Marsha
said nothing about it, she'd obviously booked it that way on purpose.
Did he embarrass her somehow? Soon after takeoff, he had to ask the
woman in front of him not to lean her seat back, because of his long
legs; she ignored him, and he had to switch places with Margarita,
just as the drink cart was coming around for the first time; now he
had embarrassed Margarita, too, because his tomato juice spilled on
his pants and he had to get a second pair out of his hand luggage;
the whole time Margarita shielded her face with her hand to avoid
bearing witness to his chaos. He changed in the lavatory and asked
the stewardess for a bag for his tomato-soaked trousers.

Outside, it was dark. As Marsha passed on her way to the bathroom, she stood there a moment, looking like she wished to ask
something before walking on.

He observed her in line, shifting her weight from one leg to the
other, swathed in a thick wool cardigan, glasses on the tip of her nose,
giant headphones over her ears. She was forty-eight now. He hated
to admit it, but there was something gratifying in her being older: he
was glad she hadn't had more kids and most likely never would.

The airplane droned, weariness enveloped him, and he lapsed
into one of those sweet daydreams that had become increasingly
rare in adulthood. At first, he thought of how strange it was that
people separated, then saw each other again after weeks, months,
or years, and just repressed all they knew about each other. He
hadn't seen Marsha in almost thirteen years, but he still remembered how she liked it in wintertime when the neighbors could
watch them while they were having sex, that she liked to be stran-
gled softly, that he had studied as others studied the Talmud how
soft or hard she wanted him to press. He tautened the mesh of his
daydream: him and Marsha lying in Marsha's childhood bedroom
in Chicago, waking in the middle of the night, jet-lagged, when was
that, Hanukkah 2005, he'd just met her parents, he thought about

how he entered her from behind, her labored breathing, not so different from her breathing in sleep; *Yes*, she murmured, and afterward she'd crept down to the kitchen, she was hungry, and she'd brought back food, American food, she almost cried again, from joy, as she wolfed it down at 5:00 a.m., and that was sexy, too, the way she scooped the frosting off the chocolate cake with her finger and sucked it, the way she lathered the bagels with Philadelphia cream cheese and piles of lox, all on a giant tray in a giant bed in a giant house. How she'd sat looking into his eyes and he grasped how homesick she'd been. And back in Jerusalem, and then in Hannover, he had ignored her homesickness, certain it would go away, had never believed her until she stopped waiting.

His dream had passed, the soft arousal had faded now that he was thinking of his errors. He hoped Selma would get better. He imagined the house without her, it didn't work, Marsha being there, Selma not. Over the years, he'd tried to overlook the traces Marsha must have left throughout the house—how she must have sat at the kitchen table just a few days before him while Selma was looking after him. What should he have done, though, deprive Margarita of her grandparents, who welcomed him and loved her madly, even if in their own crazy way? He turned to Marsha, who toasted him with a plastic cup of red wine, and smiled.

* * *

Only once they'd landed did Margarita really grasp that they had flown to Chicago. The Hancock Center came closer, looking stamped in relief; the blue of Lake Michigan was below them. Her heart leaped as she remembered that her grandmother lay somewhere in this web of streets, that she would see her in the next couple of hours, most likely; she was scared, and the airplane seat felt less uncomfortable than it had before.

Marsha was mum in the taxi, she didn't look especially tired, the flight apparently hadn't done her the way it had the rest of her ex-family.

It was afternoon when they reached Hyde Park and hauled their luggage out of the trunk. The house looked just as it had twenty-six days earlier, when she had left it, lilies and roses were blossoming in the front yard. Blackstone Avenue was quiet, a few schoolkids were walking home from school.

Marsha rang the doorbell. "Dad," she shouted into the call box, "it's us."

Grandpa opened the door. A mezuzah hung from the doorframe, as always. Is this really a Jewish house, Margarita wondered. She asked herself what her grandfather thought. He wasn't particularly observant, which made the whole thing more confusing, somehow; he wasn't the one who insisted on the mezuzah in the doorway or separating the cutlery. He was a scholar, that much Margarita knew, he believed in the tradition, but not in God, believed in scrolls, in black on white, in language. She looked at Avi as he shook Dan's hand, touched his arm, nodded with an earnest expression. Margarita had never thought of the contrast between her father with his music and her grandfather with the seven languages he spoke fluently and the five more he could read; together, perhaps, they made one perfect Jew.

They took their bags inside. Marsha hugged her father clumsily, clapped him on his arched back. Margarita was surprised not to see a tiny cloud of dust rise up from him. The house smelled musty, of fragrance-free detergent with its sour stench of vomit. Marsha went to the kitchen and poured a glass of water. Dan scampered behind her. When Margarita joined them, they fell silent. Marsha wiped her face frantically.

"What's wrong?" Margarita asked.

"I'm going to go put away my things," Marsha said. "Visiting hours are over, they won't let me in at the hospital. We can't see Mom till morning."

Dan murmured he was going to fix up the couch in the office for Avi, and clunked in his heavy house shoes up the stairs. She heard the toilet flush, the American rush and gurgle it made, then Avi emerged from the small powder room and joined them in the kitchen.

"Where are you going?" Margarita asked.

"Home," Marsha said.

"I thought Grandpa didn't know."

"I told him I was going to stay with a friend."

"What you tell him?" Avi asked in his terrible English.

"That-I'm-staying-with-a-friend. I didn't want to overwhelm him. You know I live downtown now," Marsha said.

"Downtown Chicago?" Avi asked.

"What else, idiot," Margarita grumbled. The conversation was dragging on and she was getting sick of it.

"So you're not sleeping here," he said.

"Eh, no," Marsha said, "sorry, I should have mentioned that. I'll be back for dinner." Then, turning to her father, who had just come into the kitchen, "Dad, should I go grocery shopping?"

"That's all right, sweetie. There's lasagna and fish in the freezer."

"Sounds disgusting," Marsha said. "Can't we just go to the diner?"

"No," he said. It sounded as if he had no words left over for clarifying or justifying.

It was awful, arriving there without Grandma; the house felt dead, no ritual greetings, no folded towels on the bed, and Dan seemed to have no sense of how he should behave when Selma wasn't there to berate him and boss him around. Margarita, too, would have just as soon gone to Salonica, where they had burgers and fries, but good ones. She remembered a few years ago when she had convinced her father to take her to the McDonald's on Greifswalder Strasse, because she just had to go to the place all the other kids in her primary school class went wild over, he had eaten nothing, she had ordered a veggie burger. She remembered how sad it made her, sitting there with him and realizing it wasn't the food from McDonald's that the other kids liked, it was their families, who had fun when they went to McDonald's, and she sat there with her quirky father, alone on that Sunday that she had to fill with something, and at night she couldn't sleep, that happened a lot in those days, she could fall asleep only on the sofa while Avi sat at the piano in the headphones he had bought so he could play quietly, and all she heard was the dull sound of the keys when he pressed them down, and afterward he'd have to carry her off to bed.

"I can cook, Dan," Avi said.

"It will be quite all right," Margarita's grandfather responded, and that was the end of the discussion.

The front door clicked in the lock. Her father dragged his suitcase behind him up the steps. They looked each other in the eyes. When he closed his own door, Margarita went to the bathroom. She showered until her fingers were wrinkly. She wished she could fall asleep in the shower. Her fingers hung there between her legs, almost automatically. In this house, in which just weeks before to satisfy herself had seemed forbidden, she now felt a precious solitude. She dried off and crept back into her room. For a moment, she pressed her ear against the door of the study, where her father was sleeping on the fold-out sofa. She heard his snoring. She lay on her bed, her fingers wandered to her vulva, wandered back again and again.

A knocking woke her with a start. "Lo," she shouted, "no," jumped up, looked for the towel, wrapped herself in it. She was cold, her wet hair lay heavy on her bare shoulders.

"Aruchat erev," her father said, dinner.

Margarita dressed frantically.

They ate at the big table in the dining room. Fish, as predicted, full of bones, the outside tasting of burnt oil, the inside not entirely defrosted. The lasagna, frozen and reheated, was even worse.

The two men ate with their mouths gaping open, squeezing the bones out between their teeth and slurping lasagna sauce from their spoons, sliding more of it onto the spoon with their fingers to be able to suck more down, and since it was hot, they blew on it as they chewed.

Margarita tried to eat, but she was firmly in the grip of disgust. She looked at Marsha, who likewise seemed sickened, but said nothing. She had to, though, Margarita thought, she was older. She excused herself, went to the bathroom, took a few deep breaths, and returned to the table. Her father was talking about the trip. In the midst of his explanation, a bit of fish flew from his mouth and landed on her plate.

"Aba," she said, "you just spit on my plate."

"Nonsense," her father said, "eat something for once."

Margarita looked at the still-full plate in front of her, the sludgy lasagna and the gob of spit next to it. She pierced fish and lasagna both with her fork and stuffed as much as she could into her mouth. Tears burned her eyes. Avi paid her no mind. Making a show of her inconspicuousness, Marsha plugged one ear with her index finger.

When Margarita tried to swallow, something got stuck. At first, it just tickled, but the more she swallowed, the more it seemed to scrape, and then, all at once, she couldn't breathe. She started panting, gasping for air, choking. Her grandfather rose at a snail's pace and kept asking if she could still breathe. Was he off his rocker?

So this is what choking to death feels like, she thought, and tried to cough it out, tried to breathe in. Marsha pounded her awkwardly on the back and gave her water. Nothing helped, it was getting worse and worse, now no air at all was getting to her. She was limp in her father's arms. Something happened, heaving motions, one or two times maybe, she couldn't tell, and the bone and bits of lasagna shot out onto the floor.

She whimpered. Marsha got a hand towel and wiped up, aghast.

Avi looked self-satisfied, as if there were a game and he'd come out the winner. Margarita murmured a *sorry* and shut herself up in the bathroom, her chest feeling narrow, even now seeming to struggle for air. She dug her fingernails as deep into her thigh as they'd go and dragged them up to her hip.

Then she rested her head on the floor. Tried to wrap her arms around her body, swaying as though in prayer. She heard the clang of dishes. A sign that the main course was over. Someone knocked on the door. She made an almost inaudible sound.

"Can I come in?" Marsha asked.

She turned the key.

Marsha squeezed in and reached back over her head to shut the door. She sat next to Margarita on the floor. "Your grandfather's in a real tizzy."

Margarita dug her fingernails back into the dry skin of her thigh.

"I know it's bad," Marsha said, "the noise. It's disgusting, frankly."

Margarita nodded.

"Here's what we'll do this evening: you'll excuse yourself from the table, and in twenty minutes or so I'll bring you a bagel and shmear. But tomorrow, you've got to get it together. Understand?"

Margarita nodded again.

Marsha reached out her hand, and the two of them stood.

"That food is vile," Marsha said, "but soon you'll grow up and you'll have to actually eat it. You won't be able to duck it anymore. For now, you're still a kid."

"You think?"

"I do."

And after twenty minutes, she really did bring her a bagel and sat on the corner of the bed while Margarita chewed. When she was done, Marsha took her plate and left. Her father didn't come wish her good night. Maybe she actually wasn't a kid anymore.

* * *

He couldn't understand the contempt in Margarita's eyes. He knew she thought he had poor table manners, and her grandparents' were still worse, but at the same time, he didn't know how you were supposed to eat without making noise. A few months ago, they'd fought about it, and he'd made the unpardonable error of calling her a fussy German, *a table Nazi*; sometimes when they were eating, she would hold her ears closed, Marsha had been the same way. But now it had escalated, and Marsha had taken over, he heard how softly she had spoken to Margarita, the doors in that house might as well be made of paper.

Once Marsha left, without saying goodbye—he had just heard the beeping the burglar alarm made when you set it—he had wondered whether he should tell Margarita good night before deciding against it. He didn't know whether he was rewarding or punishing her when he left her alone, but it didn't matter, he was so tired he fell asleep.

His hunger woke him in the darkness, it was as if he hadn't eaten dinner, normal; his body thought it was midday already. Something was rattling nearby, probably Margarita was in the same boat, he wondered what she had piled up onto Selma's fine porcelain.

A message from Marsha glowed on his cell phone screen: *Yo. You up.* It was 4:11, just a few minutes later than he'd guessed. He had an almost eerie sense of time, one of the reasons he'd thought for so long he'd make an excellent pilot, but then, a sense of time and a sense of timing were two different things; and timing, he had that only when he was deep in his music, whereas in everyday life, with other people, he'd often said or done things at the wrong time.

Yo, he wrote back. He had to laugh. *Yo, yes.*

Next door, the TV turned on. *Are you crazy?* he wrote his daughter. The TV turned off, and she wrote, *he's deaf tho.*

Can I call, Marsha wrote.

Before he could even answer, his phone rang. "Yes," he whispered.

"Are you there?" Marsha shouted into the telephone, always this shouting, why did Jews have to shout all the time.

"Mm-hmm," he said.

"I didn't want to talk about it anymore yesterday so Margarita wouldn't hear, but my mother's in bad shape, apparently she's getting worse by the day, she's just babbling nonsense and sleeping all the time. And Dan is just apathetic, he might as well have had dementia for the past thirty years. He drives there every day, though. Today, too, and it would be good if you could pick me up. Avi, I'm so scared."

"When?"

"Around ten."

"Okay, see you then."

Marsha didn't hang up.

"Something else?" he whispered.

"Um. They don't know that I got the job at the university, maybe you could tell him, I mean; I'm surrounded by boxes over here, I really haven't moved in yet, I should have told them. But now, in this situation . . ."

It was always the same with her, he thought. She left without saying goodbye, showed up without notice, and you ended up being even happier about it because she was so unreliable that it was like an act of mercy when she deigned to communicate with you. "Yofi."

"Thank you," she said, "thank you thank you. I'll take you out to lunch when we're at the hospital. I just hope she gets better, otherwise I don't know what . . ."

"Everything will be fine, I'm sure of it, we're here now."

"Okay," she said, and hung up.

Well then: if she was making phone calls that early, she must be living alone. He had the feeling, almost, that there was a part of her life that still belonged to him, but that was probably a lie he told himself, that everyone who had been left told themselves when they took a peek at their former father-in-law's ancient computer in his study, the login data pinned to a corkboard next to it, to see if she who had left had logged in to check her emails and not logged back out, and found with disappointment that only the deadly dull messages of their former father-in-law opened up for them.

He took down one of the many books off the shelf over the fold-out sofa to distract himself. A book about the origins of the Dead Sea Scrolls, which Dan had written decades before, Avi had followed the debates about them—political and scholarly—with interest—but he'd never actually read the book. He knew how much Marsha had suffered from Dan's expectations, but at least there were footsteps to follow in, whereas he, when he thought of his parents, was full of shame, they were burdensome, trying, Marsha had barely managed to conceal her disgust at their apartment, all the food moths in their kitchen, like someone who knew what *habitus* meant, but not what it smelled like. His parents' habitus had smelled of rotting tomatoes and cleaner.

He had rediscovered that expression on Marsha's face a few years later on his daughter's, the woman from the day care had used the term *antagonizing* to describe not just that expression, but the wailing that had followed it; for him, there was something particularly German about this word, just as there was in the word *integration*. He wasn't really sure whether the word had a subject— the child antagonizes—or an object—the child antagonizes some-one, something. This was another concept Marsha had explained to him, intransitivity, verbs typically required a subject and an object, but with *antagonize*, this was just suggested: to antagonize presup-posed an antagonist, to antagonize the antagonist was a good thing, an antagonist was a healthy thing to fear, but antagonism as such was a shortcoming, there was a balance to be found there, a ques-tion of measure. Until that moment, Margarita had antagonized as though her life depended on it, maybe it did for that matter, she had screamed *Abababa, Mommymommymommy*, and the kinder-garten teachers in Hannover had taken it for granted that Mommy was dead, and had treated him like a king, raising a daughter as a single father, and he'd let them, because no one else ever told him he was doing anything right. Everyone was an antagonist, the Germans, the Jews, even the other Israelis in Hannover, however few of them there were; either they weren't Jews or they weren't Israelis or they weren't single fathers, and he antagonized, too, perhaps antagonized himself as he pushed his child around in the cheap stroller and felt stranger and stranger, and the stranger he felt, the more he estranged the others, and this made his relations those of antagonist versus antagonist. Only at the keyboard, only singing or at the end of prayer, did he become less of a stranger to himself.

When he couldn't take the hunger anymore, he slipped down to the kitchen. It was ghostly, this house without Selma, who oversaw everything that happened there, morning, noon, and night, who got up for gymnastics at five in the morning and started making breakfast at seven at the latest.

He found the ingredients for the pancake recipe tacked up behind the gigantic gas stove and started stirring and frying, found melons, and just as everything was ready, found his daughter, who was standing behind him in her nightshirt. He piled her pancakes onto a glass plate. She drowned them in maple syrup and ate greedily as he prepared his own. When they were ready, she stuck her plate in the dishwasher.

"Hey," he said, "won't you at least wait for me?"

She gave him a pleading look, but said nothing.

He sighed. "Yofi. We're going to see your grandmother at ten."

"How is she?"

"Not good, Margarita."

She stared at the floor.

"I'm glad we're here, motek. They thought it was just the morphine and the concussion that had confused her, but they need to give her another MRI, it's like an X-ray, it takes a magnetic image of the brain, they put you inside this tube, it's really loud. They need to see if she's suffered some kind of brain damage."

"Yeah, but if they don't know, maybe that means everything's fine!"

"I'm just trying to prepare you. It's possible she'll be a totally different person from before. Or that she won't even be able to talk to you. Her situation's changing by the day. She may die, motek."

"Then what will we do?"

How she whispered that. It reminded him of those movingly naive questions she used to ask him as a child.

"We'll be sad."

"Is Grandpa going to die, too?"

"No, nudnik. Grandpa's healthy."

"You can die of a broken heart, too, though."

"Where'd you come up with something so corny?"

She didn't say.

"Besides," he said, "look at your poor Aba, he's still kicking."

"Did Marsha break your heart?"

"That's none of your business."

"Okay," Margarita said, and left.

Avi ate his cold pancakes alone, without saying brachah; he'd already skipped his morning prayers since night had transitioned imperceptibly into day. When he'd finished, Margarita's grandfather came downstairs in a shirt and tie. Avi made pancakes for him, too. As he sat down with Dan, he had the feeling he was taking care of his own father, which he'd never actually done, had Itzik looked so wizened, papery skin, hair, nails? Dan smiled at him with his mouth full.

The first time he flew to Chicago, when Margarita was five years old, Selma had begged him to come, the year before she'd gone with Dan to Berlin, but Selma wanted deeply to have her granddaughter in her home, they paid for everything, the flight, all the meals, she had set up an entire bedroom for Margarita, bought children's books, and when she realized Margarita didn't speak English, she bought more of them in Hebrew, which Dan would read to her in his dense, American-accented Hebrew, they did everything as though Marsha were always on her way home, that second summer there was still the hope that she might pop up sometime, but he had never asked her, he was too proud, and if Margarita's mother had come home out of the blue, it would only have confused her, anyway.

When Margarita was eight, Selma had organized a get-together, she went for afternoon tea at the Drake Hotel with Margarita and Marsha, Avi wasn't invited, Marsha had ruled that out. And when Margarita was eleven and he let her fly there for the first time alone, Marsha had even spent a few days with her, but then she had vanished for years, Margarita seemed stoically to have let it slide. That was just how things were, no begging, no whining.

"Those are some excellent pancakes," Dan said. "Not like my Selma would make them, of course, but very good."

Avi looked at him, this haggard old man bent over his pancakes. The thought of him left on his own . . . He asked him cautiously how he was doing.

Dan slurped his coffee, set his cup down with twitchy fingers. He had a soft smile, muted, unlike his wife, who was always beaming and bellowing. "I'm very worried," he said, slow and loud, the way Avi had to speak with him, because his hearing aid didn't work and he struggled to understand Avi's accent. He used to always ask him to speak with him in Ivrit, but what Dan really knew was biblical Hebrew, and the conversations had devolved into nonsense.

"You know, she was really still quite healthy. And it's awful to see her like that, she looks so small, and sometimes when I'm there she just sleeps, sometimes she recognizes me, sometimes she asks after Marsha and Margarita, sometimes she doesn't even know who I am, and she can hardly walk. She's still in a great deal of pain." Jittery, he took another sip, another slurp, of his coffee. "She might have lasting damage. We might have to find someone to move in here, or we might have to move ourselves, I don't know yet. The doctors say it takes time, she'll need to stay at least another week in the ICU, there could be a change any day, yesterday she was just talking a bunch of nonsense, it was terrible."

Old Dan seemed to have spoken to no one in days. And though he knew that now, when it was calm, was the right time, Avi couldn't manage to tell Dan about Marsha's move, he just suggested he play the piano for a bit, until it was time for them to leave. Dan's reaction was enthusiastic, he scraped what was left on his plate into the noisy garbage disposal, which could probably shred a child's hand, and slunk off to the living room.

There he pointed to the small cabinet where they kept Avi's sheet music, which Selma had bought for him years ago because the copies he'd always traveled with were nearly in tatters: Bartók's *Romanian Folk Dances*, Satie's *Gymnopédies*, the Scriabin that had driven him insane for months. He placed Chopin's Second Sonata on the music stand, he had struggled with it bitterly years before, he tussled, stumbled, it was like driving a car, you actually could unlearn both things. Even as he blundered through the beginning, it struck him that the middle section was a renowned funeral march, not for Jews, it was true, but still, not the best thing to play while Dan was lying on the sofa next to the instrument.

In an instant, Avi's head was empty, his fingers hovered over the keys and he was endlessly, endlessly exhausted. Only a single melody came into his mind, a few bars, and he began to play along, imagining his teacher, Shenia, behind him, she was actually supposed to be Margarita's teacher, but Margarita's objections had been so peremptory that he'd finally left her in peace. Shenia was a retiree from Ukraine, she had come to Germany in the early years of her adulthood and was making a bit of extra cash on the side, in her drafty prewar building on Greifswalder Strasse that always smelled of braised meat. She practiced whatever he liked with him, and he didn't have much trouble learning; unlike her other students, music was his profession, and once he'd played whatever she'd shown him three times, they had long conversations, him on his piano stool, her on her Ikea swivel chair, sometimes she showed him curiosities she'd discovered on YouTube, Villa-Lobos's *Bachianas brasileiras*, Arvo Pärt, whose *Für Alina* he was playing now from memory, it was a simple piece, clear, the long pauses it contained almost as important as the tones themselves.

Shenia, Russian Orthodox, idolized Pärt almost as much as Jesus and his mother Mary, whose images hung all over her apartment. It was strange for Avi, this figurative religion, but he did understand her veneration of Pärt; when he played *Spiegel im Spiegel*, she accompanied him on the violin.

The tones now filling the living room seemed like the unearthed words of a language that could at last express the concepts of waiting, traumatic brain injury, induced coma, medically prescribed diet—pale blue the tones were, sterile surgical forceps tugging at the valves of the heart.

On the very last beat, the phone rang. He stood up to get it, Dan sat awkwardly.

"Avi here," he said.

"I just called the hospital," Marsha shouted into the receiver, "we can see her now. Get the others and come over, I'll send you the address. I need to see her."

He called for Margarita. Then he turned to Dan, who was standing next to him with a quizzical expression. He needed to get it over with, quick and painless, but nothing in English felt quick and painless for him, especially not when he was muddling through his jet lag, like sleepwalking but in language—speechwalking. "Dan," he said, "we can go see Selma now."

He saw Margarita leaning down over the banister into the foyer. "Are we going?" she asked in Hebrew.

Dan looked up a long time, then down at his leather shoes, which Avi was tying methodically. Margarita tramped down the stairs.

"Motek, turn off the TV," Avi said.

She obeyed. He had thirty seconds.

"Dan, I have news about Marsha," he said, translating directly from Hebrew, the way he'd planned it. "It is actually some nice news. She's been appointed professor," this last word he pronounced with his rough, rolled *r*, he had never managed the soft American *r*, "at Northwestern, she lives downtown."

Now Margarita was standing there again.

Dan looked confused. Avi was worried he hadn't grasped what he'd just said, but Dan raised an index finger, as though he wanted to chastise Avi, and yelled, "Northwestern! In Chicago, it is the U of C or nothing, she should know that. It's an empty discipline, all that humbug of hers, that's not real science, that's just messing around, nowadays nobody dares to really do anything, nobody discovers anything anymore!" Now he pointed directly at Margarita, "You, Rita, will do something better with your life!"

Margarita nodded. She looked at Avi, who raised his eyebrows. Was there a tiny grin in the corner of her mouth?

Dan shook his head. "She had so much potential," he said. "But she always had to be special, different. Obstinate as a mule!"

Avi wanted to protest, but he didn't know how. So he simply said, "Anyway, she doesn't live far from here now," and Dan responded, "Great. Now she can help me see Selma off into her grave. If the *principessa* finds the time."

Margarita laughed almost scornfully. "She calls *me* that all the time," she said to Avi in Hebrew. He would happily have heard more about it, but he was overwhelmed.

"We're picking her up at her new apartment, Dan, and then we'll go to the hospital afterward."

"Why doesn't she take a taxi? Does she not make enough to take a taxi so she can go see her dying mother?"

Helpless Dan had turned into a wrathful patriarch. Margarita was visibly frightened, she was already out the door.

Avi called Marsha. "He wants you to take a taxi," he said, marching off to the living room to keep an eye on his daughter through the windows opening onto the front yard.

"Why? It's early, it's just twenty minutes away."

"How about if we take you back afterward?"

"Fine," Marsha said, "in thirty minutes at the hospital."

The University of Chicago hospital was a gigantic complex, the university logo glowed all over in Bordeaux red. Dan headed straight for one of the blocks. Elul's light flooded the campus.

Unlike in Germany, no one was smoking in front of the building, in Germany the smoke would have permeated the vestibule, in Hannover it had seeped all the way into the operating room where Margarita came into the world. Here, though, on this clean campus where everything oozed money, no one was smoking. The lungs weren't what got you here, it was the heart, Avi thought, because people here all ate giant steak sandwiches day after day. He had always been fascinated by this country, its debased capitalism that destroyed the social system, the horrible racism, he knew he'd gotten that from his parents, who had detested America their whole lives long, he also knew many of his judgments were nonsense, he had loved an American; however much it pained him to admit it, he had a somewhat American daughter, and what country wasn't full of racism?

The woman in reception already knew Dan. They waited, the old man leaning against the counter, until Marsha appeared, she had on high heels, ran click-clacking in the morning silence through the vestibule and kissed Margarita on the head. The gesture surprised him, so natural, free of spite and theatrics. Strange troupe that they were, they walked, almost ran, to the elevator, nearly dragging Dan behind them, his own steps were mincing and followed in quick succession. Gray steps that squeaked on the gray plastic flooring.

* * *

As soon as the elevator doors had closed, Margarita felt a novel kind of vertigo, not the tired, humming kind, but a rebellion of the circulatory system. She had never been to a hospital before as a visitor, just as a patient in the emergency room with a laceration on the forehead, normally it was the other kids at school with bumps and bruises, she was so careful, nothing ever happened to her. She knew her father told a story about her having whooping cough when she was three, but she didn't remember, and one time a spider had bitten her in her grandparents' yard here in Chicago, but a doctor they were friends with had taken care of her. The vertigo induced a slight panic when she remembered she had wanted to become a doctor.

Marsha was in such a hurry that she nearly fell down when she emerged from the elevator. The scent in the hallway was caustic, and there was beeping and buzzing all round.

Grandma lay alone in room 693, Margarita was sure she'd gotten a single room not so no one would disturb her, but so that she would disturb no one else with her loud food-smacking or her louder voice. That voice, her father said, had come from the fact that her grandmother had taught elementary school for decades, but for Margarita, that only made it worse, Mrs. Markovitz sounded like one of those awful teachers who always yelled at their students. But when they entered the room, no one cackled, no one moaned. Her grandmother was no larger than a child in that bed. A child with a cervical collar and very little hair on her head, attached to countless machines.

Marsha stayed standing in the doorway and whimpered. Margarita walked farther in. It was horrible to see Selma that way, but in some way, it wasn't surprising. In Margarita's eyes, her grandmother's body had always been precarious, sexless; she had never seen her naked, and now, as she remembered this, she realized she'd always assumed her grandmother had the round, smooth genitals of a Barbie doll.

She was sleeping when they barged into the room. Marsha crouched down next to the bed and took her mother's hand. Her high heels made it look like she was peeing in the bushes. "Hey, Mom," she said, "can you hear me?"

The blanket over Grandma rose and fell.

"She's asleep, Marsh," Grandpa said.

Margarita looked searchingly into her grandmother's face, blue veins under white skin, a Jewish body, Margarita thought, battered somehow, drained; she thought of what she'd learned in school about the *New Jew*, the new ideal of the Jews in Palestine, where the bricks of the buildings had been laid by men in suits who wished no longer to be merchants and weaklings, but strong, impetuous musclemen, and she asked herself then was this even a Jewish body at all—looked at the pinkish eyelids, the cheekbones under the skin, overwhelmed by a sudden horrible fear that her secret would be stowed away in that body forever and she would not have another chance to ask her grandmother about it. That Marsha would one day take it with her into a hospital like this one, and leave her alone with it for good. As though she had never even uttered it. Margarita knew better: there were things a person shouldn't talk about, and Selma and Marsha had broken this rule, but Margarita wouldn't make the same mistake, she wouldn't torment anyone like that.

"Rita, talk to her a little," Marsha said.

"What should I say?"

"Just think of something." Marsha laid her head down on the hand of her grandmother, who was lying in the bed like a dead fish.

"Hi," Margarita said, and took a deep breath. "I'm sorry you're doing so bad. I hope you wake up soon and everything's okay. I'd be really happy if we could bake chocolate cake together again."

A nurse came in. Margarita felt watched, all those people around the bed, and she had the chance to do something better, something more appropriate, but how—she didn't know.

"Grandma?" she asked in one last attempt, but the nurse said they should leave her alone, she only rarely woke, and even then not entirely, "It's the morphine and the concussion." But her grandmother's eyes did flicker, roll around slightly, you could see she was trying to open them; and for a moment, she managed it, she clutched her head, her face brightened, she pointed to Avi and Marsha, "You two, here together," mumbled, gripped Marsha's hand, looked at Margarita, and shouted, "What's up, guys?"

Margarita looked at Marsha. The two of them couldn't help but smirk. That was it, a flash of her real personality, her Grandma-ness. Like a life preserver thrown to the people gathered around her bed.

"Hush, hush," the nurse said, and addressed them: "The doctor will be with you in twenty minutes. Mr. Markovitz, would you like a sip of water?"

Selma looked back and forth, trying to understand what was happening. Margarita wanted to tell her something, but couldn't think of anything. Then her grandmother closed her eyes. When Margarita stood, everything started to spin. She held her father tight, he carefully took her in his arms. He smelled of their Berlin apartment, of olive oil soap and parsley.

They stood there, her grandfather rubbed his mustache, the noise made Margarita listless but she knew she couldn't run away, Marsha upbraided her father, at the very least he could have brought his wife her own pillow from home, or a shawl; it was true, Margarita could feel the chill on her bare arms, in one of the hospital series she liked to watch, she'd learned they kept it cold in hospitals because germs liked it warm, her grandmother had to be freezing.

A doctor entered, nodded to all of them, greeted her grandfather with a *Hello, Dan*, they seemed to know each other. He told them Selma had been moved from the ICU to the step-down unit, because she could talk a little bit and recognize people, but she was still sleeping most of the time and showing deficits. "And she threw up again this morning. That's why we're going ahead and giving her the MRI with anesthesia, otherwise she might wake up and get scared."

Margarita noticed her grandfather's fingers were trembling. She walked over to him and took his hand. To her surprise, it felt nice to hold it, familiar.

Marsha asked whether it was normal to spend so long in the ICU after a concussion. She said something about the Wernicke's area, and the doctor asked her, surprised, what she did for a living. She told him she was a linguistics professor.

"Wow," Dr. Johnston said. "Like father, like daughter!"

Dan sat in his chair unmoved, just holding Margarita's hand. Marsha looked as though her face might crumble to the floor, and Avi as though he'd like to keep it from doing so, but didn't know how.

Her grandmother woke again, but this time looked around baffled, breathed through her mouth, seemed not to be able to focus on the room. Dr. Johnston stood near the bed. "Nice view you've got here, Mrs. Markovitz, huh?" Grandma looked out the window by her bed. The Gothic tower of the Institute for the Study of Ancient Cultures rose high between low modern buildings. Margarita knew this tower well, her grandfather's office was there, she used to go often. It was a riddle to Margarita, why anyone would voluntarily listen to his lectures, which dragged on at a snail's pace, but he seemed to still be popular, before the Covid years he would ride his bike to the Institute every day, even on his eightieth birthday on August 13; he had crowed on about that for some time, not long after Margarita left for Israel.

"Yuh," Selma said, looking outside.

They all stood in a circle around her bed.

"I'm not dead yet, people," she shouted. That croaking voice was still there. It was true, she wasn't dead yet.

"I love you, Mom," Marsha said. Margarita nodded.

"Yuh," Selma said again. "I'm tired."

Dr. Johnston left, telling Dan, "See you tomorrow." Before Dan could answer, Marsha jumped in. "Thank you, Dr. Johnston," she said, "see you tomorrow."

Dr. Johnston shook Dan's hand, but not Marsha's. Was that sexism, or was Marsha just annoying? Margarita watched as her parents looked at each other. Marsha rolled her eyes, Avi grinned. He appeared to feel comfortable here, in this role. Something about that got to Margarita. She had always been enough for him, at least he'd said so before, and she hadn't really missed Marsha, either, showing up every few years with gifts in her handbag and sitting with her in her grandparents' backyard staring at her like a foreign object.

The mugginess had settled over the streets as they walked out of the hospital. As soon as they were outside, the world inside seemed unreal to Margarita, and the image of her grandmother being slipped into a noisy cylinder was suddenly distant. She almost wanted to go back in, take a look around, help out. Because out here, she was powerless.

Marsha sat in the driver's seat in her parents' car. "Who's hungry?" she asked, driving down Lake Shore Drive.

"Me," Margarita said.

"What a surprise," her mother responded.

Avi snorted. Contemptuously, Margarita thought at first, but it was laughter. She felt herself turning red. Did she eat too much? A bitter taste spread across her tongue. She looked down at the tight top she was wearing, saw her belly rolls underneath. Her throat tightened as when she had to cry. Not now. Not over something so silly.

264 DANA VOWINCKEL

Marsha drove to a restaurant. Margarita ordered a salad with bits of deep-fried avocado. She ate two of them and left the rest. Her father pushed her to eat. She said she wasn't hungry anymore.

Dan said they should take a stroll. They walked to the lake, Marsha sprayed her face with a small bottle of French thermal water. Margarita nudged her and got sprayed as well. Avi's expression was a little strange, as though he were jealous. Actually it was nice, being together like that, and knowing this got to Margarita, but with her grandmother, an outing like this wouldn't have been possible, it was too far, too hot, she would have wanted to take the car or go shopping instead, they walked to the Navy Pier, bought ice cream at Ben & Jerry's, Margarita wanted a sorbet, Marsha's comment had stuck with her, but at the last second she opted for mint chocolate chip. They decided to ride the Ferris wheel, Avi looked at Marsha with surprise, "Aren't you afraid of heights," he asked her, she waved him off, "I got over it," they sat together in one of the gondolas rising over the deep blue lake, Margarita, Avi, and Dan on one side and Marsha on the other; they took a photo.

Avi gnawed at his ice cream, it didn't even bother her, she just looked outside, at the highest point of the Ferris wheel you could see everything, the Willis Tower and the red rails of the L, the grid of the city Margarita loved so much, the pools on the roofs of the skyscrapers, America.

* * *

Marsha had gotten into the gondola as if she had something to prove to him. As if it were a triumph for her not to be the same person as thirteen years ago, not to be afraid, because in front of Margarita she could be another person, a mother without a fear of heights. Maybe she thought a mother shouldn't be afraid.

After they were done with the Ferris wheel, Dan looked as if he needed to lie down. Avi could still recognize it in children and old people, the midday nap expression, some skills you never lost. He said they should drive back to Hyde Park. No phone had yet rung to communicate the MRI results.

"I'm getting off at my place," Marsha said when they got into the car. After only a few minutes on the road, they stopped in front of a high-rise, smaller than all the others around it and yet likely taller than the tallest high-rise in Berlin. Marsha tossed Avi the car keys.

"Drive safe," she said, "and take care of my daughter."

It was supposed to be a joke, but he didn't think it was funny. "*You're* the one who lost her," he said.

Margarita rolled her eyes.

"You don't want to show us your place right quick? I'm sure Margarita would like to see it, too."

Marsha sighed. She was no more confident now than she was thirteen years ago. "It's a total mess, and I don't know where we can park the car."

Avi pointed to the sign for the building's garage. Marsha looked unnerved. She was definitely hiding something from him. If she wanted to keep spending time with his daughter, she shouldn't have any secrets, though—right? He got out and opened the passenger-side door for Dan.

"Avi," Marsha said, "don't do this."

He didn't know what he was doing, though; he was just curious, and she owed him something, he felt, if not for the last thirteen years, then for the simple fact that she'd forced him to tell Dan about her move, what was he supposed to do, twist her arm, hadn't he already done that enough, what was he even doing here if not? "Maybe your father would like to see your new apartment," he said, one last attempt.

"I want to go home," Dan said.

"Fine," Avi said, and sat behind the wheel.

Marsha just waved. The doorman held the door open for her. The smile she gave him was friendlier than any she'd given Avi those last six days. That, too, was so American, that relentless friendliness, so fake, he thought, then readjusted the seat.

He missed his piano, the thick carpet underneath, the ring of it streaming out into the courtyard like the scent of içli köfte from the apartment of their Turkish neighbors two floors up. Years ago, he had heard Martha Argerich in the philharmonic, had excitedly bought two tickets and had found no one to accompany him, he'd gone anyway, alone, and it had been worth it. Marsha would have gone with him, he knew, but Argerich would have had to play in Carnegie Hall or here in the Chicago Symphony Orchestra. Margarita complained about his driving, he told her to shut her trap.

* * *

Of course, Dr. Johnston had called the landline, of course the hospital had no one's cell number, of course everyone around her was utterly, completely useless. And now it was late afternoon and they'd missed two calls from the doctor. Margarita would probably have to be the one to organize her grandmother's funeral if she died of a subdural hematoma.

Subdural hematoma. That was what Dr. Johnston had said on the phone, her grandfather had needed to turn up the volume to understand it, they were asked not to come back until the day after tomorrow, the hematoma would need to be drained and then tomorrow they would operate.

"Do you know what a hematoma is?" Avi asked in Ivrit. "It's like a bruise."

Margarita said of course she knew what a hematoma was. But actually she didn't. A bruise. That didn't sound so bad.

Marsha wouldn't pick up the phone.

They sat a long time at the kitchen table. Margarita had a stale taste in her mouth, a furry tongue, her throat had hurt since they'd arrived in Chicago. Now she could hardly ignore it. Dan turned on the television, CNN crowed through the narrow room, another presidential election was coming, the *Obama 2008* sticker on her grandparents' car looked like something from another era, that had been just a year before she was born, the car was old now, too, every year they meant to replace it, Margarita had even gone to a car lot with them once, but then her grandmother had said they'd die soon enough anyway, what was the point in a new car. Don't you dare die now without buying that new car, Margarita thought.

Marsha called back. Her voice was shrill through the speaker; alarmed, Avi stood, Margarita heard him running up the stairs, the door closing. She got up, too, wandered around, Marsha was crying in the background, Grandpa trying to calm her down, all over were tchotchkes, vases from various trips, little pictures of Marsha in frames with scrolls and flourishes, on one wall photos of Margarita: as a baby, eyes still somewhere between brown and blue, at her school commencement, at her bat mitzvah. For a year, she had practiced the haftarah with her father, which verse you said when you were called on, and at the end they had written a homily together, his part in Hebrew, she had translated it; that summer in Chicago, her grandmother had bought her a dress even though the bat mitzvah was in winter, and by the time winter hit, it was a little too tight in the breasts, and throughout the celebration all she could think about was her breasts except when she was standing there hidden under the tallit being pelted with candy, she had thought to herself that she was supposedly a woman now, but she didn't believe it, the three crinkly pubic hairs certainly didn't make her one, and her father had restrained himself, he didn't want to overshadow anyone, least of all give the impression he thought he could sing better than the female cantor, whose singing was higher than his and just plain different, as if she were singing to a different God, Margarita thought at the time, as if she were singing to a goddess.

The door rang and pulled Margarita abruptly from her thoughts. Her mother. Hadn't she just been there crying on the phone?

"I took a cab," Margarita heard her say, then loud sobbing.

Benumbed, Margarita stood before the photos in the living room. She asked herself what she would feel like if Marsha died, and felt nothing. The thought that something could happen to her father shook her. It was just three days to Rosh Hashanah. Would Grandma make it to the New Year? She went up to her room and googled *Subdural hematoma.*

Fifty percent mortality. The majority of patients who survive a brain hemorrhage suffer long-term damage.

Was it better to be responsible for her grandmother's death or for her grandmother to become a vegetable, soft like the broccoli from the steamer in their kitchen?

She took the book Marsha had given her from her suitcase, laid it on her nightstand next to the volume of poems her grandparents had placed there at the beginning of summer. Then she opened it to distract herself.

A knock at the door: Marsha, a glass of red wine in each hand. Margarita was surprised, in America you couldn't drink till you were twenty-one. Her mother left the glasses on the dresser by the door and leaned against the doorframe. She looked exhausted, but stubbornly beautiful nonetheless, Margarita envied that, the fine features of her face.

"She's in an induced coma, they're draining the fluid. Tomorrow they'll operate. They're drilling a hole in her skull," Marsha said, almost choking on the words.

Margarita nodded. Her stomach growled loudly, her jet lag made her permanently hungry. Marsha either didn't notice or ignored it. She spoke no more, took the glasses, closed the door behind her.

Margarita turned off the lights. She was still in her street clothes, the hunger and tension kept her awake, and her eyes fluttered so much she decided to stop trying to close them.

Muffled voices next door. Avi trying to convince Marsha of something, but she couldn't make out the words. *You can't blame her*, maybe, but that was probably wishful thinking, probably the *t* hadn't been there, the plosive, as Marsha had taught her, and if I was a sound, I'd be a plosive, Margarita thought, but not one that marked a difference, a superfluous plosive that chopped everything to bits—words, the world, others, herself.

* * *

"You can't blame her," Avi said softly. "I know you'd like to. But she's fifteen, and I'm sorry, Marsha, but you were never really there, and she obviously wasn't comfortable."

"Don't worry, I know I'm a bad mother, that's why I left you."

"You know that's bullshit."

"You said it yourself, Avi, once was enough."

"We never should have seen each other again, huh? In the end, it was fine the way it was."

"You have no idea whether it was good for me. I didn't leave because I thought I'd be happy. I left because I was in despair in Germany, and because of you. You drove me nuts."

"I thought you wanted us to come after you. I thought I *took her away* from you."

Marsha kneaded her hands. "Not now, Avi."

She was right, not now. But also not ever. "How long will the operation tomorrow take?" he asked.

"It depends," she said. "I'm so hungry, I'm dizzy. In a series, when something like this happens, everything stops, no one has to eat. But I'm starving."

"Okay," he said. Finally, something he could do. "Salonica must be open?"

She nodded. "Is Margarita still asleep? How can she sleep now?"

"Like I said: she's fifteen."

"Not for much longer," Marsha said, "are you going to throw her a sweet sixteen party here in the garden?"

Her birthday was in a little more than two weeks, five days after Yom Kippur, September 29. "Marsha," he said as dryly as possible, "we'll be back home by then."

"Not now, Avi," she said again, and left the room.

He looked at the wall over the desk where the certificates hung, honorary doctorates, a framed letter, the whole house was full of things in frames, even a Picasso sketch, next to it a drawing in wax crayon of Selma with the letters *ATIRAGRAM* in carefully drawn block letters. In the living room, over the fireplace, stood a ketubah from the sixteenth century and a photo of Selma, Dan, and Marsha, a mortarboard was on Marsha's head. She looked proud then. And now she seemed to be the opposite of proud, or proud only in the sense of being invulnerable to criticism, not proud of what she had built, not like him, he was proud of his job, his child, his life, however much it grated on him. No, Marsha seemed unhappy, not just about her mother, but unhappy in general, did she regret something, leaving or ever having been there in the first place?

He remembered fighting, and afterward he'd always told her it was normal, healthy even, to fight, but she was right, yelling like that was awful, they were ugly and mean to each other, that was human, though, wasn't it, when a person was so worn out? Perhaps that had been their undoing, that Margarita hadn't woken up enough, no matter how loudly they argued.

Marsha had taken their fights harder than he, she was always a bit faster, always more ornery, but also more blithe, but in these battles she would end up begging him at some point to tell her he loved her, begging for it to be over, her body would hunger for consolation, she'd fetch Margarita from the bed and force Avi to sleep with them, not on the living room couch, however much he needed a refuge, and he had lain there awake, listening to Margarita's snoring and the hum of Marsha's shallow breathing getting deeper.

You only ever understood you had power when you lost it. Most people, lovers, dictators, lost their power slowly. But Avi's was taken away in an instant, he hadn't heard the shouts and threats, he was too convinced that he was the weaker one. Marsha had pulled the power out from under his feet and left, and from then on, he really was the weaker one, because Margarita was always put above him; he would do anything for her.

He crept to Margarita's room, the door was ajar, the light was off. Was she asleep already? He turned on the lamp. Margarita had pulled the sheet up under her chin. "Motek," he said. She didn't react. He sat on the corner of the bed. A little hand emerged from under the sheet. Margarita was big, but she still had a child's hands. He took her hand in his. He sat that way awhile and prayed—for the first time in days, it was an actual prayer and not just a sequence of syllables— the blessing of the children, even if she was bat mitzvah; prayed for the health of her grandmother; prayed that she would forgive him.

He thought about this year, as every year, Elul had been too hectic to make Cheshbon HaNefesh, an inventory of the last year, his deeds good, bad, and indifferent. He had always striven for a clear vantage, a lens through which life could be seen in sharp relief, but the only thing that was really clear, unmistakable, was the notes when he sang and forgot, on Yom Kippur; this earnestly intended Avinu Malkeinu made everything else seem as if it hadn't happened, had only been dreamed, a joke, and then it was over, a new year was beginning, and nothing was any clearer than before.

He remembered the good advice one of the rabbis-in-training from the college had given him, one of the only ones he'd really liked, because he wasn't as arrogant as the others, who thought they were little gods because they would be rabbis in Germany, whereas in Israel and

America this wouldn't have been enough to get their names in print
every other week. This rabbi had become his friend, they'd often had
a beer together after lessons, over the years Benny had learned to ask
the right questions and Avi had learned to open up. Benny had told
him you made Cheshbon HaNefesh not to apologize, not to atone, but
to reconcile, and that meant with yourself, too.

"Motek," he said, "are you not dying of hunger?"

Margarita pulled down the covers. Her eyes were glassy, her
cheeks beet red. He laid a hand on her forehead. She was only so
hot because she'd been covered up for so long, surely.

"Yeah, hungry," she said.

It was still humid out when the three of them walked down
Blackstone Avenue. Dan was already in his blue pajamas watching
TV. Margarita was between them, only a few sprinklers were running, even here people had started to realize how wasteful it was to
water your lawn every day, this was Hyde Park, though, bourgeois,
no American flags in the yard, just university banners. It smelled
of flowers and warm asphalt, and he briefly envied the people who
lived here, the families playing board games at their antique dinner
tables, ignorant of Israel's gruffness or Germany's cold.

Margarita ordered soup. He looked at her perplexed, no fries,
just soup, her cheeks glowed red again. She said she was cold. The
restaurant was air-conditioned, but not enough to make a person
freeze.

Marsha ignored Margarita. She wanted to talk about her mother.
About her fears. She said she had reached the doctor again, her
mother was back in the ICU. She was going to give up the fellowship in Jerusalem, she'd have to pay back the money, but she
had her place in Chicago already, she'd make it through the three
months without income before her professorship started.

He asked her about Rosh Hashanah. Marsha's mouth opened as
she looked at him, Margarita curled up in the booth.

"Seriously?" Marsha asked. "*That's* what you're thinking about right now?"

"There's not much we can do," Avi said, "and it's Rosh Hashanah, and I have to go to the synagogue, your father probably, too, he can just tell them I'm coming along, right?"

"You *have to*? Who says? God?"

"Marsha. It's Rosh Hashanah. I should actually be in Berlin leading prayers, you know that. I am going to synagogue."

"You don't have to explain everything to me. If you tell me one more time that it's Rosh Hashanah, I'm going to lose it. Go back to Berlin, then!"

Margarita reared up, as though she'd awakened from a deep sleep. "Figure your shit out. I'm going home," she mumbled, stood, grabbed her cell phone from the table, and left before he could say anything.

He threw a couple of bills onto the table and tried to stand up and follow her, but Marsha stopped him.

"She's old enough," she said, "let her go."

"Don't tell me what to do," he said. Stayed sitting there. "For years I've led the High Holy Days myself, and this time, for you two, I bowed out, even though I know half the people only go because I'm there."

"You didn't have to come."

"It's what Margarita wanted. She ran away, Marsha, if it wasn't for me, she'd have flown back to Berlin."

"Maybe that's what she should have done."

"She's trying so hard, can't you tell? And I feel like she's getting sick, I want to see how she's doing, I think she's got a fever."

"Okay, super-dad. Tzaddik."

He sucked in a breath, ready to answer, but then he remembered Marsha's situation, her worries about her mother, and his conscience bothered him.

They walked out into the moist air. Far off, he heard sirens. For a moment, he wasn't sure whether they were howling in his mind or a few streets away. Every fifty feet stood a campus emergency phone that immediately dialed the University of Chicago police. They remembered Margarita had walked home and automatically sped up. Everything was dark by the time they stepped into the cool house.

"I'm going to sleep on the couch in the basement," Marsha said, "in case the hospital calls. My father can't hear the phone with his hearing aids out." She seemed almost angry that Dan slept without them. Or that he was sleeping at all.

He wondered how Marsha had found out that his parents had died. And why she'd never even sent an email. Had he forgotten to check his spam folder?

Margarita turned away when he entered her room. "Sorry," she whispered, and he asked, "Do you need anything, motek, is there something you're missing?" All she could murmur was "Sorry, I didn't mean to get sick."

"Self-pity is a sickness, too, nudnik. What is it?"

She pointed to her throat. "It hurts."

"Can you sit up so I can have a look?"

"I want to go to sleep."

"Just a second."

She sat up. It smelled of teenager sweat, but she swore again that she was cold. He turned down the air. Her mouth looked like it had been smeared with lotion, her tongue, her tonsils, even the inside of her lips.

"Shit," he said. He'd never seen anything like that, and he'd seen everything, hand, foot, and mouth disease or whatever that nasty childhood illness was called, thrush, scarlet fever, strep throat. "Motek, we need to go to the doctor."

"Not now," she said. "Leave me alone."

He got her water, painkillers, another blanket. Back on his uncomfortable couch, he googled until he was tired. Something had to be inflamed. He wondered if he could get infected, the unending worry over his vocal cords, afraid of every cold Margarita brought home from school. If he were in Berlin, he'd be cleaning and shopping like a madman, making a meal for Rosh Hashanah, doing voice exercises, listening to recordings of all his favorite cantors, from Nachama to Sirota. Maybe he should cut a CD soon, a bit of eternity couldn't hurt, but first, he needed to take care of Margarita. She had always reacted to fears and disturbances by getting sick. All the worse now, when it was about her grandmother, whom she loved so much, as he knew. If you knew her, you couldn't help but love her, loudmouthed Selma, who herself loved like no other.

* * *

Inflamed tonsils, thrush, the doctor said, Margarita had kept getting worse and for the second night in a row had a bad fever, and finally they dragged her off to the hospital and convinced someone to get a doctor to look at her throat and prescribe an antibiotic.

Super. So she had a vagina fungus in her mouth, her grandmother was half dead because a casserole dish had fallen on her head, and it was her fault, and her mother was freaking out because she'd used Margarita's spoon to scoop up the rest of her broth and was worried that she, too, had caught the mouth-vagina fungus, and Margarita's breath under the mask was unbearable, and every time she had to swallow she wanted to cry out in pain.

But the operation had gone well, the doctor said, they'd wake her grandmother in the coming days, up until then she'd be in an induced coma. Margarita hoped she'd revive soon, then she could finally ask her whether she should tell her father the story about the adoption and get back home before she missed more school.

Dr. Johnston told them what had happened: a concussion wasn't usually life-threatening, but her grandmother had diabetes, Margarita knew this, that's why she always took her own crispbread to restaurants in her handbag and had pancakes made with whole wheat flour, and diabetes caused *vascular damage*. The first MRI hadn't shown anything conclusive, only on the second one had the hematoma been visible. They still couldn't say whether it was acute or chronic. Chronic was better, acute ones were usually fatal. Chronic ones were easily treated, the blood would just trickle out slowly, and since the casserole incident had happened a week ago, her chances were good.

Avi told Margarita in Hebrew that chronic didn't necessarily mean *forever*. He seemed to have just learned that himself.

Dr. Johnston said, "The dura mater, the outermost meninges," Margarita knew what meninges were, she'd gotten an A+ when she'd had to label the brain in her biology class, the cerebral membrane "and the arachnoidea," that was the spider skin, the middle membrane that looked like a web, not to be confused with arachnophobia, the fear of spiders, which Margarita had had since she was bitten in the garden, "both layers of the meninges are full of blood vessels. And when something tears through one or both of these layers, say, when something strikes you on the head, blood can leach into the brain. But the operation went well, the effusion was removed, with the diabetes, though, there's always the risk of more blood getting in. We'll know how bad the damage is when she wakes up."

Dan shouted: "Can't we get a second opinion? Isn't there anyone more competent here? This is my wife, I'm a professor at the university!" He threw his arms in the air. Marsha rubbed his shoulders. It was like a movie, except in the movies no one ever got a yeast infection in their mouth.

Dr. Johnston said, "As you know, Miss Markovitz, her language abilities may be affected. Her motor skills and memory, too."

"Could she die?" Marsha asked.

"Potentially," Dr. Johnston said, sending them home, and in the afternoon, Margarita called Anna, who again seemed more distant than usual. The nostalgia she'd felt all summer was now like a divine punishment, the fungus in her mouth an outgrowth of the sorrow in the pit of her stomach. Or maybe the mold on her heart had spread to her throat?

She lay back in bed and slept. She could feel her fever, dreamed she was falling further and further, but before she hit the ground, she awoke, then she dreamed she was counting, that she had to count to a hundred thousand, she didn't make it far, kept having to start over.

When she woke again, Marsha was sitting on the other side of the bed, just sitting there, Margarita had no idea how long she'd been there. She whispered, "Creepy."

Marsha smiled her cool smile. "Hi."

"Sorry. I didn't want to get sick."

"Are you sure?"

Margarita felt heavy again, heavy and tired. She closed her eyes.

"It was a joke, Rita."

"I deserved it."

"What, the joke?"

"No, getting sick."

"No, you didn't, Rita."

"What if Grandma dies?"

"She didn't die. She seems to have pulled through okay."

"We don't know that yet."

"But we can hope."

Margarita felt her drowsiness tugging at her. Luring her.

"You want some ice cream? Soup?"

"Why are you here?"

"To look after you."

"Where's Aba?" Margarita opened her eyes.

"He's here. Why?"

She didn't know what she should say. Because he should be taking care of her. Because only he could. Because she didn't deserve this, Marsha taking care of her, Aba having something better to do. "This must be my punishment," Margarita said.

"Me taking care of you?"

"The tonsillitis."

"Margarita, stop with the nonsense."

A tear flowed down Margarita's cheek. Her mouth was raw, swallowing was agony.

"There is no such thing as poetic justice," Marsha said, "and, my darling, that is the cruelest and the kindest thing about our lives." Then she left.

Margarita kept dreaming, she dreamed of flying mushrooms multiplying within her, she dreamed of honey flowing into her gullet, the honey tasted stale, it tasted of Nico's sperm. Someone in her dream said kaddish, the kaddish was now of black milk, *Black milk of morning we drink you at night*, she clutched her blond hair, she was Margarete, was Shulamith, and again it was night, Margarita dreamed of ice cream, cold succinct happiness, severed limbs, arms, the steel toe of a boot, a bone, hers, it was revealed in an examination of the body, Margarita was a skeleton, and held a rib in her skeleton hands and was meant to shape from it a mother. Something smoked, was it the chimneys, someone made her a bagel, it smelled of toasted sesame, Margarita sat up, panted, was roasting, pulled her hair into a ponytail and whimpered for Aba until he came, he brought water, brought aspirin, brought a clean sheet, brought himself, Margarita closed her eyes, asked herself was he the rib, the night ceased to swallow her, it cradled her softly, a light was on, it stayed on, it made her dreams brighter.

Part Six

When they unpacked the rattles, he couldn't stop himself from laughing. The prayer room reminded him of a garage, the rabbi was like a parody of a rabbi, and there was no chazzan, the rabbi led the prayers himself with the backing of a choir, with guitar playing and rattles, while those present spoke in low tones. The entire service was streamed on YouTube, and the rabbi prayed more for the camera than for the people sitting across from him.

Avi watched the show, increasingly baffled. He had always thought it was as normal to be Jewish in America as it was in Israel, but apparently it was even more normal, so normal it was banal and assimilated. And that was one thing you couldn't reproach the Israelis for: They weren't assimilated. Because there was nothing there you had to assimilate to.

He only opened his mouth to say *amen*. Irritated that the speaker skipped over the passages meant to be said aloud when Rosh Hashanah fell on Shabbat, he rushed through them, feeling harried. And yet, as though the year 5783 were surging once again, on this second to last day of Elul, as if his spine were straightening and a new chamber of his lungs opening up, he breathed in deeply, deeper and deeper, and when he expelled the air, resonant sounds escaped him.

It had been a long time since he was a guest on any of the High Holy Days, it was hard not to sing along, not to outdo the rebbe in Chicago, who stumbled through the morning prayer like a yodeler. He knew if he sang, everyone would turn around to look at him, and so he hid himself under his tallit, wore it like a hood over his head, and prayed as he could, trying not to think about home.

He didn't even stay for the apples and honey, walked down Hyde Park Boulevard to Blackstone Avenue, took off his kippa from habit, he'd been wearing it since before he went to the synagogue.

Nothing about today felt holy, nothing pure or clear, and though he always thought that in Berlin, too, there were bright New Year's moments there, here everything was unceremonious and fake. While the cars honked around him and people did their shopping, he thought of the weariness of his first Yom Kippur in Hannover without Marsha, the first Yom Kippur after, before he had realized it was an after. He'd been frantic then, taxed, could think only of how he could fix things as quickly as possible, the shards of their life were like safety glass, it was almost impossible to cut yourself on them. He, too, was dull. Hazy.

This weariness during Margarita's childhood had become a permanent hangover, bearable only because he and Marsha took turns sleeping on the sofa, so that each could have a break for a night, but then there were three weeks without any breaks, Marsha was gone, and only occasionally was there a lucky night when Margarita wouldn't wake up, between the fever nights, the teething nights, the thirsty nights, the scared nights, the vomit-and-diarrhea nights, the screaming nights. It was just a matter of time, he told himself, till Marsha returned, she wouldn't be able to stand missing Margarita's birthday, but Margarita's birthday had come and gone and Marsha hadn't appeared.

Margarita had spoken German with him then, or a little English, no Hebrew apart from *Aba* and the names of animals from her favorite book, *kof* was ape, *hipopotam* for hippopotamus, these were animals she'd never actually seen, they didn't have them at the zoo in Hannover. In Hannover he didn't think easier days would come, in Hannover was the hardest Kol Nidre of all, his voice was the only one in the room, in Israel they pounded the benches and pounded themselves on the chest, they saved the serious stuff for thoughts of the dead, for Yizkor and Yom HaShoah.

In Germany, it was bitterly earnest, every Kol Nidre a postscript to the Holocaust, the entire Community wore white, not just he, no, everywhere were white shirts, white kippot, white sneakers, it was as if there were no light needed, as if the angels were enough. He asked God to forgive him, not to abandon him, because he'd already been abandoned; he asked God to send Marsha back to him, and as he prayed, he got an email that said *come, what are you waiting for* and he left Margarita at day care and himself in safety, in a new prayer that had accompanied him ever since, the prayer that he could work it out.

Instead of his voice, it was sorrow that swelled his breast, a devastation that would never really leave him, and already then he had known that as he sang Viddui, beginning with *teschuva*, he knew all of it was true; *ashamnu*, we have sinned, a blow to the chest; *bagadnu*, he had broken trust, for Marsha had trusted him to make a life for them both that was also hers, and he had failed, he felt the black hole inside him; *gasalnu*, done wrong; *dibarnu dofi*, spoken ill; *heevinu*, left the path of the righteous; *v'hirschanu*, tempted to sin, he thought of sex with Marsha, the darkness of it, and the hole got bigger, he felt as if he were slipping into the void; *zadnu*, acted arrogantly, thought of the application he'd sent off in secret to Berlin, hoping it would be a pleasant surprise; *chamsnu*, done violence; *tafalnu scheker*, dishonored himself by lying; *jaatznu ra*, planned evil; *kitzavnu*, spoken falsely; *latznu*, mocked; *maradnu*, complained, he thought of all that complaining when they'd had to get up early for Margarita, they were both late risers, if only she'd come back, he'd never complain again; *niatznu*, blasphemed; *sararnu*, reviled the good, the rabbi looked to the side, thumping his chest so hard his voice shook, he had spurned the good, that was the worst thing; *avinu*, offended; *paschanu*, run up debts; *tzararnu*, hated, he thought of Marsha's hatred of the Germans and his own hatred of this hatred; *kishinu oref*, he was obdurate; *rashanu*, had rebelled; *shichatnu*, had destroyed, more a question than a sin—what had he destroyed?—fasting wouldn't be hard this year, he wasn't hungry anymore; *tiavnu*, acted undignified, he nearly laughed, his white cloak should be black, black like a black hole, black like the hot tar that the teshuvah poured in; *tainu*, erred; *titanu*, led astray, deliberately, and it was sin, it was shame, it was the hope of slicha, the response to Viddui, to every confession belonged forgiveness, divine forgiveness.

He rang, no one opened the door, but the patio door was open, so he walked through the yard and into the house and found Margarita sleeping in bed while the television blared.

The antibiotics seemed not to be working, the only thing was her appetite was gone, all she wanted to drink was Coke, she asked him to rest his cool hands on her forehead and he could never not forgive Marsha, because she had given him Margarita, stubborn, clever Margarita, who had wished him *shana tova u metuka* even with a fever, who asked how it had been and how he was doing in her brief moments awake and as always, when she asked him, he replied, "Beseder, motek, yesh li *Heimweh*."

* * *

After these tough days, the time was now flying past, as though with the new year the earth would rotate at a new tempo, and two hours passed every time Margarita closed her eyes. Everything in her body was burning, the pain medications gave her stomach cramps, she had pills for that, too, the antibiotics made her thrush worse, and she wasn't supposed to drink much because of the cream to treat the thrush, so it burned when she had to pee, and so Aba had gotten her tablets for the thrush and another antibiotic at Walgreens, and now she was bleeding again. Dark, clumpy blood.

Between the short hours were minutes that occurred in slow motion, when her parents entered the room and wanted to talk with her; her father to complain about the synagogue, her mother to *get things in order*, call the hospital, one day she cleaned the kitchen and bought a step stool that Dan nearly tripped over.

Margarita had asked whether her grandmother could receive a Jewish funeral if she died someday, she'd even said it that way, *someday*, and Marsha had replied, furious, "I want to take it back." Margarita knew she meant that she wanted to take back having told her the secret, but probably also that she wished she'd never invited her to Israel, so she said, "Me, too," and Marsha shrugged, that thin shield of ice overlaid her eyes again and she shut the door behind her.

Margarita asked herself whether that ice ever melted when Marsha was alone, or whether it was growing thicker and thicker, whether there was a permafrost in Marsha and whether she could come by one of her own, please, because everything, every single thing, shattered the ice inside her and melted it. She thought of the ice melting all over the earth and wondered why she had cared about climate change so little these past few weeks.

* * *

It was seven days until Yom Kippur, that was his neither-nor period between one year and the next, *zwischen den Jahren* the Germans said, and rhapsodically; here in Chicago, too, everything was standing still, no snowfall, just a fine mist from the sprinklers in the front yards. Margarita seemed to be doing better, and he would soon book their flights, would stop going alone to the puppet theater on Hyde Park Boulevard. Never had he thought he'd miss a German Yom Kippur.

In this between-the-years moment, between days, actually, a person prayed differently, not just judging oneself, as he did throughout the year, but doing penance. On these days of reversal, Avi did penance for his discontent, for his sorrow; he prayed his midday prayers, prayed: *May your name be praised and exalted for all this, our king, forever and ever, and may those who share your covenant live righteously.* He prayed, *Adonai, HaShem, Hamelech, may you inscribe their names in the Book of Life, Margarita, Selma, and him*, he left Marsha out at first, but then he added her in, Adonai, HaShem, Hamelech, forgive him, he would confess he had done all he could, and would do more to be written into the Book of Life, even if he harbored ill feelings. And he prayed, *Elohai, eternal one, still my tongue's wickedness and my lips' deceit*, he prayed for his wounded ego and the wounded world.

* * *

Avi had cooked for them all on the last evening of Rosh Hashanah and had asked Margarita to sit with them, so she peeled herself out of bed, heard the familiar kiddush, her grandfather stuttered along, as though his manhood depended on showing he, too, could make kiddush, even if Dan, unlike Avi, knew Aramaic.

Marsha looked somewhat less tense. It had even occurred to her to ask Margarita how her mouth was doing, and when Margarita said she could take a look if she dared, Avi shouted, "Don't do it, don't do it," and Marsha grinned. For a moment, everything seemed resolved, Grandpa farted absentmindedly, and Margarita and Marsha bent over laughing while Avi scolded them.

When she woke, the morning after, it barely hurt to swallow, and she no longer had a fever. That almost irritated her, it meant she had to get up and get dressed.

Her grandmother was still in a coma, and Anna was getting impatient. Yesterday on the phone she'd said it sucked without Margarita there, all day Margarita had been happy about that.

Marsha's voice echoed through the house, she had one Zoom meeting after another in which she explained the *current situation*. In the meantime, clumsily, she tried to take care of Dan, but Avi had taken the wheel, he was the one who cooked and looked after everyone. For hours, Grandpa sat in front of the TV or read the *New York Times*. Margarita had the sense he didn't care who was or wasn't there. All he said when he saw Margarita was that he missed Selma.

Margarita put on makeup for lunch, and Marsha asked if she didn't want to go downtown with her, to get her mind off things before they went to see her grandmother, she could see the apartment, *check out a bookstore*. Avi wasn't invited.

They drove over the long, curving road beside the lake, the skyline crept closer, the passenger seat felt familiar, so did her mother's profile cut out against the driver's side window, Margarita asked herself whether she'd miss Marsha.

The bookstore was closed, so they drove to Marsha's apartment. The building had a parking deck and a doorman. It was forty-four stories high, there was a pool on the roof. Marsha cursed, she had forgotten to tell Margarita to bring a bathing suit. Margarita told her three times it wasn't a problem, but already in the elevator, Marsha said she'd lend her one. She opened the door to the apartment on the thirteenth floor. It was cold, there were drop cloths all over. The open kitchen and living room were full of boxes. Marsha guided Margarita by the shoulder to the window. "If you've got good eyes, you can see the Ferris wheel."

Margarita had good eyes.

"I'm waiting for the new bed and mattress. I'm sleeping on the couch for now." Margarita walked into one of the two bedrooms that branched off the living room–kitchen. The apartment wasn't small, but it was compact, the rooms almost square, certainly nothing as spacious as her grandparents' home, she felt sealed in, the windows didn't look like they opened, and she was too high to see the faces of the people strolling on Walton Street when she looked down.

Margarita heard Marsha cursing. She stepped into the doorframe and saw her mother digging through boxes of clothes. "It has to be here somewhere," Marsha said, rooted around some more, opened one box, then another, emptied everything out onto the floor.

"It's okay," Margarita said, "really I shouldn't be swimming."

Marsha shot her a quick look and went on searching, emitting a frustrated, throaty squeak.

"It's not such a big deal," Margarita said.

"I can't do anything. Anything, anything at all."

"Just drop it. I doubt I'd even fit in your bathing suit."

"I just want to find it. What's the point of having three bathing suits if they all disappear?"

She wouldn't let it go, so Margarita went to see the other room. It was empty, just two boxes standing in the corner. From the window, the entire street below was visible, packed with toy cars.

In the next room over, Marsha kept up the pursuit. Margarita would have liked to send Anna a voice message, but she was scared of her mother, who was acting rash and out of control. So, paradoxically, was Avi, in a way she'd never seen, because Avi lost control only when he couldn't find things, once he'd hit the glass pane in the bathroom door so hard he'd shattered it, but he was allowed to do that, Marsha wasn't, her theatrics got on Margarita's nerves, "Get your shit together," she said, first timidly, then distinctly, "Get your shit together." It took all the courage she could muster.

"I don't have the strength for a fight," Marsha said, "I just wanted to do something nice for you."

"I don't want to swim, though, do you not realize that? Why won't anyone just listen to me?" She asked herself why it was impossible to do a single thing with Marsha without it escalating or someone raising their voice.

Marsha rubbed her eyes. "Fuck," she whispered, "fuck, fuck." She leaned on one of the boxes, which gave, and she fell forward, her elbow crashing inside.

Margarita couldn't help but laugh, the entire situation was beyond her and she had an almost bodily yearning to be with people who weren't adults.

"I wanted it to be different," Marsha said, "I always want it to be different, it never works, I just wanted to ask you something, but probably the moment's passed."

"What?" Margarita asked.

"The apartment's nice, right?"

Margarita's forehead furrowed. "That's what you wanted to ask me?"

Marsha nodded.

"Yeah, the apartment's nice," Margarita said, confused.

"Okay," Marsha said.

"Can we go now?"

"Where to?"

"The hospital."

"I thought we could use a little time together, just the two of us."

"What do you want to do, then?"

"Do you like cupcakes?"

The afternoon was getting worse and worse. Margarita just wanted to go back to her room. "I guess," she said.

They bought the cupcakes in a sterile shop called Sprinkles. All around them were women in yoga clothes who didn't look like they ate cupcakes. There was nowhere to sit, and outside was unbearably hot, so they took the elevator back up to the apartment and sat on the floor.

Margarita kept looking nervously at her cell phone. She was almost relieved when Marsha's own phone rang. She scrolled through her Instagram feed and read in the school chat what homework she needed to work on that evening. Slowly she was getting scared she wouldn't be able to catch up.

"Sorry," Marsha said, "it's the university in Jerusalem, they're mad at me."

"Oh."

"Everything's falling apart."

Margarita didn't know what she should say about it. She had said sorry so many times that she didn't feel like it anymore. And somewhere deep inside, she found it unfitting, how often her mother complained to her, even though she knew Marsha was just trying to take her seriously, share adult things with her. Unlike Avi.

Margarita looked out the window. She asked herself how they'd clean the windows here. Asked aloud, just to bridge the silence.

Marsha looked at her. "Wanna find out?" she asked.

"What do you mean?"

Marsha was quiet. Then she said, "Whatever."

"What's that supposed to mean?"

"We need to go. Otherwise we'll miss visitors' hours." Marsha looked past Margarita into the second, empty room. "I can't change," she whispered, and then, louder, "I like my life. I like my job, and I don't regret leaving Germany. But I missed you, I missed you so bad, it was like someone had torn off one of my legs. But to get it back, I would have had to trade an arm. Whereas now, I have the feeling I can be something whole."

"No," Margarita said.

"Will you not let me finish?"

"No," she said. "I would never do that to him."

"He'd manage. You could go to the lab school, there's a bus that stops here. Or you could even drive, get a license, we'd buy you a car. You could go visit him. Once my salary starts coming in, I'll make more than enough."

"No," Margarita said again. "We need to go." She stood up.

"Margarita. Please." Marsha looked up at her.

Margarita felt sick. Not in her body, but in her head. Sick, broken. "You can come to Berlin," she said, "but I won't move in with you. That won't happen. Don't you have to go back to Jerusalem? Did you even ask Aba?"

"No," Marsha said, "I wanted to talk to you about it first. I gave up the fellowship, because of Grandma."

"You'd be kidnapping me. You don't have custody."

"Margarita, I don't want to kidnap you. Calm down."

But who ever calmed down when someone asked them to. Margarita didn't calm down. Margarita took Marsha's untouched cupcake and threw it, soft icing side first, into the wall. She stared into Marsha's eyes. Her mother looked afraid of her. Strangely, that made her even angrier. She took as deep a breath as she could and roared, never had she heard herself so loud.

"I WILL NOT CALM DOWN.

"I WILL NOT CALM DOWN.

"I WILL NOT CALM DOWN."

Marsha stood. She walked, crouching, into Margarita's room, colored sprinkles clung to the wall next to the door. Margarita couldn't stop. She was shaking, but she couldn't stop. "I HATE YOU," she bellowed through the open door, "I HATE YOU."

Marsha looked at her like a wounded animal. "You're right," she said, "you're right. I don't know what I was thinking."

"Me neither," Margarita said.

Marsha began to make pitiful choking noises. Margarita wanted her to stop. She told her so, "Stop it," but it just kept getting worse.

"I've failed," Marsha shrieked, "I've failed you. I've failed every-one. I've failed my mother, and I've failed at being your mother."

"Stop it," Margarita said again. She couldn't take it anymore. She was burning inside, but Marsha kept going. "Stop!" Margarita yelled. "Stop saying it!"

"I'm so awful," Marsha said, "I'm awful, I'm terrible, and noth-ing makes sense anymore." She started scratching frantically at her forearms.

"Stop," Margarita said. "You're not awful." She just wanted it to end.

"I am, though," Marsha grunted, "I've fucked everything up, my whole life. It's not worth it. I wish I could just disappear. I wish I didn't exist anymore." She beat herself on the arms, first the left on the right, then the right on the left, back and forth, with a smacking sound.

"STOP!" Margarita shouted, but it kept getting worse, the slapping louder, her self-degradation graver.

Margarita couldn't leave, her feet wouldn't carry her, however much she imagined it, imagined getting into the elevator and run-ning far, far away.

Marsha said she'd never wanted to get pregnant.

Margarita reached out as if impelled from within. She had never hit anyone, but it was surprisingly easy, her mother's cheek surpris-ingly soft when it met her hand. Marsha stumbled back and crossed her arms over her head, protecting herself.

Margarita was panting. "I'm sorry," she said softly, "I'm so sorry, I didn't mean it, I didn't know, I didn't, I . . ." She felt faint.

"No, you were right," Marsha said, "it's true. I need to pull my-self together. I shouldn't have lost control like that. I deserved it, I deserved it. I'm not a good person, Margarita."

Oh God, Margarita thought, oh shit. "That's not true," she said.

"It is," Marsha whispered, "it is, and I deserved it, probably you should hit me again, I deserved it."

Margarita was overwhelmed, and she just wanted it all to stop, she felt bad for her mother, she couldn't have wanted all this.

Marsha touched her cheek. "I deserved it," she said again, "I failed you. And I was naive. Like you'd have ever wanted to live here."

She must have been terribly alone.

"No, that's not what I meant," Margarita said, "maybe we could try it, it's a nice room, maybe I just need to get used to the idea," she was trying to salvage something, "I can talk to Aba."

Marsha looked like she couldn't breathe, like she was hyperventilating. "No," she said, "it's okay, honey, it's okay, it was a terrible idea, just nonsense, your mother's an idiot."

She looked brave, how she stood there. Margarita wasn't brave. It had been cowardly, hitting her mother. It was brave to forgive it. "I'd like to live here," she said, regretted it in that very second, and hoped Marsha knew it was her guilty conscience speaking.

Marsha asked if Margarita would hug her. She shook her head. Cowardly Margarita. Willing to strike her mother, not willing to hug her.

Marsha left the room, she looked bent and small, vanished into the bathroom, Margarita heard running water. She lay down on the wood floor, there was a fireplace on the wall next to her. She closed her eyes. The wooden slats on her face were cool. Cold lava, she thought, just as I have inside me. She got up at some point, carefully shut the door to the room, lay back down, stared out the window, and wondered how to back out of this one, how to keep this room from becoming her room, wondered how she would manage to break neither her father's nor her mother's heart, just her own, because she could take it better, that much she was sure of.

* * *

He went grocery shopping so no one else would have to bother, slowly the freezer was starting to empty out; anyway, he needed to move. When he returned, the car was no longer in the drive-way, probably Dan had gone to the hospital. This time the patio door was locked, too, so he placed the groceries in the shade where nothing would go bad, fortunately he hadn't bought any meat, and sat on the swing. He remembered when he had pushed Margarita all the time on that swing, her happy face coming back toward him, the closer it was, the blurrier.

He thought of the first Yom Kippur in Berlin, the sun had gone down much earlier than the year before, he'd put a kosher chicken in the oven, had watched Margarita as she absentmindedly sucked the bones, had put her in her stroller and left her with Mareike, a student from his Hebrew class, they were fifteen minutes late, be-cause three buses, one after another, were full to bursting and the stroller wouldn't fit inside. After he said goodbye, he had to run to the synagogue, and minutes into his fast he was dying of thirst.

And yet, as it began, the candles were lit, and he had shaken the rabbi's hand and gathered himself, this Kol Nidre became a new be-ginning after a year of mourning, still today he thought of it as per-haps the most important one of his life, it was rare that Yom Kippur fell on Shabbat, many things were left out and others were added, no Avinu Malkeinu, because on Shabbat, you weren't supposed to ask God for material goods, but Psalm 92 was spoken, a thicket of images, a poem to God: *The righteous shall flourish like the palm tree: he shall grow like a cedar in Lebanon.* He himself became one of the righteous, simply by standing there.

When he picked up Margarita afterward, she was crying as if something ached, she lay curled up on the ground, Mareike was supposed to take care of her the next day, but instead he'd asked the professional nanny, whom Margarita had coolly accepted, to come over, took a taxi during his midday break, broke all the rules and spent money and used his cell phone. Taking her with him wasn't an option. Had never been an option. He forgot to remove his kippa, and the taxi driver called him a *Jew bastard* after he'd paid.

At five in the evening, he said to hell with it, drank water from the tap, and ate a Snickers bar before returning to the synagogue.

As he opened the gate to the front garden, a stray swan flew so close overhead that he could feel the breeze from its wings, flew higher, over the roof of the synagogue, which had remained standing only because of the residential buildings neighboring it that people hadn't wanted to destroy during the pogroms.

A few weeks later, he'd had sex with Mareike on the couch while Margarita was sleeping in her crib in his bedroom. It repelled him that she kept speaking German with him while they did it, saying *yes* and *deeper*. He liked her, but broke off contact, she was a medical student and clever and a little too young for him, not so much in age terms, but something about her was tighter wound, less stale. She thought he was a hero because he was a single father, and he wasn't, he was just a victim of the matriarchy who happened to know his daughter's shoe size, her favorite animals, and put her in the child's seat on his bicycle every Sunday to take her to the zoo, where she'd press her sticky fingers to the glass, stare at the animals, he was always afraid the window would shatter and they'd both end up in the maw of the hippo or tumbling into the bear pen. The first nightmare she told him about was that the polar bears at the zoo had broken free and were hunting her. So the zoo frightened both of them, and they both kept going back.

At Sukkot, he read a long email from Marsha that he never answered. She wrote that she wanted to visit and asked for photos. As though he'd kept Margarita preserved in a box with her maternity clothes. He moved her emails to his spam folder and deleted the photos of Marsha from his cell phone. At Hanukkah, his daughter shone. Maybe she'd forgotten there was such a thing as mothers. Marsha never sent presents, only her parents did, apologetically, vast quantities of toys and fancy clothes. When he googled Marsha's name, the computer spat back accomplishments at him, and he was almost happy for her.

In 2014, the rabbi got sick and he oversaw the entirety of the prayers, rarely had he been so proud, he had just seen his first class off to the college, ordained two cantors, and his students came to the synagogue to support him. He was no longer thinking of Marsha by the hour, sometimes not even until he was back in bed, exhausted from a day spent with Margarita. The Avinu Malkeinu that morning brought him to the furthest edge of what he'd ever felt when praying, first the quiet part, almost without melody, and he asked God, his king, for compassion and kindness, for brighter days, bright like the eyes of the gabbai, bright like Margarita's laughter when he tickled her awake in the mornings, pretending to be a monster with a thousand arms.

At some point, Margarita was old enough to spend the High Holy Days on Oranienburger Strasse or at home, as she preferred, when he allowed it and she promised not to turn on the stove.

In 2018, she stayed on her own for the first time, and he had led Yizkor, those who still had both parents left the room, and the orphaned and half orphaned remained behind with the widows and widowers, there were those who had lost both parents and spouse, there were those who remained seated because they'd lost their best friend, were mourning their son, what did he know, just that they were united in having lost someone, and the happy ones waited in the garden, ignorant of how happy they were, but all of them would one day remain in their seats, even if the Torah reading went on forever, even if they were looking forward to a walk through the leaves, and Margarita would be there among them.

At home, he found her on the couch, the apartment was dark, she hadn't turned on the lights, and he tried to shake off his thoughts from before. His child would never say Yizkor. He would be the first immortal father in the history of the world.

He wondered for a moment whether the swing could topple over. No, that wouldn't happen.

Then came 2019. When he thought of 2019, he thought of how all the Germans suddenly knew what Yom Kippur was. *The most important Jewish holiday*, they called it on the news, which also informed people that Hanukkah really wasn't such a big deal.

He thought of how the survivors stayed hungry, because they didn't get to their kosher food.

He thought of Jana and Kevin and Kiez-Döner.

And he remained disconsolate, the blue sky he swung into behind the brick building an indecency.

In 2020, everything changed. The seats were sectioned off, the usual walk-ins stayed away, so did the old people, and no one was allowed to sing along. Before then, the pandemic hadn't been so grave for him, they'd made themselves comfortable, stayed healthy, Anna came to see them every day, his social bubble was the Lang family, it didn't bother him as long as Margarita didn't suffer, and he prayed in the empty synagogue in front of the live stream camera, that was an adjustment, but he came to like it, and it was a lifesaver, being able to keep his job.

Then came the Yom Kippur *afterward*, and he didn't trust the police, that was why Margarita had gone to the Langs' instead of to Oranienburger Strasse, the Langs didn't fast, but he couldn't have cared less as long as the kid was safe.

They blew the shofar in the garden so that the ba'al tekia wouldn't spray his spit from the horn into the synagogue's interior. The garden, separated from the street only by a fence, where the policeman's booth stood. The worshippers who couldn't get a seat had been told to come to hear the shofar blasting, and now it was full, with children everywhere. Children wherever you looked. He wore his tallit over his white garments, his machzor for Yom Kippur in his right hand. He hadn't shaved in the morning, it was chag, and it irked him when someone took out their phone to take a video of the prayers, a cell phone on Yom Kippur, and it was hardly an emergency; besides, there wasn't much he hated worse than being photographed or recorded, he always looked so terribly tired, with thick bags under his little eyes.

When the first note, the tekia, sounded, he thought, perhaps for the first time, that he should emigrate again, in the opposite direction, Aliyah 2.0, the shevarim, three staccato notes, a call for forgiveness, then the t'ruah, nine short ones, he counted them.

Past the fence, parents he'd never seen before lifted their children onto their shoulders. Someone pointed at him. It lasted a moment, then he realized: at the fence were people who didn't know what was happening, strollers, passersby, lifting their children to give them a better look at the Jews.

The police looked condescendingly at those they were meant to protect. As if the Jews should be thankful for their protection. The next time one of them came into the synagogue to use the bathroom without a head covering, he'd complain, he swore to himself.

On this Yom Kippur, he stopped praying for forgiveness. What he wished was that someone would ask him for forgiveness for once, and he'd say no, I don't forgive you; but no one asked, no one excused themselves, in the eyes of those Germans he knew so well, what was present, above all, was accusation.

In 2022, more than ever, there was bickering about who was a Jew and who wasn't, what to do with the converts, everyone had their say, and it spiraled out of control, at one point a woman wrote him a blistering email telling him to leave his watch with its leather band at home, every year it upset her, he didn't even know who she was, and he needed the watch to know whether he was going too fast or too slow, the breaking of the fast would not be delayed a few precious minutes on account of this Christine, and anyway, what kind of Jew was named Christine, with Margarita's help he wrote her a decorous reply: the watch band was synthetic leather.

The synagogue was full for Neilah, again you could attend without registering, without social distancing, people just came, he looked around, on edge, there was a man without a kippa, his backpack on backward, headphones, he looked like he'd wandered in by accident, Avi's heart froze as the gabbai told the man to cover his head, Avi heard him say, "Too many rules here," the man turned around and left.

He tried, in general, to stick to the sidelines, told himself he was apolitical, but the horror after February 2022 wasn't political, the horror at the war of aggression against Ukraine, at Israel's role in it, wanting to declare itself *apolitical* even as its democracy was going down the drain. No: there was no such thing as apolitical.

* * *

When she emerged from the room, Marsha was there cleaning off the doorframe. "Sorry about the cupcake," Margarita said.

"It's okay. I licked some off the wall."

Margarita had to laugh.

Marsha pointed to something lying on the couch: a bathing suit. "Just a quick dip?" she asked.

There she was again, the strong, aloof mother.

The roof deck gave a vertiginous view into the distance, to Lake Michigan and to the edge of the city stretching almost endlessly into flat Illinois.

"I still can't believe I actually live here," Marsha said.

Margarita got into the shallow end of the pool. The water hardly reached her knee. She didn't have another tampon with her and didn't want to walk around with a tampon soaked in chlorinated water. After two minutes, she got out. Marsha looked disappointed, but she squeezed out a smile. Margarita responded in kind.

They went to the hospital in silence.

Tell her everyday things, Dr. Johnston had said, but as Marsha and Margarita stood by Selma's bed, nothing occurred to them. They just dawdled, equally defeated, equally lost.

Marsha still looked wounded, raw. She covered Grandma and cautiously said they had gone swimming and that Avi would cook that night. "You know, he's a great cook, Mom." That was apparently all she could think of. Margarita couldn't hold it against her, food was what Selma liked to talk about most, and Marsha had given it her best.

"I threw a cupcake against the wall today," Margarita said.

"What about that, Mom. She has my temper. Who knew."

Dr. Johnston entered. Margarita was starting to get the feeling he lived at the hospital.

"Seems like you live here, Mr. Johnston," she said.

Dr. Johnston told them it was a chronic subdural hematoma, a teeny-tiny one.

Marsha heaved a theatrical sigh. "This one here wants to become a doctor," she said, and Margarita could feel herself turning red. How did Marsha know? She definitely hadn't mentioned it.

Dr. Johnston smiled. "There's a great premed program at UChicago."

Marsha nodded enthusiastically.

"When will you wake her up?" Margarita asked.

"It's a long process," Dr. Johnston responded, "she's heavily sedated, we'll need to decrease the dose slowly. I'd say it'll be a week at the earliest before she's awake."

"Oh," Margarita said.

"I need to go," Dr. Johnston said. "We'll speak soon."

They drove to Blackstone Avenue. Dan was sitting on the couch asleep. As Marsha told him the news, he nodded, seeming to understand nothing. She repeated the same thing three times, then left the living room. Margarita sat down next to him. He looked at her.

"You're going to do incredible things one day, you sweet girl," he said, and patted her knee. Then he turned the TV back on.

Marsha returned with a glass of red wine in her hand. It was five in the evening. Margarita ran upstairs to tell her father hello. He wasn't in the study. Margarita was confused. She looked in her room, he wasn't there, either. She heard a creaking. He was sitting on the rusty swing Grandpa had set up for her in the yard. He kept leaning back, trying to swing higher, stretching his legs out in the air. Flying.

For the first time since he had opened the door for her at the apartment in Jerusalem, she wondered what was going on inside him. Higher and higher he swung, faster and faster. And his body grew longer, lither. She stood there awhile and observed him. He only looked up when she closed the balcony door.

* * *

He had closed his eyes. Felt the wind on his face. When he opened them, Margarita was standing at the Juliet balcony on the second floor and looking into the garden, grown, unmanageable, and when their eyes met, she closed the door.

And Abraham was old, and well stricken in age, he thought, the first sentence of the parsha in Genesis that they would read in a few weeks, when he was back in Berlin. He stood, the earth swayed under his feet; for a moment, his dizziness blinded him. Stricken in age. Not old, but not young, either, he could sense that at times, in his back, in his knees. Perhaps no more days could fit inside him.

As a few pearls of sweat ran down his temples, he decided: he had to get back to his congregation, he couldn't celebrate Yom Kippur in Chicago. The patio doors glided open smoothly this time when he tried them, Margarita must have unlocked them. Before he put away the groceries in the fridge, he wrote an email to Frau Wagner, letting her know things had resolved themselves, and he would lead the Yom Kippur prayers, she could tell his replacement he wasn't needed. She'd be pleased, that much he knew, because it meant she could get back to her organizing: putting his name on the schedule, crossing the other one out, he would escort his congregation into the new year, the September light would break through the colored glass and the bulletproof windows in front of it, and next year, everything would be different.

* * *

Margarita couldn't fall back to sleep, though she tried for hours. As the red numbers on the alarm clock glowed six o'clock, she gave up and looked for the Nina Chuba song she had listened to so many times with Anna: *You can't stop the time when it's time that you go*, she got chills, thought of the feverish longing that gripped her sometimes, thought of Lior, thought of Nico. Thought of the repulsion after she'd puked outside his front door one winter night before stuffing three sticks of gum into her mouth and running up the stairs because she'd gotten that one measly message, *place is empty, want to stop by*, and she'd answered, *def, when* and he hadn't responded again until two in the morning and she'd spent the whole time with Anna downing too much vodka and juice in front of the all-in-one shop on Rosenthaler Platz.

That night, Nico had thrown on a condom and moved around inside her for a bit, it felt good, vague, dull, not at all painful; before then, the first time, she'd just had his dick in her mouth, and even after this moving around inside her, he hadn't held her, and she thought it was true what she'd read on Instagram, that sex didn't require penetration, so in a way, penetration wasn't sex, and she told herself this sex hadn't really happened.

Maybe the infamous *first time* had really been with Lior, that made more sense to her, but she'd never see Lior again. She bit her lip. The only thing she wanted was for someone to think she was beautiful. Could she be someone new here in Chicago? Someone others found beautiful?

She shooed these thoughts away. Tiptoed to the kitchen for something to eat that she could secretly gobble up in bed. She found a ziplock bag full of oatmeal cookies. Would her grandmother notice if they were gone when she returned? Dr. Johnston had warned them she'd have memory gaps.

Would she remember her own secret?

Would she know what her name was before she was adopted?

How old was she, even?

There was suddenly so much she wanted to ask her grandmother, and so little time.

Would Grandma know how she had met her Dan, on a boat trip on the Chicago River?

Did Margarita know any more than that? What did she actually know about her father? Her mother? Her parents' past, her grandparents', was like a thicket, dark and impenetrable.

She ate the cookies and listened to more music.

She made deals.

If Grandma dies, I'll leave.

If she survives, I'll stay here.

If she's alive but her head's messed up, I'll stay.

If she doesn't wake up before Yom Kippur, I'll go.

If I stay, I'll tell Aba Grandma's secret.

Wasn't that why Marsha had left, after all? Had that not been a good reason, a human one? One that now she didn't want to admit? Because it couldn't have been so bad between them. There was no way her father had refused to go to the USA for no good reason. He was too much of a foreigner in Germany for that. And who liked being a foreigner? Her heart fluttered briefly as she imagined him without her in Berlin, sitting alone in a restaurant, worrying, always worrying. But wasn't it vain to think he couldn't exist without her? Just then, she seemed to be getting supremely on his nerves. But a whole year without her, or however long Marsha wanted to keep her there, maybe until she graduated from high school? He couldn't allow that. It relieved her to recall that he was the only one with custody of her. Maybe he would put his foot down, tell her no. Maybe that was the way out. Because she could hardly see another one. Making a huge fuss or getting her school involved weren't options.

But she owed it to Marsha. Every time she thought of hitting her, she crinkled up inside. She wondered how she could redeem herself, but nothing occurred to her. She was responsible for her dilemma.

She thought of the clean hallways of the Laboratory Schools, the stories the other students in the writing class had told her about sports clubs and lit class, and how all that had made her a little jealous.

Maybe she didn't want a way out.

Avi knocked. He asked if she wanted to go to breakfast. Dan had a doctor's appointment, he would drive there on his own.

She hadn't had the heart to tell him anything the day before, not that at least a week would have to go by before she could leave, not about her room in that tall, unfamiliar building. At breakfast, then. "What about Marsha?" she asked.

"She needs to take a break for a day, motek. She said she's going to meet a friend. I'm here, though."

"Yeah," she said, and smiled at him. He was there.

* * *

The wooden benches at the Medici looked the same as they always had, with initials carved all over them, and the students the initials belonged to were biting wearily into their sandwiches. He liked the atmosphere here, and he was happy to have an afternoon alone with Margarita. She immediately opened the book he'd bought her the day before. Only when he complained did she close it, reluctantly. Now, once again, he was in a bad mood.

"Grandma won't for at least a week wake up," Margarita said. Her syntax in Hebrew was twisted up. Avi corrected her, as he always did. She rolled her eyes.

"Beseder," he said, shoving a piece of omelet into his mouth, "then you can visit for spring break."

"Okay," Margarita said.

"Yofi."

"What about if we just stayed here. I could definitely get back in, they're still in the drop/add period, I could actually change all my classes still. Aba, what if she dies?"

"Margarita, I don't want to fight right now."

"I want to stay here, though."

"What? Why? I thought you wanted to go back to Berlin. We came here to take care of your mother and Grandpa, the operation was a success, everything's going to be fine. You begged and begged to go back home, and now we can go back home. Come on."

"I need to know what's going to happen to her."

"You'll find out, there are cell phones, there's email, you can video chat with Marsha. But we've got obligations back home."

"I thought you called out of work."

"You've got to go to school, motek! The principal said two weeks, tops."

"She'll bend, she's got the hots for you. You just need to call her."

He was surprised. She normally used that spiteful tone only when she really wanted something.

"Don't talk like that. Not after what you've put me through this summer."

"What about what I've been through this summer? I've had to take care of other people constantly. You're not supposed to have to take care of your parents. Your parents are supposed to take care of you."

"Motek."

"Don't call me that!"

"Fine. Margarita, we have to go back to Berlin. The summer's over. I don't feel right living with Marsha's parents, and you can imagine it's not easy for me to spend this much time with your mother when I haven't seen her for almost thirteen years."

"From what I hear, that wasn't just her fault."

He lacked the desire, the grit, to fight about it. "Hey. That hurts, motek, sorry, Margarita, you know that."

"What if I needed her."

Her words hurt him. "I always gave you everything. Didn't I?" He was being serious. Had he not always given her everything?

"Sure," Margarita whispered, "but what if you flew back without me? I can come later."

He shook his head. She had funny ideas about autonomy, this fifteen-year-old girl. He shouldn't have sent her to Israel on her own. "No, Margarita. That's not how it works."

"Why?"

"Because you have to go to school. Because you're about to turn sixteen. At home. We're not celebrating your birthday here."

"But you get along so well with her!"

"Excuse me?"

"You're two peas in a pod, you and Marsha."

Now he had to laugh. "Margarita, let's get a grip. It's been a very, very long time since we last saw each other. We have our own lives, but we share something, something amazing, and something extremely trying, and that's you, and I would love for you to build a relationship with her. But you have to go home."

"Do you know? Did she tell you?"

"What, motek?"

"Nothing."

"What do you mean?"

"It's not important."

"Have you hidden something from me?"

"No, Aba. It doesn't matter."

But he felt lied to, kept in the dark, and had to force himself not to pound the table.

"She's got a second bedroom," Margarita said.

He didn't understand what she was saying.

"Ima. She's got a second bedroom. In her apartment."

"And?"

"It's for me."

If that was the big secret, then it wasn't so bad. "That's nice. You can go stay with her for spring break if you like. I'm glad."

"Aba," she said, "she wants me to stay here."

He laughed. "Haisha hasu metorefet." *The woman's delusional.* Margarita wouldn't be staying in Chicago, there was no room for argument.

"She really means it," Margarita said.

"No," Avi said, "no. Out of the question. No chance." He pulled two bills from his pants pocket and left them on the table. Margarita stood and left the restaurant.

"You're welcome," he said, catching up to her. "In Berlin we won't be able to go out to eat again until I get my year-end bonus."

She rolled her eyes.

"Come on, Margarita." He thought for a moment of grabbing her, but she'd probably make such a scene someone would end up calling the police. Still, as they reached the corner of Blackstone Avenue, he couldn't hold it in anymore, and started shouting. She marched off as he cursed at her and ordered her to stay there, shouted about gratitude, which she had apparently never heard of, about how she was spoiled, how she ought to behave, people must have thought he was a criminal. Margarita stood there with her hands over her ears. That only made it worse. Pedestrians stared at them, but he saw understanding in most of their eyes, as if they knew what hell it was, having to bawl out a teenager in public. Margarita ran off. Ran all the way to the house, he ran behind her, shouting as she reached the door. No allowance, he yelled, no going out, no back talk.

Poor, confused Dan opened the door. Margarita stormed off up the stairs and shut herself in the bathroom. Avi pounded on the door. "Margarita," he said, "come out. Come out. We need to talk."

She didn't come out. He sat on the floor.

"Go away," Margarita shouted. "Fuck off."

"Slicha," he whispered, "slicha," and then he broke down in sobs. Like a loser. Like an outcast. But he didn't leave.

* * *

"It's not your fault," her father said, and took her in his arms as she left the bathroom and sheepishly said she was sorry.

She didn't know what *it* was. Or what she should be saying sorry for. She just knew that this summer had to end. And that it was a good thing that time would banish it definitively.

"You're not really considering it, are you?" he asked.

Margarita shrugged.

"Then I'm going to have to tell you no, Margarita. I've got full custody."

She knew he hated telling her no, everything was supposed to be fair, a deal, a compromise, he took her seriously, didn't forbid, rather pleaded: Please be home at such-and-such a time, please do your homework, please don't start smoking. Cut the shit, Margarita, please. But now he wasn't pleading. Now he was deciding.

Again, she closed the door. She felt locked up in this gigantic house. What would it be like to be able to leave again that evening? What would it be like to tell Marsha about school, to spend time with her and her grandmother? Wasn't Anna busy with Zoé, anyway?

She didn't even have her things here. What if she flew to Berlin and thought it over there?

Margarita felt abandoned. Anna wouldn't pick up her phone. Her father was making a fuss in the kitchen. She squeezed herself into the closet in the corner of the room with her book and read by the light of her phone.

Avi called her for dinner. When he opened the door, Marsha walked through, he didn't even say hello to her.

"Do I get some, too?" she asked.

He didn't respond.

Marsha's forehead furrowed. "What?" she asked.

He shrugged and grabbed another plate.

Only Marsha spoke throughout the meal, about the university, her apartment, how all her books were still in storage. Every few minutes, Dan said, "Whaddyasay?"

Margarita put her plate in the dishwasher and sat down in the living room. She hoped her father would play the piano later, that would calm everything down. And buy her time.

Dan sat down next to her. "Do I know you from somewhere?" His favorite joke.

She laughed, tired. "I'm your granddaughter, Grandpa!" They played this little game all the time.

He looked at her over his glasses, his bushy brows nearly covering his eyes. "Whaddyasay!" he shouted, and turned to his *New Yorker*. He didn't seem to hear what was happening at the other end of the hall. But Margarita heard every word of it.

Heard: "Are you serious, Marsha?"

Heard: "I was, yes. I don't want to steal her. I thought it might be a good idea. She seems to be taking to it."

Heard: "She has a life. You can't even imagine. You're welcome to visit her, in her life. But not the other way around. It doesn't work that way. Veto."

"No veto."

"Sorry, but yes. There are rules. I wrote them, because there was no one else to do it, and you have to follow them, both of you. She's got school."

"She can go to school here. They already know her, my father can even get us a discount on the tuition. He and Selma would pay for it, Dan already told me."

Margarita's heart beat as hard as it had when Nico had written her, in the seconds before she unlocked her phone with Face ID.

"Cut the shit. You're crazy. No. Berlin is her home, end of discussion."

"Because you decided it was."

"You're a liar, Marsha. You're lying to her. You left us, and now you have to live with the consequences. I'm not in the mood for more of your rigmarole."

"I begged you to come for me!"

"I couldn't. I had already accepted the job in Berlin, you know that."

"Without telling me!"

"I thought you'd be happy!"

"Sure, great," Marsha said, "another dreary, depressing city without any career options for me!"

"We had to eat."

Grandpa remained immersed in his magazine. Maybe he, too, was pretending not to hear anything.

"You hurt me, Avi. It's not that simple. I didn't just up and leave."

"You ran off to the rabbi instead of coming to me, remember?

You confided in him, and then you shoved off. And you still expected us to come running to you after that?"

Something broke, a plate, maybe a glass.

"Fuck!" Marsha said. "Fuck!"

"Here, I've got it, don't cut yourself."

"I can do it myself."

"How do you see this going, anyway?" Avi asked. "You're just going to suddenly turn into supermom? You may not realize it, but you have to wake her in the mornings, you have to ask her three or four times whether she's done her homework, you have to make sure she doesn't become anorexic like the rest of her class. Have you even asked yourself whether she wants this?"

"She wants it."

"Did you pressure her?"

"Of course not, are you out of your mind?"

"You do that. You manipulate people. You don't even know her. She's not your friend. And she's not a doll."

"Go pray, Avi, that's what you're good at!"

"Marsha, you know it yourself. You're acting like an asshole. You can't take her away from me."

"She said she wants to stay here!"

"You twisted her arm. She has no idea what a move like that would mean."

"She's not as stupid as you think."

"Yeah. You are, though."

Margarita jumped up and ran into the kitchen. Her parents weren't standing as close together as she'd imagined, Avi was at one end of the room, Marsha at the other. Both of them turned to her.

Margarita looked at them. They said nothing, just froze with their hands in the air, as though someone had pressed the pause button.

"Shame on you," she said.

No one followed her when she ran upstairs.

* * *

He opened Margarita's door without knocking. He never did that, but he knew if he asked, she'd just say no.

"Leave me alone," she said.

"Haha," Avi said, "no chance. I'm the one who makes the decisions here, Margarita. This summer has gotten completely out of hand. And you've abused my trust too many times."

"Why are you talking to me like this?"

"Because I'm your father, dammit."

"Marsha doesn't talk to me that way."

He was silent. He nodded slowly. She knew exactly what she had to say to hurt him.

"Sorry," Margarita said.

"Too late. But still, I can't imagine you actually want to stay here."

"I don't know what I want," she said softly, "but you could at least include me!"

"No. Not this time."

"Why not?"

"Because your mother is not in a position to offer you a stable home. Because a move is much more complicated than you think. Because we don't have the money. Because you need to go back to Berlin. Because the school year is well underway."

"None of those are real arguments."

He struck his head against the doorframe, hard enough that it ached a bit. "I don't need an argument," he said, "because it's a fact. We're flying out tomorrow, I'm buying the tickets now."

"We can't leave tomorrow!"

"We can, though. Today is Thursday, tomorrow is Friday, after that is Shabbat, and Yom Kippur starts on Sunday. It's the only way it works."

"You drove a car on Shabbat."

"That was different and you know it."

"I can't leave tomorrow. I need to see Grandma again. I'm not your property."

"Margarita, if you don't come with me tomorrow . . ."

"What?"

He couldn't think of anything. Or rather, he could. He said it before he could think better of it. "Then you're not my daughter anymore."

She yelped in pain. As if he'd struck her. And it felt terribly satisfying. He was capable of self-defense.

"Aba," she shouted. She howled so loud it couldn't be real. She knew she would always be his daughter, of course she knew that. She knew what it meant to use rhetoric as a weapon.

"Margarita, calm down. We're leaving tomorrow. End of discussion."

"I can't fly out tomorrow," she said, "and anyway, I'm not a Jew, I can fly on Shabbat, if I even have changed my mind by then."

"Slicha?"

"I'm not a Jew."

Something, some kind of utter tripe, had gotten into her head. "What are you talking about?"

"Grandma's adopted. Her biological parents weren't Jewish."

He saw Selma's face before him, the light gray hair, almost heard her laughter echoing up from the kitchen.

He still had to pack his bag. Not forget his razor again. Look for the house key so he wouldn't have to dig around for it when he was at the front door. He took a deep breath. Sighed. "So you thought I didn't know that," he said, and shut the door.

* * *

Fine, Margarita thought, fine. Like a voice she couldn't turn off, fine, fine, fine, she nodded, "Fine, yofi, fine." Now we've all left each other in the lurch.

Only then did the fear grip her. His room was empty, orderly, why hadn't she woken up, their rooms were side by side, she must have hurried off to the bathroom eight times that night, squeezing teeny droplets of urine out of her because she thought if she just went one more time, she could finally get to sleep. And then she'd accidentally slept till one in the afternoon and nobody had woken her up.

הטירגרמ was written on the envelope that lay on her grandfather's desk. She opened it. A printed ticket slipped out, for the next day, Saturday at 3:50 p.m., Lufthansa, overnight to Zurich, then a connecting flight to Berlin on Sunday morning. The ticket was in her name, *Margarita Rachel Fuchs, unaccompanied minor*. She would travel on Shabbes and reach Berlin just one hour before the start of Yom Kippur. While she was on her way home, her father would be standing in front of the bimah.

She ran to her room with the ticket and shut the door.

She listed the things this could mean, counted them down on her fingers like a child.

First, it could mean that her father agreed with her. That she wasn't a Jew. If he was letting her fly on Shabbat.

Second, it could mean that she didn't have a choice.

Third, it could mean that she did have a choice.

She thought of her grandmother. This woman, so Jewish. What was a secret anyway, if the point of it was that it was secret and it never had actually been secret? Had he really known and never told her?

Was that why he was livid with Marsha? Had he not known, and had she screwed up everything?

Was she not his daughter anymore?

It was as if life were drowning her.

It was as if she heard the beeping of the machines by her grand-mother's bed all the way in her room, as if they were beeping so loudly, one over the other, that she couldn't understand them. As if she could understand, if only she could listen closely. As if they were beeping what Grandma would say to her.

She heard it, when she really concentrated. They screeched, "I'm old, Rita," shouted, "It's okay," consoled, "I forgive you, dear heart, my dear, dear heart, no crying, Margarita," told her, "Just a minute now, just a minute." They didn't stop. Beeped, echoed, shouted.

Epilogue

They were there, people unseen for a year or four months, new babies, partners, new clothes, new hairdos, new laughter, new tears.

There were the two boys who, in a hurry, driven like sheep into the prayer room for the children's prayers, had forgotten their kippot. One slapped himself on the head and rolled his eyes, the other quickly grabbed two kippot, they were always there in a little basket at the entrance, for goyim or just for the forgetful.

There were the seconds when they closed their eyes and felt the gooseflesh rise on their back because everything felt so right: the blue of the bulletproof glass getting bluer, the yellow of the chandelier warmer, the clear tones they were all a part of in the good times, the wariness of penitence, the euphoria of the new year, a solidity in prayer and in gratitude that could be found only in hunger and thirst.

There were the minutes when the cantor could sit while the weary-looking rabbi gave his sermon. There were the prayers at the open ark, the thick rolls of the Torah wound back to the beginning, a shofar embroidered with golden thread on festive cloaks.

There was the cold air from the cracked window, there were the police and the two security guards, there were the almost eerily sweet melodies, so tender, so fragile, you must forget them the whole year, because otherwise, they would ruin all other songs for you, and everything would be special and for that reason, nothing would be special at all.

There was Avinu Malkeinu, the most earnest, perhaps, of the ten days of penance: "Our father, our king, remember that we are dust," there was dust, but also light, many small lights in the memorials near the entrance, light for the dead, light for the dust, "Avinu Malkeinu, our father, our king, do it for your sake and not for ours, Avinu Malkeinu," more plaintive, more pleading, "Our father, our king, hear us for the sake of your great mercy, for we have done no great deeds, show us clemency and favor, help us," and perhaps this prayer was the prayer of Judaism itself, the symbiosis of tone and plea; it was true, they wanted God to help forgive, to indulge, it was humanity itself that had to forgive and ask for forgiveness, to forgive one another, to forgive themselves, all they needed was a little help. "Avinu Malkeinu," they sang, "Avinu Malkeinu. Avinu Malkeinu," they wanted to be better, fight less, curse less, give more, be gentler, to actually do it this year.

The cantor joined in a little late, probably because he was praying faster, more reading than singing, with just a slight modulation; he clung to the bimah, pulling himself forward and back, and they imitated him, gripping the benches and swaying their bodies, each individual so softly you could barely tell, but all together in a palpable wave.

It was getting darker in the synagogue, the early arrivals slowly got bored, some were thirsty, others hungry and light-headed, their vocal cords quivered, or so it seemed, but the cantor kept praying and they followed along, they hadn't seen him for a while, his voice filled the whole room; did it not become more beautiful by the year, this final prayer, and during the singing, a door creaked, a shoe squeaked on the floor, there was someone, a stranger, a girl with long, dark hair, and the cantor turned, all at once his face wasn't so grave, was less concentrated, there was a smile there, and they smiled along with him, a bit bemused, smiled into the eternal light and their new year.

Acknowledgments

I finished working on this novel in the fall of 2022—a year before the events in Israel and Palestine following October 7, 2023. It is set in the summer of 2023 and ends two weeks before the Hamas massacre in Israel and the following war on Gaza. It is set in a region of the world in which civilians have been going through incomprehensible and unconscionable suffering.

I told the only story I could tell. I could not write it again the same way, for the world it unfolds in is forever changed. I hope this novel can, although it was written before these events, be read as a refusal to take any side but the side of humanity.

I want to sincerely thank Adrian Nathan West for his precise and beautiful work in translating my novel. He has transformed it into an artwork that is as much his as it is mine.

I thank my family: Joel Golb, Jack and Annette Vowinckel, Ruth and Norman Golb, and Joachim and Brigitte Vowinckel.

Thank you to Daniella Wexler, Juan Mila, and Alfredo Fee at HarperVia and to everyone at Suhrkamp Verlag, especially my editor Martina Wunderer and foreign rights director Nora Mercurio. I also thank my agents, Elisabeth Ruge and Mimi Wulz.

Thank you to my incredible friends for holding my hand and sometimes my whole body.

And to Ruben Regenass, I am in disbelief over your generosity, your humor, and your intelligence every day. You are the harshest, softest critic. Thank you.

Glossary

Ba'al Tekiyah: One who blows the shofar

Bimah: Lectern in the synagogue where the Torah is placed to be read

Birkat Hamazon: Grace said at the end of meals

Brachah, -ot: Blessing, benediction

Cheshbon HaNefesh: Spiritual accounting

Elul: The last month of the Jewish (lunar) calendar

Erev: Evening, in a religious context the beginning of a holiday

Gabbai, gabbaim: Lay leaders of a synagogue; a non-clergyman who assists with the running of the synagogue

Gibush: Tryouts for the Israeli military

Goyim: Non-Jews

Haftarah: Reading from the books of the prophets on Shabbat following the Torah reading

Halakha: The entirety of Jewish law and its interpretations

Havdalah: Ceremony at the end of a holiday

Kotel: The Wailing Wall in Jerusalem

Maariv: Evening prayers

Machzor: Prayer book for feast days

Matkot: Popular beach ball game in Israel, played with wooden paddles

Mincha: Afternoon prayers

Mitzvah, -ot: Good deed; more generally, a commandment in the
   Talmud

Modim: Prayer of thanksgiving

Neilah: Final prayer of Yom Kippur

Nigunim: Traditional melodies of religious songs

Nusach: The exact text of a service; the musical style of a
   congregation in recitative prayer is also referred to as Nusach

Parsha: Section of the Torah read in the synagogue on Shabbat
   and holidays

Payot: Sidelocks

Seder: Traditional meal on the first two evenings of Pesach

Shiva: Week of mourning after the death of a relative

Shofar: Ram's horn

Shtreimel: Traditional head covering of fur, usually worn by
   Hasidic Jews

Siddur: Prayer book

Tallit: Prayer shawl

Tefillin: Phylacteries

Teshuvah: Penitence (literally "turning back"), the most important
   religious aspect of Rosh Hashanah and Yom Kippur

Treyf: Not kosher

Tzaddik: "Righteous one," an honorary title in Judaism for a good
   person

Tzitzit: Tassels worn on the tallit or shawl

Yeshiva, -ot: Talmudic school for the training of rabbis and
   scholars

A Note from the Translator

I am always bemused when translators enthuse over collaborating with their authors. It is not that I don't think it's an author's right to make certain their work is well treated; it's simply that there is no point to a translation that can't be called into question, nothing that can't be done another way, and once you change this, it makes sense to change that, and in the end, you may find yourself compelled to put your name to something that is no longer really yours. This hasn't happened to me, or has only once, and in that case I didn't really care—and this is as good a place as any to thank my authors for their generosity and understanding—but still, some fifty books along in my career, I dread it every time I send a manuscript in. My default answer, when I imagine objections I might encounter, is that the author is the expert in his or her language, and I am the expert in English, and I think it's a good argument for keeping people's mitts off my use of register or colloquialisms, my changes in punctuation or syntax.

What happens, though, when the author is bilingual—when she knows your own language as you do, when she knows the one you learned from books as a native, and when the excuse that what this really means in English is such-and-such won't fly? Well, you do the same as you always do, obeying the principles that better is better and that good enough is not good enough, and you hope you and your author see eye to eye. With Dana Vowinckel, I was very fortunate in this regard.

Misophonia is a tale told in German, the action of which takes place mostly in English and Hebrew, in conversations between the German protagonist, Margarita; her Israeli father; and her American mother and grandparents. So it is not just that the words have to be right—they have to sound like the ones this person would say. This person—that is, a European girl around one-third my age. Whatever. I hold the unfashionable belief that people actually can understand each other, within limits, across the divides of sex, language, and nationality; the contrary notion, that identity is absolute, is intellectually fallow and boring; translation as such is premised on the faith that the distances that separate one person from another are to be bridged rather than despaired at.

I wasn't as ill-equipped as some people: the childhood years when my mother served as a Shabbos goy left her with an abiding fascination with Judaism, so I had some grasp of the rudiments of Jewish culture as described in the book even if I myself have never been religious. I do know Berlin, one of the settings for the novel, and have stepped out for liquor from the Späti, a type of convenience store, the translation of which was one of the questions Dana and I discussed as the novel came along. Chicago—where Margarita's grandparents live—is one of my favorite cities, so it, too, was familiar ground. Other aspects of Margarita's experience I am less acquainted with. In these instances, the translator must listen and try his best and not be presumptuous.

It's a commonplace that mistakes are inevitable in translation. They really aren't, but they're hard to avoid and harder to root out once a draft is done, and I would like to mention one that made it into the final version of the book in English. Mycology is not among my specialties, and just once—in my defense, I hadn't yet had my coffee—I broke my rule of not googling everything even vaguely unfamiliar and translated *Fliegenpilz* (fly agaric) as *flying mushroom*. Dana good-humoredly pointed this out, but decided she liked the image and left it in, and so this once, to quote Borges, we may say that "the original is unfaithful to the translation."

—Adrian Nathan West

About the Author

Dana Vowinckel was born in Berlin in 1996 into an American-Jewish-German family. She grew up bilingual and bicultural, living in Chicago and Berlin, and studied linguistics and literature in Berlin, Toulouse, and Cambridge. Her debut novel, *Misophonia*, won, among others, the Mara Cassens Prize and the literature prize of the Association of Arts and Culture of the German Economy, and was shortlisted for the prestigious Leipzig Book Fair Prize. She lives in Berlin.

Here ends Dana Vowinckel's
Misophonia.

The first edition of this book was printed
and bound at Lakeside Book Company
in Harrisonburg, Virginia, in April 2025.

A NOTE ON THE TYPE

The text of this novel was set in Melior, a serif type-face designed by famed calligrapher Hermann Zapf. Of particular note is the width of Melior's uppercase family, especially the *O*, which Zapf based on the mathematical superellipse, a closed curve. It has been suggested that Zapf took inspiration from Danish polymath Piet Hein, who throughout his work promoted the qualities of the superellipse, thinking it an ideal shape for design. Since Melior's release in 1952, it has been prized for its exceptional legibility, ideally suited for more formal texts because of its strong and readable letterform.

HarperVia

An imprint dedicated to publishing international voices, offering readers a chance to encounter other lives and other points of view via the language of the imagination.